Olivia Drake is a *New York Times* bestselling author who lives in Texas. Her novels have won critical acclaim and numerous industry awards including the prestigious RITA.

She invites you to visit www.oliviadrake.com

Also by Olivia Drake:

Seducing the Heiress
Never Trust a Rogue

Olivia Drake

Scandal of the Year

1 3 5 7 9 10 8 6 4 2

First published in the United States in 2011 by St Martin's Press

Published in the UK in 2012 by *Rouge*, an imprint of Ebury Publishing
A Random House Group Company

The Random House Group Limited Reg. No. 954009

Addresses for companies within the Random House Group can be found at: www.randomhouse.co.uk

A CIP catalogue record for this book is available from the British Library

The Random House Group Limited supports The Forest Stewardship Council (FSC®), the leading international forest certification organisation. Our books carrying the FSC label are printed on FSC® certified paper. FSC is the only forest certification scheme endorsed by the leading environmental organisations, including Greenpeace. Our paper procurement policy can be found at: www.randomhouse.co.uk/environment

To b

Chapter 1

From his seat on the floor with the general audience, James Ryding lifted the opera glasses and studied the balcony that stretched in a semicircle around the theater. The dimness of the gas lamps suited his covert purpose. While the actors traded witticisms on the stage, drawing laughter from the spectators, James scanned the aristocratic guests until he spied his quarry.

A small party occupied one of the private boxes reserved for the upper crust. In the front sat a middle-aged man and woman, along with a young lady. Although the girl was not the object of his scrutiny, James found himself pausing to observe her through the magnifiers.

She was strikingly pretty in a low-cut yellow gown that displayed her voluptuous charms. Coppery curls tumbled down to one of her shoulders. As she turned her head to whisper to a pair of gentlemen sitting to the rear, her lips formed a laughing curve.

The sight of that flirtatious smile sparked a visceral heat in James. He imagined them entwined in each other's arms while he kissed her. He craved to know her scent and her taste, the feel of her curves beneath his hands. The fantasy was so vivid that heat rushed to his loins.

A tug on his sleeve yanked James back to the crowded

theater. Clamping his teeth around an irritated growl, he lowered the opera glasses and frowned at the elderly man seated beside him on the bench.

Percy Thornton had bony shoulders hunched inside an ill-fitting brown coat. His gray eyebrows were raised in inquiry above his pale blue eyes. "Do you see them, sir?" Thornton whispered anxiously. "*Are* they your cousins?"

James cudgeled his thoughts back to the present. "I can't say for certain just yet."

He peered through the glasses again, this time studiously ignoring the girl and focusing on the older couple beside her. A stout gentleman with thinning brown hair, George Crompton wore a crisp white cravat and a tailored blue coat. His wife, Edith, looked rather youthful in a bronze gown with the sparkle of a diamond tiara nestled in her upswept russet hair.

James struggled to reconcile the picture of husband and wife with the memory of his last visit with them more than two decades earlier. Alas, the mists of time had blurred their images. The only clear picture from the past that he'd retained was of playing with Edith's pet spaniels.

"Are you sure you don't recognize either of them?" Thornton prodded.

"I'm afraid not. They're too far away. And kindly keep in mind, the last time I laid eyes on them I was a mere lad of ten."

James kept his voice low even though the laughter of the audience masked their conversation. Everyone around him was engrossed in the play. Besides, no one would be expecting a gentleman to be seated down here with the common folk. Not when he was connected to the finest families in England. And not when he'd been away in Barbados for so many years.

There, he'd been master of a thriving plantation, the largest on the island, until a massive storm had flattened his ripening crop of sugar cane and reduced his house and outbuildings to kindling. Rebuilding would necessitate an influx of cash, but he'd sunk all his spare money into expanding his acreage. The notion of taking out a bank loan left a bad taste in his mouth. After witnessing his father being hounded by creditors all those years ago, James had vowed never to sign any IOUs.

For that reason, the arrival of the letter from Thornton had been a godsend. The old man had once been manager of the estate in Lancashire belonging to George Crompton. A trusted employee, Thornton had stayed on to watch over the place while the Cromptons had moved to India long ago.

In the letter, Thornton wrote that when he'd called on George Crompton to settle the matter of a neglected pension, Thornton had made a shocking discovery. The couple living in the Berkeley Square mansion were not the same people who had once employed Thornton.

George and Edith Crompton were imposters.

At first, James had dismissed the wild notion. Such a deception seemed impossible to accomplish. How could two criminals take over the lives of his cousins without anyone noticing?

Yet when a second letter had arrived from Thornton, urging James to take action, he'd paid closer attention. George Crompton had amassed great wealth during his twenty-year sojourn in India. His extensive holdings were rumored to rival the riches of the royal family. If Thornton was correct, and the man sitting up there in the box seat was *not* James's cousin, then foul play had been committed.

Assuming George Crompton's wealth had been embezzled, at what point had it happened? Years ago or only recently? The woman must be privy to the crime, too. Somehow, they'd managed to pull off the bold scheme with no one the wiser. Yet surely someone, a coworker or an acquaintance in India, would have sounded the alarm.

And the bigger question was, What had happened to the real Cromptons? Had they been murdered?

James intended to find out. If the story was true, then justice must be done on behalf of his cousin. James also acknowledged that in the process he himself would reap a king's ransom for exposing them as criminals. As the only male relative, James was heir to the Crompton estate in Lancashire and much of the family holdings.

Few people knew his full name was James Ryding Crompton. Dropping the use of his surname had been an act of defiance against a father he'd despised.

His gaze flitted again to the young lady sitting in the box seat. She was still flirting over her shoulder with the two gentleman seated behind her. The spring social season had barely begun, but already she had acquired an entourage of admirers.

"Which daughter is the girl with them?" he asked Thornton.

"The youngest . . . I believe her name is Miss Blythe Crompton. There are two older sisters, but they've already married into the aristocracy."

James narrowed his eyes at the laughing girl. Wealth had bought her acceptance into the highest circles. How much did Miss Blythe Crompton know of the swindle perpetrated by her parents? Was she a full-fledged party to the deception? Or had it happened when she was too young to remember?

The answer didn't signify. If George Crompton was a charlatan, he must suffer the full force of the law.

"What will you do?" Thornton whispered. "Will you join society and call on them?"

James glanced over at his companion. "No. That would only serve to put them on their guard."

"But you must do *something*, sir. Those two mustn't be allowed to get away with such an offense."

"I quite agree. However, it would be best if I could observe them for a time without their knowledge. To study them closely and find proof of their crime."

And James knew the perfect way to do so.

Chapter 2

"You dance like an angel, Miss Crompton. The privilege of being your partner was pure heaven."

Blythe Crompton batted her lashes at the earnest, balding man who had just brought her back to her mother. "Why, Lord Ainsley, you'll turn my head with such extravagant compliments. I cannot imagine the other gentlemen here will appreciate that."

A chorus of assents rose from the small group surrounding her. She smiled at each man in the circle: Lord Robert Fortingham, dour yet ardently devoted to her; Mr. Mainwaring, handsome but for an unfortunate rash of freckles; Viscount Kitchener, a dandy with golden-brown curls and intense blue eyes.

Blythe was enjoying every moment of the party given in her honor at her parent's mansion on Berkeley Square. The ballroom teemed with aristocratic guests who mingled and danced, drank champagne and conversed in dulcet tones. At one end of the long, high-ceilinged room, the musicians rested between sets while gentlemen sought out their next partners. Hundreds of candles in crystal chandeliers cast a glow over the tall gilded columns and polished parquet floor. Mama and Papa had spared no expense in launching their youngest daughter into society.

How Blythe loved it, the dancing and the gossip and the finery! She felt like a princess in her gown of white gauze with a pale blue silk underskirt, her hair done up in Grecian curls and crowned by a gold diadem. Most of all, she adored the admiration from the highborn gentlemen. As the wealthiest heiress in the Marriage Mart, she could choose from an array of noble partners. Truly, she couldn't fathom why her two older sisters had ever complained about being the center of attention.

One of the gentlemen pushed forward and seized hold of her hand. "May I have the pleasure of the next dance?"

"Thank you, Mr. Mainwaring. But as we've danced once already, I really must consult with my mother."

"I'm afraid your kind request is impossible." Slim and youthful in striped plum silk, Mrs. Edith Crompton appeared beside Blythe and firmly pushed away his hand. "My daughter has promised the next set to the Duke of Savoy. Ah, I see His Grace right now."

A stately man of middle years approached them. The throngs parted as people gave way to his dignified passage. With the proud tilt to his chin and his exquisitely tailored garb, he drew adulating looks from the other guests.

"Smile, darling," Mrs. Crompton whispered, bending close to Blythe. "Remember what I told you."

Blythe needed no instruction in making herself agreeable. The prospect of being singled out by none other than the Duke of Savoy gave her great pleasure. It was the crowning glory of a night that had been designed to elevate her in the eyes of society.

The duke afforded her a slight bow. "Miss Crompton. Will you dance?"

She sank into a deep curtsey. "It would be an honor, Your Grace."

The gentlemen in her entourage looked disconsolate. She oughtn't derive any satisfaction in their disappointment, yet she appreciated knowing how very much they desired her company.

As Blythe started toward the dance floor with her gloved hand resting on the duke's forearm, her mother stood beaming with the other matrons. Blythe noticed a few disapproving looks among the ladies, their heads bobbing and their mouths clucking like a flock of old biddy hens.

They must be discussing her marriage prospects. There were those among them who frowned upon a commoner being courted by such a high-ranking nobleman.

Not that Blythe cared a fig for their small-minded opinions.

Pleasure buoyed her as she and Savoy wended their way through crush of guests. Although the middle-aged duke had lined features and a somewhat portly form, he was the most eligible bachelor of the Season. He had been widowed the previous summer and was said to be seeking a new wife from among the crop of young debutantes. Since he had only one daughter, a girl of Blythe's age, he needed a male heir.

Perhaps he would choose Blythe to be his duchess. Perhaps he would fall madly in love with her, and she with him.

The prospect fired her imagination. As they made their way toward the dance floor, she lost herself in a pleasant dream of being elevated to the stature of Duchess of Savoy. Her dinner parties and balls would be the most coveted of invitations. There would be no more whispered talk or censorious looks from the other ladies. She would win the duke's heart, and they would live happily ever after.

The fantasy sustained Blythe as they joined the other dancers. The men formed a long line opposite the women and the music commenced, as restrained and proper as the duke himself. Bowing to her in accordance with the dance, Savoy cut a fine figure in a maroon coat lined with pale pink satin. A snowy-white cravat enhanced the ruddiness of his face and the hints of gray in his dark hair.

He was quite old enough to be her father.

Blythe banished the off-putting notion. Affection knew no boundaries of age, and once they grew better acquainted, surely a lasting warmth would develop between them. Besides, her parents regarded the duke as an excellent marital prospect for her, and she trusted their judgment implicitly.

Performing the prescribed steps, she aimed a flirtatious smile at him, but Savoy gave no sign of noticing. His expression remained aloof and sober, his blue eyes focused just beyond her shoulder as if he were immersed in his own private world.

Perhaps his thoughts dwelled upon his late wife.

Sympathetic curiosity niggled at Blythe. How dreadful to have endured the tragic death of one's spouse. Had he dearly loved the late duchess? Even if it had been an arranged marriage, there must been a bond between them, and the loss of that companionship would have left a hole in his life.

Perhaps a little banter might serve to distract him as it did her Papa when he became too preoccupied with business. As she took the duke's gloved hand and stepped around him as the other couples were doing, she murmured, "I daresay this is all rather humdrum to you, Your Grace."

For the first time his gaze settled directly on her. Unfortunately, he did so with a frown. "Eh?"

"Attending balls. Dancing the night away. Conversing with silly young girls like me."

"It is what one does at such events."

He had not denied her silliness as a besotted swain

would have done. And yet his gaze flitted to her mouth, a sure sign of his interest.

Blythe dipped her chin slightly and gazed at him through the veil of her lashes. "Are you certain you do not mind squiring me, then? Perhaps you would rather be playing cards or smoking cigars with the gentlemen in the library."

"Rest assured, Miss Crompton, I am perfectly content."

The dance steps separated them, but Blythe was pleased with the little exchange. There had been a flash of awareness in his eyes before he'd turned away. By not playing the mouse, she had accomplished her goal of distinguishing herself from the multitude of other debutantes. When Savoy looked back on this evening, he would remember her as a woman able to converse with him.

For the remainder of the set, she savored the vivid scene of gentlemen and ladies moving in harmony. All those dull lessons with a dancing master had been worthwhile. But how very different this was from when she'd practiced her steps right here in this ballroom, and she and her two sisters had taken turns partnering each other.

A pang struck her. It was a pity they couldn't have been here. Lindsey lived in London, but she'd given birth to a daughter a fortnight ago. Portia's young son had taken ill with a cold, so she'd remained in Kent to nurse him back to health.

Blythe wouldn't let their absence dampen her spirits, though. Tonight was the culmination of a dream, and she would enjoy every moment of it.

As the music ended and Savoy escorted her off the dance floor, she murmured, "Thank you, Your Grace. I hope you won't think me forward, but perhaps we shall have an opportunity to meet again soon."

He grunted in what she hoped was an assent.

Had she displeased him? Blythe couldn't quite tell

from his somber expression. But she had high hopes that once they grew closer, he would favor her above all others. There had never been a male, young or old, that she couldn't twist around her little finger.

His hand on her elbow, Savoy guided her through the throng of guests. People stepped back as if they were royalty. The men bowed and the ladies curtsied. Such deference was shown to Blythe and her parents only by the servants. But soon she would elevate her family's position through a grand alliance. And the Duke of Savoy ranked at the top of her list of potential husbands.

Blythe cast about for an excuse to prolong her time with him. She scanned the crush of guests in the hopes of seeing a familiar face with whom to stop and converse. By lucky chance, the sea of ladies and gentlemen parted and her gaze fell upon a group of debutantes chatting near the tall arched doorway.

"May I trouble you with a request, Your Grace?"

"If you wish."

His closed expression wasn't encouraging, and Blythe had no wish to annoy him. At the same time, it was imperative that she forge a close connection between his family and hers.

"Would you afford me the honor of escorting me to your daughter?" she murmured. "We were introduced in the receiving line, and I would enjoy the chance to further my acquaintance with her."

"I've no notion where the girl might be in this squeeze."

"I spied her a moment ago, if you'll permit me to show you."

Blythe didn't give Savoy a chance to refuse. She deftly guided him in the direction of the door.

Judging by the way the three girls had their heads close together, they were exchanging confidences. From time to time, one of them would cast a sly glance around the ballroom as if to seek out a new subject for gossip. Then they would whisper and giggle behind their fans.

Blythe instinctively recognized the type. They were an exclusive clique of blue-blooded ladies who had grown up in this rarified world. Unlike the gentlemen present, the girls would have little interest in befriending the daughter of a common merchant—no matter how rich the Crompton family might be.

But they didn't know the extent of Blythe's determination. As she and Savoy approached, she donned a gracious smile. One of the trio, a petite brunette, spied them and spoke to the willowy blond beside her.

The duke's daughter, Lady Davina, turned to look at Blythe. Those blue eyes narrowed ever so slightly and her patrician features took on a coolness that radiated arrogant disapproval. The other two girls dipped their curtsies to the duke.

Gliding to her father, Lady Davina placed a proprietary hand on his arm. "Dear Papa, there you are at last. Are you feeling quite well? You appear a trifle flushed."

A smile touched his lips, warming his stern features. "'Tis the dancing you may hold to blame, my dear girl. I vow I haven't cavorted so much in two score years."

"Perhaps you need a rest. You mustn't overtax yourself." Lady Davina slid an accusatory look at Blythe as if the state of his health were all her fault. "I would be most happy to sit out the next set with you, Papa. Come, let's find a quiet spot elsewhere."

He patted her hand. "I assure you, I am not quite doddering enough to require a nursemaid. However, Miss Crompton would like to have a chat with you, so perhaps you can sit with her."

His daughter ignored the request as if Blythe didn't

exist. "If you insist upon dancing, you should ask Lady Ellen to be your partner. She hasn't yet had the honor of your company."

Lady Davina signaled one of the other girls forward. Short and somewhat stout, Lady Ellen made cow eyes at the duke over her fan.

"I hear the music starting," Lady Davina went on. "Run along now, you mustn't delay or you'll miss the opening steps."

Her desire to separate the duke from Blythe could not have been any more transparent. But Savoy seemed oblivious to the ploy. He politely took his leave and escorted Lady Ellen off into the crowd.

The ease with which he'd been maneuvered by his daughter interested Blythe. If he was malleable, so much the better. It meant that he was susceptible to being charmed by those he held dear. She had only to win his love, coax him into a proposal, and then her life would be perfect.

Of course the other side of the coin was Lady Davina, who appeared to thrive on directing those around her. Such a trait was usually seen in a matron much older than a lady in her first season. Yet was not her animosity understandable? She must be appalled at the notion of having a stepmother so close to herself in age.

Blythe extended her gloved hand to the other girl. She was a plain-faced brunette with slightly protruding teeth.

"I don't believe we've met. I'm Blythe Crompton. And you are—?"

The girl glanced warily at her companion, then touched Blythe's fingers and stepped back. "Lady Anne Oglethorpe. Davy and I grew up together."

"Davy?"

"A childish nickname," Lady Davina said, frowning at her friend. "One that is to be used only at home."

Anne ducked her chin. "Oh! Forgive me. I-I quite forgot."

Her distress stirred Blythe's sympathies. So the duke was not the only one who was subject to Davina's bullying.

"I wanted to bid you both welcome to Crompton House," Blythe said by way of a distraction. "I'm most pleased that you could attend tonight."

Davina's gaze roved over the vast ballroom with its vaulted ceiling and the chandeliers aglow with hundreds of tapers. "This will always be Herrington House to me," she said with a sniff. "It was named for the Earls of Herrington, although when the last earl died without issue some two score years ago, the title went extinct."

The comment somehow made Blythe feel like an outsider in her own home. No doubt that was the intent. "It seems you know more about this house than I do," she said lightly. "Perhaps you would come to call one day and tell me more of its history."

"I'll have to check my schedule," Davina said with an air of cool boredom that indicated she would do no such thing. "Now, come along, Anne, we'll take a turn about the room. It is a tolerable assembly, I suppose. Although I must admit to being a trifle . . . disappointed."

With effort, Blythe held on to her resolve. She would not let the girl's sour nature deter her from being pleasant. "If there's some delicacy or drink you prefer, I should be happy to send someone to fetch it. Perhaps you'd care for champagne?"

As Blythe turned to look for a servant, a footman in blue livery appeared right beside her, as if he'd been standing within earshot awaiting her summons. Startled, she took half a step backward.

He was tall—so tall that her gaze was on par with his broad shoulders and she had to tilt her head back to view his face. Beneath the customary white powdered wig, he had arrestingly handsome features and swarthy skin as if he'd spent a good deal of time out in the sun.

He wasn't one of the regular staff. Perhaps Mama had hired additional footmen to help out at the party.

He held forth a tray of crystal glasses filled with golden champagne. "My ladies," he murmured, extending the salver to them.

As he did so, he turned his head to look straight at Blythe. His dark, penetrating eyes caused an involuntary clutch in the depths of her body. The reaction disconcerted her as did the novelty of a manservant staring at her as boldly as a gentleman of the highest rank. The fellow deserved a reprimand for overstepping his bounds. Yet she felt mysteriously bewitched by that keen gaze.

Lady Davina's voice broke the spell. "We've had quite enough champagne," she said, waving the footman away.

Lady Anne had been reaching for a glass, but she furtively drew back her hand. "Yes, of course we have."

"You've mistaken my meaning, Miss Crompton." Davina lifted a haughty eyebrow at Blythe. "It isn't drink that I want. My disappointment tonight lies with the entertainment."

Blythe struggled to focus her thoughts. The footman had moved back out of her view. Freed from his magnetic stare, she wondered if she'd imagined that odd little interlude. "The entertainment?"

"Quite. I would have expected you to make a much grander entrance tonight . . . perhaps by riding into the ballroom on the back of an elephant."

She cast a droll glance at her friend, and Lady Anne giggled behind her fan.

Heat flamed in Blythe's cheeks. She had been subject to whispers about her upbringing in India, but never before had she been mocked so openly. Her fingers tensed at her sides. How dearly she would like to slap the superiority off Lady Davina's face. Or at the very least, respond with a cutting jab about ill-mannered shrews.

Blythe knew the folly in making a scene. A brawl would hardly serve her hope of becoming the next Duchess of Savoy.

Mustering every bit of restraint, she kept an agreeable smile on her face. "What a remarkable notion. The next time we have a party here, I really must consult you in the planning of it."

But Davina wasn't pacified. If anything, the cool contempt on her face grew more pronounced.

Stepping closer, she murmured, "Pray be forewarned, Miss Crompton. I will not be used as a contrivance for you to loiter near the duke in the hopes of tempting him into wedlock. I would never permit my father to marry so vastly far beneath him."

With a chilly nod, Lady Davina took her friend's arm and they strolled off into the crowd.

Chapter 3

Blythe stood frozen in the doorway. All the magic of the evening abruptly evaporated. Her smile felt stiff, her chest filled to bursting with mortified humiliation. Never in her life had she been insulted with such undisguised malice. To be denied the satisfaction of a sharp rejoinder only rubbed raw her affronted emotions. To make matters worse, some of the guests were looking at her curiously and whispering.

A desperate need to escape besieged her. Turning, she walked out of the ballroom and headed rapidly toward the back of the house. Ladies and gentlemen strolled along the grand corridor with its tall columns and Greek statuary. She kept her chin down to avoid conversation.

I would never permit my father to marry so vastly far beneath him.

Fury nipped at her heels. How dared that nasty girl debase Blythe in her own home! What a hoity-toity snob! A score of scenarios played through her mind, all of which ended with Lady Davina falling to her knees and begging Blythe's forgiveness.

Not that *that* would ever happen.

At the end of the passageway, she veered sharply to the left. Here, the buzz of noise from the party was diminished and there were no guests to witness her extreme agitation. Picking a door at random, Blythe entered a shadowy sitting room that was lit only by a coal fire on the hearth.

She stormed straight to a chaise, snatched up a pillow to her mouth, and screamed. The crewel-work muffled the sound, but at least the release of tension made Blythe feel marginally better.

"Termagant!" Clutching the pillow to her bosom, she stalked back and forth while giving voice to all the names she'd wanted to call Lady Davina. "Selfish, vile, wicked *snob.* Conceited, overbearing blueblood!"

In the midst of her tirade, someone cleared his throat.

Aghast, she whirled around to see a towering male figure outlined in the doorway. His identity struck her at once. It was a footman carrying a tray . . . the same footman who had stared at her in the ballroom.

The realization that he'd witnessed her outburst appalled Blythe. What trick of fate had brought him to intrude on her privacy?

Unless it was no coincidence.

She gripped the pillow to her bosom. "You followed me," she accused.

"Please forgive my presumption, Miss Crompton. I thought you might need this." He set down the tray on a table, selected a glass, and stepped forward to press it into her hand. "Go on," he murmured, "drink it down."

In her present state, being issued an order by anyone, let alone a servant, should have sparked rebellion in her. Yet she found herself obeying his directive. The bubbles burst on her tongue and the refreshing liquid slid easily down her throat.

Tilting her head back, she drained the glass. Almost immediately a warm glow soothed the raw edges of her emotions.

"I'll have another," she snapped, then was ashamed of her sharpness. "Please."

He chuckled under his breath, a sound she'd never heard from any member of the staff—at least not here in England. In India, however, the servants had been more open and relaxed in their manners. As a child, she'd often eavesdropped on the cook and the maids as they went about their duties, chattering in Hindi and laughing at the slightest provocation. Blythe hadn't realized until this moment how much she'd missed that warm, happy banter.

The servants in London were all so stiff and proper. They kept their heads down and allowed themselves to fade into the background.

Except for this one impudent footman.

Warily, she watched as he took her empty glass and walked back to the tray. His command of the situation exuded an authority that was highly unusual in a servant. Even his long strides revealed him to be a man who was confident of himself.

He returned with the drink. A slight smile quirked his lips as he handed her the second glass. In the process, his gloved fingers brushed hers.

The keen awareness of him as a man coursed through her body. The sensation settled in the pit of her stomach and made her realize how alone they were here. The distant hum of the party only served to underscore a sense of intimacy.

What was wrong with her? He was only a servant like so many others. It was just that her emotions had been rattled by that incident with Lady Davina.

"It isn't my place to advise you," he said. "However, you may wish to sip this one more slowly."

"I'll do as I please."

Despite her tart tone, Blythe took only a small swallow.

He was right; it would be a disaster if she were to stagger drunkenly for the remainder of the evening. Not, of course, that she had any desire to return to the ballroom just yet. The heat of humiliation might have subsided, but her resentment toward Lady Davina still smoldered.

The footman stepped back and stood in the shadows a respectful distance away. She found his air of self-assurance unnerving. Why didn't he depart and leave her alone? Any other servant would have vanished out the door by now.

His gaze flitted to the pillow that she still clutched in one arm, reminding her that he had witnessed that hysterical outburst. Perhaps he thought her a madwoman in need of supervision.

Fighting a blush, Blythe walked to the chaise and returned the pillow to its resting place. She wanted him to go . . . and yet she didn't.

"What is your name?" she asked to fill the awkward silence.

"James."

"My mother refers to all of the footmen as James. She finds it easier than trying to discern who is who."

"Then she will make no mistake with me, for I assure you that truly *is* my given name."

Blythe found herself rather liking the way he spoke to her so easily. It could be so tedious when a servant wouldn't even look her in the eye. "I don't recall ever seeing you on the staff. Are you here just for the party tonight?"

"No, I accepted a post in your house only yesterday . . . when *James* left."

She surprised herself by giggling. "Which one? The one with the big nose? The shy one who stuttered? Or the one who always squinted a bit? Oh, well, I don't suppose it matters."

"We do all look alike in livery and wig," James agreed.

He was wrong. Although footmen were chosen for their height and muscular build, Blythe found this man utterly unlike any of the others in the house. He was taller, more broad of shoulder, more imposing. His bold manner gave her the distinct impression that he regarded himself as her equal.

Savoring another taste of champagne, she speculated on the color of his hair underneath that formal wig. Was it as dark as his eyebrows? Would it be thick or thin, curly or straight? Would it feel soft to the touch of her fingers?

The force of her curiosity jolted Blythe. Good heavens. A surfeit of wine must have addled her brain. How absurd was it to be lingering in the company of a footman when so many fine gentlemen awaited her in the ballroom?

Absurd, indeed!

It was time to go back, yet she felt uneasy knowing that James had witnessed her unguarded flare of emotion. "You are not to gossip to the other servants about . . . anything that happened here."

"I had no intention of doing so."

Could he be trusted to keep his word? She hoped so. "Thank you for the champagne. You may go now."

"As you wish." James bowed to her, picked up his tray, and headed toward the door. Then he turned back to regard her one last time. "If I may be permitted to say so, Miss Crompton, you would have looked magnificent riding into the ballroom on the back of an elephant."

He disappeared into the passageway. Left speechless, Blythe listened as the tapping of his footsteps faded away. The distant lilt of a waltz drifted to her ears. Again, she was struck by how out of the ordinary the footman behaved.

Even more curious, she felt invigorated by his compliment. By the heavens, he was right. She *would* have been magnificent.

Chapter 4

The next morning, James cursed the success of his plan to infiltrate the Crompton household. He had been cleaning lamps in this tiny workroom since breakfast. The messy task left his hands black with ash and oil, and he'd been forced to don an apron to protect his footman's uniform. Yet still he wasn't finished.

He had served endless rounds of drinks in the ballroom until the wee hours. The head footman, a slave master by the name of Godwin, had allowed the staff no extra sleep. At dawn, James had been up gathering all the soiled glassware from the formal chambers on the first floor. Then he had been assigned the task of tending the oil lamps. Another footman had fetched dozens from all over the house. They had been brought to this dank cellar room so that the mess of refilling the kerosene and trimming the wicks wouldn't disturb the family.

Scowling, he polished a brass lamp with a mixture of oil and emery powder. It had taken a handsome bribe to convince the previous footman to give up his position so that James could apply for the post. Now he wondered if it had been worthwhile. He had envisioned having endless opportunities to search the house during the performance of his duties.

But things hadn't worked out according to plan. If he wasn't cleaning the lamps or the silver, he was running errands or standing duty at the front door. He had not yet had the freedom to go around the house, including the office used by George Crompton.

James hadn't even had a close look at his quarry yet. At the ball, George and Edith had been surrounded by guests. The only family member James had met face to face had been Miss Blythe Crompton.

He rubbed at a stubborn bit of tarnish on the base of the lamp. What the devil had possessed him to follow her to that deserted sitting room? He had risked ruining his masquerade by acting more like a gentleman than a servant. He was supposed to be inconspicuous, an anonymous footman unnoticed by the family.

But the hurt in those expressive hazel eyes had caught him off guard. He had expected a wealthy heiress like Blythe Crompton to be a frivolous feather-brain. He'd amended that image to cunning social climber after watching her dance and flirt with a succession of titled men, including the Duke of Savoy, a man who was old enough to be her father. It disgusted James to see that she was using her rich dowry to purchase a titled husband.

Yet she hadn't been impervious to Lady Davina's insult. Miss Blythe Crompton had continued to smile although her eyes had revealed a depth of feeling that defied any shallow label he'd assigned her. She had been distraught enough to leave the ballroom and seek a secluded spot in which to give vent to her emotions.

He grinned in spite of himself. How embarrassed she'd been to realize he'd observed her little tirade. It was a miracle she hadn't sacked him on the spot. Instead, she'd actually seemed amenable to conversing with him. There had been surprisingly little haughtiness to her demeanor, and he didn't know quite what to make of that.

Carefully pouring oil into the well of the lamp, James mulled over the prospect of altering his investigation. It might prove useful to ingratiate himself with Miss Crompton. She could be privy to information that would prove her parents to be imposters.

God knew, she might even be a party to their ruse. A girl whose family owed its wealth to trade would do anything for the chance to wed into the rarified world of the aristocracy.

And if he was wrong about her? He wouldn't allow himself to be troubled by the possibility. If George Crompton had absconded with the inheritance that rightfully belonged to James, then justice must be done.

"'Ello, James."

The Cockney voice came from behind him. He swung around to see a maidservant sauntering through the doorway of the butler's pantry. A few wisps of coal-black hair escaped the white mobcap on her head. Despite the drab gray gown buttoned to her throat, she managed to convey an impression of lush femininity.

He stifled a groan. From the moment he'd been introduced to the staff in the basement kitchen two days ago, Meg had been watching him with predatory brown eyes. James had given her no encouragement, not that it had made any difference.

He schooled his features into a bland expression. "Yes?"

Meg strolled toward him. "I come to bring ye a message."

"What is it?"

She pretended to examine his handiwork. "My, ye've done a fine job. I like a man 'oo's good wid 'is 'ands."

Her bosom brushed his upper arm. Annoyed, James stepped back to place the newly refurbished lamp on the table with the others. A high standard of behavior was expected of the staff. The slightest infraction could result in immediate dismissal. James had no intention of being tossed out on the street before he had unmasked the Cromptons.

He wiped his hands on a rag. "What is the message?"

She sidled closer. "Ye're a fine gent, ye are. Where did ye learn yer fancy manners?"

"I've no time for idle chit-chat. Now, answer my question."

Meg pursed her lips in a pout. "There's a parcel come for Miss Crompton. Ye're to deliver it to 'er above stairs."

The news galvanized James. "You should have said so at once."

He went to wash his slimy hands in a basin of water. A sliver of cheap soap did little to clean the black oily tarnish from beneath his fingernails, but he scrubbed hard, driven by the prospect of seeing Miss Crompton again.

No, he was merely grateful for the chance to escape the confines of the butler's pantry. Having an excuse to roam the house might help him further his investigation.

Meg had flounced out of the room, apparently discouraged by his lack of interest in her. So much the better. He needed no distractions from his purpose. This might be his chance to find a way to discredit the Cromptons and claim their ill-gained wealth for himself.

⁂

"Lady Davina has the power to ruin everything," Edith Crompton said. "That is why you *must* make a concentrated effort to befriend her."

Seated at the dressing table, Blythe frowned at her mother's reflection in the oval mirror. In a gown of olive-green muslin, her russet hair piled atop her head, Mama looked more wide awake than anyone ought after staying up until nearly dawn.

And certainly more wide-awake than Blythe felt herself.

She had lain in bed, her thoughts restless, until the first fingers of sunlight had crept into her bedchamber. Her mind had been fraught with memories of the ball, the squabble with Lady Davina, and even that notable interlude with James, the footman. When she'd finally slept, her dreams had been unsettling. Only a few minutes ago she'd arisen feeling out of sorts and uncharacteristically irritable.

And now she faced this inquisition from her mother, who had pried out of Blythe the truth about what Lady Davina had said.

"Must we continue to speak of this right now?" Blythe asked, picking up a silver brush and running it through her unbound hair. "I haven't even had my breakfast yet."

Mrs. Crompton glided to the window and reached for the cord to draw back the draperies. "Perhaps the sunlight will revive you."

"Mama, please. I've a slight headache."

Leaving the curtains closed, her mother hurried to touch Blythe's brow. "No fever. I'm sure you'll feel better once your tray arrives. Now, do reassure me that you understand my concern about Lady Davina."

"I understand that she despises me." Blythe twirled a lock of hair around her index finger. How could she explain her sudden reluctance to pursue the duke? It was far more than the incident with Lady Davina. Blythe couldn't forget the involuntary attraction she'd felt for James. Nothing like that had happened with His Grace. Yet how wonderful it would be to be courted by a gentleman who could arouse such a thrill in her. "Mama, I've been thinking that perhaps I shouldn't wed the Duke of Savoy, after all."

"I beg your pardon?"

"You allowed Lindsey to marry an earl and Portia a viscount. Who am I to aim higher than them?"

Edith Crompton frowned. "Don't be absurd. You're different from your sisters. You've always been more appreciative of all that society has to offer."

"But I told you, Lady Davina insulted me—and you and Papa as well." Blythe mimicked the hateful words that were branded into her memory. " 'I would never permit my father to marry so vastly far beneath him.' "

Her skirts rustling, Mama bent down to hug Blythe. Her lilac scent wafted over Blythe and their eyes met in the looking glass. "I know what she said is awful, darling, but you mustn't let Lady Davina discourage you. Remember, her mother died only last summer. It's understandable for her to be possessive of His Grace. Can you not find it in your heart to forgive her?"

A natural tendency toward kindness rose to the fore of Blythe's emotions. She knew how protective she herself would be of her own father in such a circumstance. Nevertheless, she resisted being maneuvered by her mother.

"That doesn't excuse her rudeness."

"You're quite right. However, people will make inconsiderate remarks from time to time. That is merely the way society functions. You cannot allow it to stop you from achieving your dream."

"But . . . what about love?" Blythe tried to fathom the soul-deep yearning inside herself that the meeting with James had somehow ignited. "What if I am not in love with the duke?"

Her mother laughed. "You've only just met him, darling. Love will come in time, never fear."

Would it? Blythe fervently hoped so. Having witnessed the closeness of her sisters with their husbands, she couldn't deny a longing to find such happiness for herself.

Straightening up, Mama patted Blythe's shoulder. "As for Lady Davina, she doesn't yet realize how wonderful a friend you can be. No doubt it was a shock for her to see how perfect you looked on the duke's arm. You were so very beautiful last night. Like a true duchess."

Had James, the footman, found her beautiful?

Blythe had a vivid memory of his tall, shadowy form entering the sitting room the previous night. Their hands had brushed when he'd given her the glass of champagne. Even now, something stirred deep inside her, but she refused to examine it. He was a servant and she mustn't think about him that way.

Better she should relish her happiness when she'd danced with the Duke of Savoy. Better she should savor the pleasurable memory of how everyone had gazed admiringly at her, how they had stepped aside and shown her deference as she'd passed. *That* was what she wanted—wasn't it? To be accepted wholeheartedly by all of society.

And if she could find love, too, then her life would be complete.

A knock sounded and the door opened. A stout maid carrying a breakfast tray entered the bedchamber. She bobbed a curtsy and went to place the tray on a round table by the window.

Blythe rose from the dressing table. "Thank you, Nan," she told the maid, who scurried over to the bed to straighten the linens. "Mama, would you care for a cup of tea?"

Edith Crompton shook her head. "I've already had my share at breakfast with your father. By the by, he was extremely pleased that you had danced with His Grace."

Blythe glanced up in surprise. "Papa said that?"

"Yes. Your father believes that a marriage between you and the duke would be an absolutely brilliant match."

As she poured herself a steaming cup of tea, Blythe felt a twinge of dismay. When it came to society, Mama had always been the ambitious one. She never seemed satisfied with their wealth, their fine home, their invitations to the best parties. She'd pushed all three of her daughters to marry dukes, although Portia and Lindsey had had other ideas.

Papa had left all the match-making to her mother. He was busy with his shipping business, yet whenever Blythe entered his office, he would always push aside his work and chat with her. He had never asked anything of her other than affection. Until now.

Now he wanted her to marry the Duke of Savoy.

Blythe added a lump of sugar to her tea. Well then, so be it, she would make her dear Papa happy by pursuing a betrothal to the duke. Surely all of the doubts she'd awakened with this morning were just a temporary fit of the doldrums. And as Mama had said, love would come in time.

"It *would* be marvelous to be a duchess," Blythe said slowly. "No one would ever dare to snub any of us ever again. I would have my choice of invitations, I'd lead the way into dinner, and I'd even be invited to hobnob with royalty."

"Indeed you would," her mother said approvingly. "I shall set my mind to the task of finding a way to win over Lady Davina. Nothing is impossible when one is determined."

While her mother paced, deep in thought, Blythe bent over the tray to uncover a dish of buttered toast. The delicious aroma caused her stomach to growl. But when she picked up a piece, it was soggy.

"Cold toast again. When I am Duchess of Savoy, I shall insist—"

Something made her look up. A footman stood in the open doorway—the door that Nan had left open. He was gazing straight at Blythe.

Her heart lurched. *James.*

Chapter 5

A flurry of awareness raced over her skin. Dropping the toast, Blythe clutched the edges of her dressing gown together. The nightclothes covered her from neck to toe, yet she was keenly aware of her unbound breasts beneath the fine lawn fabric.

She curled her bare toes into the soft Axminster carpet. How long had he been standing there? Had he overheard her nattering on about becoming a duchess?

What did it matter, anyway, if he had? The opinion of a servant held no significance.

Beneath the powdered wig, his chiseled features were impassive. "A parcel for Miss Crompton," he announced.

Only then did she notice the salver he carried in his gloved hands. On it sat a small box wrapped in cream paper.

"Oh . . ." She pulled her scattered thoughts together. "Will you place it on the table by the hearth?"

"It may be from His Grace," Mrs. Crompton said, sweeping forward to pluck the box off the salver. "Draw the curtains, James. We'll need more light."

He bowed, and there was something inherently proud in his bearing. "Yes, madam."

He started toward the bank of windows behind Blythe.

Picking up a spoon, she pretended to be engrossed in stirring her tea. All the while, she studied him from beneath the veil of her lashes. He had the wide shoulders and muscled physique of an Adonis—although no lofty Greek god would have donned stiff blue livery with gold buttons. Her wayward mind produced an image of James in the pose of a classical statue with a naked torso and a loincloth slung low on his hips.

She fought off a hot blush. Whatever had made her imagine *that*?

To make matters worse, as her gaze returned to his face, James had the audacity to wink at her.

As if he were privy to her fantasy.

Her foolish heart stumbled over a beat. Quickly she stared down into her teacup. Never had she encountered a footman who seemed so oblivious to the boundaries between them. Yet it was ridiculous to feel so flustered. What was wrong with her?

She ought to chastise him for his boldness. But to do so in front of her mother would have consequences. Mama would likely sack him on the spot, and as much as Blythe thought him cheeky, she couldn't bear the notion of being the architect of his dismissal.

From behind her came the rustle of draperies. A moment later, sunlight flooded the bedchamber. He went to each window in turn, proceeding past the bed where Nan was plumping the pillows.

Blythe took a sip of her tea. She'd never before thought anything amiss in allowing a male servant to enter her bedchamber. The staff had been taught to be respectful and unobtrusive, and she scarcely noticed their presence.

But she couldn't say the same of James. She was entirely too aware of his intrusion in her private sanctuary.

"Won't you open this?" Mama asked.

Blythe blinked, realizing her mother stood nearby, holding out the small parcel. "I'll do it later."

Mrs. Crompton arched a fine eyebrow. "Well! You truly *are* in a snit today. Is it time for your monthlies?

"Mama!"

"Now, now," her mother said, giving Blythe a soothing rub on the upper back. "I'm only trying to fathom your ill humor. If you're suffering from the curse of Eve, it's perfectly understandable that you might feel out of sorts. It certainly isn't like you to be so averse to opening a gift."

"I'm sure it's merely sweets or another set of embroidered handkerchiefs," Blythe said, to distract her mother from the indelicate topic. "You may open it yourself if you like."

Her only consolation was that James gave no hint that he had heeded the exchange. Her gaze furtively sought him out. He had moved to the last window, where he drew back the blue draperies and looped the tassel around a hook on the wall. Then he strode to the fire to add a few more coals from the hob. His presence in the bedchamber made it difficult for Blythe to concentrate.

Mrs. Crompton untied the string around the parcel and removed the heavy cream paper. "Well, *I* certainly would like to see what this is. Ah, there's a card on top. And oh! Look who it's from, darling—the Duke of Savoy." With a triumphant smile, she waved a printed calling card.

James picked up the poker to stir the coals, causing the flames to hiss and flare. Seeing that her mother was waiting for a response, Blythe murmured, "How very nice."

"Don't you want to know what it is?"

"Oh . . . certainly."

Mrs. Crompton peered down into the box. "Chocolate

bonbons, the very finest, you may be sure of that. His Grace is renowned for his excellent taste. Do try one and you'll see."

It was customary for a gentleman to send out gifts the day after a large party. As the package contained no personal message, Blythe suspected the duke had sent the exact same thing to every girl with whom he'd danced.

But her mother was insistently holding out the box, so Blythe took a bonbon and popped it into her mouth. The rich sweetness melted on her tongue, and the sensual delight had a soothing effect on her rattled senses. "Mmm. Delicious."

James had put down the poker and stood waiting by the door. His gaze flicked from her mother to Blythe.

The intensity in his dark eyes made Blythe wonder if there was a smudge of chocolate on her lips. Turning away, she ran her forefinger over her mouth. Why did he tarry here? He should vanish from the bedchamber as Nan had done when she'd finished making the bed.

"Pardon me," he said. "Will that be all?"

"Yes!" Blythe said.

"No," Mrs. Crompton countered, frowning slightly. "Blythe, darling, sit down and write a thank-you note to His Grace. If the footman delivers it straightaway, the duke will know you to be a lady who is prompt in her duties."

"But Mama, I'm not even dressed yet." Immediately Blythe regretted the poor choice of words. She oughtn't have drawn attention to that fact with James present.

"A task delayed is a task that will likely never be done," Mrs. Crompton said. "It will only take you a moment."

Blythe wrestled with the urge to refuse, then swallowed her pride and padded barefoot to the dainty writing desk in a corner. She sat down and pulled a note card from one of the cubbyholes. While she selected a quill pen and uncorked the inkpot, her mother kept up a stream of instructions.

"Take care to use your finest penmanship. Don't rush as you are often wont to do. Now is not the time for blots or crossed-out words."

"Of *course*, Mama."

"Now, as to the wording." Mrs. Crompton walked back and forth while dictating, " 'To His Grace of Savoy, I am delighted to be in receipt of your excellent gift.' " She paused. "No, change that to 'your *superior* gift.' That way he will know you consider it to be much finer than anything sent by your other suitors."

Blythe compressed her lips. Did Mama think her incapable of writing a simple note? Apparently so, but with James standing within earshot near the door, she was loath to make a fuss. Releasing her breath in a huff, she dipped the sharpened end of the quill into the ink and began to write, the pen scratching over the paper.

Mrs. Crompton went on, " 'It was extremely kind of you to have sent my favorite chocolates. Please know that your thoughtfulness has brightened my day.' Start a new paragraph. 'Last evening was a very special night for me.' "

For no reason at all, Blythe saw herself back in the sitting room with James as he'd pressed a glass of champagne into her hand. She blocked the image at once. How irksome to keep dwelling upon that inconsequential scene.

She continued to write as her mother dictated, " 'I hope you will not think me too forward in confessing that I will forever treasure the memory of our dance together. I shall wait with great anticipation for you to call upon me at your convenience.' "

"I can't say that," Blythe objected. "It sounds as if I'm commanding him to visit me."

"And why shouldn't you? Men are very flattered to

know that a beautiful young lady is pining for them. Especially one as wealthy as you."

"But—" Blythe bit her lip to keep from blurting out that she wanted to be liked for herself, not for her dowry. Yet wasn't that what the Marriage Mart was all about, the upper crust entering into alliances based on money and rank? She knew that well, for she and Mama had devoted weeks to weighing the merits of potential husbands.

The Duke of Savoy was the catch of the season. Although stuffy and a bit patronizing, he seemed to be a pleasant enough man, and she had confidence in her ability to breach his reserve in time.

So why was she put off today by her mother's maneuvering? Perhaps it seemed crass because James stood there at attention. She didn't like to appear cold and covetous, not even to a servant.

"Now where was I?" Mrs. Crompton said. "Oh, yes. 'Please convey my deepest regards to Lady Davina. Yours very truly, etc.' "

Blythe completed the note, although toning down the gushy bit about treasuring their dance together and expecting him to call on her. Then she sprinkled a bit of sand over it to soak up any excess ink. After tapping off the fine grains into a waste bin, she folded the paper before her mother could check it for accuracy.

She was reaching for the small gold knob embossed with her initials when James appeared at her side. "Allow me," he murmured.

He held a lighted candle which he used to melt a little blob of red sealing wax onto the paper. Blythe impressed the oval of her stamp to close the note. She was far too conscious of him standing only inches from her. Schooling her features into an impassive mask, she glanced up to give him instructions as to where to deliver the letter.

But his attention was focused on the door.

A plump Hindu woman waddled into the bedchamber. Her thin gray hair was scraped in a knob atop her head, and she wore a purple sari edged in orange silk.

In India, Kasi had been *ayah*, or nursemaid, to Blythe and her sisters, a substitute mother during those carefree childhood years when Mama had been busy with the local English society or resting in her chamber from the effects of the heat. Three years ago, Kasi had been the only Indian servant to make the long journey to England with them.

The old woman placed her leathery palms together and bent at the waist in a deep salaam to Mrs. Crompton. In her sing-song voice, she said, "*Memsahib*, I bring you message. Missy Portia come to London tomorrow."

Springing up from the desk, Blythe uttered a happy cry. "Oh, Kasi, that's marvelous news. I'm so very glad to hear it."

⁂

James stood riveted by the glow of pleasure on Blythe Crompton's face. It transformed her from the aloof, wary girl he had observed upon entering the bedchamber. The sight gripped him in an involuntary fist of heat. He wanted to see that joyous expression on her face as she gazed up at him in bed.

James buried the fantasy, though he could not fault himself for his lust. Clad in a pale dressing gown with a rich mass of coppery hair flowing loose to her waist, she looked absolutely delectable, every man's dream.

But Miss Blythe Crompton wasn't destined for just any man. She would be the bride of a duke—if she and her mother could coax Savoy into making an offer.

"Well!" Mrs. Crompton said with a sniff. "It's a pity she and Ratcliffe had to miss our ball last night. I do believe they could have made more of an effort to arrive sooner."

Blythe's face portrayed exasperation with her mother. "You know precisely why they couldn't come any earlier," she said. "Little Arthur developed an unfortunate case of the sniffles. Thank heavens, he must be much improved now." To Kasi, she added, "They *are* bringing my nephew, aren't they?"

Beaming, Kasi bobbed her head. "Yes, I fix nursery."

"That won't be necessary," Mrs. Crompton countered. "It is best they stay with Lindsey and Mansfield. The house on Park Lane has ample room in the nursery. Besides, Portia will appreciate the chance to meet her new niece."

They were speaking of Blythe's older sisters, James gathered. From downstairs gossip, he'd learned that Portia, the eldest Crompton daughter, had a young son and had recently announced she was pregnant with a second child. Lindsey had given birth to her first daughter only a fortnight ago. Now, he found it telling to note Edith Crompton's seeming lack of interest in her grandchildren.

Was it evidence of a cold-hearted woman capable of committing fraud and thievery on a grand scale?

He observed Edith closely as she stood in the sunlight streaming through the windows. There were surface similarities between her and the woman he remembered visiting when he'd been a boy of ten. They both had reddish hair and hazel-brown eyes. Both were slim and feminine.

But there were also differences. The Edith he remembered had been more quiet and shy while this woman was clearly a social butterfly. The old Edith also had exhibited a natural warmth of manner, giving him a kiss before sending him outdoors to play with her pet spaniels.

James's memory grew hazy beyond that. The facial features of his cousin's wife remained indistinct in his mind, no matter how hard he strained to call forth the image of her. He cursed the fact that he couldn't make a definitive judgment on her identity.

"I was so looking forward to seeing Portia," Blythe was saying to her mother. "They always stay with us."

"I'm sorry, darling, but a young child will cause entirely too much disruption in the household. We cannot afford any distractions while you're seeking a husband."

"But Mama—"

"Enough. You will have ample opportunity to visit your sisters at Lindsey's home. Meanwhile, you must concentrate on enticing the Duke of Savoy into making you an offer. Your future depends upon it."

Mrs. Crompton glided toward the desk and retrieved the note that Blythe had written. She handed it to James and made a dismissing motion with her fingers. "Deliver that to His Grace at once."

"Yes, Madam."

She had scarcely cast a glance at him. He might as well have been invisible.

So much the better because it gave him the opportunity to take one final quick scrutiny of her. The hair color was similar, but there was no gray. If this woman really was his cousin's wife, she must be nearing her fiftieth year. Yet the few fine wrinkles around her eyes and mouth seemed to suggest a somewhat younger age than that.

Was there a portrait of her hanging in the Cromptons' manor house in Lancashire? Damn it, he ought to have had the foresight to make the two-day journey there before taking this post as footman.

But he had believed his memories of Edith and George Crompton to be clear and distinct. He hadn't anticipated having trouble identifying them.

Now James was trapped here. Even if he were to concoct a grievous tale about a dying relative, he surely would lose his position if he were to beg a few days' leave. After all, it wasn't as though he was a valued retainer who had worked for the family for a long time. He was new and thus expendable.

A prickly sense of disquiet raised the hairs at the back of his neck. The Indian woman named Kasi stood silently to the side, her dark currant eyes fixed on him.

Realizing he'd tarried too long, he gripped the note and started toward the door. He had one last glimpse of Miss Blythe Crompton in that form-fitting dressing gown. She was watching him, too; then she blushed and glanced away. A pity they hadn't been alone so that he could have charmed her into revealing information about her parents.

But there would be other opportunities. When the moment was ripe, he fully intended to exploit her interest in him.

Chapter 6

That evening, Blythe had the opportunity to advance her hopes with the Duke of Savoy when she and her parents attended a musicale given by an acquaintance of her mother's, the Marchioness of Wargrave.

The Cromptons arrived to find the guests milling in the reception hall. From inside the drawing room came the sounds of a string orchestra tuning their instruments. Slowly wending their way through the crowd, Blythe and her parents chatted with several acquaintances. Whenever an unmarried gentleman approached, however, her mother deftly steered Blythe in another direction. All the while, Mrs. Crompton strained to see over the multitude of people.

"You're taller than I," she said to Blythe's father. "Do you see the duke?"

"There," Mr. Crompton murmured, nodding toward the doorway of the drawing room. "But he's surrounded by ambitious mothers with marriageable daughters. I will not permit you to behave so badly as to push your way through that crush."

Blythe stood on tiptoe to see that her father was correct. The throng milling around the duke appeared to be comprised of ladies vying for his attention. "I quite agree, Papa. I don't relish the notion of appearing overly eager."

Mrs. Crompton guided her family to an alcove filled with statuary and ferns. "Wait here," she said. "I must have a word with Lady Wargrave. Perhaps she can secure a seat for Blythe beside His Grace."

With that, she vanished into the colorful swarm of ladies and gentlemen, leaving Blythe alone with her father.

He looked at Blythe, and a wry grin deepened the lines on his weathered face. "Your mother is forever scheming," he said, patting Blythe's hand, which was tucked in the crook of his arm. "I don't know what she'll do once you're married and there are no more daughters to manage."

"She'll start choosing future spouses for her grandchildren among the babies of society."

They shared a laugh, and Blythe reflected on how safe and happy she felt with her father. Papa was stout and solid and had a faint, ever-present scent of pipe smoke. Although he often was busy with his shipping business, he had always been her hero, the man she admired above all others.

She treasured the rare occasions like this when she had him all to herself, if only for a few moments. The twinkle in his blue eyes brought back memories of the times in India when he had taken her for a Sunday drive in the *palka-ghari* or taught her the rules of *kabaddi*, a fast-paced game played by the natives.

The humor faded from her father's face, and he gave her a keen look. "So you are quite settled on Savoy, are you? I must say, I am well pleased by the notion. It would be an excellent marriage for you."

Blythe shifted her eyes as if to scan the crowd. She didn't want him to guess that she longed for love. Papa so seldom asked anything of her and if he wished for her to wed the duke, then she would do so gladly. Besides, who was to say that she and the duke wouldn't fall in love? She needed only to have the chance to be in his company.

"I like His Grace very much." She spoke confidently, reminding herself of all the reasons the Duke of Savoy would make a splendid husband. "He's refined and well-mannered and respectful. As his wife, I shall be quite happy to be a grand hostess of the ton."

"My only concern is that he's a bit old for you," her father said. "You're a spirited girl, but you know little of the world."

"Oh pooh," she said airily, striving to erase the hint of concern on his face. "I've watched my sisters. And I've lived abroad and traveled halfway around the world. I'm sure to know my own mind more so than any other girl my age."

Mr. Crompton studied her pensively for another moment; then a smile tilted the corners of his mouth. "You are indeed an original, my dear. My fondest wish is for you to be happy."

His heartfelt declaration brought the sting of tears to her eyes, and she leaned her head against his shoulder. She did love her father so. If only she could have a husband who was every bit as wonderful as him.

For no reason at all, she thought of James. A man of his station would marry a maidservant or a shopgirl, while she herself would take a husband from the highest ranks of the ton. That was the natural way of the world. She had observed it here in London and also in India, where the caste system was even more rigorous than in England.

But it served no purpose to dwell upon her attraction to a footman.

A chime sounded, signaling the imminent commencement of the concert. The aristocratic guests began moving en masse into the drawing room to find seats among the rows of chairs.

Mama came scurrying out of the flock of ladies and gentlemen. From the brittleness of her smile, it was clear that her mission to secure Blythe a place beside the duke had been less than successful.

"No luck, my dear?" Mr. Crompton asked.

"Hmph. These past three years I've nurtured a friendship with Lady Wargrave and it's all for naught. I should have known she would be a stickler for precedence."

It hurt Blythe's heart to see her mother looking so disappointed. "It's quite all right, Mama. I'll have a chance to see him later when refreshments are served."

"Indeed you shall. I will make certain of it."

Mrs. Crompton took her husband's arm and with Blythe on his other side, they joined the guests already in the drawing room. There, people were settling into the rows of gilt chairs that faced the musicians' dais. Blythe caught a glimpse of Lady Davina and her father making their way toward a place of honor in the front.

When the duke's daughter glanced back toward the Cromptons, Blythe lifted her hand in a friendly wave, but the girl gave no acknowledgment of having noticed. Her gaze passed over Blythe as if she was invisible.

As the Duke of Savoy took his seat in between two young ladies, Davina remained standing to speak to someone else in their party. Blythe recognized him at once. The dandified gentleman in the leaf-green coat was Viscount Kitchener, who had partnered her in a dance the previous evening.

All of a sudden, the two of them turned to look straight at Blythe.

She stiffened, resisting the urge to self-consciously straighten her pale yellow gown. So Davina *had* seen her, after all. Were they gossiping about the wealthy interloper who had invaded their exalted ranks?

Let them talk. A bit of tittle-tattle would not deter Blythe. It only made her all the more determined to be gracious. Perhaps after the concert there would be an opportunity to soften that haughty manner of Davina's. After all, Blythe had never met anyone who could withstand an assault of relentless charm.

As commoners, the Cromptons were relegated to the back row. Blythe didn't mind because it would allow her the freedom to observe the guests during the concert. If she had to sit for an hour without fidgeting, she might as well enjoy herself by studying the hairstyles and gowns of the other ladies, and deciding which of the gentlemen was the most dashing and handsome. Having only been out for the past fortnight, she found such events new and exciting. It was certainly a vast improvement over being confined to the schoolroom, taking endless lessons in dancing and drawing and deportment.

"May I join you, Miss Crompton?"

She looked up to see one of her suitors towering over her. He had an attractive thatch of reddish hair with the most unfortunate rash of freckles marring his face. The hopefulness in his brown eyes touched her heart. "Mr. Mainwaring, how good to see you again. I would be happy to—"

"I'm afraid Lord Kitchener already has a claim to Miss Crompton."

Lady Davina appeared beside the hapless young man, who took one look at her cool patrician face and scuttled away before Blythe could even form a protest. Davina had Viscount Kitchener in tow, and she aimed a frosty smile at Blythe's parents.

"Mr. and Mrs. Crompton," she said by way of greeting.

"We appear to be one chair short in the front row. I do hope you don't mind if Lord Kitchener sits back here with you."

Mrs. Crompton wore a look of dazzled enthusiasm. "Why, of *course*, my lady, we're more than happy to accommodate him. Perhaps after the concert, you and your father could join us, too?"

"Perhaps for a moment. Although I'm afraid we are leaving directly afterward to attend another engagement." Her voice held a hint of icy incivility as she gave Kitchener a nudge. "Now, do be a good fellow and sit down. The music is about to begin."

As she turned to go, a smirk played about her lips. Davina's words at the ball echoed in Blythe's mind. *I would never permit my father to marry so vastly far beneath him.*

She could only surmise that the girl must be hoping Kitchener would distract Blythe from pursuing Davina's father.

What a ridiculously transparent ploy!

The viscount plopped down in the adjoining chair without taking his usual fastidious care to avoid wrinkling the tails of his coat. On the handful of occasions when they had met, Blythe had observed his self-absorbed nature. Kitchener cultivated the image of a romantic poet with a tumbled mass of golden-brown curls and an affectation for staring into the distance as if he were contemplating some deep philosophical conundrum. He was also a slave to the latest style, as evidenced by the leaf-green coat, yellow breeches, and the intricate white cravat that must have taken the better part of an hour for his valet to tie.

His dandified appearance came at a price, however. Kitchener was rumored to be in dire need of a fortune in order to pay off his tailor bills.

Her fortune.

"Hullo," he said to Blythe in a rather loud voice. "You are truly an angel to behold! Your beauty shines as bright and clear as the moon against a black velvet sky."

"Thank you, my lord."

His syrupy compliment held no sway over her. She was too busy puzzling over his glassy-eyed stare and overly ebullient manner.

Was he foxed?

He had to be. Now it became clearer why Lady Davina had directed him to sit back here. She knew he'd been drinking. And she must be hoping he would humiliate Blythe by embroiling her in some sort of scene.

Blythe controlled a surge of temper. Davina had played a nasty trick, but that didn't mean Blythe had to fall blindly into the trap.

As the musicians began to play, the viscount continued to chatter. "What a divine harmony of sound," he said without making any effort to lower his voice. "I do believe such a melody must have been given to mankind by the gods on Mount Olympus. Do you not agree, Miss Crompton?"

Several guests turned around to scowl at him. A gray-haired matron tut-tutted while shaking her head.

Catching the viscount's eye, Blythe put a finger to her lips. "Shh," she whispered. "You must be quiet now."

Kitchener nodded solemnly and mimicked her action by placing his forefinger over his own mouth. Then he smiled abashedly at the people in front of them, who then returned their attention to the stage.

Relieved that he seemed to have fathomed the error of his ways, Blythe settled back to enjoy the music. The light, vibrant tune helped to soothe her sense of annoyance. She would not permit anyone to ruin the evening.

Her gaze wandered over the aristocrats in the drawing

room. She spied white-haired Lady Grantham leaning forward, cupping her half-deaf ear to better hear the music. A few rows ahead sat blond, vacuous Miss Frances Beardsley with her betrothed, Lord Wrayford. Candlelight glinted on the bald spot at the back of his head.

Blythe studied Wrayford with interest. He was the scoundrel who had tried to abduct Lindsey the previous year, although the scandal had been averted when Mansfield had ridden to her rescue. Portia had had a similar adventure two years ago when Ratcliffe had kidnapped her in order to stop her from wedding the wrong man.

What dashing heroes her sisters had married, Blythe thought wistfully. Somehow, she couldn't imagine the Duke of Savoy bestirring himself to perform such daring exploits on her behalf.

But James would. Blythe knew that with instinctive certainty.

She pressed her fingers into the arms of her chair. Why did thoughts of a footman continue to plague her? She knew nothing of him beyond the boldness of manner that set him apart from the other servants. They might reside in the same household, but they were worlds apart in all that mattered.

She didn't crave romantic escapades, anyway. Such childish dreams had been left behind when she had entered the world of high society on a mission to find a husband.

Blythe glanced over at her mother and father, who were absorbed in the music. They looked so elegant, Mama in steel-blue silk that offset her stylish russet hair, and Papa in his tailored gray coat. It wasn't fair that their common blood should make them any less important than the aristocrats gathered here.

It would make them so happy if she became the Duchess of Savoy. And *she* would be happy to elevate their position in society. Once she bore the duke a son, Mama and Papa would be honored as the grandparents of the heir to a dukedom.

The hopeful vision faded abruptly when Viscount Kitchener shifted in his chair beside hers and began to mutter.

"The notes dance upon the sky so airy / for ye are lovely as a fairy / and in your arms methinks to tarry / for 'tis safe from the . . . from the unwary." He leaned closer to Blythe and said in a stage whisper, "What else rhymes with airy?"

For the first time, she noticed that he exuded a sweetish smoky scent that smelled vaguely familiar. It brought to mind the men in India who would crouch around the hookah, passing the pipe to one another until they all sank into a stupor.

The truth jolted her. The viscount's inebriated state wasn't due to an excess of wine or brandy. Rather, he must have smoked opium shortly before his arrival here. She had heard rumors that such behavior was practiced among the scoundrels and riff-raff on the fringes of society. Opium-eaters, they were called.

"I need more rhymes," he complained, raising his voice so that people turned to glower at them again. Not that Kitchener noticed. "Airy, fairy, tarry. Do help me out, Miss Crompton."

Mrs. Crompton placed a warning hand on Blythe's arm and frowned at her as if the situation was all her doing.

Aggravated, Blythe whispered to him under her breath, "Hairy, scary, dairy." She certainly wasn't going to give him any ideas by saying *marry.* In his present state he might fall to his knees and beg for her hand in front of the entire assemblage. "Now, pray be silent."

"But you adore poetry," Viscount Kitchener whined. "Davy said you did."

Her lips tightened. Blast Lady Davina, what other lies had she told him? "She is sadly mistaken. I'll not hear another word from you."

Blythe gave him a stern look that must have penetrated his cloudy senses. His voice fell to a barely audible muttering about maids of dairy and lads so hairy. Thankfully, the orchestra had launched into a lively melody and no one else paid them any heed.

Then a blessed reprieve happened. The viscount's chin sagged to his cravat and he dozed off. Other than an occasional light snore, he remained silent for the remainder of the concert. Blythe sat unmoving for fear of awakening him and causing another disturbance.

At last the music drew to an end and the guests applauded politely. People arose from their chairs, the hum of conversation growing as everyone discussed the performance on their way to the supper room where refreshments would be served.

"Hurry," Mrs. Crompton whispered to Blythe. "We must make haste to seek out the duke."

"Yes, Mama."

But when Blythe attempted to get up, she realized to her dismay that Lord Kitchener's shoe was firmly planted on her hem. As she tried to tug herself free, it became clear that the fine gauze of her gown would rip if she pulled any harder.

She discreetly poked the viscount in the arm. "Wake up, my lord."

He made no response, his eyes never opening, his chest rising and falling in slumber, his head still tilted askew in a ridiculous pose. What was worse, a few people had noticed the pair of them, the ladies laughing behind their fans—as if her companionship had put him to sleep.

"Savoy is coming down the aisle," her mother prodded. "Do stand up at once or we'll miss our chance!"

Blythe glimpsed the duke advancing through the throng with Lady Davina on his arm. A bevy of debutantes trailed him. Blast! There was no time to waste.

With renewed effort, Blythe bent down to shove Kitchener's foot aside. The awkward task was like moving a leaden weight. While her mother hovered and fretted, at last Blythe was able to slide the hem free, albeit with a black scuff mark marring the pale yellow fabric.

Unfortunately, the duke already had moved past the last row. While proceeding through the open doorway, Lady Davina glanced back over her shoulder and sent Blythe a triumphant look.

"You should not have dallied," Mrs. Crompton scolded. "Come now, we can still catch up to them."

"No, it's too late," Blythe stated. "They're departing for another engagement, remember?"

She had no wish to humiliate herself by pushing and shoving. At least she could be thankful that Kitchener had not embroiled her in an even more horrid scene by falling off his chair or attempting to kiss her in front of everyone, as Lady Davina must have intended.

That hateful voice resounded in her memory. *I would never permit my father to marry so vastly far beneath him.*

Lady Davina had declared war. She had done so in words and by her actions tonight. She may have won the first skirmish by catching Blythe unawares, but Blythe would not make the mistake of underestimating the girl again.

Rather than slink away in defeat, Blythe felt more determined than ever. She would win in the end. After all, the best possible outcome would be for her to win the love of the Duke of Savoy.

Chapter 7

Since dawn, James had been cleaning silver utensils in the butler's pantry near the cellar kitchen. It was late morning now, and the heap of dirty rags beside him had grown into a mountain. So had the pile of gleaming knives and forks. God only knew what ingredients were in the pasty concoction he was using, but it stunk to high heaven. The stench blocked out even the aromas of baking bread and roasting meat wafting from the kitchen.

He rubbed at a stubborn bit of tarnish on a soup spoon. A family dinner party was scheduled for this evening, and of course the table couldn't possibly be set with the same silver service that had been used at the ball a few nights ago. That would have been far too convenient.

But at least he'd been assigned to serve tonight. After three days on staff, he finally would have the chance to take a close look at George Crompton.

Was the man his cousin—or not?

James cooled his simmering impatience. As the newest man on staff, he had been assigned every dirty task disliked by the other footmen. His temper was further eroded by the fact that he was isolated down here in the cellar, where the only natural light trickled through a window slit located high in the wall. Having spent most of his adult life in the West Indies, he was accustomed to being out in the sunshine and fresh air, not buried away like a mole in a dank burrow.

He itched to join the other servants working above stairs. At least then he might finagle a way to search for evidence to prove that George and Edith Crompton were imposters.

Hearing voices, he stepped to the doorway and peered into the dimly lit corridor. Outside the laundry room, a stout maid was handing a pile of folded linens to the Hindu servant, Kasi.

The sight galvanized James. He had wanted to interrogate the old woman ever since his arrival here. She was the only one who had lived in India with the Cromptons. But Kasi had been forever upstairs, tending to the needs of the family. She didn't even take her meals with the staff.

Blast the silverware. He could not waste this prime opportunity.

Tossing down the spoon, he seized a clean rag and scrubbed the black tarnish from his hands. He snatched up the obligatory white gloves and tugged them on as he rushed out into the corridor.

The laundry maid had vanished. So had Kasi.

But luck saved him. He caught a glimpse of her orange sari as she rounded the corner and disappeared from sight.

In hot pursuit, James strode swiftly down the passageway. The scents of starch and dampness hung heavy in the cool air. He spied the Indian woman as she started up the narrow wooden staircase that led to the upper floors.

"Wait, please!" he called.

Holding the pile of folded undergarments, she stopped on the second step and turned to gaze impassively at him. A tiny red dot glinted on her forehead in between her eyes.

Was that the Evil Eye he'd heard whispered about by the other servants? They all seemed in awe of the woman.

"Pardon me," he said, giving her a respectful bow. "I hope you'll permit me a moment of your time. I wanted to inquire as to how long you've worked for the Crompton family."

"I am *ayah* to *sahib*'s little girls."

"*Ayah* . . . is that a nursemaid or a governess?"

Her plump brown features took on a placid look. In her musical voice, she said, "*Ayah* feed babies, play games, sing to sleep."

Questions gripped James. If Kasi had been with the Crompton girls since they were born, then she must be privy to the truth. She must know if the master of the house was the real George Crompton—or a swindler who had cheated James out of his inheritance.

Of course, Crompton would have paid this woman handsomely to keep his secrets. He would not have taken the risk of bringing her to London with the family without being absolutely certain of her loyalty.

James needed to win her trust. So he formulated a lie that would explain his interest in the family's background. "You've known them for quite a long time, then. I was wondering what manner of man is Mr. Crompton? You see, I would like to move to India someday, and I'm curious if you think he might write me a reference."

Kasi shrugged. "You ask *sahib*. I do not know."

"Don't go yet." James mounted the steps in an effort to stop her from leaving. "Please, I would merely like to know your assessment of him. Is he a kind master? Is he honest and obliging? Or is he perhaps cold and ruthless in matters of business?"

The Indian woman stared at him. Under the scrutiny of those dark currant eyes, a prickling ran over his skin, and he had the sudden illogical sense that she could read his mind and see his true purpose.

Nonsense. He couldn't have given himself away with a few questions. No one here knew that James was really George Crompton's cousin and heir.

The scuff of approaching footsteps broke the silence. A maidservant in mobcap and gray gown trudged around the corner. She was toting a large breakfast tray. Upon seeing them on the stairway, she halted so fast that the dishes clattered.

It was Meg, the saucy maid who had given up on flirting with James. Her startled attention was focused on Kasi.

The Indian woman scowled, her eyes narrowing to slits. Meg sucked in an audible breath, stepped swiftly backward, and bumped hard into the wall.

The breakfast tray tilted. James leaped down the few steps and grabbed it from her. But he wasn't fast enough to stop one of the covered dishes from flying off. Toast and china scattered all over floor. Miraculously, the plate didn't break.

Halfway down the long corridor, a man stepped out of the kitchen. James silently cursed the bad timing. Godwin, the head footman, was a nitpicking taskmaster who'd kept a close watch on James.

"What's the matter there?" Godwin snapped.

"It was merely a slight mishap," James called. "No harm done."

"See to it that the mess is cleaned up," Godwin ordered before vanishing back into the kitchen.

Meg was still staring at the staircase. "'Tis the Evil Eye," she whispered.

James would have laughed out loud had she not looked so genuinely terrified. And if he wasn't so frustrated from being thwarted in his interrogation of Kasi.

The Hindu woman had vanished up the stairs. Blast it, he would have to delay any further questioning until another time.

"Don't be ridiculous," he told Meg. "Kasi is harmless. Now, you'll need to replenish this tray. Where were you taking it?"

"To-to Miss Crompton."

All of his senses snapped to alertness. Luck had handed him an opportunity on a silver platter—quite literally. "You're too shaken to carry something so heavy. I'll deliver it myself."

Chapter 8

After donning a foam-green morning gown, Blythe dismissed the maid and finished her toilette herself. She had no engagements until the requisite calls in the early afternoon and for the moment, she preferred to be alone with her own thoughts.

Lifting her skirt slightly, she stepped into a pair of soft leather slippers. She really ought to have gone downstairs to join her parents for breakfast. But no doubt Mama would have launched into a litany of schemes designed to ingratiate them with Lady Davina and her father.

Still stung by the dirty trick Davina had played, Blythe pursed her lips. In the carriage going home the previous evening, Mama had shrugged off Blythe's assertion that Davina had purposefully set up a situation whereby Viscount Kitchener would embroil Blythe in a scene. They must be forgiving of Davina, Mama had argued, if Blythe ever hoped to become the Duchess of Savoy.

Blythe *did* want to achieve the stellar marriage. Not so much to satisfy her mother's ambitions, but to please Papa. It was clear he wished to see her well settled. Wedding the duke certainly would be the crowning glory of her London season.

But she drew the line at groveling before Lady Davina.

In regard to Savoy, the duke's daughter might as well be a fire-breathing dragon barring entry to a castle. It would take cleverness to figure out a way to defeat the girl at her own game.

Pondering the problem, Blythe left the dressing room and went into her sunlit bedchamber. Perhaps her sisters would have some advice on the matter. During their own seasons, they too must have encountered such snobbery.

Her spirits lightened at the notion of seeing them again. Portia and Ratcliffe were due to arrive from Kent in the late afternoon along with their young son. They were staying with Lindsey and Mansfield, but they would be coming over for dinner this evening.

It would be just like old times. The whole family would be gathered together, laughing and talking, exchanging news about their lives.

The happy prospect made Blythe smile as she sat down at the dressing table to arrange her hair. This would be the first evening in a fortnight that she wouldn't attend any social events, but she didn't mind in the least. Strange, she had spent her adolescent years impatient to grow up and join the ton. She had never quite appreciated the blessing of having sisters. Now, Portia and Lindsey mattered more to her than an entire ballroom filled with glittering nobility.

Blythe was adding a few final pins to her hair when a firm knock sounded on the door. Leaning closer to the mirror to check for any loose strands, she called, "Come in."

The door opened and her fingers froze in place. In the looking glass, she saw the tall reflection of James entering the bedchamber. His unexpected arrival caused her heart to lurch.

He was carrying her breakfast tray. "Good morning,

Miss Crompton," he said, appearing remarkably handsome in blue.

Unable to resist, she turned her head to watch as he crossed the room to place the tray on the round table by the window. A keen awareness of him hummed over her skin. "Where is the maid?"

"She had a minor mishap below stairs, so I took it upon myself to deliver this." He fixed his gaze on Blythe. "I do hope you don't mind my presumption."

That direct stare unnerved her. It was so very unlike the other servants. Intrigued, she found herself wanting to unravel the mystery of him. What in his background had made him so bold?

Realizing she still had her hands raised to her head, Blythe returned her gaze to the mirror and pretended an interest in adjusting a few stray copper strands. "It's perfectly fine."

She refrained from adding that she might have been undressed and therefore didn't appreciate his intrusion into her sanctum. But it wouldn't do to put a picture of herself in a state of dishabille into his mind.

Continuing to primp, she observed him from the corner of her eye. James didn't immediately depart. Instead, he was lifting the silver covers off the plates. He picked up something and walked to the hearth, then crouched down in front of the grate.

Curiosity overwhelmed common sense, and she swiveled on the stool to see what occupied him. He had a slice of bread on a long fork and he was toasting it over the flames, turning it to brown both sides.

"Why are you doing that?" she blurted out.

"Yesterday, when I delivered the parcel from the Duke of Savoy, I heard you mention that your toast is always delivered cold. No wonder, for the kitchen is quite a distance from here. But as you can see, the problem is easily remedied."

Blythe sat in utter amazement. No other servant had ever proposed such a solution. His consideration touched her heart. "That's very clever of you."

"I would call it practical." James rose to his feet and returned to the table, where he placed a pat of butter on top of the toasted bread. "You may wish to eat while it's hot, or my efforts will be for naught."

He held the chair for her, helping her slide in close to the tray. She picked up a knife to spread the melting butter, then added a dollop of strawberry jam. The first bite was buttery and sweet yet still warm and crisp the way she liked it.

"Mmm," she said around a mouthful. "Delicious."

James took another slice of bread over to the hearth and began to toast that one over the flames as well. "I'm glad to hear it. No young lady should have to endure the affliction of cold toast."

Hunkered down, he cast a wry grin over his shoulder and Blythe found herself returning the smile. They might have been a lady and a gentleman bantering at a ball. How peculiar to feel so at ease with a footman. His audacity seemed to be an innate character trait, and it only made her more curious about him.

She brushed the crumbs from her fingers. "You haven't always been a servant, have you?"

As he came forward with the second piece of toast, he cast a hooded glance at her. "May I ask why you say that?"

"You speak well, you look me straight in the eye, and you're more candid than anyone else on staff."

Lowering his gaze, James immediately assumed a more servile posture. "I beg your pardon, Miss Crompton. I shall be more unobtrusive."

She frowned, irked to have ruined the camaraderie

between them. "You haven't offended me. But do answer my question. What is your background?"

His gaze returned to hers. "I grew up in the country as companion to the son of a gentleman. Thus, I was fortunate enough to have reaped the benefits of a superior education."

"Ah." That explained a lot. How difficult was it for him to be in possession of a gentleman's skills, while being relegated to the lowly role of household servant? "Why did you not seek employment as a secretary or a land agent, then? Those positions surely must pay a higher salary."

He buttered the second slice of toast for her. "There was nothing like that available at the agency. And I did hold a better position as a valet for a time. Alas, my master died on our voyage here from the West Indies."

"The West Indies!" No wonder his skin was browned from the sun. "Had you lived there very long?"

"For a time. The master was inspecting some properties he owned there. Upon his death, I was left without recourse. Especially since . . . but never mind. I'm sure you aren't interested in my tale of woe."

"Oh, but I *am*. Do finish."

His face solemn, James clasped his hands behind his back. "Upon my arrival in London, I left the ship, intending to spend a brief time touring the sights here. That's when all of my savings were stolen by a gang of footpads near the docks."

Aghast, Blythe paused in the act of pouring a cup of tea. Her father often went to the docks, but he always had a coachman and guard with him. "How terrible! Had you nothing left at all?"

"Not so much as tuppence in my pocket. I'm most grateful there was an opening here in this household. I appreciate the chance to earn enough coin for my passage."

"Passage?" She set down the teapot to stare at him.

"You're leaving England again? To return to the West Indies?"

He shook his head. "Since taking employment here, I've become most admiring of your father's accomplishments. Perhaps you'll think me above my station, but I've resolved to travel to India myself and seek my own fortune."

Blythe regarded him in astonishment. How very remarkable to meet a servant who held the dream of bettering himself. Never in her life had she known anyone of the lower classes to have aspirations beyond his station. It was just the way life was, with everyone accepting of the position in which he was born.

She very nearly asked James to sit down and join her. But such an act was forbidden. Who'd ever heard of a lady partaking of a meal with a servant as if they were equals? And in her bedchamber, no less!

At least the door stood ajar. Anyone who might look in on them would see nothing out of the ordinary.

"I shall speak to Papa," she said. "Mayhap he can find a better place for you in his offices near the docks."

James shook his head. "It may be difficult to understand, Miss Crompton, but I would very much like to make my own way in the world without anyone's help." He paused. "However . . ."

Blythe leaned forward. "Yes?"

He strolled to the window, then turned back, looking as if he was weighing his words. "However, there is a way in which you could assist me, if it isn't too much trouble. You could tell me about India."

"What did you wish to know?"

"I'd like to learn more of the native customs, the countryside, the Englishmen who trade there, and so forth. Pray forgive me if such a task is too bothersome."

"No! I'm happy to help. But I scarcely know where to begin."

James glanced around the bedchamber. "You haven't any Indian artifacts on display. Does that mean you disliked living there?"

Blythe had never really noticed there was nothing of her old life in the elegant blue-and-white bedchamber. "No, Mama oversaw the decoration of this room. I'm afraid she never cared much for India. But I liked it very much. It was all I knew for the first fifteen years of my life."

How clearly she recalled the hot, earthy, colorful chaos of India. There had been ash-covered madmen, half-naked beggars, cobras and tigers and elephants. Strange, she'd once thought England to be much more exotic than the familiar trappings of her youth. Mama had always spoken of London as being a place of refined elegance where the nobility attended parties and balls, where style and grace reigned supreme. It had all sounded so wonderful, like something out of a fairy tale. . . .

Blythe realized that James stood patiently waiting for her to continue. "I suppose you could say that India is a place of great extremes. In the heat of summer, it never, ever rains. But in the monsoon season, the showers pour in torrents for days on end. I would sit on the porch while sheets of rain came down, reading with my sisters or playing with one of our pets."

"What sort of animals did you keep?"

"Usually a monkey or a cockatoo. I had a lemur once, too, with a beautiful long tail and a glossy coat that I liked to comb." Blythe smiled at the memory. "But one day it escaped its cage and made a puddle inside one of Mama's hats. She bade the *mali* return it to the jungle. I cried for days."

"*Mali*?"

"The gardener. You will need to study the language, of course. Many of the English never bother to learn Hindi, but Papa did. He always said it gave him superior bargaining power when trading with the maharajahs."

"Maharajah . . . isn't that a king?"

"Yes, but unlike England, there are many maharajahs, each one ruling over a particular region. They're fabulously wealthy, often wearing rubies and diamonds the size of eggs. My sister Portia very nearly married the son of a maharajah herself."

James picked up the teapot and refilled Blythe's cup. "I cannot imagine your parents would be agreeable to her wedding a native, no matter how many rubies and diamonds he might own."

"Yes, Mama was extremely angry when she found out they were sweet on each other. That's how she convinced Papa to move here from India in the first place. She said it was past time that my sisters and I returned to civilization."

Sipping the tea, Blythe recalled how envious she'd been when Arun had traveled all the way from India to London to seek her sister's hand in marriage. But Portia had fallen in love with Viscount Ratcliffe, and Arun returned to his native land, whereupon he had taken a Hindu princess as his bride. Not long ago, he had written to Portia in glowing terms of his happiness upon the birth of his first son.

Such was the way of the world, Blythe reflected again. There could be no breeching the rigid boundaries of one's own social circle. It simply wasn't done. Yet as she glanced up at James, she acknowledged a twinge of regret, for he was more captivating than any of the idle gentlemen who courted her.

She banished the foolish thought at once. Her parents would be horrified if they knew she'd harbored such a notion about a footman.

James continued to gaze at her, his dark eyes full of mystery. "How very fascinating it all sounds," he said.

"Perhaps." Flustered under his scrutiny, she pushed back her chair. "By the by, you're mistaken to think I haven't kept any mementos of India. I've some pieces tucked away, embroidered shawls from Kashmir, gold bangles, beautiful ivory carvings. I'll show you one of my favorite things."

Blythe stepped into her dressing room and returned with a spray of peacock feathers in a white vase. She fingered the long, delicate fronds of turquoise, green, and brown. "We had a flock of peacocks in our garden in India. Have you heard of the birds? They're quite large and have a very raucous cry for so lovely a creature."

James came closer to examine the plumes. "I've read of them. The male bird displays a fan of feathers to attract the female for purposes of mating." He paused, then added, "One might say it's rather like the dandies of society, strutting and preening to catch a lady's attention."

She laughed, thinking of Viscount Kitchener in his leaf-green coat and elaborate cravat. But she didn't want to talk about society, not when memories of India shone so brightly in her mind.

Blythe traced the egg-shaped eye of one feather. "Because of their beauty, the plumage of the peacock is the symbol of royalty. The natives also believe these feathers can ward off the Evil Eye."

"Perhaps I should borrow one, then. The other servants seem convinced that your Indian servant, Kasi, has the power of the Evil Eye."

"Truly?" Blythe asked in surprise. "I suppose I used to

believe that, too, when I was a child and she scowled at me for misbehaving. She does seem to have an uncanny way of knowing things."

James wore a slight smile that didn't quite reach his eyes. "How long has Kasi been with your family?"

"For as long as I can remember. Why do you ask?"

"I merely wondered since she seems so close to you and your mother. I imagine she's privy to all the family secrets."

Blythe started to laugh again, but the alertness of his manner made her suddenly uneasy. Was he seeking tittle-tattle to spread among the other servants?

She hoped not because that would mean she'd grossly misread his character. "I'm afraid we Cromptons are a rather dull lot. We haven't any secrets—aside from Portia and Arun, of course."

"Of course." Gathering up the remains of her breakfast, James replaced the domed silver cover over her china plate. "I hope you'll forgive my curious nature, Miss Crompton, but have you visited Lancashire since your return to England?"

"Lancashire?" As Blythe set down the vase of peacock feathers on a table, the question caught her off guard. "Do you mean Papa's estate?"

"Yes, one of the other servants mentioned that your parents lived there a long time ago. Before you were born."

She relaxed. "I see. Well, I haven't ever visited the place. I suppose Mama and Papa prefer to remain in London."

"Most other fine families divide their time between the city and the country. They're only here for the social season."

Wondering at his persistence, Blythe plucked out a feather and ran her fingers through the silky fronds. "That's true, but why would it be of concern to you?"

His face bland, he looked up from the tray. "I merely

wondered if I might be expected to travel with the family. You see, I grew up not far from there."

"You're from Lancashire, too?" The connection intrigued her. "What is your given name? Perhaps Papa or Mama knows your family."

He frowned. "I assure you, they do not."

"How can you be so certain?"

"I was an orphan of no consequence." James skewered her with his sharp gaze. "And I must beg you not to trouble your parents with trivialities."

"But you said you were companion to the son of a gentleman. Maybe they knew him—"

"Please do *not* mention it," he reiterated. "Pray take into consideration my position here. Above all, I am to be inconspicuous, a nameless, faceless servant. Calling undue attention to myself could result in me losing my post."

Understanding flooded her. For a few short minutes they'd chatted as equals and she'd nearly forgotten he was a member of the staff, subject to strict rules and regulations. She could never bear to be the instrument of him being tossed out onto the street with no funds and nowhere to go.

Seeking to reassure him, she stepped swiftly to him and touched his arm. "Of course I won't tell. You may trust me on that, James."

He stood very still, looking down at her. She had a sudden keen awareness of the muscles beneath his coat, the heat of his body, his faintly spicy scent. Her pulse throbbed in response to the innate masculine power of him. The shocking desire to experience his kiss held her motionless. From the way his gaze flitted to her lips, she was thrilled to realize that he too felt the same forbidden urge.

Abruptly, he stepped back and broke the spell. "I

appreciate your kindness, Miss Crompton. Now, I'm afraid I've overstayed my welcome here. Good day."

He picked up the breakfast tray and strode toward the bedroom door. Feeling oddly bereft, Blythe watched him go. How imprudent of her to feel an illicit attraction to a *servant.*

Impulse made her call out to him. "James, wait!"

He stopped, looking back at her in cool inquiry.

Snatching up the peacock feather, Blythe ran to him and placed it on the tray. She graced him with a warm smile. "You forgot this."

He glanced down at the feather, then at her. "So I did."

His dark eyes revealed nothing of his thoughts. He had become a remote stranger again, as if their friendly conversation had never occurred. Turning away, he disappeared out the door.

Blythe stood wishing she had another excuse to summon him back. Foolish as it was, she couldn't deny her fascination with the footman. Knowing that he hailed from Lancashire only added another layer of mystery to James. Why had he suddenly turned cool when she'd suggested asking her parents if they knew of his family?

Blythe was determined to find the answer to that question—and many others. Whether it was indiscreet or not.

Chapter 9

A line of footmen, identical in blue livery and white wigs, walked along an upstairs corridor. Their steps echoed on the pale marble floor. Each servant carried a serving piece still steaming from the kitchen. The delectable aromas of roast beef and browned potatoes wafted through the air.

Bringing up the rear, James bore a covered oval dish in his gloved hands. The more senior footmen had been assigned duty during the soup and fish courses, and it had seemed for a time as if he might never have the chance to go above stairs. He had cooled his heels in the kitchen until he'd been summoned by Godwin, the fox-faced head footman jokingly referred to behind his back as *God*.

Now, a keen anticipation gripped James. This moment had been more than three days coming. At last he would have the opportunity to take a close look at the master of the house.

Was George Crompton really James's cousin—or an imposter?

The tall arched doorway of the dining chamber loomed midway along the passage. One by one, the footmen disappeared into the room. James followed in their wake, his fingers tensed around the handles of the dish. He kept his face sober, his gaze focused straight ahead as he'd been instructed.

From the corner of his eye, he took in the intimate gathering. Matching silver candelabra cast a soft glow over the room. He'd spent the better part of an hour assisting in laying out the white linens, the array of silver utensils, the china plates and fine crystal. Now, glasses and cutlery clinked as the family prepared to partake of the main course.

There were seven of them in all at dinner. George and Edith occupied opposite ends of the table. Two gentlemen who must be the husbands of Portia and Lindsey sat with their backs to the door. On the other side, Blythe was positioned in between her sisters, and appeared to be engaged in a lively conversation with them.

He was struck by the sight. Surely three more winsome females could not be found anywhere in England. Portia and Lindsey had dark hair, pale skin, and startlingly blue eyes. By contrast, Blythe with her coppery hair looked uniquely delectable in cream silk cut low at the bosom.

He wanted to stare at her, but he dared not risk more than a glance. It would be idiotic to focus on her, anyway. She was merely a distraction to his purpose here.

"Arthur was quite the handful in the coach," one of the sisters was telling the group. She must be the eldest daughter, Portia, who had traveled here from Kent. "Thank goodness his papa very kindly offered to take him up in the saddle to ride for a time."

"He'll make a fine horseman someday," the man across from her drawled. "If ever he can learn not to piddle all over his father's leg."

Everyone laughed except Mrs. Crompton, who mildly chided her son-in-law about inappropriate dinner conversation.

Walking past the table, James risked another look at Blythe. She held a wineglass to her lips, her face bright with merriment and her hazel eyes sparkling. His blood beat with the same lust that had assailed him that morning in her bedchamber. She had been open and friendly, almost as if they were equals. Her attraction to him had been obvious. She had touched his arm and given him the peacock feather. The egalitarian nature of her behavior had caught him off guard.

Now, as her sisters continued to chatter, she glanced across the room and looked right at him. Her cheerful expression sobered somewhat, though in surprise or alarm he couldn't tell. Their gazes held for the space of a pulse beat. Then, she broke the contact and resumed talking to her sisters.

As if he didn't exist.

Jaw clenched, James marched after the other footmen to the sideboard. He felt unaccountably annoyed as if she had delivered the cut direct to him in a ballroom. What the devil had he expected, that she would beckon him closer and make introductions? A lady was supposed to ignore the servants. He had no true interest in Miss Blythe Crompton, anyway, except as an unwitting informant.

Earlier in the day, he'd deliberately fostered a sense of trust between them. The task had been simple enough. He had played upon her goodwill by asking questions about India, and she had fallen into his trap with all the naiveté of a green girl. Now, it was a matter of biding his time and awaiting another opportunity to continue his interrogation of her in private. Somehow, he had to lead her into revealing what she knew about her parents.

He noticed Godwin frowning in his direction. The head footman was a stickler for rules. If the fussbudget had caught James looking at the family, he'd be in deep trouble.

James busied himself at the sideboard by removing the domed cover from the dish of green peas in cream sauce. He selected a silver serving utensil, one of the spoons he'd spent hours polishing. The need for vigilance burned in him. He mustn't forget, not even for an instant, that he was playing a role here. One false move and he'd be tossed out of the house on his ear, his ruse in ruins.

Thankfully, Godwin had turned his attention elsewhere. With as much pomp as one would afford the crown jewels, the head footman carried a platter of sliced roast beef to Mrs. Edith Crompton. Once she had served herself a portion, he moved on to the other ladies and the next footman took his place, this one offering a dish of potatoes au gratin to the mistress. Having been instructed in the strict order in which the dishes were to be served, James held back and awaited his turn.

He turned his gaze to George Crompton. Unfortunately, James stood a short distance behind the man, which made identification impossible. He summoned forth the image of his cousin from the mists of memory. The most distinguishing characteristic—at least to a boy of ten—had been George's thick mane of dark, wavy hair.

From this vantage point, however, James could see only a thinning cap of graying brown hair. Of course, such a difference could be attributed to age. A man could change a lot in twenty years, especially when he'd been exposed to the harsh elements of India.

Impatience gnawed at James. In a matter of moments, he would have a better look. The footman ahead of him was carrying a dish of butter-glazed endives toward the table.

It was nearly James's turn.

While he waited, he was struck by how much Portia and Lindsey resembled each other, both dark and willowy. Blythe was petite like her mother, with coppery hair and a pert nose. Odd, how little she resembled her sisters. He would never have taken them for siblings. . . .

"Ella is so fretful in the evenings," one of the sisters was saying as she served herself a spoonful of potatoes. "I cannot fathom what it is I'm doing wrong. It takes her ever so long to settle down to sleep."

The speaker must be Lindsey, who recently had given birth to her first child.

"Give her over to one of the nursemaids," Edith Crompton advised. "That is what servants are for."

"Oh, Mama, I could never do that," Lindsey said. "I can't bear to think of Ella being comforted by anyone else."

"Arthur was fussy like that, too," Portia assured her. "I like to say that I carried him for another three months after birth. Wouldn't you concur, Colin?"

Viscount Ratcliffe gave his wife an indulgent smile across the table. "Of course, darling. He's always been quite a handful." He glanced over at his brother-in-law and added in a stage whisper, "One must always agree with one's wife. It makes life far more enjoyable."

Fingering the long scar on his cheek, Lord Mansfield chuckled. "How well I know."

Then it was time for James to join the procession of footmen around the table. Carrying the white porcelain dish by its handles, he concentrated on verifying the identity of the elder Cromptons. He approached Edith from the left and lowered the dish for her access.

With nary a glance at him, she picked up the silver spoon and ladled a dainty portion of peas onto her plate. He might have been a statue for all she noticed.

So much the better.

He had already seen her from a close vantage point on that one occasion in Blythe's chamber. Now, he once again noted the lack of wrinkles that seemed unusual for a woman nearing her fiftieth year. Either she had discovered the Fountain of Youth in India, or she was younger than his cousin's wife ought to be.

But how could he prove that?

"I'm looking forward to visiting the little dears on the morrow," she told her daughters. "In the meantime, the both of you need a rest from all this talk of feedings and naptimes."

"I quite agree," Blythe said. "Mama, I've been meaning to ask you something. Why do we never go to Lancashire?"

James nearly dropped the dish. He cut a sharp glance toward her, but her gaze was trained on her mother.

Good God, did the minx intend to reveal their conversation after she'd sworn not to do so? He should never have mentioned that he hailed from Lancashire. To know that she had the power to draw undue attention to him made his blood run cold.

Edith clutched the silver serving spoon, her knuckles white. "Lancashire! Why on earth would you bring up that place?"

Blythe shrugged. "No particular reason. I was just thinking today that you and Papa lived there a long time ago. Yet I've never laid eyes on the estate and I wondered if we might visit there sometime. Perhaps in the summer, after the Season is over."

Edith took an inordinate interest in tapping off a few stubborn peas that stuck to the spoon. "The house is in ruins; I've told you so before. It's uninhabitable. Besides, your father cannot be away from the docks for so long and we wouldn't wish to leave him behind."

"Your mother is right," George said from his end of the table. "I'm not one for idling in the country as the nobs are wont to do. It's best we remain in London."

In spite of his tension, James felt the burn of interest. It made sense that George and Edith wouldn't wish to travel to Lancashire. There was too much danger that one of the locals might question their identities and expose them as charlatans.

Edith returned the spoon to the dish. "Enough about Lancashire. There are far more important things to discuss. Portia and Lindsey, you may be interested to know that the Duke of Savoy has shown a marked interest in your sister."

James was relieved when Blythe didn't attempt to say more about Lancashire. Perhaps she wouldn't betray him, after all.

Noting how swiftly Edith had changed the topic, he carried the dish to Portia. The eldest Crompton daughter paid no heed to him, either, for she was frowning at her mother.

"Oh, Mama. Pray don't tell me you're still trying to snag a duke as a son-in-law."

"I am, indeed," Mrs. Crompton said, her chin high. "It would be a feather in Blythe's cap to be chosen by Savoy. I will do all that I can to arrange matters in her favor."

"Your *arrangements* nearly proved to be a disaster for me last year," Lindsey said darkly. "Have you forgotten so quickly how Lord Wrayford tried to abduct me?"

"I still regret not thrashing that villain to within an inch of his life," Lord Mansfield growled. "However, one cannot deny the matter turned out quite well regardless."

He and his wife shared a secretive smile across the table.

"Let's hope Wrayford has finally learned his lesson," Portia said, taking a spoonful of peas, then waving James away. "As I recall, he had a nasty habit of staring at all the ladies' bosoms."

As James approached Blythe with the serving dish,

he had a clear view of *her* bosom. He was hard-pressed to keep from gawking at her decidedly feminine curves. From so close a stance, he could detect her scent, something light and flowery, yet with a hint of mystery. He wanted to bury his face in her breasts and see if she tasted as delectable as she looked.

Blythe took no notice of him as she picked up the spoon to serve herself. Did she even know who was standing beside her? Or was he a mere plaything for her to practice her flirting?

"Speaking of Wrayford," she said, "I saw him last evening at Lady Wargrave's house. You'll never guess who he's engaged to wed. Frances Beardsley."

Portia and Lindsey glanced at each other and broke into giggles.

"Now there's a well-suited couple," Portia said drolly. "A busybody and a lecher. They deserve each other."

"A match made in Hades," Lindsey said, her eyes gleaming. "Frances in particular would have everyone believe she's a pillar of society. Yet I seem to recall she was once caught kissing a footman."

The spoon clinked as Blythe dropped it into the dish. Her gaze flicked up to James, and for one heated moment their eyes locked before she looked away again.

So she *had* known it was him.

At least no one else appeared to have noticed the brief fiery awareness between them. The other footmen were engaged in serving the family members, and the banter between the sisters continued unabated as they discussed the scoundrel named Wrayford.

James walked around Blythe's chair and went to Lindsey. What had that ardent glance meant? Had Blythe herself thought about kissing a footman—him? He could have sworn it was so this morning in her bedchamber when she'd touched his arm and gazed soulfully into his eyes.

A primal heat gripped him. He wanted to do more than kiss her. He wanted to find the nearest bed and explore every inch of her luscious body. The fantasy smoldered like an ever-present fire in his gut.

Irked with himself, James kept his gaze lowered while he served her middle sister. He'd be a fool to overstep his bounds. He was here for a clandestine purpose, nothing more. If he found proof of foul deeds, it would be a rude awakening for George and Edith Crompton—and for Blythe.

"Now, girls, such gossip is beneath you," Mrs. Crompton chided. She looked down the table at her husband. "Do stop chattering about those dreary ships, George, and scold your daughters."

George had been conversing with his sons-in-law. A twinkle now entered his eyes as he regarded the women. "Why would I ruin their entertainment, dear? Scandals are to be enjoyed so long as they don't happen within our own family!"

James was struck by the man's cheerful smile and relaxed disposition. No knell of recognition sounded within his own mind. The cousin he recalled had been a rather dour, humorless sort who was absorbed in his own pursuits.

Could siring three daughters have changed him so drastically?

His mind alive with questions, James walked forward. He stopped directly beside George and presented the dish while cataloguing the man's physical characteristics.

Stout and balding, George looked every inch the prosperous businessman. His maroon coat was well tailored, as had been the garb of James's cousin, but that was only to be expected for a wealthy man. He had a straight nose, slightly ruddy features, and deep lines around his eyes and mouth.

Although he was sitting, he didn't appear to be as tall as James remembered. Yet perhaps all adults looked towering to a boy of ten.

Damn! He had a stronger sense than ever that the man was an impostor, yet he could not make a positive identification. The mists of memory obscured more than he'd anticipated. He had thought to take one close look and know for certain that this man had stolen the identity of his cousin.

He couldn't win a court case on the basis of intuition. So how the devil was he supposed to proceed with the investigation?

Then the moment of scrutiny was over. It was time to move to the opposite side of the table. As he served the other two gentlemen, James set aside his frustration and returned his attention to the conversation.

"I'd like to know more about the Duke of Savoy," Portia was saying to Blythe. "Isn't he a bit ancient for you?"

Blythe cast a pensive glance down at her plate, then flashed a determined smile at her sister. "Two people can fall in love no matter what their age. Besides, His Grace is very kind and thoughtful, and he's sent me many gifts."

James would have relished the chance to challenge her on that point. It annoyed him that she was so willing to sell herself to a man who was old enough to be her sire. It seemed her sisters agreed, for they both cast worried looks at her.

"Gifts!" Lindsey scoffed. "You should be far more concerned about the man's character."

"Indeed," her husband said blandly, "it's good to know

that I needn't bother giving *you* any more gifts. My character should be sufficient to please you."

Lindsey made a mock scowl at him while the others laughed. "You know what I mean," she said. "The most important consideration in choosing a husband is to have shared interests, for how else can one fall in love?"

Blythe looked unperturbed as she cut her beef. "I've no wish to solve crimes as you and Thane are wont to do, nor to dig in the garden like Portia and Colin. I shall be very happy as Savoy's wife, for we both enjoy going out in society. Besides, I have always wanted to become a great hostess."

James was relieved to be finished serving because it kept him from glaring at her. His lips compressed, he returned to the sideboard and replaced the cover on the dish. The chit was a social climber, after all. He should never have imagined otherwise.

He joined the other footmen who stood at attention by the wall until they were needed to clear the plates. The position allowed him to observe the party without being conspicuous.

"The duke is indeed the catch of the season," Edith declared. "I will not have anyone discouraging such a perfect match."

"But to marry simply to gain an exalted title is wrong," Portia said with a disgusted shake of her head. She looked down the table at her father. "Papa, it would be a terrible mistake. You mustn't allow it."

"Now, don't badger your mother and sister," George said. "You and Lindsey were permitted to make your own choices. And fine choices they were, too."

"But we married for love. Can you not see the importance of—?"

"What I *see*," George interrupted sternly, "is that your

sister is a grown woman now. She has expressed a wish to wed Savoy, and all of you must honor her decision."

At that, Blythe did something utterly unexpected. She slipped out of her chair and went to her father, bending down to wrap her arms around him in a hug. "Dearest Papa. I shan't disappoint you, I promise. I'll always make you proud."

He laid down his fork and returned the embrace. With a tender smile, he reached up to stroke her cheek. "Just be happy, my sweet."

James was struck by the genuine warmth between them. It was clear that she loved her father, and that George felt the same strong affection for his daughter.

The sight caused a visceral tension in James's chest. His own sire had been too preoccupied with dice and wagering to take notice of his son. It had been a welcome day when the profligate finally had been lowered into his grave.

As Blythe went back to her seat and resumed chattering with her sisters, James watched her broodingly. Her eyes bright, she glowed with happiness. And little wonder. Miss Blythe Crompton led a lavish, carefree life. Having grown up in the lap of luxury, she was secure in her position as the premier heiress of the season.

What would happen when he exposed her parents as imposters? She would lose everything: her inheritance, her home, her place in society, and her chance to wed the duke. Her life would be in shambles.

Laughing and talking with her family, she could have no idea of the grim future that lay in store for her. Nor did she have any inkling that the new footman would be the engineer of her downfall.

James hardened his heart. He refused to let sentiment sway him. The righteousness of his cause outweighed any consequences to her. For all he knew, his cousin could have been murdered. Justice must prevail. But first, James had to find a way to prove that the man sitting at the head of the table was not the real George Crompton.

If only he had a portrait of his cousin . . .

James had a sudden inspiration as to how to achieve his purpose. There might be a way, after all. Tonight, once everyone was asleep, he would put his plan into motion.

Chapter 10

Later that evening, Edith was nearly finished preparing for bed. Instead of her regular maid, Kasi had helped out, and the old Hindu woman still lingered in the dressing room. Draped in a tangerine sari, she hummed to herself while folding a discarded petticoat.

Tonight, the woman's presence irritated Edith. She had so much to ponder. Of utmost importance was the task of seeing Blythe safely married to the Duke of Savoy. This was Edith's last opportunity to link herself to the very highest ranks of society.

Nothing—and no one—must interfere with that goal.

She dipped her fingers into a green glass jar and slathered rose-scented lotion over her face, working it into her skin to prevent wrinkles. While performing the nightly ritual, she watched the stout woman in the pier glass. "Tell me, has Blythe ever mentioned Lancashire to you?"

Kasi turned around. In a sing-song voice, she said, "Lanca-sheer . . . that is where you and *sahib* live long ago."

"Yes. Now, what does Blythe know of the place?"

The Hindu shrugged. "Missy say nothing to me."

Edith relaxed marginally. Perhaps she'd overreacted at dinner. Blythe had been making conversation, that was all. Yet one could never be too careful. "Well, if she happens to do so in the future, tell me at once."

The cream silk robe swished around her ankles as she stalked into the sumptuous bedchamber with its gilt and white decor. A coal fire hissed on the hearth, the dim light augmented by a branch of candles on the bedside table. The covers had been turned down, and the feather pillows were plumped and ready.

But Edith felt too restless to sleep.

She paced to the closed connecting door and debated whether or not to knock. What was keeping George? She needed to reaffirm his dedication to guarding their secret. Given his innate integrity, there was always the remote possibility that he could suffer from an attack of conscience. That fear had dogged her all these years. . . .

Kasi had followed Edith into the bedchamber. From across the room, those knowing black eyes stared at her.

"What is it?" Edith snapped.

"*Memsahib* be frightened."

"Stuff and nonsense. Whatever would I be frightened of?"

"Lanca-sheer."

The name breathed cold fingers down Edith's spine. Folding her arms to contain a shiver, she paced the bedchamber. "I fear nothing of a place. Who are you to suggest such a thing, anyway?"

Kasi waddled forward and took hold of Edith's hand, turning it over to peer at her palm and trace the lines there with a stubby forefinger. "When people in Lanca-sheer see you, they know who you are. They tell the truth."

A knell of alarm struck Edith. Was that some sort of prophesy? The girls believed that Kasi could predict the future by reading palms, but Edith had always disdained such native nonsense.

She snatched her hand free. "Enough of your superstitions. Go to bed at once."

Kasi made a deep salaam. "As *memsahib* wish."

The old woman trudged out of the chamber, and Edith drew several deep breaths to calm herself. It was absurd to think that one's fate could be divined from looking at a hand. She had always believed in taking firm charge of her own future. Kasi had made a calculated guess based on what she knew of the past.

There was nothing more to it.

Yet the fact that Kasi knew their secret weighed heavily on Edith. Perhaps it had been a mistake to bring the woman to England after all. Keeping the woman under strict supervision was turning out to be more dangerous than leaving her in India, where any slip of the tongue might have been ignored as the ranting of a madwoman.

Edith consoled herself with the reminder that Kasi would never betray the girls. She was much too devoted to them to stir up a scandal. As for George, he also knew the danger of returning to Lancashire. He would never permit the family to travel halfway across England, anyway, merely to lay claim to an estate that held such dismal memories.

As long as they remained in London they would be safe.

⁂

Blythe walked barefoot across the rug and blew out the candle on the bedside table. A soft darkness descended over the chamber, and the glow from the dying fire cast flickering shadows over the walls. The setting usually made her sleepy, but for some reason, she felt wide awake tonight.

She perched on the edge of the bed, drew up her knees, and hugged a feather pillow to her bosom. What was the reason for her nagging discontent? Certainly, she had enjoyed having the family together again. The dinner party had been just like old times—almost.

It *was* a little sad to realize that nothing would ever be exactly the same ever again. Her sisters led separate lives now. They might come to visit every now and then, but they were busy with their husbands and young children.

Was that the source of her malaise? Did she feel a wistful yearning to settle her own future? To know that she would someday be as happy and content as they were?

Would she be happy marrying the Duke of Savoy?

Of course she would! She mustn't allow herself to think otherwise. Papa approved of the match, after all, and she trusted his opinion. If only she could spend some time alone with the duke, surely love would grow between them. Yet they'd scarcely had any opportunity at all to converse. The obstacle was Lady Davina.

I would never permit my father to marry so vastly far beneath him.

Those hateful words still burned in Blythe's memory. After the incident the other night when Davina had finagled the situation with Viscount Kitchener, Blythe had been wracking her brain to think of a way to outfox the duke's daughter.

She had a half-formed idea, but it would require an accomplice. Mama was too awed by Lady Davina's rank to participate in a scheme that could result in humiliation for the girl. To recruit Portia or Lindsey was out of the question, too, considering their animosity toward the duke.

Perhaps James would help her.

Blythe clutched the pillow tighter. The mere thought of him caused a disturbance deep inside her. She had no right to ask him to risk his position here for the sake of her own ambitions. Yet the more she pondered the notion, the more she believed he was the perfect man for the task.

But would he do it?

Tossing the pillow aside, she sprang up from the bed and paced the darkened bedchamber. She'd been hard-pressed to concentrate on the conversation with her family while he'd helped to serve dinner. His face had been sober and impassive—at least until she'd asked about the family estate in Lancashire. Her impulse to do so remained a mystery to her. Had she wished to spark a reaction from him?

That must be it. He'd been extremely adamant that she not mention his place of birth to her parents. Why? Was it just that he didn't want to draw attention to himself, as he'd claimed? She sensed a mystery about him, something intriguing that she longed to uncover.

Deep in thought, Blythe stopped at the window overlooking the rear garden. Night veiled the trees and shrubbery. By day, the garden contained neatly manicured beds of roses. Now, moon-silvered shadows draped the concentric pathways, and the stables loomed like a black monolith at the rear of the yard.

The sight enhanced her vague sense of melancholy. The utter stillness made it seem as if she was all alone in the world. . . .

Something shifted in the gloom.

Startled, Blythe wondered if she'd imagined the movement. Then a moment later, she saw it again: the tall shape of a man slipping through the trees. His gait was furtive, as if he was making an effort to keep out of sight.

She was struck by something curiously familiar about him.

The figure paused at the stone fence along the rear of the property. As he glanced back at the house, the faint starlight illuminated his features. Even though he wasn't wearing his footman's white wig, she knew him at once.

James.

Instinctively, Blythe shrank back behind the draperies. She didn't know why, but it seemed important for him not to catch a glimpse of her at the window.

What was he doing outside? All the servants should be fast asleep at this late hour, since they had to arise before dawn.

She cautiously peered around the edge of the curtains in time to see him slip out the back gate. He vanished into the pitch-dark mews. Pressing her nose to the glass, she watched for a few minutes, but he didn't reappear.

All lay still again.

Blythe put her hand over her thudding heart as she tried to fathom his purpose. The household rules forbade the servants from venturing out in the middle of the night. Yet James had disobeyed. Why?

More important, where was he going at this late hour?

A distasteful possibility wormed into her thoughts. Perhaps he had a tryst arranged. The more she pondered the notion, the more logical it seemed. James had led her to believe he had no family or friends in London. And she would stake her reputation that he wasn't a thief or a footpad.

Therefore, he must be meeting a woman.

Blythe scowled into the darkness. She told herself to forget his indiscretion. It was irrational to feel affronted. What a servant did while off duty was of little concern to her. Nevertheless, she stood gazing out the window for a time, hoping to see him return.

But he was still gone half an hour later when she finally gave up and went to bed.

⁂

James rapped hard on the plain wooden door. Glancing up and down the pitch-dark lane, he kept a close watch on his surroundings. Thankfully, only a stray cat slunk through the shadows. This rundown neighborhood off the Strand boasted no watchmen patrolling the streets as in the posh area of Mayfair.

James didn't want any trouble tonight.

The chilly breeze carried a fishy odor from the Thames. Two o'clock in the morning was far too late to be paying calls, but he'd had little choice in the matter. His days were filled with endless duties. With the way Godwin watched the footmen, it was a miracle James had been able to sneak out of the house at all.

For a moment in the garden, he'd feared he'd been spotted. There had been a flash of movement in one of the upper windows. But upon closer inspection, he had concluded he'd been mistaken. The family had retired early, as had all the servants, so he had nothing to fear.

The occupants of this small house must be dead asleep as well.

James pounded his fist on the door. He hoped he wouldn't have to resort to shouting, which would awaken the neighbors and draw undue attention. Then, much to his relief, the muffled sound of footsteps came from within. A key rattled in the lock and the door squeaked open a few inches.

An elderly man in a nightcap and long shirt peered through the crack. He held up a lighted candle. "What the devil's all the commotion about? Oh! Mr. Ryding!"

Percy Thornton opened the door all the way, allowing James to enter the tiny hall. There were very few furnishings, only a chair and a side table. By the window, the sleepy chirp of a finch came from a covered cage.

"Forgive me for disturbing you," James told the old man. "It was the only time I could escape my duties."

"Never mind, I'm eager to hear your news," Thornton said. "Come to the kitchen and Roland will make a cup of tea for you."

James followed the retired estate agent along a narrow corridor leading to the rear of the house. The light of the single candle cast elongated shadows on the peeling wallpaper, and the odor of boiled cabbage tinged the musty air.

They headed down a steep flight of stairs to the cellar kitchen, where James had to duck his head to avoid hitting the lintel. Banked coals glowed in the hearth, casting a faint illumination over a lumpy pallet on the dirt floor in front of the fireplace.

The blankets shifted and moved as if a mole burrowed deep inside the blankets. Then out popped a gangly bald man with ebony skin and a flash of white teeth.

He rubbed his eyes. "Mister James, suh! Praise the Lord, you come back."

"I trust you've been behaving yourself, Roland. No sacrificing of chickens on the back stoop or anything of the sort?"

Roland shook his head. "No live chickens a'tall in this devil's town. Where dey get dere eggs from, I dunno."

"He's been a big help with the chores," Thornton said. "Please don't think it's been any trouble at all for him to stay here."

For many years, Roland had been valet, manservant, and all-around helper to James. He'd trusted no one else to accompany him on the long voyage from the West Indies. It had been a godsend when Thornton had agreed to house Roland for the duration of James's employment at Crompton House.

"A pity he can't come and help with *my* daily chores," James said with a grimace. "I've developed a new appreciation for the hard work of servants."

A deep chuckle came from Roland as he stirred up the coals into flame and then put the kettle on for tea. "Dat be somethin' I like to see, mon. You, bowin' to dem fancy gents and ladies."

Thornton nodded sagely. "The house must be busy, what with Miss Blythe Crompton making her debut. Such a pretty girl surely attracts many suitors."

James frowned, unwilling to discuss her. "Yes, but most of the time I've been stuck in a basement room, cleaning lamps or silver spoons."

Except when he'd taken the tray up to Blythe's bedchamber. They'd shared a long conversation about India, and at the end of it, she had given him the peacock feather along with a flirtatious smile. The memory burned in him, as did the fervent look she'd aimed at him at dinner only a few hours ago. Her attraction to him was unmistakable, as was his own lusty reaction to her. He didn't know what the devil to do about it except to avoid her.

And *that* wouldn't help his investigation. He needed to encourage her interest in the hopes of gleaning information to prove his case.

"What is your news?" Thornton asked, setting the candle down on a rough-hewn table. "Have you been able to verify that the Cromptons are imposters?"

"Unfortunately not," James said. "That's why I'm here. I was hoping you could help me with something."

Thornton waved at the table. "Pray sit down, sir, and tell me how I may be of assistance. Or would you be more comfortable upstairs in the parlor?"

"This is perfectly fine. I dare not linger more than a few minutes, anyway."

They settled into hard wooden chairs across from each other while Roland scattered tea leaves in the simmering water in the pot. Thornton looked old and drawn, and James had a sudden concern that he was asking too much of the man. But as the former manager of the Cromptons' estate in Lancashire, Thornton was the ideal person for the task at hand.

"I need you to make a journey for me," James said. "I'd go myself, but obviously that's impossible at the moment."

Looking mystified, Thornton cocked his grizzled head. "As you wish, sir. Where am I to go?"

"To Lancashire. My memory of the Cromptons is not quite as clear as I'd hoped it would be. So I'd like you to visit the estate on my behalf and see if there might be any paintings of George and Edith in their younger days."

"Ah." Thornton nodded sagely. "And you want me to bring these portraits back here to you?"

"Precisely. Not only will it help in identifying them, it will also give me the necessary proof when the case comes to court."

They paused for a moment while Roland silently brought them mugs of tea.

Thornton added a lump of sugar to his cup and stirred it with a pewter spoon. "But is there not a housekeeper or caretaker who will question my presence there? Mrs. Barnaby is retired now, and her replacement won't recognize me."

James reached inside his coat. "I've forged a brief note of introduction for you. The penmanship is a fair imitation of George's."

After serving dinner, James had been lucky enough to spot a business letter addressed in George's hand and left on a tray in the entry hall for delivery in the next day's mail. He had spirited it away to his room and hastily practiced the man's handwriting.

Now, he passed the folded paper to Thornton. "I've explained that you've been tasked with fetching some paintings to London. You're to have full access to all areas of the house. If you cannot find any pictures of the Cromptons in the main rooms, be sure to search the attics, too."

James had no doubt that an imposter would have sent orders for any incriminating paintings to be put out of sight. He only hoped they hadn't been disposed of entirely.

"A very wise plan," the elderly man said with a nod. "When shall I depart?"

"Preferably on the mail coach in the morning. Roland will give you money for the fare." James looked at his servant, who was sitting cross-legged on the pallet, drinking his own cup of tea. "Providing he hasn't squandered all my coin on useless trinkets."

Roland flashed a grin. "I bin stay right here, mon. I guard your money right dere."

He pointed beside him to his pallet, and James realized that the lump he'd assumed to be a pillow was actually the outline of a strongbox.

James chuckled as he blew on his hot tea. "You're a good man, Roland. Remind me to give you a bonus when this is all over."

"Well, then!" Thornton said, rubbing his palms. "If all goes well, I should be back in about a week or so."

"In the meantime, I'll continue to look for evidence myself," James said. "I'm hoping to find something when I search George's desk. The sooner I can bring those two charlatans to justice, the better."

Roland scrambled to his feet. "I can help, suh. You pluck one hair from George and one from his wife, and I make *gris-gris* magic. Den I stick a pin in each one"—he mimicked stabbing an imaginary doll in his hand—"and real quick, dem two be sorry dey stole your money."

"Voodoo won't be necessary," James said with an amused shake of his head. "I intend to rely upon the English court system to handle the case."

"Maybe den you bring fingernail clipping from Miss Crompton? I make a powerful potion so she fall in love with you, suh. That be a fine revenge on her momma and daddy."

James sat up straight as if he'd been pricked with a *gris-gris* pin himself. He gripped his teacup hard. "For God's sake, *no.* There'll be no witch doctor deeds at all, and that's that."

Rising from the chair, he ignored Roland's crestfallen look. The fellow didn't know it, but the last thing James needed was a love potion. He was already far too obsessed with Miss Blythe Crompton.

Chapter 11

Blythe needed to finagle a measure of time alone with James so that she could broach her plan about tricking Lady Davina.

With that in mind, Blythe ordered a breakfast tray brought to her bedchamber the following morning. Unfortunately, one of the maidservants delivered it. James was nowhere in sight, either, when she sought out a footman to accompany her to the shops on Bond Street. She was loath to ask for him specifically since that would draw undue attention to her interest in him.

At noon on the second day, she descended the grand staircase with Kasi. They were preparing to take a stroll to Lindsey's house on Park Lane and visit the children. But upon reaching the entrance hall, Blythe spotted her quarry in an antechamber.

Although his back was to her and he wore the traditional white wig and blue livery, she recognized James at once. No other footman had those broad shoulders or that self-assured stance.

Determination took fire within her, but she hid the reaction behind a cool demeanor. She knew from long experience not to stir the suspicions of her *ayah*.

Going to one of the long windows that flanked the front door, Blythe made a pretense of peering out into the gray day. "Oh, pooh, I do believe it looks like rain. We had better postpone our walk until later."

Kasi's dark eyes narrowed to slits. Too wise by half, she glanced from Blythe to the antechamber, then back again. "We take coach, missy."

"That is an excellent solution," Blythe said. "Why don't you order it brought around? Tell the coachman that half an hour from now will suffice."

Kasi gave her another suspicious look. Nevertheless, she put her palms together and salaamed, then shuffled away down the corridor leading to the rear of the house.

Blythe lost no time in scurrying across the marble floor and through the door of the antechamber. "James, how fortunate that I found you here."

He turned sharply, a stack of letters in his white-gloved hand. The rugged masculine angles of his face looked at odds with the sober garb of a servant. Certainly, his gaze skimmed her in a way no member of the staff ought to look at a lady.

His bland expression revealing nothing of his thoughts, he gave a slight bow. "Good morning, Miss Crompton. How may I assist you?"

"I wondered if there was any mail for me today."

"The usual collection of posies arrived earlier," he said. "The housekeeper put the flowers in vases in the morning room. Oh, and there was a note, as well."

He flipped through the letters in his hand, selected one, and held it out to her.

She ignored the offering. "Bring it to my chamber," she said coolly. "At once."

Turning on her heel, Blythe breezed out of the room. How haughty he must think her to be unwilling to carry one measly little note by herself. But he would understand her purpose soon enough.

His footsteps sounded a short distance behind her. She felt a trifle breathless, and the sensation had nothing to do with the slight exertion of mounting the stairs. It was the giddy anticipation of being alone with James.

Instantly, Blythe lectured herself. She *must* overcome this girlish mooning over a handsome footman. Marriage to the Duke of Savoy had to be the foremost objective in her life. To accomplish that goal, she needed to convince James to take part in the scheme to hoodwink Lady Davina.

Upon reaching the family quarters, she kept a sharp lookout. To her relief, the corridor with its gilded pillars was empty in both directions. Mama was busy in her chamber, writing out invitations to a card party she was planning for the coming week.

That was her mother's solution to the problem with Lady Davina. They had gone to another ball the previous night, and the duke's daughter had snubbed Blythe yet again, refusing to allow her access to Savoy. Mama couldn't seem to grasp that Lady Davina would not be diverted by fair means.

So Blythe would use foul.

The plush carpet muffled their footsteps. Her hips swaying, she knew that James would be lagging a respectful distance behind her. What was he thinking as he followed in her wake? Was he watching her? Did he admire her figure and envy the gentlemen whose rank allowed them to court her?

Blythe grimaced. How imprudent to speculate on the thoughts of a servant. James might be handsome, even fascinating in his distinctive way, but their lives were irrevocably separated by rank. Nothing could ever come of her attraction to him. She knew full well the necessity of avoiding even the slightest breath of scandal.

Consequently, no one must find out about this clandestine meeting.

Outside her bedchamber, she took another glance around and then proceeded inside. A moment later, James stepped through the doorway. He was holding a silver salver on which sat the letter.

His shrewd gaze met hers, but he said nothing. He must know something was up, but he would leave it to her to make the first move.

Blythe closed the door, then hastened past him to take a swift glance into the dressing room. It was empty. No maid lurked anywhere within earshot. The last thing Blythe needed was for gossip to spread below stairs, because then it would inevitably reach Mama's ears.

James stood waiting in the same spot. He lifted the salver slightly toward her. "Your letter."

An undercurrent of irony in his voice revealed his suspicion of her request to come here. But he could have no possible notion of her true intention.

She took the letter, saw that it was from Lord Kitchener, and then tossed it onto the bedside table. Another silly rhyme, no doubt. The viscount had been sending them every day, thanks to Lady Davina's assuring him that Blythe loved poetry.

Better she should think about James. He might lose his position if he was caught assisting in her scheme. Was she wrong to ask him?

She shook off her misgivings. Instinct told her that now was not the time to equivocate. She must win James over by treating him like a friend, an equal. To that end, she must be frank.

"I'm sure you've guessed that the letter is merely a

pretext," she said. "I asked you to follow me here so that we might have a word in private."

"As your servant, I'm always happy to oblige you."

She flushed. The swift beating of her heart made her feel light-headed. He couldn't have meant anything salacious . . . could he? Certainly not. Envisioning the two of them locked in a passionate embrace was the product of her own wayward imagination.

She took a deep breath. "I've a favor to ask you in regard to Lady Davina. You do remember her, don't you?"

"The daughter of the Duke of Savoy."

"Yes." Beset by restlessness, Blythe walked back and forth in front of the fireplace. "You witnessed her rudeness toward me at the ball here. She has made it very plain that she opposes a marriage between me and her father."

"She was quite clear on the matter," James agreed in a neutral tone.

He seemed so cool and distant today. What had happened to the camaraderie they'd shared the morning he'd brought her breakfast?

Folding her arms, she continued her pacing. "Since then, Lady Davina has kept to her word. She's done everything in her power to separate me from her father. A few evenings ago, she even played a nasty trick by creating a circumstance in which I would be embarrassed by Viscount Kitchener."

James cocked a dark eyebrow. "Indeed?"

Blythe didn't want to hearken back to that incident, but perhaps it would gain James's sympathy. "My parents and I attended a musicale at Lady Wargrave's house. Davina arranged for Lord Kitchener to sit beside me. You see, she knew he'd been smoking opium and she hoped he would embroil me in some sort of distasteful scene."

"But you're not in disgrace, so I must assume she failed."

"Luckily, Kitchener fell asleep before he could do any harm to my reputation. However, I confess to being worried about what she might try next. And whether or not she will succeed next time in humiliating me in front of society."

James set down his silver tray on a table. He clasped his hands behind his back and regarded her. "Forgive my forwardness, but perhaps you should find another nobleman to wed—someone with more amenable kinsfolk."

If only it was so simple. Like her sisters, he couldn't fathom Blythe's situation. He didn't know that Papa had his heart set on this union. Mama had said so in no uncertain terms.

Your father believes that a marriage between you and the duke would be an absolutely brilliant match.

Blythe lifted her chin. "My parents wish for me to marry well. Having the duke as my husband would elevate not only my status, but theirs as well. No one would ever again dare to snub them."

He frowned. "Your sister is wed to an earl and your other sister to a viscount. Is that not sufficient?"

"No," she said firmly. "There are still those who look down on us. That is why I am determined to wed the duke. However, Lady Davina is an impediment. I'll need to find a way to distract her so she'll lower her guard and allow me access to her father."

"Distract? In what way?"

"I've decided to play matchmaker and find a suitor for her, a man who will divert her attention. There's only one problem."

Faint amusement tilted one corner of James's mouth. "Let me guess. No man in his right mind would court a shrew like her."

It should be shocking to hear such a condemnation of a lady coming from a servant. Yet James seemed set apart from the rest of the staff, a man unique unto himself.

"There is that," Blythe said. "But I meant Davina is such a snob that only a very few gentlemen meet her high standards. I cannot imagine her settling for any rank less than a duke. And at present, there *are* no dukes—or their heirs—on the Marriage Mart besides her father."

"A pretty pickle for you, then."

"Not entirely." Blythe slowed her steps to watch him closely. "I was thinking that I might have to find a royal for her . . . a prince, to be precise."

"Surely you cannot mean the Prince Regent," James said. "Forgive me, but from what I've heard of the man, I doubt you would have any influence over him."

Blythe shook her head. "I don't want someone known to society. That would be far too difficult to manage. Rather, I was considering a foreign prince."

"Considering? Did you have one in mind?"

"Yes. Perhaps . . . Prince Nicolai of the tiny nation of Ambrosia."

James stared at her, then threw back his head and laughed. "You cannot be serious. You're intending to *invent* a prince—as well as an entire country?"

Miffed by his incredulity, Blythe said, "The hoax *can* work, truly it can. I've thought it through and formulated a plan."

"I can't wait to hear it."

Her skirt rustling, she walked back and forth. "Ambrosia is a small kingdom nestled in the mountains north of the Caspian Sea. It is so remote that very few Europeans have ever traveled there."

"But it must be rich beyond compare, lest Lady Davina turn up her patrician nose at your prince."

"Quite so. The prince will own fabulous reserves of

gold and precious stones. And he will be exceedingly handsome. You see, I will put out the word that I met him once, when he visited the Maharajah of Mumbai."

"I'll concede such a ruse would not be entirely impossible." All humor vanishing, James regarded her with a strange intensity. "It can be easier to fool people than one might think. They see what they expect to see."

"Precisely." Blythe quickened her steps. "I'll whisper in a few ears and start a rumor about the imminent arrival of the prince in London. Soon, everyone will be abuzz with the news. Then Lady Davina will begin to receive letters from Prince Nicolai. He will say that tales of her legendary beauty have traveled all over the globe."

James cocked an eyebrow. "I presume *I* would be expected to deliver these letters."

"Would you?" Stopping in front of him, Blythe laced her fingers at her waist and looked at him from beneath the screen of her lashes. "I promise you will not suffer any trouble for it. I'll make absolutely certain of that."

James knew he was being maneuvered. Yet as he gazed down into her beautiful face, he lost all ability to think. Those come-hither hazel eyes were almost green today, and her lips formed a pleading pout that drove him half-mad with lust. Were he not clad in this damnable footman's outfit, he would demand a kiss to seal their bargain.

Not that Blythe would acquiesce. A passionate encounter with a servant would run contrary to her stubborn insistence on selling herself to the Duke of Savoy.

James cudgeled rational thought back into his brain. "So you'll attempt to distract Lady Davina with flattering notes from an imaginary prince. I must say, I fail to see how such a scheme will wrest her from her father's side long enough for you to entice Savoy."

"Oh, I have a plan for that part, too." Blythe strolled

to the bed and wrapped her arms around the post, leaning against it while again giving him that sultry look. "You see, she'll have to actually meet the prince."

"But the fellow doesn't exist—" James bit off his words as her meaning struck him like a fist. "What the devil. You expect *me* to play this prince?"

"Of course. What else did you think I meant?"

He shook his head, feeling like an utter fool for not realizing her intention from the start. He had been far too caught up in dissolute fantasies to consider all the implications. "No. Absolutely not!"

She dipped her chin and gave him a beseeching look. "But you'd be perfect for the role, James. You're handsome and well-spoken—and I suspect you can be very charming with the ladies, too. I, of course, would provide you with the proper attire for a foreign prince. It would only be a matter of arranging a few discreet assignations with Lady Davina."

Like hell! James had a vision of his own plans going up in smoke. He wanted to unmask her parents, not play dangerous games that could result in him being tossed out of this house, his mission in ruins.

"You ask the impossible. I haven't the freedom to play at such a scheme."

"I'll require you to accompany me about town. That should give us ample time to accomplish the ruse."

"I'm sorry, Miss Crompton, but you've put me in an awkward position. I've too many duties to perform right here. If I fail, I'll face the wrath of God."

Confusion wrinkled her brow. "The wrath of . . . ?"

"Godwin, the head footman," James explained. "He's quite the fierce taskmaster, and since I'm new, he's keeping a close eye on me."

"God is watching you." She clapped her hand over her

mouth and giggled, much to his surprise. "How terribly irreverent of me to say such a thing."

James found himself grinning back at her. "God really will punish me if I set one toe out of line." His face sobering, he willed Blythe to abandon the ludicrous proposal. The last thing he needed was the complication of pretending to be a prince. "In all sincerity, Miss Crompton, I must beg your understanding. Surely you can see that I dare not partake in this intrigue of yours."

He felt confident that she wouldn't order him to participate. In the short time he'd known her, Blythe Crompton had proven herself to be a fair-minded girl who would respect the wishes of a servant. She would find some other means to accomplish her scheme, leaving him alone to conduct his own detective work.

But in the next breath, she shattered his assumptions.

"James, you told me that you wanted to travel to India. If you cooperate in this, I shall give you the means to go." She stepped closer, her gaze intent on him. "Fifty pounds."

"What?"

"You heard me. I'm offering to pay you more than two years' salary to become Prince Nicolai."

James went cold all over. For the second time in five minutes, he felt as if she'd knocked his feet out from under him. She couldn't begin to guess how neatly she had backed him into a corner. No footman in his right mind would turn down such an enormous sum for the work of a few hours.

Still, he had to try. "You'll be in trouble if your parents discover what you're doing."

"They won't find out." She gazed up at him with the charming entreaty of a seasoned flirt. "Please, James. Won't you do it for me? I truly need your help."

That winsome smile did him in. He resigned himself

to his fate. There was no way for him to refuse, anyway, without stirring her suspicions.

He bowed. "As you wish, Miss Crompton. I'll play the prince."

Chapter 12

"Do straighten your necklace," Mrs. Crompton instructed in the coach that evening. "The clasp is showing, and it's essential that you look your very best tonight."

Blythe obediently reached up to rearrange the dainty pearls around her neck. "There, is that better?"

"Lovely," Mrs. Crompton said with a nod of approval. "I daresay, you are certain to attract the attention of His Grace tonight. That pale green is perfect with your complexion and so are the white rosebuds in your hair. It would not surprise me to see Savoy fall to his knees and propose at the sight of you."

"Oh, Mama. Don't be silly."

"Well, then, your dowry will sweeten the pot. Either way, you *will* be the Duchess of Savoy."

The coach swayed slightly as it inched forward in the line of carriages outside Almack's. The soft glow of a lamp illuminated the plush interior with its crimson velvet cushions and the gold fringe on the window shade. Elegant in cobalt-blue striped silk, Mama sat with her hands folded in her lap. She looked utterly cool and confident.

Glancing out into the purple dusk, Blythe hoped her

mother was right. Given half a chance, Blythe could charm the duke. But would she have that opportunity tonight? It was doubtful, since there would be scores of other pretty girls in the ballroom, bluebloods who would not inspire Lady Davina's bile the way Blythe did.

I would never permit my father to marry so vastly far beneath him.

Mama still clung to the belief that the duke's daughter could be coaxed into approving of the match. But the trick she'd played with Lord Kitchener had erased all such illusions in Blythe. Her future couldn't be left to happenstance. She needed to orchestrate the situation to her advantage, which meant removing Lady Davina from the picture.

That was why Blythe had commandeered James as her ally.

She frowned out the window. *Unwilling collaborator* was a more accurate description of his role in the scheme. His initial refusal had been understandable. After all, she was asking him to take a great risk that might jeopardize his position in the house. But then she had offered him a very generous sum—and yet still he had seemed reluctant.

Why?

Perhaps James was worried about his ability to convince Lady Davina he was really a prince. That had to be it. There was no other rational explanation. When Blythe had dismissed him from her bedchamber, his gait had been stiff, his expression closed. She had not seen him since.

Well! At least James would have a few days in which to accustom himself to the notion. She would allow him plenty of time to practice, too, if he liked. But first, she had to set the stage for the hoax by spreading a rumor that a foreign prince was on his way to visit London.

Whispering the news in a few key ears was Blythe's task for the evening.

"Ah, here we are at last," her mother said as the coach came to a halt. "A pity your father couldn't have come with us tonight."

"Papa would have been bored silly. From what I've heard, there's nothing to do at Almack's but dance and drink warm lemonade."

"Well, darling, you are extremely lucky to have received a voucher. Neither of your sisters had that honor until they were betrothed to noblemen."

A footman opened the door and let down the step. To Blythe's regret, the fellow was not James. Somehow, she had to finagle a way for him to accompany her on trips around the city. When the time came for James to pose as the prince, it would be necessary to have a reason for the two of them to go off together. The thought filled her with a sense of giddy excitement. That moment could not come soon enough to suit her.

Almack's occupied a rather modest building with arched windows. Emerging from the coach, she saw a stream of well-heeled guests flowing past the iron gates to the nondescript entrance.

Mrs. Crompton caught hold of Blythe's arm. "What luck!" Mama whispered, nodding toward the doorway. "There's Savoy and his daughter right now. Their coach must have been just ahead of ours. Come, we must make haste and catch them."

Blythe spied the pair disappearing into the building. Pleased by the prospect of furthering an alliance with the duke, she accompanied her mother in pursuit. Perhaps, just perhaps it wouldn't be necessary to put her subterfuge in motion, after all. Perhaps a miracle would happen and Lady Davina would prove friendly this time. . . .

Perhaps elephants would fly.

Mrs. Crompton presented their vouchers at the door and they entered a foyer filled with people. A small crowd milled near the cloakroom where attendants were taking the wraps of the guests.

Blythe spied the duke handing his top hat to a servant. "There, Mama."

Her mother deftly wove a path through the throng. "Your Grace," she called. "May I beg a word, please?"

Savoy turned with Lady Davina on his arm. Of a similar height, they looked as if they'd coordinated their garb, she in blush-pink gauze and he in a coat of claret superfine with buff knee breeches and buckled shoes.

Blythe curtsied along with her mother. The duke gave a regal nod to accept their obeisance. He had the customary haughty tilt to his chin, and his ruddy features held a polite smile. "Ah, Mrs. Crompton, Miss Crompton. What a pleasant surprise."

Lady Davina's patrician face wore a mask of icy civility. "A surprise, indeed. I didn't realize *you* two had vouchers."

Her voice dripped with disdain. It conveyed the belief that the nouveau riche should be barred from this exclusive club. So much for hoping the girl might have softened her enmity.

Blythe arched a cool eyebrow. "I'm very much looking forward to the dancing. I presume you and His Grace are, too."

"I shall be keeping Papa company. He will need me to screen his partners. I shan't allow him to dance with just anyone."

"Now, Davy," the duke said, patting his daughter's hand while looking completely oblivious to her rudeness. "It's kind of you, but I am more than capable of managing on my own. Why, look at Miss Crompton for example. I'm sure she would accept my—"

"I've already arranged your program, Papa," Davina cut in. "Come, you'll want to greet the patronesses before the crush of people becomes too great."

She started to draw him away, but Mrs. Crompton scurried into his path. "Your Grace, may I mention one item before you go? This afternoon, I sent out invitations to a small card party at Crompton House on Tuesday next. I do hope you and Lady Davina can attend."

"A card party?" he said, his eyes lighting up. "I would be most happy to accept."

"Papa!" Davina chided. "You mustn't agree before I consult my calendar."

"My dear, you needn't attend if you've another engagement. But you know how very much I enjoy wagering on a few rubbers of whist."

"Apparently, others know that, too." Casting a black look at Blythe and her mother, Davina steered him away into the throng. She had her head bent to him, talking, as if she were apprising him of the dangers of associating with riff-raff.

Mrs. Crompton looked positively gleeful. Taking Blythe by the arm, she whispered, "There, you see? I knew the card party would appeal to Savoy. His daughter may be a bit difficult, but I'll manage her, you'll see."

"A *bit* difficult?" Blythe murmured. "She prevented His Grace from asking me to dance."

"Pish posh, the important thing is our party. Once we have the duke under our roof, it should be simple enough to ensure that he is seated right beside *you* for the entire evening."

Blythe hoped so. But she suspected Lady Davina would concoct a scheme to spoil Mama's party and separate Blythe from the duke. For that reason, she deemed it wise to proceed with her own plan to divert the girl with a trumped-up romance.

First, though, Blythe was required to greet the patronesses, who were seated on a dais at one end of the ballroom. She made her curtsies to each lady in turn, countering their critical examination with a modest smile. She was then dismissed with a cool nod by such illustrious leaders of society as the Countess of Jersey, Lady Sefton, and the Viscountess of Castlereagh. It was clear that tonight was a test, and Blythe would have to pass muster or see her voucher revoked.

She welcomed the challenge—at least until she laid eyes on the last of the patronesses. The shrewd, dark-haired beauty in her early thirties was the Countess de Lieven, wife of the Russian ambassador and a lady known for her political salons.

A jolt of alarm struck Blythe as she dipped a curtsy. The countess was well-versed in European affairs of state. Which meant that in creating her fictitious prince, Blythe must be extremely careful to avoid attracting the woman's attention.

Should she abandon the scheme until a safer time, when the countess wasn't present?

Blythe fretted over the question as she and her mother strolled the ballroom with its huge mirrors and elegant draperies. A soft golden glow cascaded from the crystal chandeliers. By rote, she smiled and chatted with acquaintances. She had almost decided to postpone her plan when she spotted Lady Davina introducing a ravishing blond debutante to the Duke of Savoy.

A sense of urgency enveloped Blythe. She mustn't twiddle her thumbs and wait for a more opportune moment. She had to act tonight before Davina maneuvered her father into betrothing himself to someone else.

Under Mrs. Crompton's watchful eyes, Blythe danced the quadrille with a succession of gentlemen before being approached by the one she'd been hoping to encounter. Lord Harry Dashwood was a younger son with no prospects other than to marry wealth.

Although women were reputed to be the biggest gossips, Blythe knew that wasn't always the case. Lord Harry's appetite for tittle-tattle surpassed that of all the clucking hens in the ton. He was perfect for her purpose.

A short man with a big nose and a thatch of brown hair, he bowed over her mother's hand. "Mrs. Crompton, you have the most lovely daughter. May I humbly beg the next set with her?"

Clearly seeking a better prospect than a fifth son, Mrs. Crompton cast a surreptitious glance over his shoulder. "Well, I—"

"I would very much enjoy having the pleasure of your company, Lord Harry," Blythe said. "If you'll excuse us, Mama."

Before her mother could object, Blythe tucked her gloved hand into the crook of his arm and they began walking toward the area where two lines of ladies and gentlemen were forming. The orchestra in the corner tuned its instruments while the hum of conversation swirled in the air.

"I confess I'm a trifle warm," she said, plying her fan. "In lieu of dancing, would you care to take a turn around the room instead? I would greatly love to hear all the latest *on-dits*."

"Absolutely!" Lord Harry said with alacrity. Then he toned down his enthusiasm. "Although pray be assured, I am no rumor-monger."

"Most certainly not. *I* would rather regard you as a keen observer of society."

"Exactly! So many do not understand that quality in me." Lord Harry glanced around to make certain no one was listening. "Speaking of news, did you know that Freddie Skidmore was caught cheating at cards this very morning? Lord Ainsley has challenged him to a duel."

"Oh, dear. When is this dreadful event to take place?"

"Never! Skidmore claimed he merely made a mistake when dealing out the deck. They'd been playing all night at White's, you see."

"Hmm. Well, I've had the honor of dancing with Lord Ainsley. I do not believe he would have made such an accusation lightly."

"Quite so. Skidmore is a known profligate. In truth, he isn't fit conversation for a young lady's ears."

As they continued to stroll a circuit around the ballroom, she said, "Then you shall have to tell me the latest reports about others in society. Being so recently out of the schoolroom, I know very little about the ton."

Pandering to his self-importance opened the floodgates of hearsay. He launched into a non-stop dialogue about the various people present. It was rather mind-boggling, she mused. If even half of what he related was true, these aristocrats led secret lives full of clandestine affairs, hidden debts, and illegitimate children.

Seeing that the dance was drawing to a close, she deemed it time to bring up her own gossip. "That is all very fascinating," she said. "I'm afraid it doesn't hold a candle to *my* news."

Lord Harry stopped short. "You have news? Pray do not tell me you are betrothed already."

Blythe smiled. "Rest assured, I am not. Rather, I only wished to mention that my sister Portia is in town with her husband and young son. They're staying at Pallister House."

"Lady Ratcliffe," Lord Harry said musingly. "As I recall, she's the one who was visited by that Indian prince two years ago."

Blythe had hoped he would bring that up. He was the sort who never forgot a juicy tidbit of gossip.

"Arun was his name," she said with a nod. "He's the Maharajah of Bombay. He and Portia are fast friends and they still exchange the occasional letter. She received a note from him not too long ago, one that contained some interesting news."

"Do tell!"

Lord Harry cocked his head toward her. He had rather large ears, she noticed, the better to listen to gossip. "Arun mentioned that a friend of his will be traveling to London soon. Apparently the prince is taking a world tour before he assumes the throne."

Lord Harry stopped dead in his tracks again. "Prince, you say? Who is he? From where does he hail?"

Blythe pretended to think hard. "If I remember correctly, his name is Prince Nicolai of Ambrosia. I believe it's a small country nestled in the mountains near the Caspian Sea."

"The Caspian—? I must remember to look for it on a map."

She urged him to continue their stroll. "I'm afraid Ambrosia is so tiny, it is often left off many maps."

As she anticipated, Lord Harry cared little about such a minor detail. "What momentous news! You should have mentioned it from the start! When will His Highness arrive? Where will he be staying?"

"I believe his ship is due to arrive momentarily. As to where he's staying . . ." Blythe lifted one shoulder in a casual shrug. "I really wouldn't know. I did have the honor of meeting Prince Nicolai once, though, at the maharajah's palace in India."

"My word! What is he like?"

"Tall and dark-haired, very handsome, perhaps near thirty years of age. And unmarried." As if something had just occurred to her, she tapped one finger on her lips. "You know, I believe Arun mentioned that Prince Nicolai is coming to England to seek a bride."

Lord Harry fairly quivered with excitement. "How very delicious, Miss Crompton. All the ton will be agog when they learn that a foreign prince is to visit our fair shores."

"Oh, you mustn't trumpet his arrival to everyone here," Blythe warned. "Did I not make myself clear? The prince is a retiring sort of gentleman who doesn't like a lot of fuss made over him."

"I would never *dream* of making a big announcement to one and all. I *can* be discreet, you know."

"I'm sure you can." The high level of his enthusiasm caused a niggle of worry in Blythe. Lady Davina mustn't discover that Blythe was the source of the gossip. "But do promise that you'll keep my name—and my sister's name—out of it. It would be dreadful if Prince Nicolai were to find out that I'd revealed his quest for a bride."

"You may depend upon me to keep your confidence." Lord Harry locked his lips with an imaginary key. "Absolutely!"

Chapter 13

It was the perfect night for espionage.

Carrying a tray with the remains of tea and cake, James walked along the upstairs corridor. The plush carpet muffled his footfalls. Candles in sconces cast flickering shadows over the deserted passageway with its gilded columns and landscape paintings.

The other servants had finished their duties for the evening. Blythe and her mother had gone to Almack's and they were not expected back for hours.

He scowled at the memory of how capably Blythe had dragged him into that wild scheme of hers. He wanted no part of posing as a prince, for it was bound to interfere with his investigation. Perhaps tonight he would have the good fortune to find a piece of evidence.

Although the time was approaching midnight, George Crompton was still busy in his downstairs office. A few minutes ago, James had walked past to glimpse the man at his desk, making notations in an account book.

There might never be a better opportunity to search Edith Crompton's chamber.

Upon reaching the end of the passage, James glanced over his shoulder before opening the door. The darkened room smelled faintly of lilacs. He felt his way around and set down the tray on a table. Then he went back out to fetch a candle from one of the sconces. He used the flame to light an oil lamp before returning the candle to its holder.

Closing the door, he held up the lamp to illuminate a boudoir decorated in shades of pink and white. The place was decidedly feminine, from the rose-colored draperies to the chaise longue by the window. A dressing table held various bottles and jars, along with a silver-backed brush.

Maybe he should take a strand of Edith's hair and give it to Roland for his *gris-gris* magic.

James's mouth twisted, half grin and half grimace. He was not yet so desperate as to seek reparations by supernatural means. Rather, he needed to find something that would be admissible in court. If Percy Thornton failed to find a portrait of George and Edith at the Lancashire manor house, then James would need some other tangible proof of the crime.

Thus far, he'd had no occasion to search George's office. Since Edith had to be an accomplice to the crime, James had come here instead. Perhaps she'd kept some token relating to her true identity. How convenient it would be to find a miniature of her as a young girl, or a diary detailing her theft of a lady's identity.

One could always hope.

He poked through the drawers of the dressing table, but found only cosmetics, hairpins, ribbons, and other feminine essentials. The single drawer of a dainty desk held pens and embossed stationery. There were no secret compartments to be found, even when he crouched down and patted the underside.

Where would she hide her valuables? Jewels would be kept in a strongbox, but might she have put incriminating evidence in there, as well?

He peeked behind a landscape painting on the wall. No safe.

Holding up the lamp, James went through a doorway and found himself in a spacious bedchamber. He scanned the French white furnishings in a slow sweep, looked behind more gilt-framed canvases, and then headed to the dressing room. Women sometimes hid things among their personal items.

A quarter of an hour later, he had combed through scores of lacy undergarments, silk stockings, garters, and petticoats. He had checked the far reaches of each drawer. He had poked into the corners of every chest and clothes press. He had searched through ear bobs and trinkets in the hopes of finding something that would yield a clue to her origins.

Edith owned a substantial array of fine garments, but that was the extent of it. There was nothing whatsoever of her past. No letters. No diary. No drawings. No knick-knacks. One would almost think that Mrs. Edith Crompton had sprung full-grown into the present day.

Frustrated, James returned to the bedchamber to see what he might have missed. The bedside table contained a single drawer. Setting down the lamp, he pulled open the drawer. There were a few folded handkerchiefs, a stash of fresh beeswax candles, and a black-bound book of devotionals.

In the back of the drawer lay a pistol.

Picking it up, he examined the pocket-sized weapon with interest. The dainty muff pistol had a short iron barrel and a curved walnut grip that was decorated with filigreed silver wire.

Why would a lady of the ton keep a handgun by her bedside? Was it merely a habit carried over from India, where she might have feared the attack of a tiger or perhaps a native uprising?

Or did Edith Crompton have the dark mind of a criminal? Did she feel the need to be prepared for any contingency—such as the exposure of herself as a felon?

Frowning, he carefully replaced the pistol at the rear of the drawer. The woman who occupied this chamber was shrouded in mystery. He now had more unanswered questions than ever.

Blast it, why did she keep no mementoes? It had to be on purpose, to hide her past. He had hoped to find proof that she'd stolen the life of his cousin's wife. But aside from the odd juxtaposition of the pistol and the prayer book, there was little here to define her nature.

Deep in thought, James picked up the slender volume and riffled through the pages. One thing was certain, he would never have expected a swindler to be in possession of a book of psalms—

A paper fell out of the pages and onto the carpet.

Bending down, he rescued the sheet and brought it close to the light of the lamp. On a folded piece of foolscap was written *Mr. and Mrs. George Crompton*, along with an address in India.

James opened the yellowed paper. Excitement flared in him. He was holding a letter, an old one judging by the looks of it. In places, the black ink had faded to brown, and he had to strain to discern the words.

To the esteemed Mr. and Mrs. Crompton,

Pray permit me to give thanks for your most generous bequest, which arrived on Tuesday last. Although your kindness will not bring back my dearest Mercy, she would have been happy to know that I am well cared for in my waning years. May God Almighty bless you both and keep you safe,

Mrs. Hannah Bleasdale

Littleford Cottage
Lancashire, England

The spidery script had a wobbly, laborious quality as if the author was not accustomed to putting pen to paper. It was dated nearly twenty years earlier.

James stared down at the note. Who the devil was Mrs. Bleasdale? And why would Edith Crompton save nothing from her past but this one seemingly insignificant note of thanks? Had it been slipped into the prayer book long ago and then forgotten?

He was inclined to think otherwise. Surely the letter had to be of great value to Edith if she kept it in the table right beside her bed. And who was Mercy? Mrs. Bleasdale's daughter or granddaughter?

More important, what connection did the two women have to Edith?

A muffled thump jerked his attention away from the note. The noise had come from the corner of the bedchamber where the outline of a white door loomed in the shadows.

It was the connecting entry to George's quarters.

The man must have concluded his work downstairs. If he were to walk in here right now . . .

James pocketed the letter, quietly shoved the drawer shut, and snatched up the lamp. Then he made a mad dash for the boudoir and the outer door that led to the passageway.

In the boudoir, James set the lamp on the dressing table. He was leaning down to blow it out when he heard the sound of the door opening and then the heavy tramp of approaching footsteps. Swiftly, he abandoned the task and picked up the tray.

Just in time.

George Crompton appeared in the doorway. Having

shed his coat and cravat, he wore a plain white shirt and dark breeches. He stopped short on seeing James. A mistrustful frown descended over the man's weathered features and his fingers curled into fists at his sides.

"What are you doing in here?" he snapped.

Rigid with tension, James lowered his gaze in order to portray an image of humble servitude. The purloined letter burned in his coat pocket. If he was taken for a thief and searched, the note would be found.

He would be hard-pressed to explain why he had it in his possession. Such a discovery would force him to reveal his true identity or risk being thrown into prison.

At all costs, James had to avoid playing his hand too early. He wasn't yet ready to openly accuse this man of being an imposter. It would be a disaster if the fellow were to burn the letter and destroy any other evidence that might be in this house.

"The tray, sir," James murmured, indicating the tea tray he held. "I was sent to fetch it."

"Why is that lamp lighted?"

"I don't know. It was lit when I came in."

James hoped the flimsy ruse would pass muster. He had brought the tea tray here for the purpose of giving himself an excuse in case he was caught. Now he wondered if it would be sufficient to exonerate him.

Against all logic, a part of him half hoped for a confrontation. James felt more certain than ever that a crime had been committed against his cousin. He was looking forward to the moment when this man would be exposed to the world as a charlatan.

George ran his fingers through his thinning hair. "Edith! One of these days that woman will burn the house down. Go on, then, off with you."

James turned to leave. He clenched his teeth to keep from uttering a condemnation of the man right here and now. To demand to know if the real George Crompton had been murdered.

Holding himself in check, James walked out the door of the boudoir. It would be unwise to make any accusations just yet. Before such an event took place, he must have an iron-clad case.

With any luck, the letter in his pocket might be the key piece of proof he needed.

Chapter 14

Blythe suspected trouble when Portia sent a terse summons to come to Lindsey's house at her earliest convenience—alone. An hour later, as Blythe stepped into the spacious foyer, she had disobeyed in one respect. She had brought Kasi with her as a foil for whatever scolding her sisters had in store.

A sense of unease nagged at Blythe. Had Portia and Lindsey found out about the ruse? Surely that was impossible.

The previous evening at Almack's, Lord Harry Dashwood had lost no time in spreading the word about the imminent arrival of Nicolai, the crown prince of Ambrosia. The air had been buzzing with the news. Much to Blythe's delight, she'd seen Lady Davina herself listening avidly to Lord Harry.

Blythe had warned him not to reveal the source of the report, and he had complied. She knew her secret was safe. After all, no one at Almack's had approached her for additional information. Then, on the way home, Mama had expressed interest in the prince's visit without betraying any suspicion that Blythe herself had started the rumor.

Standing in the sunlit foyer with its tall windows, she ordered herself to relax. The summons could have nothing whatsoever to do with the hoax. Rather, it was far more likely that her two sisters intended to lecture Blythe on the folly of marrying the Duke of Savoy.

Let them try. She had no intention of being dissuaded from the course she'd set for her life.

Informed by the butler that the ladies were up in the nursery, Blythe and Kasi ascended the grand staircase. The previous summer, Lindsey had wed Thane Pallister, the Earl of Mansfield, and they had moved into this mansion on Park Lane. As always, Blythe felt awed by the splendor of Pallister House.

If she married the Duke of Savoy, she too would have a beautiful home in which she could play hostess. She could hold balls and dinners for the ton. Yet for some reason, the prospect held little interest for her today. Was it because she'd been so frustrated in her efforts to have a moment alone with the duke?

That must be it. And the problem would be solved very soon, once she'd enacted her scheme to distract Lady Davina. Blythe could scarcely wait to see James garbed as Prince Nicolai. . . .

Upon reaching the top of the steps, she heard the sounds of laughing voices and childish squeals emanating from the far end of the broad passageway. She and Kasi followed the happy noise to a large, sunny schoolroom that had been converted to a playroom with a rocking horse, dolls and games, and other toys.

They paused just inside the doorway. Across the room, Portia stood with Lindsey, who cuddled her infant daughter, Ella. Nearby, Thane leaned against the windowsill, his arms folded. He stood grinning at his brother-in-law, who was chasing Arthur around the playroom.

Shrieking with laughter, the little boy toddled as fast as his chubby legs could carry him. Colin pretended to catch him, while letting him escape at the very last moment. Round and round the room they ran until Arthur collided with a stool and flopped backward onto his padded bottom. A startled look came over his face; then he let out a howl that was more indignant than distressed.

Portia rushed to kneel beside him and dry his tears. "Poor baby. Are you hurt?"

"He's perfectly fine," Colin said. "You needn't cosset him."

Sure enough, Arthur stopped crying and stretched up his hands to his father. "Up," he demanded. "Up, Papa."

"Goodness," Lindsey said. "He's learning more words every day."

"My nephew is quite brilliant," Thane replied, coming close to gently cradle the sleeping baby's head in his hand. "However, little Ella here will be giving him competition soon enough. Only look at what a clever mother she has."

He and Lindsey shared a private smile. Lifting up on tiptoe, she kissed his scarred cheek. "I was clever enough to marry you."

In the throes of wistful yearning, Blythe watched them. With all her heart, she ached to experience such closeness with the man of her dreams. She imagined herself being held by James while he gazed at her with loving tenderness. . . .

James? How jarring that *he* would enter her daydreams. She had no interest in the footman other than to ensure that he cooperated in the ruse to trick Lady Davina.

Colin took hold of Arthur and swooped him up high in the air. Reaching for the ceiling, the little boy burst into gales of infectious laughter that made Blythe smile.

Portia waved at Blythe and Kasi. "Why, look who's here."

"Go give your Auntie Blythe a kiss," Colin said, setting his son down and giving him a gentle push toward the doorway.

Arthur came rushing toward Blythe, his cherub features alight with joy. "Tiss!"

"Do you mean kiss?" She bent down to hug him tightly and to kiss him on the cheek. How small and sturdy he felt, how very dear. A rush of love squeezed her heart. He felt so perfect in her arms. How wonderful it would be to become a mother herself.

She ruffled his black hair. "How is my favorite boy? Have you been good since I saw you yesterday?"

Being too young to answer her questions, he took hold of her face in his chubby hands. He landed a loud smack on her cheek, then giggled at the noise he'd made.

Breaking free, he toddled to Kasi and threw his arms around her legs. She beamed down at him, murmuring to him in her singsong voice.

Blythe looked across the playroom and caught Lindsey and Portia exchanging a telling glance; then they each nodded to their husbands. Clearly, it was time for the men to leave the women to their talk.

Colin strode forward to hoist Arthur up to straddle his shoulders. Arthur wrapped his arms around his father's neck and chortled with glee. "Well, my lad," Colin said, "we're to make ourselves scarce. What do you say we go look for frogs in the garden?"

Arthur babbled his assent.

Portia smiled, though observing them with a hint of anxiety. "You do have a firm hold on him, don't you?"

"Have a little faith, darling. I won't let my son fall."

As the men departed with the boy, Blythe tried to picture the Duke of Savoy abandoning his dignity to play chase with their child, or to give him a ride on his shoulders. The image refused to take shape in her mind. But she could easily envision James in the role of doting father.

Irked, Blythe banished him from her mind. Her future depended upon becoming the Duchess of Savoy. Nothing and no one must rob her of that opportunity.

Lindsey passed the sleepy infant to Kasi. "Would you be a dear and put Emma for her nap? If you need me, we'll be in the drawing room."

"Yes, missy." Kasi spared a single piercing glance at the sisters before turning away. Clearly she suspected something was up, though she made no attempt to follow them. Heading into the adjoining room, she crooned a soft song in Hindi while rocking Ella in her arms.

Blythe ached to hold the baby herself and escape the coming inquisition. Nevertheless, she joined her sisters in walking toward the grand staircase.

"Where is Jocelyn today?" she asked. A year younger than Blythe, Jocelyn was Thane's ward and still in the schoolroom. The previous spring, she and Blythe had become fast friends. "I haven't seen very much of her since my come-out."

"She and Miss Underhill went out to Green Park for her sketching lesson," Lindsey said. "So you needn't look to her to rescue you."

"Rescue me?" Blythe said, sending a cool glance back at her middle sister as they descended the stairs. "That sounds ominous."

"Quite," Portia murmured. "By the by, I asked you to come alone."

"So you did, but I could scarcely leave without a chaperone. Be thankful I didn't bring Mama with me."

"I suspect you'd have been very sorry if you had."

"Why? Mama is most anxious to see me wed His Grace of Savoy. She won't take well to the two of you trying to convince me otherwise!"

Portia frowned, but refused to say any more until they were seated in chairs in the sunny yellow drawing room with its tall windows overlooking the verdant stretch of Hyde Park. A servant wheeled in a tea tray at once, apparently having been given orders to prepare it on Blythe's arrival.

Lindsey poured three steaming cups and distributed them. Blowing on her tea to cool it, Blythe braced herself for the usual arguments against the Duke of Savoy. She felt secure in her decision to marry him, and she only wished her sisters could support her.

"I had an unexpected visitor this morning," Portia said. "To say that I was surprised would be an understatement."

"A visitor?" Blythe said, wracking her brain. Had Lady Davina come here to enlist support in her crusade to keep Blythe from marrying the duke? "Who?"

"The Countess de Lieven."

Blythe nearly spilled the tea in her lap. The cup rattled in the saucer as she stared at her oldest sister. The stern look on Portia's face boded ill. *Dear heavens.* So this meeting wasn't about the duke, after all—at least not directly.

Out of sheer cowardice, Blythe prevaricated. "The wife of the Russian ambassador? I wasn't aware that you knew her."

"You're right—I don't. Or at least I *didn't.* I must say, it was extremely awkward to be questioned by a near-stranger about an imaginary letter I'd received from Arun."

"Oh." Blythe felt a flush spread up her throat and into her face. What exactly did the countess know? Perhaps she had merely been fishing for information. "I . . . um . . . might have mentioned last night at Almack's that you still correspond with Arun on occasion."

Lindsey snorted. "Well, that's a mild way of putting it. Apparently, you invented a friend of his, a Prince Nicolai of Ambrosia. He *is* an invention, isn't he? Because the countess said she'd never heard of the country. Why on earth would you spread such a mad rumor?"

Blythe held up her chin. "It isn't mad at all. It's perfectly logical." Her fingers gripped tightly in her lap, she gave Portia an anxious look. "But first, I must know exactly what you said to the countess. Did you tell her I was lying?"

"I said that I wasn't willing to discuss the content of my private letters, and that you should not have done so, either. When she left, she was less than happy with me."

"That's all? You didn't reveal that Arun never wrote about Prince Nicolai?"

"Of course not. I didn't want to land you in hot water." Portia raised a chiding eyebrow at Blythe. "However, you might have warned me that you're up to some scheme. I was hard-pressed to determine what you meant in telling such a colossal fib."

Awash with relief, Blythe sprang up to embrace Portia. "Bless you! You're the best sister in the world."

Lindsey cleared her throat.

"As are you, of course," Blythe added hastily, giving her middle sister a hug, too. "Please don't tell anyone about this. It's crucial that no one in society questions the story."

"Then do us the honor of telling *us* the truth," Lindsey said. "I for one am most intrigued."

Wondering how much she should reveal, Blythe walked back and forth in front of the tea tray. She didn't dare divulge the full extent of her plan. They didn't know James as she did, and they would object to her trusting his ability to pull off the ruse. . . .

Her sisters were staring at her, Lindsey drumming her fingers on the arm of the chair, and Portia absently smoothing a hand over her barely rounded midsection. The last thing Blythe wanted was a dressing-down from the two women she loved most in the world.

"You know that I wish to wed the Duke of Savoy." Seeing them frown in unison, she held up her hand. "I don't want to hear your objections. Just accept it as my decision. The trouble is, the duke's daughter, Lady Davina, opposes the match."

"As well she should," Lindsey muttered. "He's too old for you."

"That isn't why she objects. Rather, she thinks that because of my common birth I'm not good enough for him. She told me straight to my face that she would never permit her father to marry so vastly far beneath himself."

Portia clucked in sympathy. "She's a narrow-minded snob. It is best to simply avoid people like her."

"That isn't all." Blythe related how Lady Davina had played several nasty tricks, including the one involving Lord Kitchener. "She's made it her personal aim never to allow me anywhere near her father. So I decided that since she won't leave his side, something must be done to divert her attention."

"Enter Prince Nicolai of Ambrosia," Lindsey said, giving Blythe an astute look. "However, if you're planning to deceive Lady Davina with this fictitious prince, then you're playing a dangerous game."

"I intend to convince her that the prince is interested in courting her. That way, she won't be hovering near the duke and I'll have a chance to charm him."

Portia set down her teacup in its saucer. "Do you mean to have this Prince Nicolai actually appear in society?" she said in an aghast tone. "How? Have you hired a Covent Garden actor to play the role?"

"Not precisely," Blythe hedged. "I assure you, it isn't anything that should worry either of you."

She strolled to the window, pretending an interest in the view of Hyde Park. Maybe they would take the hint that she didn't wish to answer any more questions.

But of course her sisters weren't known for their tact.

Lindsey marched forward and turned Blythe back around to face them. "We *will* worry if you don't tell us exactly what you're planning. Now, give it out. Every last bit, no holds barred."

Blythe bit her lip. She didn't want to cause trouble for James. Nor did she want to confess all to her sisters. But it was obvious from their determined faces that she had to tell them *something.*

"I've found a footman who's willing to play the part. He's well-spoken and he'll be perfect for the role."

Her sisters glanced at each other, then back at Blythe.

"Who is this man?" Portia asked. "Can he be trusted?"

"More to the point," Lindsey said in a scoffing tone, "how can a mere footman ever hope to convince anyone that he's a gentleman, let alone a prince?"

Blythe bristled at the unfair attack on James. He was a fine, upstanding man with hopes and dreams like everyone. He'd told her he wanted to go to India and make his fortune. She very nearly blurted out an argument in his defense. But the last thing she wanted was to reveal his identity because then her sisters might find some way to interfere.

"He was raised as a companion to a gentleman, and he's quite adept at mimicry." Blythe said in an offhand tone. "Truly, you're both making far more of the scheme than I ever intended. It'll involve just a minor flirtation or two, a brief meeting in the privacy of a garden, perhaps. Then, while the prince is with Lady Davina, I'll have my chance to speak to the duke. The very moment that His Grace makes me a marriage offer, Prince Nicolai will leave the city, never to return."

Or at least she prayed it would be that simple.

"It sounds tremendously risky," Portia said, looking troubled. "This footman may speak well enough, but what if he's questioned by members of society? What if the Countess de Lieven looks into his background and exposes him as an imposter?"

That possibility worried Blythe, too. Yet she refused to retreat at the first sign of a stumbling block. "He won't be around long enough for anyone to send for information about him from abroad. So you needn't fret. I promise you, his participation in society will be minimal."

"I should like to meet this footman," Lindsey said. "If you insist upon such a rash course of action, the least we can do is to help outfit him in the proper clothing. He'll also need to be instructed in the ways of society and how to charm a lady."

James was already charming enough. He had proven himself to be a fascinating conversationalist, one who could make a woman feel special and admired. The very thought stirred heat in Blythe. She wanted to see him adorned in royal garb. But transforming James into a prince was a task she would keep for herself.

It was *not* for her interfering sisters, however well-meaning they might be.

She crossed her arms. "Both of you are much too busy with your children. Besides, I'm perfectly capable of handling the matter myself without any assistance. Everything will work out just fine, you'll see."

"I certainly hope so," Lindsey said, one eyebrow arched in doubt. "Because if this scheme of yours is exposed, the footman will lose his post."

"Even worse," Portia added with a stern look at Blythe, "*you* may find yourself embroiled in the scandal of the year."

Chapter 15

"Check every room above stairs," Godwin instructed James in the cellar kitchen. "Leave no candles burning unattended. And you must see to it that the oil lamps are not—"

The head footman broke off into a fit of coughing. Seated in a rocking chair next to the hearth, he looked feverish, his normally pale features flushed and his eyes reddened. Though a rough woolen blanket covered his lap, he shivered from a fit of the ague.

"I'll make certain the lamps aren't smoking," James finished for him. "The wicks must be trimmed low so there's no threat of a fire."

Godwin nodded as he honked into a large handkerchief. He wiped his nose before grumpily adding, "See to it that the task is done properly. I shouldn't be handing over such an important duty to a new man like you. But Laycock must man the front door and the other footmen are attending the family coach at Lord and Lady Wortham's ball."

James made a respectful bow. "Thank you, sir. I'm mindful of the great honor you've afforded me. Pray know that I shall not fail you."

Taking a candle to light the way, he left Godwin to his

misery and strode out into the shadowed passageway. Most of the other servants had retired for the night or had lain down to catch a few winks while waiting for the family to return home in the wee hours.

James was exhilarated to be given free rein to roam the upper floors. He'd been waiting for this chance to conduct a thorough search of the place. There had to be more evidence somewhere, something that would prove the Cromptons were not who they claimed to be.

Discovering the old letter in Edith's bedside table three nights ago had been a boon to his investigation. Since Percy Thornton had departed already on his journey to find portraits of George and Edith, James had forwarded a message to the former estate agent. He had asked Thornton to track down Mrs. Hannah Bleasdale at Littleford Cottage and to inquire as to why the Cromptons had sent the woman a generous bequest for someone named Mercy.

For all James knew, he could be chasing a ghost. Mrs. Hannah Bleasdale might be long dead. However, it would be worth the extra day or two it would take for Thornton to find out for certain. If Mrs. Bleasdale was still alive, she might know information that would shed light on the mystery.

But James couldn't bank on that hope. He would need a rock-solid case in order to convince a judge to arrest such an influential couple as the Cromptons.

Candlestick in hand, he mounted the narrow wooden stairs that led to the ground floor. He pushed open the door and stepped into a large, dimly lit passageway near the front of the house.

A few steps led him to a gloomy foyer. The formal rooms on either side lay in darkness. The only illumination came from an oil lamp that flickered near the footman on duty.

Laycock had fallen asleep on a stool beside the double front doors. The freckled young footman sat with his bewigged head tilted back against the wall. Soft snores emanated from his open mouth.

James celebrated another stroke of luck. There would be no witnesses at all to his explorations.

Cupping the candle flame against any drafts, he made a quiet retreat. He was supposed to be checking the bedrooms. But first he intended to have a look in George Crompton's private office.

As James headed for the rear of the house, the faint hollow scrape of his footsteps echoed down the length of the wide corridor. At intervals, the feeble light from a few sconces made a valiant attempt to penetrate the deep pools of shadow. With its tall columns and marble statuary, the place might have been the palace of a king.

George Crompton owned this mansion. But not for long. As soon as James secured the irrefutable evidence, he would expose the man as an imposter—and quite possibly a murderer. George and Edith would be convicted in a court of law and a judge would determine their punishment. Then James would lay claim to his rightful inheritance.

And what would happen to Blythe?

He wanted to ignore the troubling question. Her fate was of no consequence to him. After all, it wasn't as if she'd be tossed out on the streets to fend for herself. One of her sisters would take her in, although Blythe would be forever tainted by the crimes of her parents. Stripped of her generous dowry, she'd become a pariah, shunned by society, no longer welcome in the best homes.

The reality of her stark future disturbed James. It shouldn't matter, he told himself. Justice must be done.

Nevertheless, he disliked being the instrument of her downfall. Not so much because of the money, but because he'd seen for himself that she harbored a genuine affection for her parents. Learning of their treachery would come as a terrible shock to a girl who'd grown up in an insulated world of wealth and privilege.

A girl who was hell-bent on marrying a title.

He grimaced. By God, he'd suffer no regrets for destroying her hope of wedding the Duke of Savoy. She should never have set her cap for a man who was old enough to be her father. In her ambition to become a duchess, she intended to resort to subterfuge in order to entrap Savoy.

Several days had passed since she'd summoned James to her bedchamber and offered to pay him an extravagant sum to play Prince Nicolai of Ambrosia. At a time yet to be announced, he was to garb himself as a foreign royal and distract the duke's snooty daughter, Lady Davina, giving Blythe a chance to attract the duke.

James wanted no part of that folly. There were too many variables that could cause matters to go awry—not the least of which was for Prince Nicolai to be unmasked as an upstart footman. It was difficult enough pretending to be a servant. James didn't need the added aggravation of pretending to be footman pretending to be a prince.

At least Blythe had made no further attempt to seek him out. A whirl of social engagements had kept her away from the house, including the ball that she and her parents were attending this evening. Perhaps she had failed in her attempt to spread a rumor about the imminent arrival of Prince Nicolai. Perhaps no one had believed the Banbury tale. Perhaps she'd snapped to her senses and abandoned the reckless plan.

His mouth twisted. Perhaps his long-dead, profligate father would rise from the grave.

Turning a corner, James spied the office at the end of the shadowed passageway. The sooner he had solid proof in his hands, the better. Then he could abandon this footman's disguise, itchy wig and all. How shocked Blythe would be to learn that he was a blue-blooded gentleman—and the true heir to her father's vast fortune.

Without a doubt, she would despise him for deceiving all of them. She would hold James to blame for the ruination of her parents. Which meant that he'd never know the pleasure of her kiss. If making love to her was off limits to him as a footman, it would be absolutely out of the question once she found out the truth of his purpose here. And *that* was a bitter pill for him to swallow. . . .

James came to an abrupt halt in front of the office door. Was he really weighing the prospect of abandoning his righteous cause in favor of indulging his lust?

No. It would never happen. Blythe Crompton might be an exceptionally pretty girl, but she wasn't worth the sacrifice of his principles—and certainly not his stolen inheritance. He had to face the fact that there were no circumstances under which he could ever claim her for his own.

Grasping the doorknob, he felt a sudden prickling of unease. He lifted the candlestick. Nothing moved in the gloom of the passageway. Only the marble bust of an ancient Roman gazed sightlessly from a pillar against the opposite wall.

Nevertheless, James kept his attention on the murky shadows of the corridor while he slipped inside the darkened office. As he shut the door behind him, he shook off the nagging sense of disquiet. Now was no time to let his imagination run wild.

On impulse, he reached up and stripped off the cumbersome wig. It would be easier to search without that discomfort. But even as he turned around with the bundle of powdered horsehair gripped in his fingers, two observations struck him in rapid succession.

First, a faint whiff of flowery perfume overlay the more masculine aromas of leather and tobacco smoke.

Second, he was not alone.

The glow of his candle reached the broad mahogany desk. And there in the shadows, a quill pen in hand, sat Miss Blythe Crompton.

He stood rooted to the floor. Disbelief slammed into him at the sight of her staring back at him. She wore a shoulder-baring gown, the white gauzy fabric setting off to perfection her creamy skin and upswept copper hair. Since she had frozen in the act of leaning forward, apparently to blow out her own candle, he had a spectacular view of lush breasts and a hint of lacy chemise.

Her eyes wide, she uttered a little gasp and dropped her pen. "James! You frightened me half to *death!*"

"I could say the same for you." In a temper over his wrecked plans—and the spontaneous combustion of lust inside him—he strode straight to the desk. "Why the devil are you in here? You're supposed to be out at a ball."

"I told Mama that I wasn't feeling well. The coachman brought me home a little while ago."

"She allowed you to abandon the Duke of Savoy?"

"He wasn't present tonight. There was no reason for me to stay."

"And so you would prefer to sit here in the dark."

"Don't be ridiculous! I blew out the candle when I heard someone coming."

Blythe willed her heart to stop racing. The reaction had more to do with James himself than with the shock she'd experienced at his abrupt entry into her father's office. For one, she'd never seen him without his white powdered wig. If she'd thought him handsome before, now he was downright gorgeous, with rumpled black hair to match his dark eyes and swarthy skin.

Clad in blue livery, he created a forceful presence that altered the quiet peace of the room. The flickering light of his candle cast harsh shadows over his strong cheekbones. She had the oddest impression of roiling emotions in him, a notion that was corroborated by his terse tone and scowling expression.

But why should a footman be angry to find her at her father's desk? Come to think of it, why had James crept into the office so furtively?

"Enough of your inquisition," she said. "I believe it's my place to inquire why *you're* here."

His features took on an impassive look. "The lamps," he said. "I was charged with the task of making certain there were none left burning that might start a fire."

"I see." It was a reasonable excuse, yet she knew he wasn't telling her everything. "And when you check each room, do you always remove your wig?"

He tossed the bundle onto a nearby chair. "It's an annoyance. I didn't think you'd mind if I did so."

"You also closed the door behind yourself. Why?"

He fixed her with an unfathomable stare. Then he set down the candlestick, strolled around to the side of the desk, and seated himself on the edge. Leaning forward, he murmured, "Because I guessed at once that you didn't want anyone to know you're in here. And besides, I find it necessary to have a private talk with my employer."

His nearness gave Blythe a tiny shiver of pleasure. Although his tale didn't quite ring true, the note of sensuality in his voice had a distracting effect on her, as did the sight of his disheveled hair. She had the mad urge to reach up and comb her fingers through it. Besides his casual appearance, his unorthodox behavior rattled her composure. Never before had she known a servant to sit in her presence without invitation. James was much too close and she really ought to order him to move.

Yet the paper lying before her was a stark reminder that she needed his cooperation.

"I'm not your employer," she pointed out. "My father pays your wages."

"A minor distinction. Nevertheless, you do wield an undeniable power over me, Miss Crompton."

Again, his silken words seemed imbued with under-currents of meaning. Was he admitting that he was at-tracted to her? Or was he merely referring to the difference in their ranks? Whatever the reason, his dark brown eyes held her enthralled. He gazed intently at her as if she was the subject of his romantic dreams. Her blood beating faster, Blythe found herself craving his embrace with un-ladylike desperation.

How imprudent even to allow such a thought. Noth-ing could be more forbidden to her than a liaison with a servant.

"Why did you wish to speak to me?" she asked.

Her question broke the spell. Sitting back, he folded his arms and subjected her to a cool stare. "It's about your plan to trick the duke's daughter. Since I'm involved, I was curious to know if you've given up on it."

"Of course I haven't given up. I've already spread the rumor that Prince Nicolai of Ambrosia is to visit London. Everyone is on pins and needles awaiting his arrival."

A brief tightening of James's mouth revealed his dis-pleasure. "Then it seems the nobility is far too gullible."

"You told me yourself that people will see whatever they wish to see." To give herself something to do, Blythe picked up the quill and twirled it between her fingers. "I'm sure you're wondering why I came home early to-night without my parents."

"You felt ill."

She shook her head. "That was merely an excuse. The truth is that I've been writing a note to Lady Davina from Prince Nicolai, and I needed to borrow a few sheets of my father's stationery. It looks more manly than mine, you see."

James picked up a blank piece of heavy cream paper and held it to his nose. "It also doesn't reek of flowery perfume, as yours does."

"How do you know—? Oh, you delivered the thank-you note that Mama made me write to the duke."

"For the chocolate bonbons that were ever so much finer than the mundane offerings of your other suitors."

His mocking tone wrested a self-conscious laugh from Blythe. How embarrassing to remember that James had been standing nearby while her mother had dictated those gushing words. Not wanting to be disloyal to the duke, Blythe said primly, "It was very considerate of His Grace to send me sweets."

"Very special, indeed. I'm sure he put a tremendous amount of thought into such an unusual gift."

Irked, she tossed down the quill. "I know you don't approve of me marrying the duke, but may I remind you, it is no concern of yours."

"Quite the contrary. In order for you to succeed in your mission, I am expected to play Prince Nicolai of Ambrosia."

James had a point there. Blythe couldn't fault him for feeling manipulated, so she strove for a more conciliatory tone. "I am rewarding you well for your trouble, don't forget. Now, you should be interested to learn what the prince wrote to Lady Davina." She pushed the paper toward him. "Go ahead, read it and tell me what you think."

He stared at her, his eyes hooded. Then he reached for the letter and angled it to the light of the candle. " 'To the most gracious Lady Davina.' " He aimed a sardonic look at Blythe. "Do they use the English tongue in Ambrosia, then?"

"His Royal Highness Prince Nicolai has had the very best tutors. He can speak English like a native."

"How convenient." One dark eyebrow cocked, James continued reading, " 'Pray forgive my boldness in writing this note, but I confess to being too eager to await the proper introductions. The tales of your great beauty have reached far and wide, luring me on a journey to the shores of England. I hope you will be so kind as to grant me an audience upon my arrival in London. Until then, I shall look forward with great anticipation to paying my addresses to you, dear lady. I remain your most ardent admirer, Nicolai Aleksander Leonide Pashenka, Crown Prince of Ambrosia.' "

Deviltry in his dark eyes, James looked at Blythe. "Couldn't you have given him a shorter name? It shall prove a disaster if I forget the order of my own identity."

"Stop teasing and tell me, is it a good letter? Do you think Davina will be fooled?"

He shook his head. "I'm afraid it won't do at all."

Affronted, Blythe sat up straight. "What do you mean? I spent the better part of half an hour debating exactly how to word it."

"It isn't so much the content, although I must say that *is* a bit syrupy."

"Then what is the problem?"

"The note obviously has been written by a woman's hand. And if I must play this role, I heartily object to the prince being perceived as effeminate."

"Oh." Blythe studied the letter with a fresh eye. He was right, there *was* a dainty quality to the penmanship. And James—in the guise of Prince Nicolai—required a more masculine style.

Sliding off the edge of the desk, he advanced on her.

"You needn't look so glum. Move aside, if you will, and I'll do it over for you."

Blythe found herself obeying, vacating the chair so that he could take her place. A belated concern struck her. He claimed to have had the education of a gentleman, but what if James had overplayed his skills in order to impress her? What if he embarrassed himself by producing a coarse, ink-spotted mess?

She hovered over him as he reached for a clean sheet of stationery and dipped a quill into the silver inkpot. He frowned down at her letter for a few moments, which only served to increase her anxiety. Then with confident strokes of the pen, he began to write. For a few moments, the only sound was the scratching of the nib on the paper. Every now and then, he reached out to refresh his ink.

Standing so close, she could touch his broad shoulders or run her fingers through the thickness of his hair. The very thought of indulging those desires stirred a secret fire in her. If only she could fathom why she felt so drawn to him. Was it merely the temptation of the forbidden?

Perhaps, for there was no denying he was the most breathtakingly handsome man in the world. Unfortunately, good looks were not what mattered in life. She was obliged to marry well in order to secure her future and her parents' place in society. And yet . . . wistful longing kept a tenacious hold on her heart.

Clearly oblivious to her wayward thoughts, James signed the prince's convoluted name with a flourish. He sanded the note before nudging it in her direction across the polished surface of the desk.

Blythe bent nearer to read it by the meager light of the candle. He had altered a few words here and there to lend a more masculine tenor to the message. The bold dark slash of his handwriting gave an air of authenticity to the letter, and she caught her breath in delight. "Oh, that's much better. It's perfect!"

Turning her head to smile at him, she felt a lightning bolt of awareness. His face loomed mere inches away, and there was no mistaking the heat in his eyes. His smoldering gaze flicked to her bosom, then returned to her face. More specifically, to her mouth.

"*You're* perfect," he muttered. "And I must be the world's biggest fool for helping you catch another man."

The husky statement sounded wrested from him by force. It sent a shiver over her skin, for never in her life had she heard such a romantic declaration.

In the grips of a powerful yearning, Blythe stroked her fingertips across his cheek. "James," she whispered. "Oh, James."

She didn't know who moved first. But their mouths met in a tentative brush that instantly caught fire like dry tinder. In a flash, she tumbled into his lap, throwing her arms around him as he kissed her with feral intensity. When his tongue demanded entry into her mouth, she welcomed the intimacy. Whatever inhibitions she had left melted away under the heat of their closeness. His taste, his scent, the sheer masculinity of him, overwhelmed her with a feast of the senses.

In all of her girlish dreams, she had never imagined a man's embrace could make her feel so wildly alive. She'd flirted and teased, much to the frustration of her suitors. But now she experienced the torment of passion herself. She craved James in every part of her body and soul.

Pressing herself to the wall of his chest, she could not seem to get close enough to him. Her fingers learned the angles of his face and the smooth silk of his hair. He explored her as well, his hands roving over the exposed skin of her shoulders and tracing the shape of her breasts. She moaned from the surfeit of pleasure. The illicit nature of their kiss only fed the hunger inside her. Clasped in his arms, in the small circle of candlelight, she felt as if the rules of the outside world had ceased to exist.

How amazing to know that James desired her with such ferocity. James, with his sardonic sense of humor and abundant charm. James, with his enticing aura of mystery. How was it that the one man who set her heart on fire had to be a servant?

Even as the unwelcome thought intruded, he lifted his head and slid his hands from her bosom down to her waist. His breathing harsh, he pressed his lips to her brow. "This is wrong," he muttered. "We should not be doing this."

His chivalry stirred her deeply. Catching his face in her hands, she brushed her damp lips over his. "It's merely a kiss. Nothing more."

"It's far more than that. You know it as well as I, Blythe . . . Miss Crompton." Grimacing, he shook his head. "There, you see? I haven't even the right to use your given name."

"Then I grant it to you." Unwilling to end the pleasure, she enticed him with light kisses. "Whenever we're alone, you may address me so."

"We won't be alone again, not if I can help it."

"Then I shall devise reasons to keep you in my company." With her fingertip, she traced the shape of his lips and the solid line of his jaw. "You'll attend me to the shops while I procure your princely garments. I'll find an excuse to stay home again so that I might teach you about the ways of society. You'll need to learn what to say—"

He caught her wrist in a firm grip and pushed her hand away. "This isn't a game, Blythe. I won't be your plaything while you prepare to marry the duke."

His sharp tone sliced through the romantic haze. Seeing the glitter of anger in his eyes, she felt the golden moment draining away, leaving her bereft. "I never said you were. It's just that . . . we both enjoyed kissing and I only thought . . ."

He shook his head decisively. "Let me make myself very clear," he said, his face cold. "I will not be satisfied with a passing flirtation. I want to seduce you. And by God, I *will* do so if you give me half a chance. Is that what you want? To lift your skirts for a footman? Do you really suppose your duke will accept damaged goods?"

His words struck Blythe like a physical slap. He had transformed the beautiful passion between them into something that was sordid and ugly. And as much as it pained her to admit it, he was right. Her destiny was to marry the Duke of Savoy. She didn't dare throw away her future for a tryst with a servant.

The enormity of her mistake flooded Blythe. What madness had come over her? She should never have kissed James. Nor should she be perched in his lap—and in her father's office, no less. How pitifully juvenile he must think her, not to have considered the consequences of her behavior! Even worse, a part of her still ached for him to pull her close and make the world go away.

Appalled and mortified, she scrambled to her feet. Unfortunately, the tangle of her gown along with a residual weakness in her legs, caused her to stumble.

James sprang up and caught hold of her arms to steady her. Even with her heart bruised and hurting, the brush of his hard body stirred base urges in her. It shook her to realize how very susceptible she was to him—now more than ever.

She thrust away his hands. "How dare you touch me. You've no right to do so."

Her attack wasn't fair; Blythe knew it the instant the words left her lips. He'd only been trying to help her. It was just that her emotions still reeled from his blunt statement, and she'd wanted to lash out at him for ruining the magic of that kiss. Yet how could she blame him for indulging his desires when she herself had done the same?

His face a rigid mask, he stepped back. "Pray forgive me, Miss Crompton. It won't happen again."

She drew a shaky breath. Much as it pained her, she owed him an apology.

She forced her chin up and met his gaze. "No, it's your forgiveness that I must beg. I'm sorry for snapping at you. Rather, I should thank you for being honest with me."

A certain wariness entered his eyes. "I had to be frank. You're too young and sheltered to realize the danger of being alone with a bounder like me."

Was that how he thought of himself? "James, you're far from being a cad. By calling my attention to reality, you behaved honorably. Would that I could say the same for myself."

Frowning, he cocked his head. "I beg your pardon?"

"I'm more at fault than you for that kiss. You're a servant, and I should never have taken advantage of you."

"Taken advantage? Of *me*?" The deferential footman vanished. James slapped his palms on the desk and thrust his face closer to hers. "I'm the one who made that brainless statement about being a fool for helping you entrap the Duke of Savoy."

In the light of the single candle, James radiated anger from the glitter of his eyes to the rigid tension in his jaw. But Blythe refused to back down.

She reached for the letter from the fictitious Prince Nicolai and carefully folded it. "Be that as it may, as a lady I've a responsibility to behave well. I should never have encouraged you to kiss me."

"What? None of this is *your* fault. It's entirely mine for lusting after you!"

Her gaze flew to his. Desire shimmered between them, vivid, undiminished, more intense than ever. It urged her to burn the wretched letter and abandon her scheme to marry Savoy. To throw her life away for a few moments of bliss in the arms of a footman.

Blythe could only imagine the reaction of her parents to *that*. They might never forgive her. Even worse, they would be devastated and hurt by her wild imprudence. Not just in their hearts but also in regard to their standing in society.

She could never bring such shame down on them.

Willing steadiness into her hand, she picked up the unlit taper, the one she'd earlier blown out. She touched the wick to the flame of his candle. "Then we shall compromise and accept that the guilt is mutual."

"It most certainly is not—"

"I'll hear no more about it. That is an order."

He glowered, opening his mouth as if to argue the point.

Before he could gainsay her, Blythe thrust the note at him. "Seal this now and see that it's delivered to Lady Davina on the morrow. Good night, James."

Chapter 16

"Your Grace, you simply must sit with my daughter. She's an avid card player and she would be quite desolate to be denied your company. Isn't that so, my dear?"

Aware of her mother's scrutiny, Blythe made a deep curtsy before the Duke of Savoy. "I confess I've been looking forward to this evening, Your Grace. It would be an honor indeed to share your table."

It wasn't difficult for Blythe to sound enthused or to give him a warm smile. After all, she was on a mission to further her acquaintance with the duke. For her mother's card party, she had taken special care with her appearance, choosing a pale bronze gown that enhanced her eyes and enduring a long session of having her hair tied up in rags in order to create the curls that came naturally to her sisters.

Oblivious to her preparations, the duke gave her only a distracted nod. "That sounds agreeable enough," he said, peering ahead into the Cromptons' drawing room. "I'm always ready for a good rubber of whist."

His daughter had lagged behind him to speak to one of the other guests. But now the elegant blonde glided forward to block their path. "Papa, pray don't forget that you promised to be my partner. And Lady Anne has requested to join us, so we will need a *gentleman* to complete our foursome."

A brunette with slightly buck teeth stood at Lady Davina's side, smiling coyly at the duke. Lady Anne, Blythe recalled, had been one of the clique who had eyed her with derision at the ball here over a fortnight ago. That was the same night Lady Davina had insulted Blythe.

The same night Blythe had met James.

The thought of him stirred a delicious warmth in her, as did the memory of that mad, impetuous kiss of two nights previous. She couldn't resist scanning the crowd of guests and looking for his tall figure. Several footmen were distributing glasses of champagne, but James was nowhere to be seen.

Thank goodness for small favors. She didn't need any distractions tonight. She'd already lost track of the conversation.

"I'm sure Lady Anne won't mind sharing another table," Mrs. Crompton was saying. "In fact, Lord Ainsley asked after her specifically."

"Did he?" Lady Anne asked, then giggled behind her fan. "He's very handsome. Oh! But . . . but *you*, Your Grace, you put all the other gentlemen to shame!"

Only Blythe noticed that in the middle of that discourse, Lady Davina had given her friend a sly pinch on the arm. It was clear that the duke's daughter had made plans with her friend ahead of time in order to deny Blythe the duke's company.

She'd had quite enough of Davina's trickery.

"Look over there, Lady Anne," Blythe said with a nod toward the grand staircase. "I do believe I see Lord Ainsley beckoning to you right now."

"Truly? Where?"

While the girl peered myopically into the throng,

Blythe slipped past her to take hold of the duke's arm. "I'm pleased we are to share a table. Do you enjoy making wagers, Your Grace?"

An avid gleam entered his pale blue eyes. "Absolutely!"

"Then I'll lay you a gold guinea that you cannot win three straight games against my partner and me."

"Wager accepted." He waved to a young man with golden-brown curls who was passing in the crowd. "Ho, there, Kitchener, you'll make our fourth. Come along, Davy, we've settled the matter quite satisfactorily. You will be my partner and Kitchener will play with Miss Crompton."

Now *that* was a stroke of bad luck. Blythe had no wish to associate with Viscount Kitchener after the incident in which he'd nearly embarrassed her while under the influence of opium. But at least she could take satisfaction in the fact that Lady Davina looked peeved at her father for overriding her arrangement.

Mrs. Crompton gave Blythe a slight smile of approval, then looked at the duke. "Allow me to show you to your table, Your Grace."

Slim and dignified in dark blue silk, she led the way into the drawing room. The place had been beautifully arranged with tall green draperies, gilt furnishings, and branches of candles glowing everywhere. The chaises that usually scattered the cavernous chamber had been removed to make space for several dozen tables with four chairs at each.

Mindful of her prize, Blythe kept her hand tucked in the crook of Savoy's arm. His Grace made an impressive appearance in a maroon coat with gold buttons fitted tightly over his slightly stout form. People stepped back to allow them to pass, the ladies curtsying to the duke and the gentlemen affording him respectful bows. His chin raised in a proud manner, Savoy appeared to take for granted all the attention directed at him.

But Blythe didn't. She reveled in the envious looks and admiring glances. She smiled serenely at the ladies who whispered to each other behind their fans, no doubt making catty remarks about the upstart heiress. She would show them up by winning the greatest trophy of all, the hand of the Duke of Savoy in marriage. She would achieve the highest pinnacle of society and have a most beautiful life. . . .

James stood waiting at their table. Clad in footman's livery and powdered wig, he stared straight at their approaching party.

She faltered to a stop. Her heart took flight, fluttering against her ribs like the wings of a caged bird. More so than before, the hot memory of their passionate kiss permeated her body and weakened her legs.

Savoy cast an irritated frown at Blythe, and she snapped to her senses. The episode took no more than two blinks of an eye; then they proceeded to the place of honor at a table in the center of the drawing room.

His face impassive, James held the chair for Lady Davina. Luckily, she paid him no heed, not so much as glancing his way. She continued to carry on a gossipy conversation with Viscount Kitchener.

Blythe's alarm swiftly turned to relief and then to anger at James. Blast him for taking such a risk! If Lady Davina were to look at him, she might remember him later. Then how would he ever succeed at posing as Prince Nicolai?

As James rounded the table to approach Blythe, their gazes met for one brief moment. A glimmer of amusement in his eyes, he winked.

Winked.

Her insides performed a cartwheel. Flushed, she looked

around the table to be certain no one else had noticed. The rest of the party behaved as normal, talking and laughing, the duke settling into his chair and then picking up the deck of cards to shuffle them. With her mission accomplished, Mrs. Crompton hurried off to see to the other guests.

There was naught to fear, Blythe assured herself. It had been such a quick action that anyone else would have taken it for an involuntary twitch. She alone knew better. Hidden behind the blank-faced mask of a footman, James had a decidedly rakish way about him. And for some perverse reason, his boldness of manner held for her a forbidden allure.

As she sat down, he took hold of her chair to slide it in. Not once did his white-gloved hands brush against her. He behaved with the utmost decorum. The madness existed within herself, this longing to haul him into the nearest alcove and demand the pleasure of another fervent embrace.

Did he feel it, too?

I want to seduce you. And by God, I will do so if you give me half a chance.

A shiver permeated her depths. His blunt assertion had been intended to snap sense into her, but somehow it had had the opposite effect. In the two days since their kiss, she had done little but dream of him. What folly! Nothing could ever come of their association, and besides, the rogue likely made such romantic declarations to all the women in his life.

Blythe pursed her lips, remembering the time she'd seen him from her bedroom window as he'd stolen out of the house under cover of darkness. He must have been going to meet a female. Not, of course, that his private sins should have any bearing on Blythe. She had made a mistake in kissing him and it wouldn't happen again.

He walked away to offer assistance to some of the other ladies in the drawing room. The duke was dealing out the pasteboard cards, while Lady Davina and Lord Kitchener traded tittle-tattle about people Blythe didn't know.

To them, James was just another faceless servant like so many others. That boded well for the ruse, but perversely, she felt miffed that no one else had perceived his striking good looks. They were so caught up in their own insular world, they would never bother to find out that he had a dry sense of humor and a keen intelligence. They would never know that a mere accident of birth had relegated such a proficient man to a life of anonymous servitude.

The unfairness of it niggled at her.

Out of the corner of her eye, she could still see him. Now he was helping her sister, Lindsey, at a table across the crowded room.

Lindsey looked up and gave him a smiling nod of thanks. Or rather, she appeared to be studying him quite closely.

A jolt of unease struck Blythe. Good heavens, was her sister intending to use her detective skills to determine which footman would play the faux prince? After Blythe had expressly warned her to stay out of the matter?

"Are you intending to play?" Lady Davina drawled. "Or shall I summon Lady Anne to take your place?"

Blythe realized everyone was staring at her. She picked up her pile of cards and fanned them out while trying not to fret over her sister's interfering nature. "I'm sorry, what is the trump suit?"

"Diamonds," Kitchener said, slouching languidly in his chair as he took another gulp from his wineglass. "At least I believe so."

The duke looked positively gleeful at the inattention

of his opponents. "Quite. Now, do lay down your card, Miss Crompton. I find myself anxious to win that gold guinea."

Blythe forced herself to concentrate on the game. A trio of spades rested on the green baize tabletop, so she played her ace and took the trick. Other than that, her hand was lackluster, so she decided it was a good time to spice up the conversation.

"Has anyone heard when Crown Prince Nicolai of Ambrosia will arrive in London?"

Lady Davina fumbled her cards. A blush tinted her porcelain skin. The mask of hauteur slipped and she appeared a trifle flustered. "Prince Nicolai? Why, I cannot imagine."

Viscount Kitchener snickered as he tossed down a card. "You needn't be so coy, Davy. Go on, tell Miss Crompton what you received in the mail yesterday."

"Oh, all right, I suppose the news will come out soon enough." Recovering her aplomb, Davina looked down her nose at Blythe. "His Royal Highness has written me a note begging an introduction upon his arrival."

"Truly?" Blythe feigned an expression of surprise mixed with envy. "But he lives abroad. How did he know of you?

Davina's lips tilted in a smirk. "It seems that word of my marital eligibility has traveled across to the Continent."

"That's my lovely girl," Savoy said with a fond smile. "But be forewarned, royal or not, this Nicolai fellow will have to pass muster with your papa."

"Of course," Davina said smoothly. "However, I must point out that it is no small event for a lady to be courted by a crown prince. And rumor has it that Prince Nicolai is seeking a high-born bride to be his future queen."

At the girl's superior look, Blythe bit her lip to hold back a gleeful laugh. Everything was going according to plan. Davina had no inkling that the letter was a forgery written by a fictitious prince. Rather, she was vain enough to consider being singled out by Prince Nicolai as quite the feather in her cap.

Lord Kitchener held up his wineglass in a toast. "To your Royal Highness, Queen Davina of Ambrosia. I shall compose a poem on the grand occasion of your marriage."

"I vow you are quite mad, Kitchy," Davina scolded, though obviously pleased at the notion of becoming consort to a monarch. "There is no certainty that Prince Nicolai will make me an offer."

"How could he not when you are the fairest of the fair?" The viscount cast a soulful look at the ceiling as if to seek inspiration from its plastered medallions. With his mop of golden-brown curls and earnest expression, he resembled the caricature of a romantic poet. "There once lived a lady and a prince / Whose great love has never been seen since." He broke off with a frown. "What else rhymes with prince?"

"Wince, mince, rinse, quince," Blythe said. "Or perhaps even hints, mints, flints."

Kitchener took a gulp of wine, then continued to spew ever more wretched verses about the prince bearing gifts of quince while the lady hid a wince since she'd been hoping for mints.

While Davina was preoccupied with the viscount, Blythe took the opportunity to smile at the duke. "Do you like poetry, Your Grace?"

"Never did," he said. "'Tis all blather and nonsense."

"What do you like to read, then?" she asked, hoping to find an area of common interest. "Is there a particular topic in your library?"

"Books? Barely cracked one open since Eton. Sends

me off into a doze every time. Kitchener, cease your prattling and play your turn."

To Blythe's frustration, the duke's attention remained on the cards in his hands. He seemed to have little care for any other subject matter that she broached. As the foursome continued to play, she noticed that he and his daughter were exchanging cunning little finger motions, along with subtle facial expressions such as raising an eyebrow or tapping a chin.

In disbelief, Blythe watched them more closely. Was it possible they were *cheating*?

They must be, for they had a whole range of signals to one another. The shock of it stunned her. Nothing could be more dishonorable. Imbibing yet another glass of wine, Lord Kitchener fell too deeply in his cups to pay heed, and she herself could think of no way to stop them aside from creating a scene.

Mama would disown Blythe if she dared to humiliate the duke with an accusation of deceit.

She tried to reason away her aversion. What did it matter anyway? It was merely a casual game of cards. The wager she'd made with the duke would barely make a dent in her pin money. Nevertheless, his cheating disturbed her, for it revealed something of his character, something she didn't care to ponder.

It also sparked in her the irrepressible desire to win.

She paid closer attention to the cards, counting the suits that had been played and calculating the odds. The task was difficult, hampered as she was by a partner who was more interested in guzzling wine and spouting drunken verses than playing whist. However, luck favored her and toward the end of the rubber, she had nearly managed to stave off their win.

At least until she glanced across the chamber and saw

something that erased all other considerations from her mind.

Carrying a silver tray of empty glasses, James was walking out of the drawing room. At the same moment, Lindsey arose from her chair and glided after him.

Chapter 17

Blythe sat riveted to her seat. Heaven forbid, had her sister gone to question James? Was she intending to bully the information out of him about his role in the ruse? Would she interfere in a misguided effort to thwart Blythe's plan to marry the duke?

Fraught with worry, she played the next few hands badly.

Savoy slapped down his last card and chortled. "There's the win. You owe me one gold guinea, Miss Crompton."

Blythe managed a rueful smile. "So I do. Alas, I seem to have forgotten my purse. Will you excuse me while I fetch it?"

The duke made an expansive gesture. "Go on, go on. We'll play with a dummy hand in your absence."

"And you'd best bring some extra coins in the event you're unlucky again," Lady Davina said with a smirk.

Wishing she dared to make a clever allusion to cheaters, Blythe pushed back her chair and headed for the arched doorway. Courtesy demanded that she speak a few gracious words to some of the guests on her way. At last, she escaped into the grand corridor and abandoned her polite smile. Only a few servants scurried here and there, readying the formal dining chamber for the midnight supper.

James was nowhere to be seen.

Had Lindsey pulled him into a deserted room? Was she even now grilling him, forcing him to admit that he would play Prince Nicolai?

Picking up her skirts, Blythe walked faster. She made haste down the passageway, glancing into the rooms right and left. When at last she found him, a disaster nearly ensued.

He was emerging from a doorway with a silver tray of full champagne flutes balanced on his open palm. She came to an abrupt halt within an inch of bumping into him. "Oh!"

James reacted swiftly. He lifted the tray high to keep from spilling its load of crystal. "Devil take it, slow down."

A whiff of his spicy scent caused an immediate tension inside her. She stood close enough to feel the heat of his body, close enough to arch up on tiptoes and brush her lips over his mouth. . . .

How absurd! She would never again be so foolish.

Craning her neck, she looked past him into a small, lamp-lit antechamber filled with wine bottles and glassware arranged on tables. "Where's Lindsey?"

"Your sister? She was playing cards when last I saw her."

Relief poured through Blythe. "Praise heavens, I was mistaken." Seeing his quizzical look, she explained, "Lindsey left the drawing room directly after you. I thought . . . well, you see, a few days ago I had to tell my sisters about the plan to trick Lady Davina."

"Had to?"

"The Countess de Lieven came to ask questions of Portia . . . but never mind, it's a long story."

An ominous frown descended over his face. James glanced past Blythe down the deserted corridor. With a slight jerk of the head, he indicated that she was to follow him. "Come," he said. "I can spare a few minutes. Especially when it involves the exposure of something I believed was a sworn secret between us."

They went into the antechamber, where James set down the tray and then closed the door. He folded his arms and pinned Blythe with a hard stare. "I must ask you to remember that I could lose my position here because of this game you've ordered me to play."

His forbidding look daunted her. So did the reality of being alone with him again, with the soft glow of the lamp and his masculine presence filling the small room. But she wouldn't be intimidated.

"It isn't a game," she said. "I'm paying you well for your participation. And I certainly *didn't* reveal your identity to my sisters."

"Then what precisely did you tell them?"

"Only the essential facts." Gripping her fingers at her waist, she paced restlessly back and forth. "When I first spread the rumor about Prince Nicolai, I had to make up a plausible reason to explain how I knew about his impending visit to England. So I said that Portia had learned of it when she received a letter from her friend, Arun."

"The Maharajah of Mumbai, her childhood sweetheart."

Blythe nodded, remembering their conversation about India when James had brought her breakfast. "Yes. You see, Arun also happens to be a friend of Prince Nicolai. You've visited his palace on your travels."

"Amazing," he said dryly. "To think I've been to India and I didn't even know it."

She tapped her chin with her forefinger. "Remind me to describe Arun's palace to you in case Lady Davina questions you about it."

His expression inscrutable, James handed Blythe a

flute of champagne from the tray. "I must say, this hoax is becoming more and more complex by the day. Now, go on with the business about your sisters."

She sipped at the fizzy wine, remembering how he had also given her champagne on the night they'd met. James seemed to have an uncanny instinct for knowing when she needed liquid courage.

"I was at Almack's when I first told the story to one of the biggest gossips in society. I swore him to secrecy. But apparently when the Countess de Lieven heard the rumor, she wormed the information out of him about Arun and Portia."

"This countess sounds like a formidable woman."

Blythe took a larger swallow, letting the bubbles burst on her tongue for a moment before finding the pluck to speak. "She's one of the patronesses at Almack's, as well as the wife of the Russian ambassador. Besides which, she's a quick wit and well known for her political salons."

James cocked an eyebrow. "Ah. Then if her husband is a diplomat, she will be entertaining doubts about the existence of the sovereign nation of Ambrosia."

"I'm afraid so," Blythe said, ducking her chin to look up at him through her lashes. "She told my sister she'd never heard of such a country. Which is why when you play the prince, we must keep you out of sight as much as possible. It's imperative that you never encounter the countess."

Nervous of his reaction, she ran her fingertip over the rim of the flute. Would he be angry at her for embroiling him in such a tangled web? What if he refused to go through with it? What if he called her bluff and banked on her not tattling that she'd seen him leaving the house late at night?

"Leave the countess to me," James said. "There's nothing for you to fret about."

"Fret? She could unmask you by asking pointed questions."

"I'll dodge them. But if you're that worried, perhaps it's best to abandon the whole charade."

"No! The plan is working; I need only iron out a few wrinkles." Clutching the champagne glass, Blythe resumed pacing. James looked entirely too confident. And no wonder. He had spent his life in the servants' hall and couldn't fully fathom the ins and outs of society. It was up to her to protect him from danger. "When the prince arranges a meeting with Davina, it must be in a garden somewhere, away from people. Under no circumstances are you to enter any ballroom or party in full view of society."

"That might work for the first assignation. But Lady Davina is certain to suspect something is amiss if Prince Nicolai behaves as a total recluse. Besides, she seems a vain sort who'll be eager to show off her prize suitor."

Blythe found the prospect worrisome, too. "We'll solve that problem as it arises. The matter depends upon how swiftly I can convince the Duke of Savoy to make an offer to me."

Her words had an immediate effect on James. His amiable expression turned cool and his jaw tightened. The easy camaraderie between them vanished as he turned away to pick up a glass of his own.

"To your success." He stepped forward to clink his flute against hers. "That *is* the point of all this skullduggery, is it not? For you to land the biggest fish in the matrimonial sea."

An undercurrent of mockery to his voice belied his smile. He made Blythe feel defensive about her plan to secure her future—and that of her parents. Who was he to deride her choices?

"By the by," she said stiffly, "I'd like to know why you

were at my table a little while ago. That was an unnecessary risk. If Lady Davina had taken a close look at you, the ruse would have been over before it had even begun."

"Come now, no one notices the servants. I was merely performing my required duties." He took a swallow from his glass. "Drink up, Miss Crompton, it's time for you to return to your card game. Perhaps you could save us both a lot of trouble by making a wager with the duke in which he might win your hand in marriage."

"Don't be absurd."

"It's no more absurd than having me skulk around in the bushes for the sake of your ambitions."

Watching him finish off his champagne, Blythe was more disturbed by his actions than by his bold disdain for her aspirations. Surely he knew that any member of the staff who was caught imbibing spirits would be dismissed on the spot.

But James was no ordinary footman. He had the air of a privileged gentleman rather than a lowly servant. If not for the powdered wig and blue livery, he would fit in as a guest in any great house—although she didn't trust him not to make mistakes. Was he merely a good mimic? Or was it his upbringing as the companion of a gentleman that lent him such careless self-assurance?

One fact was certain: Blythe had the distinct impression of secrets behind those masculine features, hidden truths that he didn't allow her to see. And the notion of discovering them intrigued her far more than it ought.

Blythe tilted her head back and drained the rest of the bubbly wine, only to find James watching her intently. It had the immediate effect of making her heart trip over a beat. Caught in the throes of desire, she felt exposed and self-conscious. "Why are you staring at me?"

"How can I not? You have the most beautiful hazel eyes."

His husky compliment sent tingles over her skin. It transported her straight back to the moment when they'd fallen into each other's arms. She had a sudden awareness of how alone they were, of how much she craved an encore to that wild, splendid encounter. Was he, too, remembering the blazing glory of their kiss?

She set down her glass with a sharp click. "You oughtn't say things like that."

"Quite the contrary. I must learn to become the charming prince. Who else would you have me practice on but you?"

"Practice would be superfluous. Behaving as a rogue comes naturally to you."

He had the audacity to chuckle. To laugh when she'd meant it as an insult.

Irked beyond belief, Blythe stalked past him. But he moved faster, blocking her path and taking hold of the doorknob. She hoped for one eager instant that he intended to stop her from departing, that he would clasp her to his hard, male body and have his wicked way with her.

But he merely said, "You mustn't be seen leaving this room. Allow me to check the corridor." He opened the door and peered out. "The path is clear."

All of Blythe's senses sprang to vibrant life as the firm pressure of James's hand settled at the small of her back. His breath tickling the back of her neck, he leaned closer and added, "I'll wait here until you're gone."

As he stepped aside to allow her space to exit, she afforded him a cool nod and headed down the long corridor. Yet her mind dwelled upon the phantom weight of his fingers at the back of her waist.

That had not been a casual move. His touch had been deliberate. And it had borne the stamp of possessiveness.

⁂

Loitering in the doorway, James watched Blythe walk off in a high dudgeon. His gaze obsessively tracked the sway of her hips beneath the gauzy bronze fabric of her gown. He needed to return to the drawing room himself, to rejoin the other footmen and pass out his tray of drinks before his absence earned him a reprimand by Godwin.

But not quite yet. James needed a moment to cool down first. It wouldn't do for anyone to glance down at his tight-fitting trousers and notice his state of arousal. Of course, that had been his near-perpetual condition ever since he'd made the colossal blunder of kissing Blythe in the privacy of her father's office.

How dare you touch me. You've no right to do so.

She had been correct to denounce him on that night, but wrong to issue an immediate apology for that censure. Blythe had erroneously shouldered the blame because she perceived herself as ranking higher than him. Little did she realize that James alone bore the burden of responsibility for the way he was tricking her and her family.

Even now, unresolved guilt smoldered in his gut. The feeling had dogged him after her departure that night. It had distracted him as he'd searched Crompton's office and come up with nothing.

Not a single shred of proof to bolster his case against Blythe's parents.

He stared moodily after her. She had reached the large vestibule outside the drawing room. A tall, slim woman in a plum-colored gown stepped into sight from the direction of the grand staircase. Even from a distance, he recognized her as the middle Crompton sister.

Lindsey glanced down the passageway, seeming to stare straight at him.

James ducked back into the antechamber. Devil take it, he was annoyed with Blythe for telling her sisters about that damned deception. The last thing he needed was for one of them to guess that *he* was the footman who would pose as Prince Nicolai. That would only serve to call undue attention to himself.

And it could wreak havoc with his secret investigation.

Picking up a bottle, he poured two fresh glasses of champagne to replace the ones they'd drunk. Blythe had a knack for complicating his life. Her blend of naïve girl and sultry woman held an irresistible appeal. James derived entirely too much enjoyment from teasing her, from watching the fire of indignation flare in those big, expressive eyes.

She posed a danger to his plan of exposing her parents. He needed to keep her at arm's length. Sentiment would only stand in the way of exacting justice and claiming his inheritance.

So why had he succumbed to impulse and touched her? He'd succeeded only in marking his own mind with the memory of her lush curves and the enticing floral scent of her perfume.

It had been jealousy, he admitted to himself. Knowing that she was returning to the duke, James had wanted to remind her of how passionately she'd responded to him that night in her father's study. Let her remember *his* seduction while she batted her lashes at Savoy.

Perhaps you could save us both a lot of trouble by making a wager with the duke in which he might win your hand in marriage.

Thank God she hadn't guessed the true source of his

vitriol. James despised gambling. His father had been a dissolute who had squandered a fortune at cards and dice, and his death in a drunken duel had left sixteen-year-old James awash in debt. All that remained had been the run-down plantation in Barbados. Years of hard work had enabled James to turn the place into a thriving estate—at least until the tempest had swept it all away.

That was why he needed to stay focused on his goal of regaining his inheritance. Miss Blythe Crompton could never be anything to him but a distraction. For when the truth came out, and he exposed her parents as thieves, she would hate him with every bone in her gorgeous body.

⁂

"He's the one, isn't he," Lindsey whispered. It was a statement, rather than a question.

Alarmed, Blythe followed her sister's gaze down the corridor and feigned confusion. "Who?"

"That footman, the tall one with the chiseled features. I must commend you. As Prince Nicolai, he'll be more than handsome enough to turn Lady Davina's head."

"Shh." Blythe grabbed hold of her sister's arm and marched her into the darkened ballroom. Glancing anxiously out into the vestibule, she said, "For pity's sake, Linds, your voice might carry."

"Nonsense. I was speaking in an undertone and besides, everyone is talking so loudly they can't possibly overhear us."

The buzz of laughter and conversation drifted from the drawing room. Her sister had always been a champion eavesdropper and she would know how far sound carried. Nevertheless, Blythe didn't want to take any chances. No one must guess at her secret scheme.

It was bad enough that Portia and Lindsey had found out about it.

"Now is neither the time nor the place," Blythe murmured. "If you wish to speak of this matter, we'll do it on the morrow."

She started to walk out, but Lindsey's voice pulled her back. "He'll fit into my husband's clothing, you know. I'd venture to say they wear exactly the same size. Thane will be gone to Bow Street tomorrow morning. You should come over then and choose a few articles for the prince's disguise."

Blythe realized it was a peace offering after the row she'd had with her sisters over the duke. What a boon it would be to have the garments. She'd been mulling over the problem of how to procure the proper costume from a tailor's shop without drawing attention.

But she hesitated to accept. That would be tantamount to admitting that Lindsey had correctly identified James. How could Blythe break her promise to him?

"Thank you, but I'll handle the matter myself. Now, I must fetch a few coins and return to my foursome."

Her sister caught Blythe's hand and gave it a soothing rub. "I'm only trying to help. Your secret is safe with me, I promise you."

"Is it?" Blythe turned squarely to face Lindsey, studying her through the shadows. "To be frank, I'm afraid you're going to try to talk him out of participating in the ruse. After all, you don't approve of me marrying the duke."

Lindsey gave her a quick hug. "It's just that I don't believe you've put enough thought into what the future will be like as Savoy's wife. Right now, you're dazzled by his title. But there's so much more to choosing a husband. I wouldn't want my sweet sister to miss out on the greatest joy in marriage . . . true love."

The soft smile on Lindsey's face revealed that her thoughts dwelled on her husband, Thane. Blythe had been surprised when the two of them had become betrothed the previous year. Lindsey had always been so strong and opinionated, so scornful of Blythe's romantic nature.

Now, the tables had been turned and Blythe had become the pragmatic one. Leaving her childish dreams behind had been part of growing up. Her father wanted this marriage for her, and she was determined to make him happy. An alliance with the Duke of Savoy would lend great honor to her parents.

Nevertheless, a wistful envy settled over her. If only she could have the closeness she saw in both her sisters' marriages. She *did* want the excitement of passion and the experience of being wife to the one man who meant more to her than anyone else in the world. A man who could warm her heart with a brash smile and a witty remark. . . .

The image of James appeared in her mind, but she thrust it away. Although she desired him, he could have no part of her future. Such a union was utterly impossible. It would mean giving up her standing in society and inflicting terrible pain on her parents as well.

Besides, James had never indicated he wanted anything other than a tryst. He might have absolutely no interest in burdening himself with a wife, especially since Blythe would be cut off without a penny if ever she was foolish enough to dally with a servant.

Realizing that her sister stood gazing at her with some concern, Blythe pulled her mind back to the conversation. "If you don't approve of the duke, then why would you offer to help me?"

Lindsey pursed her lips. "If marrying Savoy is truly your dream, I'll support you, of course. And so will Portia. However . . ."

"Yes?"

"However, I do hope that as you come to know the duke a little better, you'll see how very unsuited the two of you are. And then you'll change your mind."

Blythe had no intention of altering course. There was no turning back now. She must forge ahead with her plan to have Prince Nicolai lure Lady Davina away from the duke's side. And Blythe suddenly thought of something that would make the charade so much easier.

She slipped her arm through her sister's and they began to stroll out of the ballroom and back into the candlelit vestibule. "Will you do something for me, then?"

"What is it?"

"First, promise me you'll refuse if it's too much trouble. I realize it's a lot to ask since you have a newborn infant."

"I do employ nursemaids, you know. I'll help so long as your request doesn't require me to be away from Ella for more than a few hours."

"Oh, it won't! Will you host a small party at your house in a few days' time and invite Savoy and his daughter?"

Lindsey glanced around the deserted vestibule, then said in a lowered tone, "Do you mean for this to be the first meeting between Lady Davina and your counterfeit prince?"

Blythe nodded. "It would be ever so much simpler than arranging something elsewhere."

A gleam of interest entered Lindsey's blue eyes. "Well! That would certainly prove a novel evening. I'd be delighted to participate!"

Blythe wasn't sure she liked that zealous look. Lindsey had a knack for subterfuge and she was sure to insist upon meeting James. Blythe would have to be very, very careful.

By the heavens, if her sisters were concerned about her setting her cap for the Duke of Savoy, they would be even more horrified to learn of her illicit attraction to a footman.

Chapter 18

Within a few days, the scheme had been arranged and invitations to the party sent out.

James had found out about the revised plan when Blythe instructed him to write another letter to Lady Davina, this one announcing the prince's imminent arrival in London and begging a rendezvous with her in the garden at Pallister House on the night of the party. Prince Nicolai asserted that he wished to have the long-awaited meeting with the beautiful lady in a private place away from any crush of onlookers.

What blather, James thought as he strode through the teeming streets of Covent Garden. To think anyone would be brainless enough to believe such a trumped-up scheme. He only wondered how Blythe had managed to talk her sisters into assisting with it.

The mid-morning sun shone down on the soot-stained buildings, the dim alleyways, and the open stalls of the market where tradesmen hawked their wares. Having delivered the letter to the duke's townhouse on Albemarle Street a few minutes prior, James had left Mayfair on an additional errand of his own making. He didn't have much time since Godwin always kept a sharp eye on the footmen under his charge.

But James had been waiting for an opportunity like this. He was impatient to see if Percy Thornton had returned from Lancashire. More than a week had passed since their last meeting, which was ample time for the retired estate agent to have completed the journey.

"Fer yer lady," wheedled a flower seller, thrusting out a grimy hand holding a bunch of violets.

For one mad moment, James pictured himself presenting the flowers to Blythe, watching her face light up with pleasure, enjoying the kiss of gratitude she bestowed upon him. . . .

Then he shook his head at the woman and strode onward toward the cramped streets near the Strand. How idiotic. He wasn't courting Blythe. And why would he think she'd want a cheap posy from him, anyway, when extravagant bouquets from her suitors arrived like clockwork every morning?

These untimely fantasies had to cease. With each passing day, she seemed to have a stronger hold on him, mind and body.

The worst of it was, he genuinely liked her. She was warm and friendly, with expressive features that revealed her feelings. After that hot kiss they'd shared, he certainly wouldn't call her snobbish, either. Nor could he condemn her as a social climber. Although Blythe was pursuing a title, that was only to be expected of a girl in her position. She'd been raised to believe that making the best possible marriage was her sole purpose in life.

Nevertheless, he disliked seeing her wed a stuffy, middle-aged widower like Savoy. She ought to choose a husband closer to herself in age. A man who had the virility to arouse and satisfy her passions.

James realized he was clenching his jaw. He forced himself to relax. It served no purpose for him to dwell on his desire to bed her. Blythe might be naïve enough to flirt with a footman, but that was the extent of it. She was off limits to him. Even though he himself was a gentleman, she'd never forgive him once he exposed the crime of her parents.

For that reason, the sooner he left Crompton House for good, the better. He had searched the place top to bottom, and the only item of interest he'd found was that cryptic letter from Mrs. Hannah Bleasdale.

Perhaps today he would find out what it meant.

Striding down a narrow lane, he located the brick row house where Thornton lived. The place looked even more forlorn in the daylight than it had in the middle of the night. Up and down the street, laundry strung from the upper floors flapped in the dank breeze from the river. A slattern leaned out her window and called out an invitation to him.

James ignored her and rapped on the wooden panel. The door opened at once. Roland peered out cautiously; then his teeth flashed in a huge smile. The dark-skinned man stepped back to let James enter the tiny foyer with its peeling wallpaper and the brass birdcage sitting in front of the single window.

"Mister James! What a surprise dis be!"

"Hello, Roland." James clapped the valet on the shoulder. "You're looking well. I trust you've been taking excellent care of the house here."

"Nothin' else to do, suh." Roland looked him up and down. "Now, dat be a sight to see, you in dat fancy wig. Better not open dis cage, or Amora be makin' a nest in dere."

The yellow finch in the cage chirped as if in agreement.

"I'm looking forward to the day when I can toss this thing into a rubbish bin." James pulled off the hateful wig and hung it from a straight-backed chair. Combing his fingers through his hair, he asked, "Has Thornton returned from Lancashire?"

"'Deed so, after midnight. I be takin' his tea up to him right now." Roland picked up the tray from a nearby piecrust table. "I'll tell him you come here."

"Pray don't trouble yourself," called a voice from upstairs. "I'm on my way down."

The elderly man appeared on the landing. Garbed in a brown coat and breeches, his fringe of gray hair still mussed from sleep, Thornton gripped the banister and hobbled down the staircase.

Upon reaching the foyer, he made a creaky bow to James. "Pardon me, sir, I'm still a bit stiff from the long ride in the mail coach. But I must say, you're a sight for sore eyes. I was just now wondering how I'd send word to you."

"Then I'm glad to have called," James said. "However, there isn't much time for me to spare. Dare I hope you met with some success on your journey?"

"I'm happy to report so, yes," Thornton said, rubbing his age-spotted hands. "Do follow me and I'll show you."

The retired estate agent beckoned James into a cramped parlor off the passageway. Bookshelves lined the walls and a pair of threadbare wing chairs sat in front of the cold hearth. Roland brought in the tea tray and vanished, presumably to fetch another cup.

Thornton shuffled over to a corner, where a long, round leather map case stood propped against a pile of books. He bent down, untied the strings, and began to unroll it.

Over his shoulder, he said, "I spent a full morning looking in every room of the manor house, but found nothing. I'm afraid the place is in a state of neglect. The housekeeper is a dull-witted sort who would have been shown the door in my day. But at least she left me alone to conduct my search."

Seeing the man struggling with the cumbersome bundle, James made haste to assist him. "Is this what I think it is?"

"Indeed, sir. You were correct to advise me to look up in the attic. The place was chock full of furniture and trunks and such. It took some doing, but I finally located this hidden behind some old boxes."

The leather bindings fell away to reveal a large canvas.

"I removed the painting from the frame so it would be easier to transport," Thornton added. "I do hope that was agreeable."

"Perfectly so."

Hardly daring to hope, James carried the painting to the window and angled it to the watery sunlight. He was gazing at the portrait of a solemn young man and a smiling woman garbed in the fashion of a quarter of a century earlier. She sat on a chair, a small spaniel curled up in her lap, while her husband stood behind her with his hand on her shoulder.

James knew at once they were his cousin, George and George's wife, Edith. This must have been painted around the time of their marriage.

He felt whisked back to his childhood. Memories washed over him, much clearer now than ever before. He'd been only a boy of ten at the time, but how well he recognized George's thick mop of brown hair, the grave features and thin lips.

This was not the face of the man who employed him. And there was another difference. His cousin's lanky height hadn't been just the vague impression of a boy to whom all adults were tall. His true cousin topped by several inches the charlatan who had stolen his name.

With mingled fury and exhilaration, James scrutinized Edith as well. Her reddish curls had a golden cast that was subtly different from the present Edith's auburn hair. The features were not quite the same, either. This Edith appeared to have brown eyes and her face was somewhat narrower.

Besides the long-eared spaniel in her lap, several more dogs tumbled and played at her feet. She had adored them, he recalled, yet the present-day Edith kept no pets.

Now he knew why. Even taking into account the aging of nearly twenty-five years, the couple in this painting couldn't possibly be the same George and Edith who now resided in Crompton House.

"What do you think, sir?" Thornton asked, hovering close. "How do the Cromptons compare to them?"

"Both of my employers are imposters. This painting proves it beyond a shadow of a doubt." The full force of rage struck James like a punch to his abdomen. His gaze snapped to Thornton's. "My God! They very nearly got away with the crime. Had you not written to me, I would never have known my inheritance had been stolen."

"It was your idea to look for the portrait," Thornton said modestly. "I merely noticed there were anomalies when I went to see Mr. Crompton—or whoever he is—about my pension two years ago."

"How did they do it?" James asked, as much to himself as to Thornton. "Why the devil did no one ever challenge them? Surely *someone* in India saw the differences in their appearance!"

"I wish I knew, sir. I wish I knew."

His mind percolating with unanswered questions, James carefully rerolled the painting and propped it against the bookcase. As he did so, Roland came in with another cup and poured their tea, then left the parlor.

Thornton added a lump of sugar to his mug and stirred it with a pewter spoon.

James was too agitated to bother with refreshments. Running his fingers through his hair, he prowled back and forth in the small room. "The key question is, what happened to my cousin and his wife? Did they die a natural death? Or were they murdered?"

"That remains to be seen," Thornton said, his mouth set in a grim line. "I must say it was a despicable act to steal their identities no matter what the cause."

James continued to think out loud. "How do you suppose they accomplished the switch? And when exactly did it occur?" In his mind, he saw the image of Blythe in her wide-eyed innocence. "One thing is certain. I cannot believe that any of the three daughters could have been aware of this wickedness. And that would suggest the exchange happened either before they were born or shortly thereafter."

"I must agree. Especially in light of the old letter you found."

James swung toward him. "Then you received my note. Were you able to locate Mrs. Bleasdale?"

"Indeed, it was no trouble at all. I remembered the woman from my tenure as estate agent to the Cromptons. She was wife to one of the tenant farmers. Now she's an old pensioner living in a cottage near the village."

"Thank God she's still alive. Do you find out the identity of Mercy?"

"She was Mrs. Bleasdale's only child." Blowing on his tea, Thornton frowned. "I recall seeing Mercy a few times, for she worked above stairs at the manor house. When the Cromptons left all those years ago, Mercy sailed off with them as Edith's personal maidservant. Unfortunately, some two years later, Mrs. Bleasdale received word that her daughter had died in a cholera epidemic."

"Edith sent her a letter of condolence along with a bequest."

"Yes, a very generous one. Mrs. Bleasdale is quite frail now, but grateful to be living out her days in comfort."

Determined to unravel the puzzle, James continued to pace. "Edith kept the note of thanks from Mrs. Bleasdale all these years. It was stuck in her prayer book. Why would she do so? What would induce a lady to save a letter from a farmer's wife?"

"I have a theory," Thornton said, his voice raspy. "You see, the two-day journey back to London gave me ample time in which to ponder the matter. And also to examine my old memories."

He stopped to take a drink of tea, and the truth struck James before the old man could continue. It seemed incredible . . . yet it would explain so much.

"You believe that Mrs. Bleasdale's daughter, Mercy, isn't dead at all," James said slowly. "She is very much alive. And she's now calling herself Edith Crompton."

⁂

"Mama, what on earth are you doing?"

Having just entered the bedchamber, Blythe blinked to see her mother, elegantly dressed in a blue-and-ivory striped gown while sprawled inelegantly on the carpet. She was peering under the four-poster bed, her arm stretched out beneath as if to pat the floor.

"Did you drop something?" Blythe asked.

The blue feathers on her stylish hat bobbed as Edith Crompton turned her head to glance over her shoulder at Blythe. "I've lost a paper, that's all."

Blythe crouched down to look from the other side.

Although sunlight brightened the room, she could see only shadows under the bed. "What sort of paper?"

"A letter."

Her mother's voice sounded terse, worried, and not at all concerned about their mid-morning appointment at the dressmaker's. Mama was always punctual, so when she hadn't come downstairs, Blythe had gone in search of her.

Blythe had been too anxious to sit and twiddle her thumbs, anyway. She needed a distraction from her own agitated thoughts. Only a short while ago, James had left to deliver the forged note from Prince Nicolai to Lady Davina.

He had been cool and distant ever since their encounter at the card party, but she wouldn't let his disapproval of the ruse bother her. The scheme was in play now. The soiree had been scheduled for a few nights hence, the invitations sent out the previous day.

It was too late to turn back.

Blythe attributed her attack of nerves to impatience. If only she could move the clock ahead and have the party happen right now, this very minute, then perhaps the knot inside her stomach would unravel.

She straightened up and smoothed the wrinkles out of her lilac muslin gown. "I can help you look, Mama. When did you last see this letter?"

"It was tucked into my prayer book in the bedside table."

Blythe stepped around her mother and peered into the opened drawer. Picking up the black-bound book, she riffled through the pages. "And you think it dropped out onto the floor?"

"Yes."

"Who is it from?"

"Just . . . someone I once knew. No one of consequence."

Blythe found it difficult to believe that her mother would go to so much trouble to find something insignificant.

Intending to see if the letter might be tucked in a back corner of the drawer, she bent down to look. Her gaze widened on a metallic gleam. She picked up a tiny muff pistol that fit into the palm of her hand. This must be the one Portia had used to shoot Colin in the arm two years ago. Blythe had overheard her sisters whispering about the incident. Lindsey had borrowed the weapon without their mother's permission, and their parents had never known about the episode.

Now, the very presence of the weapon puzzled Blythe. It seemed out of character for her modish, fashionable mother to own a gun.

"Why do you keep this pistol?" she asked.

Mama flashed a glare up at Blythe and then struggled to her feet, hampered somewhat by the slim-fitting gown. "Put that away at once! And do stop poking through my private things."

Startled, Blythe replaced the gun in the drawer. Her mother was often firm, but seldom snappish. "I'm sorry, I didn't mean to pry. I was only trying to help."

Mrs. Crompton stepped past her to peer behind the bedside table. "Never mind," she said in a distracted tone. "Run along downstairs. I'll join you in a few minutes."

Blythe deemed it wise not to ask any more questions. But as she left, she couldn't help noticing that her mother was frowning down into the drawer as if her very life depended upon it.

⁂

"You are correct, sir," Percy Thornton affirmed. "To my best estimation, Mercy Bleasdale is now posing as Mrs. Edith Crompton. Once I worked that out, the resemblance became clear to me. I'm only sorry I didn't put two and two together sooner."

James strode across the tiny parlor to lay a hand on the older man's bony shoulder. "Your work has been excellent. I couldn't have managed without you."

"The case is far from resolved, sir. For one, I've no notion whatsoever as to who is pretending to be Mr. George Crompton."

Hands on his hips, James resumed pacing. "Perhaps Mrs. Bleasdale knows him. We must bring her to London so she can identify her daughter and give testimony at the trial."

That was the moment James desired and dreaded in equal measure. He wanted to find out the whole truth of what had happened to his cousin. He craved to see justice done on George's behalf. But in the doing, he would also cause unspeakable pain to Blythe and her sisters. Their lives would never be the same. . . .

"I'm afraid that's impossible," Thornton said. "She's an old woman and far too frail. Two long days in a coach surely would be the death of her."

"Are you certain of that? Perhaps the journey could be taken in small increments."

Thornton pursed his lips doubtfully. "It would be a tremendous risk to her health. It wouldn't do for your only witness to fall ill and die. Is there no way to lure the Cromptons to Lancashire? Then the confrontation could take place there."

"In any other case, I would agree. But for obvious reasons, Lancashire is the last place on earth those two charlatans wish to go."

James had seen that for himself at the family dinner when Blythe had expressed a desire to visit the manor. Edith Crompton had looked aghast at the notion and had cited numerous reasons why such a journey was out of the question. George had concurred in no uncertain terms.

Thornton picked up the teapot and refilled his cup. "I quite understand your point, sir. There is the social season, as well, to consider. Since they are marrying off the youngest girl, the family will wish to stay in London."

Blythe wanted to affiance herself to the duke. If the truth came out before the wedding, Savoy would toss her aside like a piece of common rubbish. If it came out afterward, he would have grounds for divorce. Either way, her life would lie in ruins.

Yet James had little choice. It was unthinkable to allow the crimes against his cousin to go unpunished.

Frustration filled him as he prowled the tiny parlor. "If Mrs. Bleasdale cannot appear in a London court, I will need a sworn affidavit from her declaring that Mercy is masquerading as Edith Crompton. Yet it's impossible for the woman to give one without coming face to face with Edith. The situation is quite the Gordian Knot."

Thornton sipped his tea and then ventured, "What if Mrs. Crompton were to receive word somehow that her mother lay dying?"

James considered that a moment. Edith had kept the last letter from Mrs. Bleasdale all these years. Did that mean she harbored a fondness for her mother that could be exploited?

Thinking of the wealthy life of privilege she led now, he shook his head. "Mercy Bleasdale no longer exists. She cut off all contact when she sent a letter announcing her own death. She'd never risk losing her status, her place in society. Not even for her own mother."

"Then what will you do, sir?"

"I don't know yet. I'll have to give the matter some thought."

As James bade farewell and left the house, the seed of

an idea took root in him. He rejected it at first as a despicable act unbefitting a gentleman. But the more he considered the notion, the more he became convinced it was the only way to lure Edith and George to Lancashire.

James would have to use their youngest daughter as bait.

Chapter 19

"This scheme is the height of lunacy," Portia fretted with a shake of her head. "There are too many things that can go wrong. It will never work."

On the evening of the party, the sisters tarried in one of the spare bedchambers at Pallister House. All three of them were dressed in their finest gowns, Portia in primrose silk, Lindsey in celestial blue crepe, and Blythe in filmy white muslin with delicate gold trim.

"It most certainly *will* work," Lindsey said. "I've seen to the details myself. Besides, I quite relish the notion of tricking Lady Davina. She was very rude to Blythe and deserves a comeuppance."

"Not at the expense of a scandal," Portia retorted. "If Blythe wishes to speak to the duke alone, I shall call Lady Davina out of the room on a pretext. Then there will be no need for such an elaborate hoax."

"Would that it were so simple," Blythe said, annoyed that they were discussing her as if she wasn't even present. "Ever since Davina realized that I've an interest in her father, she has stuck to his side like a burr. She will be drawn away by nothing less than the meeting with Prince Nicolai, and that's that."

"If indeed a footman can play a credible prince," Portia said. "I shall have to see him to believe it."

They all turned in unison to stare at the closed door to the dressing room, where James was changing into his costume. Blythe had accepted Lindsey's offer of the borrowed garments, after all. In the end, it had seemed too pigheaded not to do so.

Now, her errant imagination supplied a picture of him in there, stripped down to his bare skin. James was built so much more powerfully than the half-clothed men she'd seen on the streets of India, and Blythe fancied herself helping him disrobe, smoothing her palms over the brawny contours of his naked body.

Feeling the rise of a blush, she strolled to a table on the pretext of picking up the porcelain figurine of a shepherdess. It would be a disaster if her sisters were to guess the direction of her wayward thoughts. They'd be aghast to know that Blythe felt such a forbidden attraction to a footman. To save her reputation, they might feel obliged to report the matter to their mother, and James would be summarily dismissed.

Blythe set down the little statue. That wouldn't happen. She had no intention of acting on her desire for him ever again.

Once had been enough.

She had spent too long preparing for this masquerade to let matters go amiss. This morning, she had informed the head footman that James was needed to assist in serving the guests at her sister's soiree. Godwin had attempted to offer his own services instead, but she'd refused him with a cool smile. Lady Mansfield, she'd claimed, required a footman precisely the height and size of James. No one else would do.

She also had made up an excuse to convince her parents that she needed to arrive ahead of them in order to help Lindsey with last-minute preparations for the party. Accordingly, the coachman had dropped her off early, along with James, who had gone in through the back entrance and then met her up here in this bedchamber.

Her sisters had joined her a few minutes later.

Now, she prayed that James played his part well. Ever since writing the second note to Lady Davina a few days ago, he had acted distant and aloof. Blythe had the distinct impression that he was angry with her. And little wonder. She had brought her sisters in on the ruse when he had expressly asked her to keep it a secret.

Had she been wrong to do so? No, the circumstances would be much easier to control here at Lindsey's house. There would be less chance of something going awry.

"It's taking him too long," Portia said, gliding to the window and glancing out at the street below. "The guests will be arriving soon."

"When precisely did he go in there?" Lindsey asked Blythe.

Jittery with nerves, Blythe glanced at the ormolu clock on the mantel. "Perhaps fifteen minutes ago. And mind, he does not have the benefit of a valet's assistance."

"Wonderful," Portia muttered. "He likely will have his shirt on backward and his cravat in a tangle."

"If so, he will have ample time to fix it," Lindsey said, plopping down on the blue coverlet of the bed and looking far more nonchalant than Blythe felt. "His rendezvous with Lady Davina isn't scheduled until over an hour from now."

The plan was that Prince Nicolai would not attend the party itself. His latest note to Davina had stated that he wanted their first meeting to be in a private place, away from the throngs of people who would be sure to swarm around visiting royalty.

"She may not have swallowed the bait," Portia said.

"Of course she did, she accepted the invitation here," Lindsey said. "A snooty girl like her won't be able to resist catching a prince."

"Meanwhile, our sister will attempt to charm the Duke of Savoy," Portia said. "Personally, I hope this ruse will have the opposite effect. I hope she will come to her senses and realize he is *not* the right husband for her."

Portia raised an eyebrow at Blythe, and Blythe stared defiantly back. She was well aware that her sisters were cooperating only because they believed that closer contact with the duke would cause her to change her mind.

They would be sorely disappointed.

But now that the scheme was finally under way, she felt the prod of misgivings. What if she'd misjudged James and he failed to pull off the scam? She couldn't bear it if her sisters found fault with him.

"The both of you should go now," she told them. "You'll want to be in the entrance hall when the guests arrive."

Lindsey languidly arose from the bed. "We've a few minutes yet. Thane and Colin can greet anyone who is rude enough to arrive early."

"Our husbands are probably speculating right now about why the three of us went off together," Portia said darkly. "I don't like keeping secrets from Colin."

"We'll tell them after the fact," Lindsey said. "Anyway, it's a harmless masquerade."

"I certainly hope so," Portia said. "Because if something goes wrong—"

The quiet rattle of the knob sounded like a gunshot. As one, they pivoted to watch as the door to the dressing room opened and James stepped out.

Or rather, Prince Nicolai.

He wore a superbly tailored coat in coffee-brown superfine over a gold striped waistcoat and buff breeches.

His cravat was perfectly tied and a ruby stickpin glinted in its folds. From somewhere, Lindsey had procured a crimson sash on which gleamed a variety of medals. A sword in a jeweled scabbard hung at his side.

He walked toward the women and gave a royal nod, regarding them with the perfect trace of hauteur. "Good evening, ladies. How enchanting to make your acquaintance."

His deep voice held the hint of a foreign accent. Blythe could only gape at him in astonishment. He was James—and yet he wasn't.

She lifted a gloved hand to her throat. Words escaped her. Even in her wildest imaginings, she had not thought he could look so magnificent.

"Oh my," Portia said faintly.

"A pity he isn't a real prince," Lindsey murmured to Blythe. "Lady Davina would be out of your way for good."

Blythe agreed, but only in part. Little could they guess that it wasn't for the sake of the duke's daughter that she wished James really was a prince. It was for herself.

Foolish, foolish fancy!

With effort, she collected her scattered thoughts. "There, you've seen that the disguise will work," she told her sisters. "Now do hurry downstairs. I must give Prince Nicolai some last-minute instructions."

"In a bedchamber without a chaperone?" Portia said, looking from Blythe to James and back again. "I hardly think that's appropriate."

Shooing her sisters toward the door, Blythe affected a laugh. "Don't be ridiculous. There's no impropriety. After all, he's merely a footman."

As Portia and Lindsey went into the corridor, Portia pulled the door almost shut, leaving a gap of a few inches. Blythe listened at the crack until the sound of their footsteps died out. Then she quietly closed the door until the latch clicked. The last thing she wanted was for any servants to come along and overhear this conversation.

When she turned back around, Prince Nicolai stood directly before her.

Blythe uttered a startled gasp. "You mustn't creep up on me like that."

"I most humbly beg your pardon, Miss Crompton. I did not mean to frighten you."

James spoke in the foreign accent of Prince Nicolai, and his deep, rich baritone sent shivers over her skin. One white-gloved hand resting on the hilt of his sword, he regarded her with cool arrogance. With the crimson sash across his chest, the medals gleaming in the candlelight, he looked every inch a royal.

Just gazing at him made her knees weak.

"You needn't pretend with me," she said. "We must go over again how you should behave with Lady Davina and what you should say to her."

"How delightful. I find myself most intrigued by the notion of being instructed by such a beautiful lady as yourself."

He continued to play the character of the prince. His dark eyes were intent on her, and Blythe found herself in danger of falling under his spell. But perhaps it was wise that he kept up the pretense. Practice would help ensure that he made no mistakes.

"Have it your way, then." She stepped around James and turned to face him. "When you greet Lady Davina in the garden, you must pay heed to her sensibilities. It is better to be somewhat aloof than to be overly charming."

"She will be enamored of me. Make no mistake about that."

James was confident, but the prince was downright conceited. It shook her to see how well he'd adapted to the role.

Blythe pursed her lips, unsure if she liked the idea of him whispering sweet nothings into Lady Davina's ear, giving her the full force of his magnetism. But wasn't that the point? To keep Lady Davina occupied and away from the duke?

"Pray remember that she will be engaging in risqué behavior by meeting a man to whom she has not been introduced, prince or not. For that reason, it may be that she will take one of her friends along to act as chaperone."

A frown darkened his face. He walked away, only to swing around to face her. "I requested that she come alone. These other fawning sycophants bore me."

In spite of herself, Blythe felt a tickle of humor. "Excellent, James. But you needn't be pompous, merely polite. And you really mustn't tease her as you do me."

He took a step closer, and his eyes held a gleam she recognized well. "You wound me, my lady. Do you not enjoy my teasing, then?"

She liked it entirely too much. Not that she would inflate his pride by saying so. "We are speaking not of me but of Lady Davina. Now, you surely have observed many of the rules of well-bred behavior. For instance, you must never sit so long as she is standing."

A half-smile crooked one corner of his mouth. "Do you truly think me so untutored? Allow me to put your mind to rest."

He held out his gloved hand and after a moment's hesitation, Blythe took it. She was keenly aware of the warm strength of James's fingers through the thin kidskin of their gloves. He led her to a chaise in the corner of the room and with an imperious gesture, bade her to sit.

Watching him warily, she sank down on the cushion. She started to draw back her hand, but his fingers retained hold of hers and brought her hand to his mouth. He kissed the back, his gaze roaming down to her breasts, then back up to her face. "My lady, you are indeed the most ravishing creature I have ever beheld."

Tingles scurried over Blythe's skin and penetrated deep within her core. Was James directing those words to her or merely practicing his role? For the life of her, Blythe didn't know.

I want to seduce you. And by God, I will do so if you give me half a chance.

The memory of that declaration made Blythe's heart race. She extricated her hand from his. "You've certainly proven yourself to be an accomplished flirt," she said coolly. "However, you cannot depend on extravagant compliments alone. I would suggest that instead you draw out Lady Davina by asking questions about her life and her interests. And for obvious reasons, it's best that you speak as little as possible of your own—or rather, the prince's—background."

James towered over her, his hand on the hilt of the sword, looking for all the world like Crown Prince Nicolai of Ambrosia. "So I am to remain a man of mystery? I find that strategy to be an insult."

"An insult? It's for your own protection."

"Yet you would deny me the chance to charm the lady. Only consider all the amusing little tales I can tell her about life at court. In particular, she will want to hear the legend behind the solid gold thrones used by the monarchs of Ambrosia. Since, as you know, she has an ambition to occupy one of them as my queen."

Blythe couldn't help giggling. "James, how wicked. Did you really make up a legend? All right, let me hear it."

A smile played at the corners of his mouth. He propped one polished boot on a footstool and casually leaned an elbow on his knee. "A very long time ago, a fair princess was captured by an evil ogre and whisked away to his mountain castle. There, he locked her in a gilded cage and commanded her to sing for his amusement every day."

"I trust she could carry a tune better than me. I was ever the despair of my governess."

"Oh, she did sing beautifully. Her voice was like the trill of a lark on the wind. The sound of it carried down into the valley, where it caught the attention of a lowly stable lad. The poor fellow was utterly enchanted, for never before in his hard life had he heard anything so pure and lovely."

When James paused, Blythe found herself caught up in the tale. Sitting on the edge of her seat, she prompted, "And?"

"And so he resolved to discover the source of that angelic song. Being a strapping young man, he set out to climb the mountain. He disregarded the warnings of the villagers about the ogre, for nothing mattered to him but rescuing the princess and claiming her for his wife."

"But she was royal. He can't have expected her to come live with him in a stable."

Ever so briefly, James touched his forefinger to her lips. "Shh. Just listen."

Blythe could not have spoken at that moment, anyway. The brush of his finger had felt too deliciously like a kiss.

"The young man had a difficult time on his journey up the mountain," James went on. "The ogre had cast many enchantments, you see, and our hero found himself wandering in freezing fogs, nearly tumbling off cliffs a number of times. Yet the musical sound of the princess's voice lured him ever upward until at last he reached the castle. There, he engaged in a mighty sword fight with the ogre."

James straightened up, drawing his own sword from its hilt and swishing it through the air. "The ogre attempted to use spell after spell, but his evil tricks proved no match for the power of true love. Once the monster lay dead, our hero freed the princess from her gilded cage and she flew into his arms for their first kiss. And what a moment that was, a kiss so perfect and passionate it would be immortalized by the bards for a thousand years to come."

He thrust the sword back into the scabbard.

The metallic clang startled Blythe out of a memory of *his* kiss. No doubt James had deliberately used a parallel to their own situation. She was the princess and he, the lowly servant.

Nevertheless, she felt compelled to hear how the story ended. "Surely her father, the king, would never have allowed his daughter to marry a stable boy."

"Quite the contrary. The king was so grateful to have her back, safe and sound, that he knighted our hero and gave his blessing to their marriage. They melted the gold from her gilded cage and used it to fashion two thrones. Upon the death of the old king, the princess and her stable lad ruled the kingdom of Ambrosia and lived a long, happy life together."

A wistful sigh escaped Blythe. What a pity it was only a fairy tale. Things didn't happen that way in the real world. She could never imagine her own father allowing her to wed a footman. Such a circumstance would devastate her dear Papa.

Why would she contemplate such an utter impossibility, anyway? It had no relation to the hoax she had planned for Lady Davina.

Blythe rose to her feet. "Well! That was an excellent performance, James. I don't believe you need any more advice from me. When this is all over, you might consider applying to be an actor at one of the theaters in Covent Garden."

Giving a cordial smile, Blythe started toward the bedchamber door. She had taken no more than two steps when he caught her by the shoulders and turned her around to face him. His fingers firm and warm against her bare skin, he gazed down at her with faint amusement.

"Am I acting . . . or not? That is the question."

His accent belonged to the prince, though the rakish glimmer in his dark eyes was pure James. With every breath, she drew in his faintly spicy scent. Her mad, romantic heart fluttered with the hope that he would kiss her again.

"You're playing a role, of course," Blythe said with as much steadiness as she could muster. "And if you will be so kind as to release me, I must go downstairs now and greet the guests."

"But there are things you haven't yet told me."

Standing so close to him, with his fingers lightly kneading her shoulders, she could scarcely form a rational thought. "What do you wish to know?"

"How long am I to keep Lady Davina distracted in the garden?"

"Oh . . . half an hour, perhaps. Or a little more if she wishes."

"Lady Davina is certain to try to coax me into the party."

"You must refuse her, of course. Tell her that you don't care for large gatherings."

"And if she becomes amorous? Would you advise that I kiss her?"

"No!" Blythe reacted before realizing he was teasing. Or at least she *thought* he was teasing. "Of course that isn't required of you. Nor would a lady ever expect it."

"A pity," James murmured in his beguiling accent. He bent his head closer to her. "Because I was rather hoping we might need to . . . practice."

His finger traced the outline of her mouth. The feathery touch set off a slow burn that descended to her depths and heated her all over. He stood so close that Blythe could see the individual lashes of his dark brown eyes. In defiance of good judgment, her lips parted and she placed her hands on his chest. Sweet heaven, she wanted to feel his arms around her again.

What harm could one kiss do?

"Perhaps," she whispered, "it might be wise . . . just in case . . ."

Their lips almost touched. Then abruptly James set her back and dropped his hands to his sides. "No, I believe you're right, Miss Crompton. Lady Davina is too well-bred to breach any rules on our first meeting. That will come later."

Nonplussed, Blythe stared at him. "Later?"

"Yes." He stepped to a gilt mirror on the wall and straightened his sash. "The Duke of Savoy cannot be expected to make you an offer at once. That means you'll need me to continue to distract his daughter. Although I must warn you"—he leaned closer to check the positioning of one of the medals—"it may prove difficult to keep Lady Davina from falling in love with me. By the very nature of this ruse, she is bound to see me as the husband of her dreams."

As he turned to face Blythe again, the embodiment of the perfect man, Prince Nicolai gave her an enigmatic smile.

No, *James*.

He was James, the footman. She mustn't forget that, not even for an instant.

And why had he not kissed her when he'd had the opportunity just now? Why had he drawn back? Was he merely being gallant?

A disquieting thought took root in her mind. Despite

Lady Davina's snobbery, she was a very beautiful woman. What would happen when James spent much time in her company? Would he find himself wanting to kiss *her* instead of Blythe?

⁂

He had her exactly where he wanted her.

As she went out into the corridor, James took one last look at Blythe's wary expression before he shut the door. She was off-balance, frustrated, and more than a little jealous.

Unfortunately, so was he.

At loose ends, he prowled the sumptuous bedchamber. Without Blythe's vibrant presence, the place now seemed forlorn and empty. It had been torture pulling back from that almost-kiss, torture to deny himself the pleasure when she had been ready and willing to fall into his arms.

But it was essential to his plan that she remain uncertain of him. That would serve to hone her desire and make her more amenable to persuasion. Besides, he wanted her to be thinking about *him* when she turned her feminine wiles on the Duke of Savoy.

Damn, she had to fail! Nothing could be more disgusting than to think of that cold, self-absorbed nobleman despoiling her innocence.

His jaw tight, James took a deep breath to calm himself and then stalked to the window. He parted the draperies and peered down at the arriving guests. Coaches lined the street, their headlamps glowing against the velvet darkness. It looked like something out of a fairy tale.

Tonight, he was the prince.

Not so much to the duke's daughter, but to Blythe herself. She didn't yet know it, but in a short while he intended to turn her little scheme upside down.

In order to expose George and Edith as frauds, James had devised a plan to lure them to Lancashire. It required him to coax Blythe into falling in love with him. As Prince Nicolai, he intended to blur the line between fantasy and reality.

The Lancashire estate lay near the road to Gretna Green, where couples escaped across the Scottish border to wed against the will of their parents. And when the time was right, James intended to convince Blythe to elope with him.

Chapter 20

The intimate party of about a hundred guests was held in the drawing room rather than the more cavernous ballroom. A quartet of musicians in the corner played a lively country tune. At one end of the long, candlelit chamber, the Aubusson rugs had been removed and dancers formed two lines.

Mingling with the crowd, Blythe kept an eye on the small group seated near the fireplace. The Duke of Savoy and Lady Davina had been laughing and chatting with the Marchioness of Wargrave for nearly half an hour.

Blythe had greeted the duke and his daughter upon their arrival. After that, she had ignored them, pretending not to see her mother's little frowns and other furtive signals. Mama wished for her to join them, of course. But Blythe needed to convince Lady Davina that it was safe for her to leave her father alone for a while. Otherwise, she might entertain second thoughts about the rendezvous with Prince Nicolai.

The tall casement clock against the wall showed less than ten minutes until the appointed hour. Was James keeping an eye on the time?

Blythe certainly hoped so. Perhaps at this very moment he was stealing down the back staircase to the garden.

Then he would wait for Lady Davina beneath the trellis of roses by the fountain. When the girl went out to meet him, he would be standing there, tall and princely, his gloved fingers resting on the hilt of his sword. . . .

"May I have the honor, Miss Crompton?"

Pulled back to the present, Blythe realized that a freckled young man stood before her. "Mr. Mainwaring! Forgive me, I must have been woolgathering."

"I only wished to know if you'd care to dance. Or . . . or perhaps we might simply take a turn around the room if you prefer."

His eager-to-please expression touched her heart. She spied her sisters dancing with their husbands at the far end of the chamber. In her present state of preoccupation, Blythe was afraid she'd miss the steps and make a fool of herself. Besides, a little conversation would allow her to keep an eye on her quarry.

"Do let's walk," she said, sliding her hand in the crook of Mr. Mainwaring's arm and giving him a polite smile. "I must thank you for the flowers you sent the other day. Daffodils are one of my favorites."

"You're most welcome. They reminded me of you."

"Of me?" she asked as they began their stroll around the perimeter of the drawing room. "I certainly wouldn't describe myself as long and yellow with a green stalk."

Mr. Mainwaring looked aghast. "Oh no, Miss Crompton! I didn't mean it quite so literally! It's just that you are always so pretty and cheerful. When you walk in a room, the place fairly glows."

His puppyish adoration made her feel sorry for teasing him. "How very nice of you to say so," she murmured, then changed the subject. "Now, do tell me, from what area of the country does your family hail?"

While he launched into a description of his father's

holdings in Shropshire, Blythe listened with only half an ear. Covertly, she glanced at the casement clock again. Only a minute or two remained before the scheduled rendezvous.

Why did Davina continue to converse with her father and Lady Wargrave? Had she not noticed the time? What if she'd scented a rat and changed her mind about meeting Prince Nicolai?

Blythe would lose the opportunity to catch the duke's attention. This party would be for naught. And James! Her steps faltered. James would be left to tarry out in the garden alone.

"Did I say something wrong?" Mr. Mainwaring asked worriedly. "Perhaps I offended your sensibilities in speaking of fox hunting. Some ladies don't care for the sport."

"Pray continue. I'm most interested in country pursuits."

As they resumed their promenade, her mind returned to James. In a little while, if it turned out that the ruse had been a failure, she could steal away from the drawing room and join him. *Yes*. Her heart beat faster at the prospect of seeing him again in his princely raiment. After all, it would be rude for her to leave him waiting out there all alone for hours. . . .

She realized that Lady Davina had arisen to her feet. The girl was saying something to her father, who remained seated on the chaise.

Fraught with tension, Blythe continued the pretense of listening to Mr. Mainwaring's chatter. But she kept her attention furtively fixed on Lady Davina.

In a gown of primrose pink with a dainty diamond tiara in her styled blond hair, the girl looked as slim and lovely as a princess. Blythe felt an instant antipathy that was fueled by jealousy. *She* wanted to be the one going out to meet James. What if he fell prey to Davina's blue-blooded beauty? Would he lose interest in Blythe and set his sights on the duke's daughter instead?

How ludicrous. James was a footman, not a real prince. In truth, she should rejoice if he managed to trick Lady Davina into falling in love with him. That would be the perfect revenge for all of her nasty tricks.

Davina beckoned to someone in the milling guests. A moment later, her friend, Lady Anne, scurried forward to take the coveted spot beside the duke. Davina then strolled out of the drawing room.

So she was going to meet Prince Nicolai without a chaperone. And apparently, she believed her father was safe in the care of Lady Anne.

Blythe pursed her lips. While Mr. Mainwaring launched into a detailed description of the hunting horses in his father's stable, she steered him toward the fireplace. When he paused for breath, she interjected, "I've just remembered something very important. Lady Anne mentioned that she was very much looking forward to dancing with you. I hope you will not disappoint her."

Astonishment painted his freckled features. "Lady Anne? But her father is a marquess. I cannot imagine why she would ever notice *me*."

"On the contrary, I believe she harbors a secret admiration for you."

It was merely a small fib, Blythe assured herself. For all she knew, the two of them might be well suited in truth, and she could be doing them a favor.

They had reached the group by the fireplace. Blythe curtsied first to the duke, who sat with one foot propped on a stool, and then to the Marchioness of Wargrave, before turning her gaze to Lady Anne.

"Pray pardon my interruption. Lady Anne, Mr. Mainwaring would be most obliged if you'd have a word with him."

The plain-faced girl looked wary; no doubt she'd been warned not to budge from the duke's side. "But Davy said . . ."

Blythe leaned close and whispered, "He's too shy to admit it, but he adores you. He'll be heartbroken if you refuse."

Lady Anne was vain enough to look pleased at the notion of the gentleman's unrequited love for her. She hopped up from the chaise and went off with Mr. Mainwaring, who still looked somewhat befuddled by the switch in partners.

As Blythe sat down beside the duke, old Lady Wargrave held up a gold lorgnette, which magnified her blue eyes with their crow's-feet wrinkles. "You're Edith's youngest. You look more like your mother than your sisters."

"So I've been told, my lady."

"You have her cleverness, too. Look at how you sent off that girl and took her place beside the most eligible peer of the season."

Blythe fought the rise of a blush. That last thing she needed was to be characterized as mercenary.

She affected a genteel laugh. "Rather, I've scarcely had a chance to speak to either of you. And I *did* promise my sister that I would help her out as hostess." Blythe turned a contrite smile on the duke, whose tailored blue coat and ruddy features lent him an air of aristocratic splendor. "I hope *you* don't think ill of me, Your Grace. I never meant to cut short your chat with Lady Anne."

He lifted his hand in a desultory, dismissing gesture. "Never mind, the girl natters too much about gowns and hairstyles."

"And would you prefer to speak of hounds and horses,

then?" she teased. "After listening to Mr. Mainwaring, I feel ready to compare your stable with that of his father."

In lieu of a reply, the duke turned his attention to Lady Wargrave. "We've traded a few horse stories this evening, haven't we?" he said. "I especially liked the one where my daughter beat your grandson in that race. Tally-ho and away we go!"

He slapped his hand on his knee, and they both laughed merrily. Having no notion of the joke, Blythe could only maintain a polite smile.

Lady Wargrave squinted again through the lorgnette. "You must forgive us, Miss Crompton, for we've been reminiscing about old neighbors in Hertfordshire. Davy had some very amusing stories to share with us."

Blythe couldn't imagine Lady Davina possessing any sense of humor at all. Or maybe she just reserved it for bluebloods.

A picture flashed into Blythe's mind of Lady Davina and James trading witticisms outside in the garden. He greatly enjoyed such banter. Perhaps they would get along exceptionally well. . . .

"She promised to tell us a jolly good one about the Huffingtons when she returns." The duke craned his neck to peer past the throngs of guests. "I can't imagine what's taking the girl so long. She left to have a word with an acquaintance, but I don't see her at all."

Because she'd gone to meet Prince Nicolai.

Blythe glanced anxiously at the doorway. Was Lady Davina at this very moment coming face to face with James in the moonlight? Would he kiss her hand and tell her she was the most ravishing woman in the world? Would he relate to her the enthralling legend of the gold thrones of Ambrosia?

Would she be so fascinated by Prince Nicolai that she would abandon all decorum and invite his kiss?

Realizing that she was clutching at the folds of her skirt, Blythe forced herself to relax. She must *not* think of James, nor should she wonder what was going on out in the garden. The entire point of the masquerade was for her to have this opportunity to attract the duke.

Unfortunately, His Grace was paying little heed to her. He and the marchioness were discussing the ramifications of a long-ago breach of manners perpetrated by someone Blythe didn't know. She was forced to sit quietly and look interested. To change the topic of conversation would have been insufferably rude.

In all of her preparations for this moment, she had fancied herself having the duke's full attention. She had worked out various scenarios in her mind and listed dozens of subjects that would spark a lively conversation. She'd planned to tease him about the guinea he'd won from her at the card party, to ask him which other games he enjoyed, and to inquire if he collected anything, since men so loved to talk about their own pursuits.

She had prepared for every contingency but this one.

Lady Wargrave presented a serious obstacle. Blythe could hardly order the venerable old woman to leave them alone. Mama might be enlisted for help, but she was nowhere in sight. Portia and Lindsey were still dancing with their husbands at the other end of the long chamber.

Blythe had to devise an excuse to lure Savoy away.

When Lady Wargrave began gossiping about a dance at which several young ladies had became drunk on the spiked punch, Blythe seized the opportunity. "Speaking of dancing," she said, aiming a warm smile at the duke, "I haven't yet seen you step out this evening, Your Grace. We ladies will very disappointed if you remain seated here."

He raised a quizzical eyebrow at her. "Would that I could, but regrettably, I've suffered a minor attack of the gout," he said, indicating the foot he had propped on the stool.

Aghast at her folly, Blythe hastened to apologize. "I'm very sorry, I didn't realize. Is there something I can provide for your comfort? A pillow, perhaps?"

He patted her arm in a fatherly fashion. "That's very kind of you, Miss Crompton. A small pillow would be most appreciated."

"I'll ask one of the servants to fetch it at once."

Blythe rose from the chaise. Maybe there would be time for her to take a quick detour to the back of the house. She did so wish to see for herself how the tryst was proceeding. It would only require a few minutes to peek out into the garden and ease her nagging curiosity. . . .

She had advanced no more than three steps when a wave of murmurs swept through the party. The buzz of excitement gathered force and penetrated her reverie. Many of the guests were turning to gaze toward the arched doorway.

Curious, she lifted herself on tiptoes to see what had caught their attention. Even the music had ceased. Had something happened? Perhaps someone had fallen ill. Or maybe her sister Lindsey had scheduled an entertainment that she'd failed to mention to Blythe.

But her view was blocked by a barricade of gentlemen and ladies. Not for the first time, Blythe lamented the whim of nature that had made her shorter than her sisters.

As if someone had waved a magic wand, the crowd began to part in order to open a path to the doorway. Blythe caught a glimpse of Lady Davina's blonde hair with the dainty tiara.

Not twenty minutes had passed since the girl had left. Why had she returned so soon?

The reason quickly became apparent. Davina held proudly to the arm of the man walking at her side.

Prince Nicolai.

A knell of alarm rocked Blythe. This could not be happening. She must be dreaming. Horror-struck, she stared at his tall figure, at the gleam of candlelight on his black hair and the medals decorating his crimson sash.

People were whispering the prince's name as the news of his arrival spread like wildfire. Ladies sank into deep curtsies as he passed. He nodded to them right and left, his cool expression reflecting a faint scorn of their adulation.

Blythe lifted a gloved hand to her mouth. Dear God, why had James come into the party? She'd expressly warned him not to do so!

Had Davina discovered his true identity? Maybe she had found out Prince Nicolai was really a footman in disguise. Maybe she intended to humiliate Blythe by exposing the hoax in front of all these people.

Her cherished plan of marrying the duke would be shattered.

Like a king and his queen, the couple walked straight toward her. A miasma of dread held Blythe immobile. The calamity was unfolding before her eyes and she could not think of how to avert it.

To her surprise and relief, however, the pair walked right past her. The haughty gaze of Prince Nicolai brushed over Blythe as if she were one of the fawning sycophants he'd earlier professed to abhor.

They stopped in front of the Duke of Savoy. The crowd fell silent as if commanded by an invisible stage director. Only the ticking of the casement clock and the rustle of clothing disturbed the quiet.

"Prince Nicolai," Lady Davina said in a ringing tone, "I would like you to meet my father, His Grace the Duke of Savoy. Papa, this is Nicolai Aleksander Leonide Pashenka, Crown Prince of Ambrosia."

A collective *ooh* rippled through the drawing room.

Using the arm of the chaise for support, Savoy levered himself to his feet and respectfully inclined his head to James. "It is indeed an honor to meet you, Your Highness."

Covering her mouth, Blythe subdued the mad urge to laugh. If only the duke knew he was bowing to a *footman*.

The Marchioness of Wargrave had arisen to dip a creaky curtsy. As Lady Davina made the introductions, she kept her back to Blythe, deliberately barring her from joining the small circle of aristocrats.

For once, Blythe welcomed being excluded. Trapped in this nightmare, she needed a moment to collect her thoughts and to figure out how to remove James from the party before he committed a serious gaffe.

He didn't know all the rules of society. There were so many mistakes to be made. Besides, people were bound to ask him about the fictitious country of Ambrosia. . . .

To her chagrin, he pivoted toward her. His admiring gaze skimmed over her face and gown. "Ah, who have we here?" he said with that beguiling hint of an accent.

Blythe found herself the focus of everyone's attention. The noble guests were agog at the novelty of having a foreign prince in their midst. They believed his status outranked everyone in the room, an illusion corroborated by his royal demeanor.

But they didn't know James as she did. Although his expression had the proud arrogance of a man born to rule, she noted the distinct gleam of deviltry in his dark eyes.

And despite the dire circumstances, her heart responded with a wild lurch of attraction.

Her shock at seeing him enter the drawing room crystallized into anger. James was enjoying himself. This masquerade meant nothing more to him than a parlor game.

Yet one slip of his tongue could cause the ruination of her. Blast him for disobeying her edict!

Aware of all the watching eyes, she forced herself to dip a curtsy. To neglect the required obeisance would only raise suspicion. "Pardon me, Your Highness. I didn't mean to intrude."

He took her hand and lifted it to his lips. "Your apology wounds me. So lovely a lady could never be an intrusion."

Chapter 21

James watched as a faint flush tinted Blythe's cheeks. He hoped it proved that she was not immune to his allure. She had to be livid at the way he'd seized control of her scheme. The subtle signs of her displeasure showed in the set of her mouth and the spark in those expressive hazel eyes.

He couldn't blame her for taking offense. But she'd be even more outraged if she knew his true purpose. Fictitious or not, Prince Nicolai stood a far better chance of winning Blythe's love than did a footman. At least it enabled James to fully participate in her rarified world.

He held on to her fingers when she would have pulled free. "May I know your name, my lady?"

Their gazes clashed. Her lips formed a taut line, though when she spoke, her modulated tone hid her emotions. "Miss Blythe Crompton."

Lady Davina aimed a look of pure venom at Blythe. Leaning closer, she murmured, "Come, Your Highness. She's no one of consequence."

Blythe merely raised a cool eyebrow. But the insult infuriated James. Davina had been irritating him from the moment she'd come out to the garden, all syrupy sweetness and toadying possessiveness.

As Prince Nicolai, he had the means to punish her rudeness.

"Miss Crompton certainly *is* of consequence to me." Knowing he dared not be too blatant in singling out Blythe, he aimed an engaging smile at the multitude of guests. "As are all the ladies here. I must commend you Englishmen, for truly you have the most beautiful women I have ever encountered in my travels around the globe."

Excited murmurs came from the ladies. A number of gentlemen called out huzzahs of agreement, and a smattering of applause echoed through the room.

Lady Davina's smile had become brittle. The rebuke had served its purpose.

Unfortunately, Blythe didn't appear to appreciate his effort on her behalf. She covertly watched the guests as if expecting someone to denounce him as a fraud. Or maybe she was just looking for her sisters, who were wending their way through the crowd from the direction of the dance floor, their husbands lagging behind.

James deemed it time to disperse the audience. "I ask for everyone to return to their merrymaking. I would not wish to disrupt your enjoyment of the evening."

As expected, the aristocrats had the good manners to heed his command. The gentlemen and ladies began to drift away, some to gather in clusters to gossip, and others to form lines on the dance floor. The string ensemble resumed playing, filling the air with a lilting melody.

"Prince Nicolai," Lady Davina said, applying subtle pressure to his arm, "my father is waiting to speak to you."

"One moment." Seeing another couple approach, James held up his hand. "It appears there are a few others who wish to greet me first."

His gaze narrowed on the newcomers. It took all his concentration to hide the hostility that twisted his insides.

Edith and George Crompton.

They were the very image of prosperity, Edith in rich green silk with an emerald aigrette in her styled auburn hair, and George wearing a finely tailored burgundy coat with fawn pantaloons. No one here would ever guess that Edith had started out her life as a tenant farmer's daughter named Mercy Bleasdale. No doubt her swindler of a husband had come from a similar background.

Edith glided straight to James. "Your Highness," she said, genuflecting before him. "If I may beg a moment of your time."

Beside her, George made a deep bow from the waist.

Their respectful posturing stirred a cynical amusement in James. Not a flicker of recognition showed on their faces. They did not identify him as the new footman who had served them at the dinner table—and certainly not as the heir of the man whose fortune they had stolen.

"You may speak," James said.

"I am Mrs. Edith Crompton and this is my husband, George. On behalf of my daughter and son-in-law, Lord and Lady Mansfield, I would like to welcome you to Pallister House." She placed her hand on Blythe's shoulder. "May I also mention, my youngest daughter, Blythe, has been launched recently into society."

"Mama, that isn't necessary. The prince and I have already met." Blythe's eyes widened and she swiftly amended, "Just now, I meant, for when else would we have met?"

James hid a smile. He found her utterly adorable when she was flustered. "When else, indeed, considering this is my first trip to England. I must thank all of you for your generosity in allowing me to join your inner circle."

The Duke of Savoy and Lady Wargrave uttered polite inanities, as did Lady Davina, although her mouth had a pinched look. She clung like a nettle to his arm, clearly unwilling to relinquish her claim on him—especially to any of the upstart Cromptons.

Portia and Lindsey joined the small group, and Edith introduced the rest of the family. While the sisters did their curtsies, Portia wore a slight frown while Lindsey exchanged a furtive glance with Blythe.

They must be itching to toss him out on his ear. But James knew they wouldn't dare make a scene for fear it would reflect badly upon Blythe. It should prove interesting to hear how they explained his presence at the party to their husbands.

A tall man with a scar on one cheek, the Earl of Mansfield offered James a firm handshake. "It's an honor to have you in my home. Although I must say my wife neglected to mention that we had royalty on the guest list tonight."

Lindsey leaned against his arm and directed a cajoling look up at him. "Darling, you're far too busy a man to be bothered with all the details. Anyway, I've been so involved with Ella that I simply forgot."

He had the guarded look of a man who thought he was being conned. "But when did you meet Prince Nicolai to issue the invitation?"

When Lindsey hesitated, Blythe and Portia spoke at the same time.

"A chance encounter on Bond Street," Blythe said.

"The prince and I have a mutual friend," Portia said.

Lord Ratcliffe sent a keen stare at his wife. "A mutual friend? Strange, I've never heard anything about this."

"Nor have I," Mrs. Crompton said, raising an eyebrow at her eldest daughter.

Portia glanced at her sisters and then at her husband, who stood at her side. "Prince Nicolai is acquainted with the Maharajah of Bombay. You do recall Arun, don't you?"

Ratcliffe shared an intense look with his wife. He placed his hand on her back in a possessive gesture. "How could I forget? But forgive me for being perplexed. How did the maharajah meet Prince Nicolai? Is Ambrosia located near India?"

"Um . . . I don't really know."

She flashed a desperate glance at Blythe, who parted her lips as if to speak. Of course, Blythe didn't dare spout expert knowledge of his native land, James thought in cynical amusement. It served her right for scheming to have him play a phony prince from a fictitious country.

"Your Highness," Blythe said, "perhaps *you* are the best one to answer our questions."

He gave her a cordial nod. "Yes, I forget that few people know of my distant kingdom. Ambrosia lies in the mountains north of the Caspian Sea. My father became acquainted with Arun's father a very long time ago in Kashmir. When I embarked upon my world tour last year, my father requested that I pay my respects to the son of his late friend."

"You've been to Bombay, then?" George Crompton said. He had been standing silently at the edge of the group, but now he stepped forward, his face alight with interest. "My shipping business is based there. I've been to the maharajah's palace many times."

James had no wish to be bogged down in a conversation about a place he'd never seen. "Then you will already be aware of its magnificence. I shan't trouble you with the details."

"Why, it's no trouble at all," George said with alacrity. "Perhaps if it's agreeable, we might talk sometime. I should very much enjoy hearing all the latest news."

"Your Highness, if I may be so bold," Edith said, "may I invite you to dinner at our house very soon? It would be at your convenience, of course."

Blythe lifted a hand as if to restrain her mother. "Please, Mama, we mustn't intrude on the prince's goodwill. I'm sure that he has many more important things to do during the *short* time he's in London."

Her gaze shot to James. But he needed no warning of the danger of sitting down to dinner at Crompton House. The upper crust might not always recognize the individual footmen, but the servants had far better powers of observation.

Godwin in particular.

"Regrettably, Miss Crompton is correct," James said. "Much of my time in your fair city will be taken up in such matters as trade negotiations and tedious dinners with government officials. You see, my country has rich deposits of gold and precious gems, and my people are depending upon me to see to their livelihood."

"Surely you will be accepting *some* invitations," Lady Davina said. "Prinny will be returning next week from Brighton, and you'll certainly wish to meet England's Prince Regent. With Papa's permission, I will plan a ball in your honor."

Blythe looked positively aghast at the prospect, as did her sisters.

Taking pity on them, he told Lady Davina, "I would never dream of putting you to so much trouble on my behalf. Especially since I may be called away at any moment."

"Called away?"

"I received a letter only this morning that my father, the king, lies ill. Should his condition worsen, it may be necessary for me to return to Ambrosia at once."

She made a murmur of distress. The fingers that seemed

permanently affixed to his arm now tightened. "How very dreadful."

James saw through the sham sympathy in those avid blue eyes. The duke's daughter was calculating her chances of becoming Queen of Ambrosia sooner than anticipated.

"I do not like to see you so unhappy over my refusal of your kind gesture," he said. "Perhaps I could arrange time for you and your father to accompany me on a drive in the park tomorrow afternoon."

"Of course, Your Highness. We would be most honored!"

James allowed her a moment of triumph. It wouldn't last for long.

He slowly scanned the small group until his gaze stopped on Blythe. She watched him with wary attention, her lips compressed. He knew exactly what she was thinking. She had created Prince Nicolai in order to divert Lady Davina. The purpose was for Blythe to have the opportunity to attract the Duke of Savoy.

But now James had turned her plans upside down.

Little did she realize, however, he had done so for a reason she couldn't even begin to fathom. To make her fall in love with *him*, instead.

"I must ask one more request," James said. "That we will make a foursome and include Miss Crompton in our party."

Chapter 22

By the following morning, Blythe had worked herself up into a lather. She was too vexed to touch the breakfast tray on the table by the sunny window. Although the ormolu clock on the mantel of her bedchamber showed the ungodly hour of nine-fifteen, she was already garbed in a gown of sky blue with her hair twisted up into a loose knot atop her head.

Soft cream slippers kicked out her skirt as she wore a path in the fine carpet. Blast James! She had not seen him since he'd bid an early farewell to Lady Davina and the rest of the party. He had walked out of the drawing room at Pallister House, and Blythe had hesitated to follow for fear of drawing undue attention. When she'd finally deemed it safe to leave the room a quarter of an hour later, his princely raiment had lain abandoned in the upstairs bedchamber. That meant he must have changed back into his livery and wig.

But he hadn't joined the other footmen serving at the party. Nor had he attended the coach that had carried Blythe and her parents home.

He had simply . . . vanished.

Where had he gone?

That question had plagued her into the wee hours of the night. She'd waited up late, thinking he might knock on her door and offer an explanation for his actions. But he hadn't. Consequently, she had slept fitfully, awakening earlier than was her custom. This morning, when she'd asked about him, her maid had revealed the startling news that he had not been present at breakfast with the other servants. On a pretext, Blythe had dispatched the girl to look for him.

She prowled to the window and looked out over the rose garden. James must know that he owed her an accounting after the way he had disobeyed her orders. He wasn't a coward to be hiding down in the cellar, afraid of her wrath. Nor was he a man who shirked his duties.

Maybe he was busy at some task below stairs. He might be unable to find an excuse to come up here.

Or what if something dreadful had happened to him?

The possibility clutched at her heart. Last night, he must have walked back alone to Crompton House. Maybe he had been attacked by footpads. He was a powerful man, well capable of defending himself in a bout of fisticuffs. But if the villains had come at him with pistols or knives, and if there had been a whole band of them . . .

A soft knocking made her pivot toward the door. James?

She flew to answer the summons, pausing only a moment in front of the pier glass to tuck a few stray strands back into place. Then she swung open the door.

Kasi waited in the corridor. An orange sari swaddled her round form, and the familiar gray bun perched atop her head. She held a gold jewel cask in her hands.

A vast disappointment spread through Blythe. "Oh . . . good morning. Please come in."

The old *ayah* waddled past her. Blythe peeked out,

half-hoping to spot James striding toward her. But the ornate passageway stretched out empty in both directions.

When she turned around, Kasi had a quizzical look on her wrinkled features. "Who you look for?" she asked in her sing-song voice.

Those dark currant eyes always seemed to know everything. Blythe said offhandedly, "I'm expecting my maid to return soon with a fresh pot of tea. Now, why are *you* here?"

"*Memsahib* tell me give you this." Kasi handed Blythe the gold box. "She say you wear for prince today."

Blythe frowned at the reminder. At four o'clock, she was supposed to depart for a drive in the park with Prince Nicolai, Lady Davina, and the Duke of Savoy. What if James failed to show up?

She had to find him. Never mind waiting for the maid to return. Blythe must go below stairs herself. Failing that, she'd don her pelisse and walk the route to Lindsey's house, looking for signs of an attack. . . .

"You open," Kasi prodded.

Realizing the Hindu woman stood waiting, Blythe unlatched the clasp and lifted the lid of the cask. The breath caught in her throat. On a bed of dark blue silk gleamed her mother's finest pearl necklace, along with a matching set of earbobs. The creamy orbs seemed to glow with a life of their own.

"These are the pearls that once belonged to the Maharani of Jaipur."

Kasi pressed her palms together in a salaam. "Yes, missy. Blessed by Shiva, bring great luck so you marry prince."

"Prince Nicolai?" Startled, Blythe shut the box at once. Had Mama now set her ambitions on Blythe becoming royal? Good heavens, what a tangled web! "I've no desire to be the wife of any foreign prince. I intend to wed the Duke of Savoy."

"You marry prince." The *ayah* touched the red dot above her eyes. "I see your destiny."

Blythe decided not to argue the matter. Kasi was often correct in her predictions, but not this time. Prince Nicolai didn't really exist and Blythe certainly could never marry the footman who had impersonated him.

Affecting casualness, she asked, "By the by, have you seen the new footman this morning? I need to ask him a question about a letter he delivered the other day."

Kasi made no reply. Her gaze shifted toward the door.

A moment later, someone knocked. Blythe whirled around to see James standing in the open doorway.

Her heart took flight. Unlike her last view of him at the party, he now wore his footman's livery and wig. She scanned him up and down in search of injury. He appeared perfectly hale, his strong, masculine features exhibiting no sign of bruising from any tangle with footpads.

Instantly, her vexation returned in full force. So her fears had been for naught. He had allowed her to stew all night and half the morning without offering any explanations.

To Kasi, she said, "You may go now."

The *ayah* looked from her to James, and back again. Then she took the box of pearls from Blythe. "I put these away for you, missy."

She shuffled into the adjoining dressing room.

Blythe fumed in silence, aware that she couldn't confront James while the *ayah* remained within earshot. Nevertheless, she turned a fierce look at him and motioned to him to enter the bedchamber. She could scarcely wait to give him a piece of her mind.

But her glare was short-lived.

As James walked in, Blythe noticed he was carrying something at his side. The large object was rounded at the top and draped with a cloth.

"Is that . . . a birdcage?" she asked in astonishment.

James nodded. "Very astute, Miss Crompton. It was delivered to you this morning."

He placed it on a table by the window and whisked off the covering. Inside an ornate brass cage, a small yellow bird sat on a perch. As soon as the sunlight bathed the cage, the bird fluttered its wings and launched into a cheery warble.

Nothing could have been designed as a more perfect distraction from her ire.

Enchanted, she hurried over for a closer look. She had seen many exotic birds in India, but none as sweet and pretty as this one. "What a darling little thing! Is it a bunting?"

"A grassland finch, if I'm not mistaken."

She glanced inquiringly at James, then returned her attention to the bird, watching as it flew down to the floor of the cage to peck at a pile of seeds with its short brown beak. "What a marvelous present. I've never received anything quite like it. Who is it from?"

"Prince Nicolai."

Her gaze snapped to James. A faint smile played at the corners of his mouth, and his eyes held a gleam of warmth as if he were hoping she would be pleased. An involuntary surge of pleasure flowed like heated honey through her.

He had given her this gift.

Why? To support the pretense that Prince Nicolai really existed?

Or was it a peace offering to get himself out of trouble?

Another possibility took hold in her heart. Maybe

James had a deeper reason. Maybe he wanted to make her happy, to see her face light up with joy. Because he had fallen madly in love with her . . .

The thought was too dangerously alluring. She must not allow herself to believe such a forbidden thing. It was far more likely that he was merely trying to mollify her after his act of insubordination the previous evening.

Regardless of his motive, the bird and its cage had to have cost him a considerable sum. Such an extravagant gift would beggar a man of his station. Since she had not yet paid him for his part in the ruse, James must have used his meager wages—the wages he'd once professed to be saving to buy passage to India and make his fortune as her father had done.

"Such birds are common to the tropics," James said. "I would venture to guess the prince acquired it on his world travels." He handed her a sealed letter. "Perhaps this contains an explanation."

Automatically, Blythe took the folded note from him. But she didn't open it. Rather, she glanced at the door of the dressing room, stepped closer, and whispered, "It's a wonderful gift, James, but truly you shouldn't have done this."

"Me? You can thank Prince Nicolai the next time you see him."

"Don't be absurd. You spent your own funds. I'll reimburse you, if you like."

His face hardened. "Absolutely not. I'll hear nothing of the sort."

Blythe hardly knew what to think. Was it pride that kept him from accepting her money? Or did he consider her offer an insult for a gift freely given? His purpose still eluded her. Even if James had meant only to salve her anger, she had to admit he had done so in a stunningly romantic manner.

And she felt a most imprudent desire to throw her arms around his neck and thank him with a kiss.

Fortunately, Kasi emerged from the dressing room at that moment, and when she spied the bird, her face beamed with delight. The *ayah* trotted forward to peer into the brass cage, bending down to cluck her tongue. The finch tilted its head and chirped in reply.

"What is name?" Kasi asked.

"I haven't yet thought of one," Blythe said, smiling at them.

"Since she's a gift from Prince Nicolai," James said, "Amora would be suitable. If I'm not mistaken, that is the name of Ambrosia's most famous princess."

Flustered, Blythe aimed a frown at James. He was referring to the princess who had been held captive in a gilded cage by an ogre until she was rescued by a stable lad. The princess who had fallen in love with her hero and lived happily ever after.

But it wouldn't do for the *ayah* to wonder how an English footman knew anything of Ambrosia's history.

"Kasi, please convey my thanks to Mama for the pearls. You must do so straightaway so you don't forget."

The *ayah* raised an eyebrow, looking from Blythe to James. Her dark gaze held his as if she were attempting to see into his soul. But she said nothing, merely pressed her palms together and bowed.

As the Hindu woman left the bedchamber, Blythe made haste to shut the door.

"I'm not one to believe in the power of the evil eye," James said. "However, I had the distinct impression just now that she knows about us."

Dredging up anger, Blythe came toward him. "What do you mean? She can't have guessed that you're posing as Prince Nicolai—despite your mention of that phony legend. Nor can she know that you disobeyed my express orders last night."

"I merely meant that she senses the attraction between us."

Her gaze locked with his. The heat of desire flashed through Blythe and she knew from the intensity of his eyes that he felt it too. He glanced at the bed, but made no move to touch her. She felt a breathless hunger to lock the door and invite him to have his wicked way with her.

Nothing could be more foolish.

"Never mind Kasi," Blythe said firmly. "I need to have a word with you about your behavior. You took a terrible risk coming into my sister's party after I'd warned you not to do so."

Crossing his arms, he propped his shoulder against the wall in a casual pose. "You haven't yet read the note I gave you."

Resisting the tug of curiosity, she tossed the sealed paper down beside the bird cage. "No more of your distractions. I would like an explanation at once. Why did you disregard my wishes?"

He shrugged. "Lady Davina began to grow suspicious when I refused to accompany her into the house. I had to do something to reassure her. Joining the party seemed the only way to allay her doubts."

His reason had merit, but Blythe wasn't ready to forgive him. "Nevertheless, you should never have done so without my permission. There are dozens of mistakes you might have made. If you'd been exposed as an imposter, there would have been a terrible scandal, not just for me but for my whole family."

James came closer, placing his hands on her shoulders. "I'm very sorry to have caused you distress, Blythe. Believe me, that was never my intention."

The sincerity of his apology threatened to disperse her

righteous anger, so she pulled out of his grasp. "I'm not through. What's worse is that you've arranged this drive in the park for today. We will encounter all manner of the ton—especially when gossip spreads of the prince's appearance there."

"You wished for an opportunity to be with Savoy. I've given it to you."

"At a time and a place of *my* choosing." Blythe needed to impress upon him the difficult position in which he had placed her. "There are many considerations you've ignored. As the prince, *you* issued the invitation, which means *you* are obliged to provide the coach. And that puts *me* to the trouble of arranging for one. Not to mention I shall have to procure another suit of clothing for you."

James looked unperturbed. "This morning, Lady Mansfield sent a message to Godwin, instructing him that she requires my services this afternoon to clean glassware from the party. I suspect she is readying the prince's garb and his coach at this very moment." A smile played at one corner of his mouth. "A very resourceful woman, your sister."

Blythe wasn't reassured. Rather, she felt as if the situation had spiraled out of her control. Frowning, she nibbled on her thumbnail. "That's all well and good. However, I don't like having to depend upon her—or you—to solve my problems."

James caught her hand and brought it to his lips. His dark eyes held her spellbound. "You must lay your worries to rest," he said in the soul-stirring accent of Prince Nicolai. "All will be fine. Trust me, my darling."

While she stood bemused, he turned on his heel and strode out of the bedchamber. *My darling.* She felt warm all over. Did he really feel a strong affection for her, or was he merely playing a part? Blythe wished she knew for certain. It was disturbing how easily he switched between the roles of footman and prince.

The sound of happy chirping drew her to the finch's cage. Whatever his intention, James had thrilled her with his gift. It showed a thoughtfulness and an originality she hadn't seen in any of her suitors.

Then Blythe noticed the abandoned letter. Curious, she broke the red sealing wax and unfolded the paper to find a message written in his bold, distinctive hand.

> *My dearest Miss Crompton,*
>
> *May this humble gift win your pardon for my neglect of you last evening. I hope you will understand that circumstances required me to pay heed to other guests when I wished only to be alone with you. Pray allow me to make amends and know that I am counting the hours until we meet again. I remain your most ardent admirer,*
>
> *Nicolai Aleksander Leonide Pashenka, Crown Prince of Ambrosia*

Blythe clutched the note to her bosom as the weakness of yearning swept through her. Anyone else would assume the note was authentic. Mama would deem it a clear indication of the prince's interest in her. Only Blythe could see the hidden meanings, that James was apologizing for upsetting her plans, that he had not meant to cause her anxiety, and that she was definitely not to think that he had any real interest in Lady Davina. Once again, he was doing so in a wildly charming way that warmed her heart.

It was a game to him, Blythe told herself. Yet that explanation no longer rang true. She had the distinct impression that James had another purpose.

He was using the guise of the prince in order to court her himself.

Chapter 23

As the open landau proceeded through the open gates at Hyde Park Corner, Blythe found herself relaxing for the first time since the shock James had dealt her the previous night. There was something about an excursion that always made her happy. How could she fret on such a splendid spring day?

Clusters of daffodils dotted the greensward on either side of the road. The harness of the horses jingled in harmony with the twittering of the birds. Lulled by the gentle rocking of the coach, she tilted up her face to the afternoon sun and relished the warmth on her skin.

"I see that you like the outdoors, Miss Crompton."

Prince Nicolai's deep voice drew her attention to him. He and Lady Davina occupied the seat opposite Blythe and the Duke of Savoy.

Looking at James, she felt a little clutch in her chest. In the charcoal-gray coat and buff breeches, he appeared every inch a royal. His transformation involved more than a mere change of clothing. He exuded the natural confidence of a man who has been born to wealth and privilege.

It remained a mystery to her how a footman could manage to impersonate a prince so well. More and more she was learning that James was a man of many talents. There could be no doubt he would succeed in life at whatever he did.

At the moment, his dark eyes held a hint of mischief. He was enjoying the masquerade, and he wanted her to do so, too. Blythe smiled at him, for now that she'd overcome the alarm of seeing Prince Nicolai in society, it truly *was* amusing to keep such a delicious secret from their companions.

"I do like the outdoors," she replied. "I grew up in India, where the sun is always hot and bright. My sisters and I spent a great deal of time outside."

Lady Davina adjusted the pink parasol to shade her face. "I cannot imagine doing such a thing. Everyone knows that the sun's rays are harmful to a lady's delicate complexion."

In her present good humor, Blythe could not take offense at the girl's pretentiousness. "That must be why Mama would so often scold us that we looked as brown as the natives."

"How vulgar." The duke's daughter tut-tutted. "Gentlemen prefer ladies to take more care with their appearance. Don't you agree, Your Highness?"

"A bit of sun can be beneficial," James said. "I've often thought that it lends an attractive glow to a lady's face."

"Surely you're not suggesting that ladies abandon their bonnets and parasols."

"In the kingdom of Ambrosia, our noblewomen have a great love for the sun. Only nuns and elderly widows cover their heads."

Davina looked so dismayed that Blythe bit her lip to stifle a laugh. How wicked James was! And how wicked he tempted her to be. She had the mad urge to untie the ribbons beneath her chin and toss her straw bonnet into the wind. How lovely it would feel to let the breeze stir her hair, to enjoy freedom from the cage of conventions required by society.

Instead, she turned to the duke. He had been sitting placidly, his gouty leg stretched out, and Blythe was chagrined to recall that she had never fetched him the pillow he'd requested the previous evening. She had forgotten everything in the drama of seeing James as Prince Nicolai.

Today she would make up for her neglect.

"What say you, Your Grace? Will you weigh in on our debate?"

Smiling, he reached out to pat her hand. "Both you and my daughter are lovely. I would not dare to disagree with either of you."

Lady Davina pouted. "Oh, Papa. You are just being polite."

Catching Blythe's eye, James waggled a dark eyebrow. He did it so swiftly that no one but she caught the movement. A bubble of mirth rose in her. Once again, Blythe had the distinct impression that he was flirting with her—just as he had done by giving her the caged finch, and just as he had done by writing that stirringly romantic note from Prince Nicolai.

James had a rakish way about him that appealed to the weakness of her bodily desires. But nothing could be more dangerous than for her to act upon her attraction to him. She must not squander the opportunity he had provided her. The purpose of this drive today was for her to become better acquainted with the duke.

The trouble was, the landau had joined the slow procession of carriages and horsemen up and down Rotten Row, a broad sandy avenue that stretched all the way to Kensington Gardens. On such a fine afternoon, all of the beau monde had come to Hyde Park in their stylish garb. It was the fashionable hour, the place to see and be seen.

The duke's attention swiftly became absorbed in nodding at friends and acquaintances as they passed in their carriages. Many stopped to exchange greetings and gossip.

But mostly, they wanted to meet Crown Prince Nicolai of Ambrosia.

Blythe marveled at all the interest in him. She had never seen so much bowing and scraping in all her life. James became the haughty, slightly bored royal who afforded his admirers a cool smile and a few words of conversation. The more proudly and arrogantly he behaved, the more obsequious they became.

Watching him, she could scarcely believe he was the same man who served her breakfast and delivered the mail. All of her worries had been for naught. James played the role of prince as if he'd been born to it. He showed not the slightest hint of his true station as a footman.

Trust me, my darling.

Warmth curled through her. She *did* trust him. He had a keen intelligence and an infectious zest for life. No gentleman could have more honor, either, for he had not seduced her even when she'd thrown herself into his arms that night in her father's office.

And she adored his sense of humor. Every now and then, while the duke and Lady Davina were busy talking to an acquaintance, James would wink at Blythe or flash her a droll look. It was a reminder that they shared a private jest on all these fawning aristocrats.

She fingered the pearl necklace at her throat. According to Kasi, it was supposed to bring great luck. Blessed by the Hindu god Shiva, it would enable her to wed a prince. How foolish was she to wish that such a silly superstition could really come true?

Very foolish, indeed!

Then she saw something that drove all other thought

from her mind. An open carriage approached from the opposite direction. In it sat a trio of ladies, all snooty patronesses at Almack's.

One of them was the Countess de Lieven.

Blythe lifted a gloved hand to warn James, then dropped it to her lap. He wasn't looking her way and what could she say in front of the duke, anyway? There was no escaping this confrontation.

The carriage slowed to a halt right beside the landau. Blythe sat with a rigidly polite smile on her face. James didn't know how much these particular ladies reveled in their specialized knowledge of pedigree and rank.

Davina introduced Lady Sefton, the Viscountess of Castlereagh, and the Countess de Lieven. "May I present to you Crown Prince Nicolai of Ambrosia."

He gave them a regal nod and a raffish smile. "To meet three such lovely ladies is indeed an honor. Countess, I have heard that your husband is the Russian ambassador."

Elegant in green striped silk, the Countess de Lieven observed him avidly from beneath the straw brim of her hat. Her scrutiny of him held a hint of suspicion. "Yes, and he is most interested in meeting you as he professes to be unfamiliar with the nation of Ambrosia. You must come to my salon next Thursday."

"If my schedule permits."

"Where shall I send the invitation?"

Blythe froze with her fingers tightly clutched in her lap. Dear God, what would James say to *that*?

"You must forgive me for not revealing the address of my lodgings," he said with majestic arrogance. "I do not care to be inundated with a flood of letters and visitors."

Lady Davina leaned forward, eagerness lighting her patrician face. "Your Highness, I would be most happy to collect any invitations on your behalf."

"How very kind, my lady." James made a negligent gesture. "So be it, then."

The flow of traffic required the vehicles to move on, and the conversation ended. Just in time, for Blythe feared Countess de Lieven would ask him probing questions about Ambrosia. The woman was too sharp by half and her face had shown subtle signs of her doubts about his background.

Blythe frowned at James, but he merely smiled back in unperturbed calm. Even with his limited knowledge of the ton, he had to realize the danger of tangling with the countess and the ambassador. Deceiving the nobility in a social atmosphere was one thing; it was quite another to fool officials in the highest levels of the government.

"What an honor for you to be invited to one of the countess's political salons," Lady Davina told James. "Not even Papa is attending—although I am sure that if he wished it, he too would receive an invitation."

"Heaven forbid," the duke said, grimacing as he shifted his gouty leg to a more comfortable position. "I cannot abide such meetings, sitting in a circle and hashing over affairs of state. It is as tedious as listening to the droning of speeches in Parliament."

"We have differing interests, then," James said, "for such an event sounds fascinating to me."

Fascinating?

Was he actually intending to *go*?

Horrified, Blythe said, "I thought you were busy with trade meetings, Prince Nicolai. You said so yourself last evening."

He turned a benign look on her. "There is always time for such an important event, Miss Crompton. After all, the diplomatic contacts to be gained could be most beneficial to the people of my country."

He had to be teasing her. She could not believe otherwise. It would serve no purpose for him to attend such a salon, for it had nothing at all to do with him distracting Lady Davina from the duke's side.

Blythe vowed to give him a stern reprimand at the earliest opportunity. This was *not* his ruse. It was *hers* to direct as she saw fit. He must not be allowed to run rogue by doing such things without her permission.

Compressing her lips, she turned her head to look out at the passing scenery. They had reached the end of the avenue, and the coachman guided the landau around for the return trip. Then they had to run the gauntlet of yet more aristocrats who clamored to meet the celebrated Prince Nicolai of Ambrosia.

James greeted them all with royal civility. Never once did he deviate from his role.

Lady Davina took great satisfaction in telling everyone that she was collecting invitations on behalf of His Royal Highness if they would care to send them to her. Several times, she aimed an arch look at Blythe as if to gloat over the fact that the prince had singled out Davina to act as his personal secretary.

The snobbish girl had no idea how she was being duped. And yet perhaps the joke ultimately would be on Blythe. Concern about the political salon remained at the edge of her mind. Would Prince Nicolai be exposed as an imposter by the Countess de Lieven? Then what would happen to James?

He would lose his position. He might even be prosecuted for fraud and end up in prison. And it would be all Blythe's fault.

As the coach headed out of Hyde Park to take them home, the Duke of Savoy directed a smile at her. "May I say, Miss Crompton, you are looking exceptionally fine today."

The compliment took her aback. "Why, thank you, Your Grace."

"I trust you will reserve the first dance for me tonight at Lord Gilpin's ball."

"Of course."

That was that. He turned to speak his daughter, whose pinched lips indicated disapproval. James raised an eyebrow at Blythe as if to mock her quick acceptance of the duke. But what else had James expected her to do? She could hardly refuse Savoy when furthering the cause of a marriage between them was the point of this drive.

Gazing out over the busy streets, Blythe wondered at her lack of enthusiasm. She felt no sense of triumph or anticipation. Was it possible she found the duke to be . . . dull?

The disturbing notion wormed its way into her mind. There could be no doubt she was more drawn to James. That was only natural, for he was handsome and dashing and closer to her in age. He made her laugh and he stirred her desires. By contrast, the Duke of Savoy was rather starchy and settled in his ways, more like a father than a suitor.

Blythe bit her lip. What was she thinking to compare the two men? A footman could never measure up to a duke. She must not forget that His Grace could give her the perfect life, or that her parents would benefit from her exalted place in society. . . .

As the coach rumbled past an alleyway, she glimpsed a sight that drove out all other thought. A gang of adolescent boys surrounded a small gray object on the cobblestones. One of them kicked at it, and it attempted to dart away, only to be encircled again by its tormentors.

Eyes wide, she turned back to stare in horror. "It's a dog," she gasped. "Those boys are torturing him."

"Street urchins," the duke said, his lips curling in disgust. "It is no concern of ours."

James sprang to his feet. "Stop this coach at once."

The coachman immediately began to slow the team of horses.

"Your Highness, surely you cannot think to interfere," Lady Davina said. "It's far too dangerous—"

He vaulted over the side of the still-moving vehicle and ran toward the band of boys. Blythe hastily unlatched the door and jumped out, too, even before the footman at the rear could fold down the step.

Stumbling, she swiftly regained her footing and dashed after James. Only one thought filled her mind, to rescue the poor animal before it was injured or killed.

Ahead of her, James gave a shout. The boys saw him coming and scattered in all directions. One attempted to snatch up the dog, but James caught him by the scruff of his neck. The brat tore himself free and took off at a run.

Blythe reached James just as he knelt on one knee to see to the cowering animal. Whimpering, the dog quivered in fright.

She crouched down, peeling off her glove to extend her bare hand to the mutt. "Oh, you poor dear. Are you hurt?"

"Have a care, he might nip."

"No, he won't. There, you see?"

The mutt cautiously sniffed her fingers and began to wag its stubby tail. Blythe continued to croon, telling the dog he was her sweet, pretty darling, even though his fur was so dirty and matted that she couldn't even discern its true color.

James gently examined the beast for injury. "It doesn't look as though she's suffered any permanent damage," he said.

"She?"

"Indeed. She's only a pup, and a skinny one at that." James had abandoned the prince's accent for the moment. "The question is, what are we to do with her?"

Blythe made an instant decision. "I'm taking her home, of course."

"Are you certain that's wise?" he said with a keen stare. "Your mother doesn't appear to like dogs—or any other pets."

"She needn't know." Petting the mutt, Blythe considered how best to elude her mother's sharp eyes. "We'll simply have to sneak the dog in the back door and let her live in the kitchen."

James arched an eyebrow. "We?"

"*I*, then. *I* will smuggle her into the house and see if one of the *other* footmen will look after her for me."

"Perhaps the prince should adopt her. It might prove amusing to convince Lady Davina that this mutt is a rare, long-lost breed that somehow escaped from Ambrosia."

Blythe giggled. She glanced over her shoulder at the landau, parked halfway down the street. With all the traffic noise, it was impossible for them to be overheard. "You wouldn't dare."

"You should know by now that I would dare anything."

The rakish glint in his dark eyes brought to mind things she oughtn't be thinking about. Things that involved kissing and caressing. Things that appealed to her far too much.

"We had better return to the coach," she said. "The duke will become impatient."

"A calamitous event that must be avoided at all costs."

On that sardonic note, James stood up, then helped Blythe to her feet. Tail wagging, the puppy regarded them with mournful brown eyes. Suddenly she hopped onto her hind legs and braced her front paws on his breeches, leaving dirty streaks on the buff fabric.

"Minx," he said, reaching down to scoop up the dog without a care for his fine coat. "That might be the very name for you. You'll need a proper bath and a brushing as soon as possible."

Wriggling with happiness, Minx washed his chin with her pink tongue.

Blythe smiled. "I do believe you have a new admirer, Prince Nicolai."

"She's far too forward, considering we've just met." He lowered his voice to a husky murmur. "A pity she doesn't realize I would sooner have kisses from a different girl."

"Lady Davina?"

"Try again." His gaze dipped to Blythe's mouth, making his meaning deliciously clear. Then he returned his eyes to hers. "Shall we go? Prince Nicolai must shame our two companions into allowing this grimy little mutt to share the coach."

As they walked back toward the landau, James carrying the dog tucked in the crook of his arm, Blythe felt a warm glow in the region of her heart. He had been quick and decisive in saving the puppy from harm. It had been the act of a fine, decent man who was noble in character if not in birthright.

So what did that make the Duke of Savoy?

She hesitated even to consider the question.

⁂

"I wonder if we should wait downstairs," Edith asked, parting the lace under-curtain in her boudoir to peer down at the street. With the weather so fair, the green square teemed with pedestrians. "That way we can step quickly outside to greet Prince Nicolai when Blythe returns."

"Is that why you summoned me from my work?" George said. "To make a decision as to where you should stand? Do as you see fit. It matters naught to me."

Edith stepped briskly to stop him from leaving the room. Her husband looked irritated, his lips thinned and his eyes frowning. It never failed to amaze her how obtuse men could be about courtship. Situations had to be orchestrated, events planned in advance, opportunities seized lest they be lost forever.

She patted his hand. "Don't be cross, dearest. I need your help. If you would just have a word with Prince Nicolai, perhaps you can persuade him to accept our dinner invitation."

"He's already turned us down. And what is this sudden interest in him, anyway?"

"Blythe was very taken with the prince last evening, as he was with her. Did you not notice the way they kept gazing at each other?"

"Frankly, no. However, she's stated several times that her wish is to marry the Duke of Savoy."

"But she can do better." Edith gripped his hands hard. "Only think, George. No one among our acquaintances has a daughter who has married royalty. Not Lady Wargrave, not Lady Grantham, not even the Duke of Savoy himself."

"What? I won't have my daughter going off to live in a remote country where we'll never see her again."

"But they'll be able to visit from time to time. Imagine, darling, our grandson could be a king."

George shook his head decisively. "Absolutely not. I forbid it. Your ambitions are taking you much too far this time."

"But dearest—"

"No, Edith. That is my final word on the matter."

Lips pursed, she watched him wheel around to leave

the boudoir. She had to concede the issue. Once George made up his mind, it was difficult to convince him otherwise. Blythe would have to wed the duke.

At the doorway, George turned back around. “By the by, did you ever find that letter?”

Nothing could have been better designed to distract Edith from her matchmaking scheme. “No. It’s still missing. I’ve searched everywhere.”

“Well, see to it that you keep looking. I needn’t warn you of the consequences should it fall into the wrong hands.”

As he left, a cold fear settled in her bones. Yes, she knew that all too well. They could lose everything: the house, their wealth, their standing in society. And in a court of law, possibly even their very lives.

She had queried the maids, moved every piece of furniture, but to no avail. Where had that blasted letter gone?

Chapter 24

After the drive in the park, James directed the coachman to deliver Savoy and his snooty daughter to their house on Albemarle Street. Then he let off Blythe in the mews behind Crompton House so that she could slip the rescued dog in through the garden.

James wanted to accompany her. Unfortunately, his disguise as Prince Nicolai required him to return the coach to Lindsey's house, where he changed back into his footman's livery. There was a further delay as Blythe's sisters grilled him about the progress of the ruse. By the time he'd arrived home, Blythe had already washed and brushed the little mutt.

He found the two of them downstairs in the laundry room surrounded by several maids. Blythe wore a damp apron over her pale green gown. Minx was curled up on a towel in her lap. Wielding a pair of scissors, Blythe clipped a mat out of the dog's fur.

Amazingly, the dark gray dog was now a pale cream color. James refrained from commenting on the transformation, since he wasn't supposed to have ever seen the animal before.

Blythe looked up at his entry. Given their audience,

she wore a polite smile. "James, you're just the person I'd hoped to see. Are you fond of dogs?"

"I am, indeed."

"Excellent. Mama won't permit animals upstairs, so I'd like for you to watch over Minx for me. You'll need to see to her meals and let her out when necessary."

He bowed. "You may depend on me, Miss Crompton."

Their gazes locked as she rose and walked toward him to hand over the dog into his arms. "See to it that you do an excellent job. Prince Nicolai rescued Minx from a gang of ruffians, which makes her very special to me."

Mirth—and something else—danced in Blythe's eyes. A deep, mysterious warmth. It made James feel as tongue-tied as a callow lad. While he held the tail-wagging mutt, she disappeared out into the corridor. A moment later, he heard the light patter of her footsteps going up the stairs.

James didn't see her again until after dark, when he was assigned to accompany the family coach to a ball. Under Godwin's sharp-eyed supervision, James held the door for the Cromptons when they arrived at the party in Grosvenor Square. His gaze met Blythe's for an eloquent moment; then she looked ahead to the torch-lit doorway and disappeared into the house.

After that one warm glance, the evening turned cold and lonely. He waited long hours out in the chilly night air, listening to the boasting and jesting of the coachmen and footmen, watching them play dice beside the long line of carriages. Having always had a distaste for gambling, he declined to join them.

Instead, he walked up and down the street in an effort to stave off irritation. He'd never been one for idling away the time; he vastly preferred to be active. The faint strains of music drifted from inside the house. He craved to be in there with Blythe, at her side, staking his claim on her. Not as Prince Nicolai, but as himself, James Ryding Crompton.

He wanted Blythe to know the truth about him. He wanted to peer into the future and be assured that she would understand he'd had no choice but to expose her parents as frauds. He hungered for the certainty of her forgiveness.

Damn, he was a fool! Hoping for the impossible would accomplish nothing. It was far more likely she'd hate him forever.

But what else was he to do? He couldn't let the false Cromptons' crime go unpunished.

Long after midnight, the noble guests began to trickle out of the house. The coachmen jockeyed their vehicles into position. Blythe emerged with her parents, and when James held the door for them, her gaze sought his. But this time, the playful warmth had vanished. Her eyes held a serious, almost troubled look.

Had something happened to upset her at the party? Perhaps Lady Davina had made another verbal jab. It frustrated James to be so removed from Blythe's life that he could neither protect nor defend her.

Once back at Crompton House, Godwin did the honor of letting out Blythe and her parents at the front door while James remained on his perch at the rear of the coach. He had one last glimpse of her before the coachman drove around back to the mews.

Godwin held a lantern to light the gloomy path through the garden. As they entered the house through the servants' door, a ball of fur barreled out of the darkness. The head footman yelped and nearly fell.

Minx planted her paws on James's legs, wagged her tail, and yapped for attention. "I see you've learned how to push open the door," James said, reaching down to scratch her long ears. "Were you looking for me?"

"That creature should be kept in the stables," Godwin said, wrinkling his fastidious nose. "There will be puddles all over the floor."

"Miss Crompton gave orders for the dog to live in the house."

Leaving the head footman to stew, James led Minx out to the grassy area of the garden. While she sniffed and explored, his gaze was drawn upward to the glow of candles in Blythe's window. He peeled off his white gloves and stuffed them into his pockets. What was the cause of that distressed look she'd given him?

The question nagged at him like a sore tooth.

Minx completed her business and ran back to him. "Good girl," he said absently. She trotted alongside him as he went back inside. The corridor was dim and deserted at this late hour. Godwin was gone, presumably having retired to his attic bedchamber.

James paused at the shadowy entrance to the servants' stairs. He was supposed to take the dog back down to the cellar kitchen.

But she provided him with the perfect excuse to visit Blythe.

It took no more than an instant to make the decision. Reaching for Minx, he tucked the dog under his arm and started up the stairs. "You're to be very quiet," he told the pup, giving her head a rub. "No yapping or whining. Is that understood?"

Minx gave him an adoring look and licked his hand. Then she looked ahead, clearly excited at the prospect of accompanying him on an excursion into new territory.

A shuttered oil lamp at the landing enabled him to see the narrow wooden steps of the servants' stairwell. James continued up until he reached the floor where the family bedchambers were located.

There, he peered cautiously out into the passageway. An encounter with George or Edith would be a disaster. They'd want to know why he'd brought a dog up here. Such an incident would draw attention to James when he needed to remain unobtrusive, just another anonymous servant performing his duties.

Happily, their suite of rooms lay at the opposite end of the floor from Blythe's. And it was, after all, the middle of the night. By now, everyone should be in bed.

Was Blythe?

A keen sense of anticipation spurred James onward. He felt lust, yes, but something more. He enjoyed being in her company, teasing her, making her smile. While playing Prince Nicolai, first at the party and then on the drive through Hyde Park, he'd had the freedom to live in her world. That was the root cause of what had been eating at him all evening. He despised being relegated to the lowly status of a servant. He craved for her to view him as an equal.

Damn! How the devil was he to persuade Blythe to run off to Gretna Green to be married? He didn't doubt she felt an attraction to him; their hot kiss in her father's office had proven that. But the Duke of Savoy had the clear advantage. The old coot possessed a pedigree no footman could ever match.

It was one thing for James to charm Blythe with witticisms and gifts. It was quite another for him to convince her to abandon wealth, family, and status. To give up her luxurious world for marriage to a nobody.

A common servant.

But he had to succeed. His need to expose the crimes of her parents depended upon him luring her north to Lancashire.

As he approached Blythe's chamber, his footfalls barely

made a sound on the plush carpeting. With any luck, her maid would be gone by now. It would be best if there were no witnesses to his visit here.

He raised his hand to knock. But before he could do so, the door opened. Blythe started to walk out, then stopped and stared.

So did he. All the blood in his brain rushed to his loins. The candle in her hand illuminated a pale cream dressing gown tied at her slim waist. Her hair was piled on her head in a careless knot with a few coppery strands hanging loose on her shoulders.

She had never looked more alluring.

"James!" Her startled gaze softened as she looked at the mutt. "Oh, you've brought my sweet little darling. I was just now going to visit you, Minx."

Blythe retreated to set down her candle on a table just inside the bedchamber. Then she took the animal from James and cuddled it to her bosom. Minx squirmed with delight, licking Blythe's chin.

Laughing, Blythe tilted her head back in an attempt to evade the washing. As she did so, her bodice stretched taut over her breasts.

Her unbound breasts. In the uncertain light, he could just see the outline of her nipples through the thin fabric.

James tried not to gawk. He wanted to be the one held in her arms, pressed to that luscious body. Damn, he was jealous of a dog. Nothing could be more pitiful.

"I thought you might wish to see her," he said inanely.

"That's very considerate of you." Nibbling her lip, Blythe gave him a soulful, serious look. "James, I'm very glad you're here. I'd like to talk to you. May I bother you to come in for a few minutes?"

Bother him? He held back a strained chuckle. Little did she know, he'd follow her anywhere, even into the fires of hell.

Chapter 25

Leading the way into her shadowy bedchamber, Blythe hugged the sturdy little dog. The animal's warmth and unconditional love were a comfort. And Blythe needed support after what she'd learned at the party. The news had festered inside her, making sleep impossible.

James closed the door. The welcome surprise of discovering him out in the corridor had been the best moment of her evening. He couldn't know it, but at that very instant she'd been wondering which of the bedchambers in the servants' garret belonged to him, and whether she dared to go look for him. She was that desperate.

He was the only one in whom she wished to confide. Not her mother, not her father, not her sisters. Only James.

When had he come to be so important to her?

A hopeless longing enveloped her as she watched him move through the gloomy bedchamber. He took the candle from the table and touched the flame to a branch of tapers. Then he picked up the poker and stirred the dying embers on the hearth, adding more coals from the hob until a cheery blaze danced in the fireplace.

Hugging Minx, Blythe wished instead to feel James's arms surrounding her. As much as she liked the dog, she felt a great need for human warmth—*his* warmth. James was everything she admired in a man—kind, witty, strong, honorable, courageous. And he made her laugh, though she didn't feel much like laughing at the moment.

But the vast gulf of rank separated them. A footman and a lady. It simply could never be. Still, she would rather have James here with her than any high-born gentleman.

He replaced the poker and turned to face Blythe. "I took her out to the garden just now," he said, nodding at Minx. "So she ought to be good for the night."

"Oh . . . thank you. She can sleep here with me."

"Lucky dog."

James's devilish gaze shifted to the bed, then back to her. The half-smile on his lips caused a pulse of heat inside Blythe. She had spoken without thinking, but now she imagined the two of them lying together under the covers, kissing and touching. . . .

To hide her hunger, she walked away to make a nest out of a spare blanket at the foot of the bed. She placed Minx there, and the pup turned around several times, then plopped down with a contented sigh, resting her chin on her paws.

"What breed do you suppose she is?" Blythe asked.

James came to stand beside her. His faint scent drifted to her, something exciting and spicy combined with the freshness of the outdoors. "Part spaniel, from the long ears. But her small size and coloring would suggest a terrier of some sort."

"I'd have to concur." Blythe continued to idly pet the dog as she glanced at him. "That's two you've given me, all in one day."

"Two?"

"My new pets, Minx and Princess Amora," she said, nodding at the finch's cage, now covered for the night. "My sisters and I always kept animals in India, but we weren't allowed here in England. Mama said we were too old for childish pursuits."

Blythe knew she was chattering to keep things light. Or perhaps because she didn't know quite how to broach the topic on her mind. How would James react to the news? Would he be displeased or indifferent? What would he advise her to do?

"It's hardly childish to keep a pet," he said. "I'm sure your mother merely wanted you to concentrate on catching a noble husband."

His blunt statement hit at the heart of Blythe's dilemma. For many months she had looked forward with great anticipation to the future. While shopping for her wardrobe and practicing her dance steps, she'd been eager to be courted by the cream of London society. But now, because of what she'd heard tonight, a plague of doubts had infected her.

James studied her a moment. Then he reached for her hand and led her to a chaise by the fire. "Sit," he commanded. "You look as though you're about to swoon."

Blythe wilted onto the edge of the cushion. She stared down at her laced fingers in her lap. She wanted to talk—yet she didn't.

He gently tipped up her chin. "You had better tell me what's disturbing you. Did something happen at the party?"

She nodded slowly. Would James understand her quandary? She herself hardly understood the seismic shift in her emotions.

"It was a bit of gossip I overheard," she said. "During one of the interludes between the dance sets, there was a group of ladies whispering. They were saying that the Duke of Savoy has crushing debts from gambling."

A stillness came over James's face. His expression turned hard and cold. "I should have known," he said flatly.

"At the card party, I noticed he had the look of a devoted gamester."

"How so?"

"It was the way he handled the cards, the avid expression on his face. And his inability to pay heed even to a beautiful woman like you sitting beside him. It reminded me of my father."

Blythe stared at James in confusion. "Your father was a gambler? But . . . you never told me he was a gentleman."

James lowered his lashes slightly, lending mystery to his dark eyes. "It isn't only the haute ton who make wagers. The common class are quite fond of squandering their coin, as well. The coachmen and footmen were playing dice tonight on the street, though I didn't join them."

The disdain in his voice told her more than words ever could. He loathed gambling because he had seen for himself the destruction it could wreak. "What happened to him—your father?"

"He lost everything and he drank to forget the troubles he'd brought on himself. He died facedown in a ditch when I was sixteen."

With her emotions already raw, the story put her on the verge of tears. Here she was, wrapped up in her own troubles, without a care for his. How had she never thought to ask James more about his past?

She cupped his cheek in her palm. "I'm so very sorry. What of your mother?"

"I never knew her. She died when I was very young." James took her hand from his face and rubbed his thumb over the back. "But never mind me. We were speaking of *you*. It's now becoming clear why Savoy seemed a bit more attentive toward you during the ride in Hyde Park."

"Yes," Blythe said, vowing to learn more about James at another time when she didn't face such a pressing problem herself. "Apparently, the duke is drawn to the considerable size of my dowry."

"As you are drawn to his title."

She blushed to hear it stated so frankly. But he couldn't know she had naïvely assumed the duke would fall in love with her if only she tried hard enough. She had hoped for affection and warmth from a man who cared only about gambling. "It's true, ever since we came to England, I've dreamed of becoming a premier hostess of the ton. But it wasn't just for myself. I also hoped to improve my parents' standing in society."

His mouth tightened. "Is it not enough that your sisters have married a viscount and an earl?"

"A duke is the highest-ranked peer. For me to wed His Grace would be the pinnacle of success for Mama and Papa. No one would ever again dare to malign them for being commoners."

"Yet I must wonder. Is this marriage really *your* ambition—or that of your parents?"

Blythe was taken aback by the question. *Had* she fallen into doing their wishes? Yes, she had wanted to please her father, who seldom asked anything of her. But she could not hold her parents entirely to blame, either. She herself had wished to make a grand alliance, to have the wedding of the season. At least until she'd met James. Now, a lavish life at the apex of society seemed shallow and empty, devoid of love.

"It was *my* ambition," she stated, unwilling to malign her parents in his eyes. "Yet . . . I never imagined marrying a lord who only wants my money to pay off his gaming debts. I-I had always assumed the duke was an honorable, upright man like Papa."

Of course, there had been that little incident when she'd noticed Savoy and his daughter sending secret signals to each other at the card party. At the time, his cheating had not seemed terribly significant to Blythe, since it had only been a casual game among friends. But now she saw it as a serious character flaw.

James sat in rigid silence for a moment. His face appeared set in stone, and she had the odd impression of dark emotions roiling in him. "It would be a mistake to bind yourself to a gambler. You had better think long and hard about what your life with him would be like."

Fraught with tension, she plucked at the skirt of her dressing gown. "I haven't told you everything, James. On the ride home tonight, Papa said that the duke had spoken to him. His Grace has requested an interview with him tomorrow afternoon. And Papa has granted it."

"Tomorrow!" James shot to his feet. He removed his wig and tossed it onto a chair, then ran his fingers through his dark hair. In obvious agitation, he walked back and forth in front of the fireplace before swinging to face her. "So. Savoy will ask for your hand in marriage. You don't suppose his daughter will try to stop him?"

Blythe shook her head. "I should have mentioned . . . Lady Davina was in the group of women I overheard. She said . . . that it appeared her father would have to marry the rich heiress, after all."

That rich guttersnipe had been Davina's actual words, though Blythe didn't want to repeat the phrase. Name-calling said more about the speaker than the subject. She knew that, yet she had been humiliated nonetheless.

"You've attained your heart's desire, then," James said, fixing her with an intent stare. "You will not be needing me to play Prince Nicolai any longer."

Her heart lurched. She could not imagine her life without the excitement of planning their next adventure together. Panic nipped at the edge of her composure, and she took a shaky breath to steady herself. "Oh, James, it's all happening much too quickly. I don't feel prepared to make *any* decision."

It was every lady's dream to marry a man as grand and important as a duke. When had her own aspirations changed?

Perhaps when she had first succumbed to her feelings and kissed James. Or perhaps when he'd donned the garb of Prince Nicolai and related that charming fairy tale. Or maybe when he had plunged into the gang of ruffians and rescued Minx for her.

James sat down beside Blythe again, so close their legs were pressed together. Taking her hand in his, he stroked his thumb over her palm. His dark gaze held her mesmerized. "Blythe, I can no longer keep silent. I must confess how very dear you've become to me. Dare I hope that your indecision might stem from your own feelings for me?"

A pulse of happiness melted her insides. She closed her eyes a moment, the better to savor it. Looking at him again, she cradled his cheek in her hand. "*Yes*. Oh, yes, James, I *do* have feelings for you. Very much so."

Something akin to triumph glittered in his eyes. He lightly ran his finger over her lips. "Then perhaps you should follow your heart."

His mouth came down on hers in a deep, searching kiss. A glorious sense of homecoming filled her as she slid her arms around him, pressing herself to the muscled wall of his chest. He clasped her tightly, as if he never wanted to let her go. The kiss went on and on, interspersed with caresses and murmurs, gradually becoming tinged with a kind of delicious desperation.

She could not get enough of him, the taste of his mouth, the roughness of his skin, the silkiness of his hair. Nothing existed but the two of them, enclosed in candlelit darkness. She'd had no idea that so much pleasure could come from the weight of his hands sliding over her body. He turned his attention to her bosom, where he cupped her breasts over the dressing gown.

"I want to see you, Blythe," he murmured, his fingers moving down to the fastening of the garment. "Will you allow me?"

The notion of disrobing for him held a wicked allure. Her throat taut, she nodded.

He untied her belt, and she shrugged the loose gown off her shoulders so that it fell into a pool at her waist. As he gazed at her exposed breasts, she suffered a twinge of embarrassment and buried her face in the crook of his neck. Her wanton behavior had gone far beyond that of any decent young lady.

He tipped up her chin. "You are so very beautiful. There's no need to feel shame, not with me. We were meant to be together like this."

"I want to believe that. So very much."

"Then do."

Their lips joined in another soul-stirring kiss. His hands were on her bare skin, lightly kneading her, doing enthralling things to the tips of her breasts. A flush of excitement spread throughout her body, making her tingle all over. "Mm," she sighed against his mouth, "I do love this."

He awarded her a slightly strained smile. There was a heaviness to his breathing, as if he fought to control himself. "If ever I displease you, just say so. You have my word that I shall stop."

"Oh, James, if you stop I'll be most unhappy."

Holding his face in her palms, she kissed him with renewed fervor while he continued to caress her. He slid his hands down inside the waist of her nightdress to clasp her bare bottom. Yet she hungered to be flesh to flesh with him. Unsteady with passion, she unbuttoned his coat and pushed it off his shoulders. He grasped his shirt at the hem and dragged it off over his head. The action caused a rippling of the muscles in his arms, and she marveled at the sight of him, the candlelight flickering on the broad expanse of his chest.

When he shifted his mouth to her throat, she arched her neck in unfettered enjoyment. He kissed a path downward to take the peak of her breast into his mouth. The pulse inside her became an insistent throbbing, and she moved against him in an effort to assuage it.

"Please," she whispered.

He seemed to know precisely what she wanted, for he peeled away her nightdress, letting it slither to the floor. It felt natural for her to be naked in his arms, with him clad in only his breeches. Surely, as he'd said, they were destined to be together. James was truly a prince among men. *Her* prince.

The hush of night somehow enhanced their delight in each other. They inhabited their own private place of pleasure away from the rest of the world. His explorations became bolder and her entire being focused on the progress of his hand sliding up her bare thigh.

Abruptly he paused. His eyes glittered in the semidarkness. "I intend to make love to you, Blythe. Right here and now. If you've any objections, you had better say so at once."

"I want this. I want *you*."

Kissing his chest, Blythe needed no time to ponder. If nothing else, she would have this one night. She must not fool herself into believing James would ask her to marry him. For all she knew, he might not even want a wife. Seduction might be his sole purpose.

Her heart ached at the thought. And yet she felt no

hesitation in giving herself to him. Beyond this moment in time, nothing held any significance. The future could wait until tomorrow.

He kissed her softly, his tongue entering her mouth. All the while, his fingers made teasing circles along her inner thighs. Then at last he was touching her *there*, in the spot that ached so exquisitely.

Blythe quivered from an onslaught of reckless pleasure. Acting on pure instinct, she parted her legs to allow him full access. Her breath came light and fast while he continued those maddening, swirling strokes. She felt like warm wax in his hands, ready to be shaped according to his will.

So this was the beauty of lovemaking. No wonder her sisters had been so concerned that she choose her husband wisely. In truth, she could not imagine allowing any other man to touch her so intimately.

James pressed her back against the pillows of the chaise. At the same time, he tore at the fastening of his breeches, shoved them down, and kicked free of the binding fabric. As he settled over her, the heated length of him lay against her thigh and a shiver of anticipation rippled through her.

James lifted his head slightly. His eyes were heavy-lidded, dark in the shadows. "Afraid?"

She shook her head. "In India, there are shrines where women worship a stone statue of the lingam." Reaching down, she glided her fingertips over him, marveling at the splendor of him. "For the first time I understand why."

He was hot and hard, yet more silken than she'd imagined. Not that her girlish fantasies of him had ever ventured this far. Heavens, she just had not *known*.

He made a sound halfway between a groan and a chuckle. "That feels far too good," he said, drawing her hand away. "I want this to last."

So did Blythe. Had she the power to command the moon and stars, this night would go on forever. As they kissed and caressed, she reveled in their closeness. His fingers plied her again, arousing a beautiful torment inside her, making her pant and sigh with need.

When she thought she could bear no more, James pressed into her. A brief pain made her catch her breath; then she exhaled slowly, closing her eyes to savor the wonder of their joined bodies. When she looked at him again, she found him watching her with a dark intensity.

"You're mine now," he muttered. "*Mine*. Never forget that."

Nothing in her life had prepared her for the sensation of him deeply embedded in her. They were truly one. An immense well of emotion overflowed in her, and she brushed her lips over his. "Oh, James. I love you so much."

For an instant, he looked almost startled, then he bent his head to kiss her. He moved within her, commencing a deep and steady rhythm that thoroughly distracted her from any coherent thought. All the while, he stroked her breasts and caressed her elsewhere, murmuring sweet endearments.

Her head tipped back against the cushions of the chaise. She moaned, clutching at him as he quickened the pace. His body felt hot and slick with sweat, and she reveled in his strength. Her breath came in labored gasps until at last the tightly coiled tension in her broke in convulsive waves of pure bliss unlike anything she had ever known.

As she lay amazed and replete, James thrust ever more deeply into her. He uttered a harsh cry of rapture, and then the weight of his body settled on top of her, his breathing gradually slowing.

They lay for timeless moments entwined in idyllic exhaustion. As rational thought returned, Blythe realized with a pang that he had not returned her declaration of love. Had she chosen the wrong moment? No, *chosen* was the wrong word. The sentiment had poured from her heart without forethought. But perhaps James had been too caught up in physical enjoyment to voice his own feelings.

He raised himself slightly to gaze down at her. With a tender touch, he brushed back a strand of her hair and then ran his fingertip over her damp lips. "What a gift you've given me," he said. "I've little to offer you in return."

"The gift was mutually shared. I've no need for anything else."

He picked up her hand and kissed her knuckles, while looking intently at her. "Will you allow me to give you the honor of my name? Will you marry me, Blythe, even though I'm merely a footman? Will you be my wife?"

She had not thought the evening could be any more wonderful. His proposal made the breath catch in her throat. She imagined being with him every night like this, sharing his life, bearing his children, growing old together.

Yet in the midst of her joy, something gave her pause.

Perhaps it was the way he was looking at her.

His gaze held that secretive darkness she'd sensed in him from time to time. There was a watchfulness about him, an elusive tension that now struck her as peculiar. She felt an odd certainty that she was missing something vital, that he wasn't being completely honest with her.

Questions crept past the haze of her happiness. How much did she really know about James? Was it possible—just *possible*—that he had romanced her for a mercenary purpose? That he viewed her as his key to achieving the life of a gentleman?

She hesitated even to think it. But the possibility must be faced.

"Do you love me, James?"

He did not answer at once. A faint frown touched his brow, and he lowered his head to kiss her fingers—or perhaps to hide the truth in his eyes. "My affections belong only to you," he murmured. "Surely you know that."

His slight hesitation told Blythe everything. His reply was not the impassioned declaration she so desperately craved from him. Her questions grew into full-blown doubts that dealt a blow to her heart.

Denying the truth served no purpose. If James did not love her, then that could only mean he'd been wooing for his own hidden purpose.

For her money.

Blythe slipped out from under him, disengaging their bodies. Snatching up her dressing gown, she blinked back tears while thrusting her arms into the garment. How could she be so blissful one moment and so filled with suspicions the next?

Behind her, she heard him rise to his feet. His hands settled, warm and heavy, on her shoulders. "Blythe, what is it? What's wrong?"

Temptation urged her to fling herself into his embrace. To forget this sudden onslaught of misgivings. But that would mean throwing away her whole life for a charming bounder.

A man who did not cherish her.

Pulling away, she swung to face him. "A marriage between us is impossible. It would cause a terrible scandal for my family."

"I can provide for you, if that's your concern. I've plans to make my fortune. With you at my side—"

"No." She shook her head. "I must ask you to leave here. I-I need time to think."

"Pray do not refuse me. Not after what we just shared." He softened his voice, cajoling her. "Blythe, you might already be carrying my child."

The notion caused a bittersweet lurch inside her. What would she do in such an instance? She desperately needed to be alone, to sort through her tangled emotions. "Please go, James. *Now.*"

Chapter 26

The following afternoon, Blythe descended the grand staircase. A summons had been delivered to her bedchamber a short time ago by one of the maids. The Duke of Savoy had arrived and Mama had requested Blythe's presence in the green drawing room.

Her every step felt leaden. She did not want to face this interview. Only a fortnight ago, she would have been thrilled to know that His Grace had come to ask for her hand in marriage. She would have rejoiced in the golden future that lay before her.

But that had been before she had fallen in love with James.

The mere thought of him threatened to open the floodgates of her emotions. She hadn't seen him since that glorious interlude in the middle of the night and their ensuing quarrel. After he had gone, she had crawled into bed and hugged Minx for comfort, eventually falling into a troubled slumber.

By the time she'd awakened, it had been late morning. The patter of raindrops on the window explained the darkness of the room. Minx had vanished, presumably taken out by the maid.

In a state of numbness, Blythe had prepared herself

for this audience. She had bathed, then donned the garments Mama had chosen for her. She had sat quietly while the maid did her hair. All the while, thoughts of James had preoccupied her. She had teetered between misgivings about his mercenary purpose and memories of the joy she had found in his arms.

You're mine now, he had said as he'd joined their bodies. *Mine. Never forget that.*

She wouldn't—couldn't—forget. He had been so tender and loving that it was difficult to believe he might harbor an ulterior motive. Perhaps her instincts had been wrong, and James wasn't a cold-hearted scoundrel. Perhaps she had simply expected more from him than he was able to express. What he felt for her might not be love, but surely it wasn't villainy, either.

Was it so terrible, anyway, that he would seek to use her family connections to better himself? Hadn't she herself intended to do the same with the duke?

Besides, James was more than intelligent enough to know that Papa would never sign over her dowry to a footman. It was very likely she would be cut off without a penny, so there would be no monetary gain for James. She would lose all standing in society, too. She would be a pariah, an outcast, scorned by the nobility who now invited her to their parties.

Would she also be shunned by her parents?

Pausing outside the drawing room, Blythe drew a shaky breath. Papa would be devastated to learn of her fall from grace. By marrying James, she would be giving up everything for a man who had not even professed to love her. If she married the duke, at least she would always have the esteem of her family.

Dear God, what should she *do*?

The final decision still eluded her. Yet the course of

the rest of her life depended upon the choice she would make this afternoon.

She forced herself to walk through the arched doorway and into the long chamber. At the tall windows, swags of gold cord held back the green brocaded draperies. Chairs and chaises in asymmetrical groupings filled the immense space.

Her mother sat alone beside the marble fireplace. She was pulling a needle and thread through the embroidery hoop in her hand.

Relief poured through Blythe. The duke wasn't here, after all. The reprieve made her so giddy, she caught hold of the back of a gilt chair to steady herself.

Smiling, Mrs. Crompton laid aside her sewing. "There you are, my dear. I was about to come in search of you." She hurried over to Blythe and eyed her critically. "The lemon yellow is an excellent color for you, although your cheeks are a bit rosy. Are you feeling ill?"

While making love, James had pressed his face to hers. She had relished the whiskered roughness against her tender skin.

"Perhaps from the sun on the drive in Hyde Park yesterday," Blythe murmured. How long ago that seemed. She had felt carefree and happy while flirting with James. In the guise of Prince Nicolai, he had rescued Minx for her. . . .

"Well, do hurry and sit down." Mrs. Crompton glanced out into the empty vestibule. "His Grace may arrive at any moment."

A knell struck Blythe. "Is he . . . still in Papa's study, then?"

"Of course. They are no doubt working out the particulars of the dowry arrangements. With so large a portion as yours, these things take time." Mrs. Crompton motioned Blythe to a chair by the hearth and handed her an embroidery hoop. "Now, concentrate on your sewing."

Blythe obediently sat. The knot inside her tightened as she noticed how happy her mother looked. Mama often seemed dissatisfied, always ambitious to improve their social standing. But now, she must be reflecting on the grand alliance Blythe was about to make.

"I despise needlework," Blythe objected. "You know I do."

"Never mind, just pretend to sew. It's important that everything look ordinary. We must act as if we don't know why His Grace is here."

Blythe jabbed the needle into the fabric. It was one of her father's white handkerchiefs. She stared down at his half-completed initials in blue thread and blinked back tears. Dear God, Papa would furious—and terribly disappointed—if he knew she had given away her virginity.

And to a footman, no less!

Rain tapped on the window, underscoring her despair. And what of the duke? Even if she agreed to marry him, it would be wrong of her to wait until their wedding night to reveal the truth. She would have to tell him today. What would he say when he found out? Would he withdraw his offer?

Perhaps not. He needed to pay off his gaming debts. The size of her dowry might be a powerful incentive for him to overlook her indiscretion, though he likely would insist upon waiting a few weeks to be certain she was not with child.

At the notion of carrying James's baby, Blythe felt the softness of yearning. Every child was a gift, no matter what the circumstances. It seemed only right and good that the marvelous joining of their bodies could result in the miracle of a son or a daughter.

She'd had no inkling that a woman could feel such

complete abandonment in a man's arms. Or that his touch could transport her to perfect pleasure. Even now, fraught with doubts about her future, Blythe felt a deep pulse of longing. She wanted to experience it again.

With James. As his wife.

But her parents would never allow the marriage. They would be devastated—and they would do everything in their power to stop her.

It wasn't penury she feared, but the loss of her family. They would suffer the consequences of the scandal every day. Her sisters cared little for society, but Mama enjoyed all the visits and dinners and balls.

How could Blythe heap disgrace on her parents in exchange for life with a man who didn't truly love her? That was the crux of the matter. If only she had time in which to assure herself of James's affection.

"Mama, what if . . . what if I *don't* wish to marry the duke? What if I've changed my mind?"

Astonishment on her face, Mrs. Crompton let the sewing fall to her lap. "I beg your pardon?"

"I've very disturbed to find out that he's a gambler. I had no idea he had so weak a character."

"Shh. Do keep your voice down." Lips taut, her mother glanced at the empty doorway. "All men have their foibles. It is nothing to fret about."

"But it's been such a shock. I-I need time to consider the matter."

Mrs. Crompton gave her a keen stare. "Does this have to do with Prince Nicolai? Have you set your sights on him instead?"

Blythe felt the rise of a blush. She glanced down at the sewing that lay abandoned in her lap. Her mother had no idea that the prince was Blythe's own creation. Or that Blythe had fallen in love with the footman who had played the role. "No, I . . ."

"You have, haven't you? Well! I cannot pretend it wouldn't be wonderful to see my daughter become a princess. And Prince Nicolai *is* quite the dashing rake." Mrs. Crompton made another dainty stitch in her embroidery. "However, you must put all thought of the prince from your mind. Your father prefers that you remain in England, rather than go off to some faraway land. It is your duty to obey him."

But I've been ruined.

Blythe couldn't bring herself to voice that confession. Anyway, she didn't *feel* ruined. Making love with James had been a private joy, and she didn't want to sully the memory with horrified recriminations from her mother. "Am I to have no choice in the matter, then?"

Mrs. Crompton gave her a fond smile. "Oh, darling, it's perfectly normal to harbor doubts. Just keep in mind what you've always wanted. To become a duchess. To be the grandest lady in society." She pulled her needle through the fabric. "This alliance will make your father and me so happy and proud."

With every word spoken by her mother, Blythe felt as if a weight were crushing her. The burden of obligation. She owed her parents the honor of making a good marriage. She had always been the dutiful daughter. It wasn't their fault that she had changed.

The sound of measured footsteps came from the doorway. A footman—not James—entered the drawing room and bowed.

"His Grace, the Duke of Savoy."

Panic flashed through Blythe. There had to be a way to escape this ordeal. Could she pretend illness? It would not be a lie, for her stomach churned with tension.

The duke walked into the drawing room. He leaned on a cane today, which meant his gout must be bothering him. Nevertheless, he made a stately figure with his neatly combed dark hair with hints of gray, tailored maroon coat, and perfectly tied white cravat beneath his haughty chin.

Like a marionette controlled by strings, Blythe found herself rising to her feet and then curtsying to him alongside her mother. He and Mrs. Crompton exchanged a few pleasantries. Then Mama said, "I've a matter I must check on with the housekeeper, Your Grace, if you'll excuse me."

Mrs. Crompton aimed a secretive smile of encouragement at Blythe before hurrying out of the drawing room. How silly to keep up such a pretense, Blythe thought. They all knew why Savoy had come here. Why not just say so and be done with it?

The duke waved his ringed hand at a chaise. "Will you sit with me, Miss Crompton? There is a matter of importance we must discuss."

The urge to dash out of the room made her sway. She wanted to run as far and as fast as possible. But in the end, there was nothing for her to do but comply.

She lowered herself to the cushions and laced her fingers in her lap. As the duke took his seat beside her, he seemed an utter stranger, a middle-aged lord who thought too highly of himself. She could scarcely bring herself to meet his eyes. There was nothing whatsoever about him that interested her anymore.

A gambler! How little she had known of him.

Savoy afforded her the benign smile one would give a child. "I have just spoken to your father," he said, his fingers curled around the knob of his cane. "If you will forgive me for speaking plainly, he has given his consent for me to pay my addresses to you."

Of course Papa had done so, Blythe thought in despair. She had told him weeks ago that the duke was her ideal husband. Then last night in the coach, when her father had informed them of the duke's scheduled visit, she had been too shocked to voice any objection.

But now, she could not keep silent. All her frustration and despair demanded to be released. "I will speak plainly, too, Your Grace. It would seem you are in dire need of my dowry."

His pale blue eyes blinked in surprise. "The state of my finances is neither here nor there. It can be of no concern to a young lady such as yourself."

"It *is* of concern to me. My father works hard to earn his wealth. Now it will be squandered to pay your gambling debts."

Savoy's lips tightened. "By Jove! You're a cheeky girl. I would remind you of how greatly you and your family will benefit from an alliance with me."

He was right, Blythe knew. Her spark of anger died, leaving the ashes of bitter desolation. Mama and Papa would be elevated in the eyes of society. And she herself would wear the tiara of a duchess. That was what she had wanted. But now, such a life seemed so cold and empty.

"As you are aware of my purpose," he continued, "I see no reason to belabor the moment." He reached for her hand and clutched it limply. "Miss Crompton, will you agree to become my wife?"

The proud tilt to his chin conveyed his unshakeable belief that she would accept. This was merely a formality to him.

Savoy cared nothing for her wishes, nor would he ever care. By marrying him, she would be forever bound to a man who believed himself superior to her, a man who lacked the ability to love her as she yearned to be loved.

But James had that ability. James had displayed his warmth and affection for her many times, most notably during the night when they had engaged in such tender lovemaking. Oh, she *knew* she could win his heart. With James, the future held radiant possibilities.

The truth of that washed through her like a balm to her battered emotions. She couldn't wed the duke, not even for the sake of her parents.

"Your Grace, I . . ."

A movement drew her attention to the arched doorway. A tall man strode into the drawing room as if he owned the world.

Prince Nicolai.

Blythe's heart did a wild leap. Without conscious thought, she stood up and pressed her hand to her mouth. James!

Dear God, what was he *doing* here? She wanted to laugh and weep all at once. She hadn't ordered him to don the costume. They had agreed it was no longer necessary.

Yet he was here.

Prince Nicolai walked straight toward them. He wore his full regalia, the crimson sash with the glittering medals, the sword at his side. His black hair glistened from the rain, and his handsome face bore a look of gallant resolve.

And with him, he brought all of the light and color that had leached from the room. Everything turned bright again—most notably, her spirits.

The duke levered himself to his feet with the aid of his cane. By the rigid set of his face, he appeared none too pleased at the interruption.

He bowed to James. "Your Highness."

"Savoy. I see you have managed to corner the most lovely lady in all of England." Prince Nicolai reached for her hand. While he raised it to his mouth and kissed the back, his dark eyes held a devilish gleam. "Have I interrupted something important?"

"No," Blythe said.

"We were engaged in a private discussion," Savoy corrected with a hint of irritation. "Perhaps you will be the first to congratulate me. Miss Crompton was about to accept my offer of marriage."

"About to? Then there is still time for her to reconsider." James dropped to one knee before her. Lacing his warm fingers through hers, he looked up at her with grave earnestness. "Miss Crompton, we have known each other for only a short time. Yet I must confess that I fell madly in love with you at first sight."

Her heart squeezed taut. His stirring declaration fulfilled all of her romantic dreams. She searched his dark eyes for the truth. Why was James saying this right now? Why had he not done so last night?

Unless he was merely playacting now. Because he believed Blythe needed rescuing from a life of unhappiness with the duke.

"See here!" Savoy objected. "I must ask you not to speak to my betrothed in so familiar a fashion. I've obtained her father's consent. We have worked out a dowry agreement."

James ignored him. He was staring up at Blythe, and she could not tear her gaze from his. "I hope you can forgive my boldness," he said in that stirring foreign accent. "I've been called back to my homeland and there is no time for delay. I would very much like for you to go with me. My dearest Blythe, will you marry me?"

She desperately wanted to say yes. But she didn't want to accept the prince; she wanted to wed James the footman.

If he truly loved her.

"That is quite enough," Savoy said. "Release her hand at once. Your Highness, you cannot waltz in here and steal my bride."

"It is up to Miss Crompton to decide whose bride she will be."

Blythe looked from one man to the other. The duke, who needed her money to pay his gaming debts. And James, who was far too adept at playing Prince Nicolai when what she really wanted was . . . open and honest love.

She pulled her hand free. "I refuse *both* of you."

Turning, she ran out of the drawing room.

Chapter 27

"There be such a quarrel above stairs," said a wiry maid named Sally whose mobcap drooped low on her brow. "Shoutin' an' doors slammin' an' such! I was polishin' the woodwork an' 'eard it all."

A cluster of servants had gathered in the kitchen, where a scullery maid stood peeling carrots at the long wooden table. Listening intently, James busied himself by mixing the contents of a jar of silver polish at the dry sink. He had just returned to Crompton House after changing back into his footman's livery. He burned to know what had happened after Blythe had fled from the drawing room.

God! She had rebuffed him again. The memory lodged like a stone in his gut. At least he could take solace in the fact that she'd also turned down Savoy and his blasted title.

"The missus locked Miss Blythe in 'er chamber," Meg told the others. "Told 'er t' stay put till she comes to 'er senses."

Sally gave a vigorous nod. "She refused to wed a duke and a prince, all in one breath."

"Cor!" said the scullery girl in awe. "Fancy that! Two at once!"

The women murmured in envy and disbelief.

Godwin appeared in the doorway and clapped his hands. "Enough gossiping about your betters," he snapped. "Go on, get your work done."

The maids scattered.

The head footman marched toward James. "You! Where have you been? You disappeared for an hour."

"Miss Crompton asked me to walk her dog," James said coolly. He nodded at Minx, who lay by the hearth, gnawing on a beef bone.

Disapproval showed on Godwin's thin, foxy face. "Next time, you will inform me before you leave the house. Or you will have no position here upon your return."

James was tempted to turn in his notice right then and there. But not yet. Not when he had made such a mangle of things.

Assuming the guise of Prince Nicolai had seemed the perfect solution, for Blythe had always found him charming. But even that ploy had failed miserably. What the devil was his next move to be when she clearly wanted nothing to do with him?

One fact was certain. He had to see her again. He was desperate to make amends somehow.

But how?

The jar of polishing mix in hand, James stalked to the tiny, dank workroom where another endless pile of silverware awaited him. Minx trotted along with him, the bone clamped in her teeth. She settled down in a corner to continue her happy chewing.

Would that he could be so easily contented.

The approach of dusk muted the already dim light from the single high window. In the semi-darkness, he ferociously attacked one spoon after another. All the while, his thoughts dwelt on Blythe. The silken feel of her skin. The taste of her breasts. The look of wonder on her face when he'd entered her.

Then the hurt in her eyes when he had failed to return her words of love.

What a damn fool he was! After she had sent him away, he'd plunged into the depths of misery. He had been wretched at the thought of losing Blythe. It was a feeling unlike anything he'd ever known. His turmoil could not be attributed merely to the failure of his scheme to entrap her.

There was only one explanation. He really *had* fallen in love with Blythe. Hopelessly, stupidly, in love.

Yet when he'd told her so as Prince Nicolai, when he had sunk to his knees and bared his heart, she had scorned him.

How could he blame her? Blythe was right to mistrust him. She sensed he had a secret purpose she likely thought him a fortune hunter. She couldn't know that his true motive was far, far worse.

He intended to use Blythe in order to expose her parents as imposters. Those two must be tried in a court of law and punished for their crime. But first, Edith had to come face to face with Mrs. Bleasdale, the elderly woman James believed to be her mother. Edith must be lured to Lancashire.

James burned to know what had happened to his cousin and his wife. His love for Blythe must not stand in the way of justice. But with every passing moment, he felt his chances with her slipping away.

Abandoning the silver, he stalked to the kitchen, Minx at his heels. The assistant cook stood at the stove, stirring a large pot.

"Miss Crompton has requested a tea tray," James told her.

The stout woman stared at him in befuddlement. “Meg took one not ’alf an ’our ago.”

“A fresh pot of tea,” James amended. “The first one was cold.”

Grumbling, the woman shuffled to the hearth to pour the hot water and add the leaves. He took the dainty porcelain pot from her, set it on a silver tray, and headed toward the servants’ staircase.

Minx trotted after him. “Stay,” he told her.

The mutt plopped down on the bottom step, head cocked mournfully and tail barely wagging.

James trudged up the narrow stairs. What could he possibly say to Blythe? How the devil was he to convince her to abandon her family and friends, to give up London society in exchange for an uncertain life as the wife of a common servant?

Of course, he couldn’t reveal that he was really a gentleman. Nor could he say that by marrying him, she would be securing her future.

Everything her father owned rightfully belonged to James. As his wife, Blythe could continue to live in the lavish manner to which she was accustomed. It would be difficult for her to endure the scandal of her parents’ crimes, but at least she would have the protection of James’s name. The gossip would die down in time. With the aid of her sisters, she might even be accepted in society again.

But would she ever forgive him? That was a question for which James had no answer.

As he walked down the opulent upstairs corridor, his steps faltered. A footman stood on duty outside Blythe’s bedchamber door.

Anger stabbed into James. Blast Edith! The dragon had actually imprisoned Blythe as punishment for refusing the two offers of marriage.

The tray balanced on his palm, he strode forward and greeted the freckled young man. "Laycock," he said with a nod. "I've been sent to relieve you. You're to finish polishing the silver."

Laycock looked perplexed. "But Godwin said—"

"He'll be angry if you don't finish the task before dinner. Now, I presume the bedchamber is locked, so give me the key. I'll need to deliver this teapot to Miss Crompton."

Laycock fished the key from his pocket, handed it to James, and took off down the passageway.

James turned the skeleton key in the lock, then rapped lightly. A moment later, the door opened a crack and Blythe peered out.

Her face looked wan, her hair charmingly mussed, her eyes a little red as if she'd been weeping. There were wrinkles in the skirt of her lemon-yellow gown. She had never looked more beautiful.

Or further out of his reach.

"May I come in?" he asked gently.

James didn't know what he'd do if she refused him. Push his way inside? Force her to listen to him? Fall to his knees and beg?

But she stepped aside to give him space to enter. Twilight had cast shadows throughout the room. A single candle burned on the bedside table. The large four-poster was rumpled, the coverlet and pillows in disarray. He ached to coax her there right now. To kiss her until they both forgot all their troubles in pleasure . . .

Amora chirped sleepily in the brass cage by the window. It was enough to snap James out of his untimely fantasy.

He carried the tray to the table, where another tea tray already sat untouched. Setting down the pot, he turned to face Blythe. She stood watching him, her back to the closed door, her arms crossed.

The guarded look in her eyes was not encouraging.

A host of charming compliments stuck in his throat. But she appeared in no humor to suffer platitudes from him. It would be cowardly to hide behind such shallowness, anyway.

"I was worried about you," he said. "They were talking below stairs that you'd had a terrible row with your parents."

She nodded. "Mama and Papa weren't very happy that I'd turned down two such brilliant offers. Of course, I couldn't tell them that one was not quite so exceptional as they believed."

"Prince Nicolai."

"Mm-hmm. By the by, how did you talk my sisters into letting you borrow the clothing again?"

"I took Minx on a walk to Pallister House. I told Lady Mansfield about the duke's visit, and that Prince Nicolai would find some way to thwart him."

Blythe's spine remained glued to the door. "Lindsey and Portia will be anxious to know everything. I wonder if they'll come to call."

"I told them afterward that you'd rebuffed the duke, and they seemed quite satisfied to hear that." He softened his voice to a husky murmur. "Of course I didn't mention Prince Nicolai's proposal—or your refusal of it."

She dipped her chin and gazed at him through the screen of her lashes. "Why did you do it, James? Why did you say what you said?"

He knew exactly what she meant. She was referring not to his offer of marriage, but to his declaration of love.

The dusk had grown so thick that he couldn't read the look in her eyes. But he had the keen sense that whatever he said next would determine his future. Although he didn't dare reveal his secret purpose, he at least could admit the truth about what she meant to him.

James took a step toward her. "I couldn't let you marry any other man, Blythe. Ever since we met, you've occupied all of my thoughts, all of my dreams. I'm obsessed with you, with the way you move, the way you speak, the way you smile." He spread his hands out wide. "I don't know if that's love. I've never been in love before. But . . . you mean more to me than anyone else in the world. Last night was the single most incredible experience of my life—"

He broke off. She had darted forward to lay her head on his shoulder and to slide her arms around his waist. "Yes, I'll marry you," she said breathily. "*Yes*."

Awash in amazement, he clasped her close. He could scarcely believe she had just agreed to become his wife. *His wife*. He closed his eyes to hold back the unmanly prickle of tears. He concentrated on savoring the faint flowery scent of her hair and the womanly curves of her body. He didn't ever want to let go of her. "But you refused me last night. And then again this afternoon when I said I loved you."

"I didn't want to accept the prince. I wanted to accept *you*, James. Only you."

Tilting her face up, Blythe stood on tiptoe to brush her lips over his. A vast tenderness filled him, a feeling that was far richer than mere physical lust. James joined their mouths in a deep kiss, threading his fingers into her hair to hold her in place for fear she might change her mind. It was humbling to realize that Blythe would give up everything . . . her family, her status, her wealth. For *him*, a man she believed to be a mere footman.

What had he done in his misbegotten life to deserve such love?

The question faded beneath the intoxicating taste of her, the feel of that shapely form pressed against him. She was everything he had ever dreamed of in a woman—and so much more. In the past, he had given only negligible thought to marriage. So long as there were experienced women who were willing to slake his needs, what was the point?

But now he understood. With Blythe in his arms, he felt . . . complete. She belonged to him, as he belonged to her. No other man could ever touch her. He wanted to spend the remainder of his life making her happy.

If she didn't hate him when she found out the truth.

Drawing back slightly, he gazed deeply into her eyes and spoke in the voice of Prince Nicolai. "Such a kiss will be immortalized by the bards for a thousand years to come."

She laughed. "But it wasn't our *first* kiss."

"It was love's first kiss. Can you forgive me for being such a fool?"

In the candlelight, Blythe had stars in her eyes. "Oh, James, of course I can." She looked sweetly naïve, at least until her fingers ventured below his waist. "Can we—? Dare we—?"

Lust threatened to swamp his common sense. "Absolutely not. There are people about. And I'm supposed to be on duty outside, guarding the door."

Blythe ran her fingertips over his erection. "We could be swift. Without completely undressing, perhaps?"

His willpower crumbled and he made haste across the room to turn the key in the lock. When he returned, Blythe sat on the edge of the bed with her skirt drawn to her waist. She gave him a sinful smile. Lord! She was every man's dream. While they kissed open-mouthed, James opened his breeches and then caressed her between her legs, finding her damp and ready.

He slid his hands beneath her bottom and lifted her a bit for his entry. As he pressed into her heat, she moaned, lying back slightly while braced on her elbows. Her fingers clutched at the coverlet while he moved rhythmically. He glanced down at the place they were joined, and saw her watching, too, her eyes heavy-lidded with desire.

Her breath coming faster, she closed her eyes. Gritting his teeth against an early release, he quickened his pace, working her with swift, urgent strokes. With stunning swiftness, she shuddered and cried out, her inner muscles clenching around him. One final plunge sent him over the edge into white-hot rapture.

He collapsed on top of her, his labored breathing gradually slowing. As coherent thought returned, he nuzzled her hair and basked in perfect contentment. Never had he known a woman quite like Blythe, so sweet and yet so sensual. Although he felt utterly sated, James was sorry the act was over. He could hold her like this forever.

He opened his eyes to find her gazing softly at him. They kissed and caressed for some minutes, a tender and gentle interlude that he relished as much as the wild passion they had just shared. The closeness he felt with her far surpassed anything he had ever known.

She took his face in her hands. "My parents will never give us their blessing."

The reminder hung over him like a dark cloud. "Indeed," he murmured. "And they'll cut you off without a penny. I only pray to God you can forgive me for separating you from them."

James held her tightly, not wanting her to see the guilt in his face. But she pulled back, saying, "We *are* going to run away together, aren't we? We'll go to Gretna Green. I am ready to leave right now."

He chuckled. "It will take a little time for me to make the arrangements. And there's the small matter of smuggling you out of the house."

"Tonight, James, *please*. I don't think I can bear to stay here a moment longer. I want to be with you, always."

His chest tightened. Everything in him balked at the prospect of causing her pain. What if he abandoned the whole scheme? What if he whisked her away to some corner of the world where no one would ever find them?

The thought held the allure of temptation. But then he would always be hiding a secret from Blythe, the truth about his identity. Their life together would be a lie.

He also would never learn what had happened to his cousin. The crimes against the real George and Edith would go unpunished. James felt the crushing weight of obligation to seek justice for them. His own wants and desires must not deter that.

A scratching sounded at the door.

Blythe gasped. She sat up and gazed at him in shock, hastily rearranging her skirt. "Is it Mama?" she whispered.

James shook his head. "I believe I know who."

He buttoned his breeches, then went to turn the key and open the door. Just as he'd suspected, Minx bounded into the bedchamber.

After a swift glance to see that the corridor was empty, James shut the door again. "I must not have securely latched the staircase door," he said. "Minx is becoming quite adept at pushing open doors."

Blythe crouched down to pet the dog. "What a clever girl! You found my room all by yourself."

Wagging her tail, Minx lapped Blythe's hand.

Blythe cuddled the dog close and gave James a pleading look. "Can we take her along with us when we go? Please?"

"I'm sure there will be space for one little mutt. But I do draw the line at bringing the bird."

"Kasi will watch over Princess Amora," Blythe said. "Now, you'll need to hire a post-chaise and horses. I'll fetch you some coins."

She vanished into the adjoining dressing room, Minx at her heels. James set his jaw. It stung his pride to take her money. He wanted to be the one providing for her. But in his role of penniless footman, there was no other way. He could hardly produce his own funds without stirring her suspicions.

What a tangled web of deception he had woven! And it was far from over. Little did Blythe realize, he was a cad of the worst ilk.

Instead of honoring her love, he would repay her with betrayal.

Chapter 28

In the soft light of late afternoon, Blythe leaned against James on the seat of the well-sprung carriage. Minx lay curled up asleep on the blanket in her lap. The sway of the vehicle had a lulling effect on Blythe, although she felt too full of life to slumber. She wanted to treasure every moment of this marvelous day.

The narrow gold band on her finger glinted in the sunlight. She was Mrs. Ryding now. Mrs. James Ryding.

The joy of being his wife made the rigors of the long journey all worthwhile.

It was hard to believe that only three days ago, she had been in London, worried about her future and wracked with uncertainty about James. Then he had come to her bedchamber and declared his love and she had never looked back. They'd left at midnight and driven through the dark, while she'd dozed against him. How James had managed to stay awake, she still didn't know. Then, the following two nights, they had stopped for a few hours at posting inns, posing as husband and wife.

Now they were truly married by Scottish law. At mid-morning, they had arrived at Gretna Green, a village right over the border. The wedding ceremony had been a hurried affair performed by the blacksmith and witnessed by his stout wife and a serving maid. Afterward, James had not wished to tarry because Blythe's father would have sent men in pursuit of them. So immediately they had headed south again, avoiding the main road this time.

Blythe felt a little pang at the thought of her parents. James had left them a sealed note, and he'd told her what was in it—a testament to his love for their daughter and his firm commitment to take excellent care of her. That would have to satisfy them for now.

For most of the day, they had been driving through the Lake District. Around every bend lay a breathtaking new sight, a crystal blue lake nestled between rugged mountains, a waterfall coursing down a sheer cliff, herds of sheep grazing on verdant hills.

"I had no idea England had such gorgeous scenery," she marveled. "Cumbria reminds me a little of the foothills of the Himalayas. We traveled there sometimes to escape the heat of the summer."

"Someday, I'll show you Lake Windermere and the area around Grasmere. Although, by the way, we're in Lancashire now. We entered it at the last village."

"Lancashire!" She looked out at the rolling landscape and the cluster of cottages in the distance. "My parents are from somewhere around here. And this is where you grew up, too, isn't it?"

James nodded, his eyes on the winding road. "I haven't been back in many years. I left shortly after my father's death."

He had been sixteen, she recalled, all alone in the world. "Where did you go, then?"

"I worked here and there, including a good deal of time in the West Indies." He laid his hand over hers, looking away from the road for a moment to search her eyes. "I *am* sorry we've had to travel so far and so fast, Blythe. You must be weary of being jostled about for days on end."

She laced her fingers with his. "I don't mind, so long as we're together."

He gave her that crooked smile, the one that always stirred heat inside her. Then he returned his attention to the horses. "There's a place I'd like to show you not far from here," he said. "But don't ask me to elaborate, it shall be a surprise."

He refused to tell her, no matter how much she begged, instead pointing out landmarks and other sights: a badger waddling through the bushes and a hawk wheeling against the cloudless blue sky.

The sun was sinking on the horizon as James drove the carriage between a pair of stone pillars and down a wide avenue that meandered through a stand of ancient oak trees. He deftly guided the horses around the potholes in the graveled road. On either side stretched more of the drystone fencing that seemed ubiquitous to the area.

"There," he said, pointing ahead. "That's what I wanted to show you."

In the pink and gold of sunset, an ivy-covered mansion sat on a gentle knoll against a thicket of trees. Mullioned windows marched across the stone front and many chimneys dotted the roof. Sheep grazed the undulating green lawn that stretched up to the house. The place had a warm, homey feel to it that instantly appealed to Blythe.

"How very lovely!" she exclaimed. "Do you know who lives here?"

"The owners are no longer in residence." James gave her a strange, tight smile. "This is Crompton Abbey, the house where your parents once lived."

She gasped in surprise, immediately scrutinizing the place again with a sharper eye. "But . . . Mama said it was a tumbledown ruin. I wonder why we've never come here in the summer. It would have been far more pleasant than staying in London."

"Perhaps your father couldn't leave his shipping business."

"It still seems as though they would have at least wanted to visit the place." Blythe could not imagine a reason why her parents would shun such an idyllic setting. "How did you know where to find it?"

James shrugged. "When you grow up in the country, you learn the location of all the large estates in the area."

"You were a boy, then. Did you ever encounter my parents?"

He glanced away, staring at the house. "No. We did not frequent the same social circles."

His voice held a hard note. Of course, James had not been a member of the upper class, though he had been raised as a gentleman. Had he felt resentment of his lot in life? Did he wish he too belonged to the gentry?

Blythe longed to heal the wounds of his past, whatever they might be. It was thrilling to know that as his wife, she would have that chance.

There was no time to ponder the matter further, for James was directing the pair of horses down the drive toward the front portico. She glanced quizzically at him. "Are we stopping, then?"

"Even better, we're spending the night here." He leaned closer to brush his mouth over hers. "Our wedding night."

Though a shiver of pleasure swept through her, Blythe felt troubled at the prospect of barging in unannounced. "But no one's expecting us."

"There will be a housekeeper and a skeleton staff, I expect. They will not turn us away, especially as you are the daughter of the owners." He flashed a roguish smile. "Consider it an adventure."

James was right. How exciting it would be to see

where her parents had lived before they'd moved to India so long ago. There was no danger of discovery, either. Papa would never think to look for her here. And even if any of the staff should chance to send word to London, she and James would be long gone by then.

As he drew the horses to a halt, she slipped her arm around him. "Oh, James, this is the most wonderful wedding gift you could ever have given me."

He stared intently at her, a muscle working in his jaw. "Blythe, I hope—"

James compressed his lips without completing the statement. Again, she had an impression of dark emotions roiling in him. What was its source? Was he perhaps reflecting on all that he could not give to her because he lacked the funds? Blythe would just have to prove to him that none of that mattered so long as she had him in her life.

The front door opened and a lumpy, middle-aged woman shuffled out onto the porch. She wore a mobcap on her head and a white apron over her gray gown. Arms akimbo, she squinted at the carriage, her demeanor radiating curiosity.

James jumped down from the high perch and came around to the other side. He set Minx on the ground and the dog went sniffing the grass that edged the drive. Then his strong hands lifted Blythe down. Her legs felt stiff from sitting and she leaned gratefully against him as they mounted the granite steps to the porch.

He nodded to the servant. "You are the housekeeper here, I presume?"

She looked him over warily. "Aye, Mrs. Grimshaw, I am."

"I'm Mr. James Ryding, and this is my wife, Blythe. Her parents are George and Edith Crompton."

Mrs. Grimshaw's jaw dropped. Her brown eyes grew large. "No one told me that family was coming."

"Well, here we are. We have been traveling all day, and we would like your best bedchamber prepared at once. We'll need a hot bath as well and a meal delivered to the room."

"Sir! I-I've little provisions for fancy folk."

James gave her a cool stare. "Cold meat and cheese will suffice. I'm sure you can manage something simple. And do send a man for the horses, will you? In the meanwhile, my wife and I shall be taking a tour of the house."

His hand resting at the base of Blythe's spine, he guided her past the dumbfounded woman and into a pleasant, though rustic, entrance hall with a suit of armor on display and tapestries on the wood-paneled walls. Minx trotted inside after them, her claws clicking on the checkered marble floor. Mrs. Grimshaw vanished down a corridor.

Untying her bonnet ribbons, Blythe tilted her head back to admire the paneled walls and the fine oak staircase. But she wrinkled her nose at the musty smell of a house kept closed up too long.

"What a pity the place has gone unused for so many years," she said, her voice echoing. "If I lived here, the very first thing I would do would be to air out the place."

"An excellent notion," James said, striding to one of the windows flanking the door. He wrestled with a stubborn latch, then pushed open the window so that a cool, fresh breeze eddied through the foyer.

Since Mrs. Grimshaw had gone to do their bidding and there didn't appear to be any other servants around, they left their wraps on a chair before exploring the house.

Arm in arm, they wandered through rooms filled with old furnishings, the chairs and chaises shrouded by white dust cloths. Minx scampered after them, sniffing all the corners. They discovered a cozy parlor for sitting, a library with tall shelves full of old books, and a breakfast room that looked out over a tangled, overgrown rose garden. The whole place had a charming air of shabby elegance.

James ran his forefinger over a carved wood mantel, and it came away gray with dust. "Mrs. Grimshaw does not appear to have high standards of cleanliness."

"Perhaps she hasn't had sufficient help," Blythe said. "Were it up to me, I would hire a team of maids to make everything shine."

"You like the house, then?"

"Very much so!" she exclaimed as they strolled into a dining chamber. She stopped to admire an exquisitely carved chair at the head of a long mahogany table. "I'm trying to imagine my parents sitting here for dinner when they were first married. Do you suppose there's a portrait of them anywhere in the house?"

James gave her a piercing stare before turning to examine the large hunting scene that hung over the fireplace. "I haven't seen one."

She tucked her arm through his again. "Well, dust or not, the house appears to be in good condition. Is there an estate agent, I wonder? If so, he must have sent an erroneous report to my parents."

"If you like, I'll look into the matter. But not tonight." Smiling, James rubbed his thumb over her lower lip. "Tonight I have other plans."

A bone-deep tremor of excitement gripped Blythe. For the first time, they would be joined as husband and wife. She could scarcely wait to lie in bed with him, with the entire night stretched out before them. "It's growing dark outside," she said, glancing at the window. "Shall we go, then, and see if our room is ready?"

She expected him to laugh, but instead he gathered her close, his arms enveloping her in a tight embrace. His hands moved up and down her back, and he murmured into her hair, "I don't deserve you, Blythe. You're far too good for me."

A little puzzled by his shift in mood, she renewed her resolve to make him happy. "I do not wish for either of us to be *good*," she said. "In truth, I vastly prefer you to be very wicked."

This time, he chuckled, and they headed upstairs. It was a simple matter to find their quarters since a straggling line of servants was hauling large tins of steaming water through a door at the end of the passageway. Mrs. Grimshaw was nowhere in sight.

"I'll give you a few moments alone while I check on the horses," James murmured before he went striding down the dim passageway.

Venturing inside, Blythe found a spacious bedchamber with heavy old furniture and burgundy hangings. A lighted branch of candles sat on a table and a wood fire burned on the grate. One maid was changing the bed linens while two others filled a brass tub in front of the fireplace. Blythe greeted them with a smile and a word of thanks, then went to open the casement window to the cool evening air.

A deep purple twilight shrouded the front lawn. Clusters of sheep huddled together against the backdrop of hills and trees. How amazing to think that this magnificent house was a part of her family's heritage.

One of the maids helped undo the buttons at the back of Blythe's gown, then Blythe dismissed the servants. She left her clothing in the dressing room and hurried naked into the chilly bedchamber.

Shivering, she gratefully lowered herself into the oval copper tub. It was scarcely large enough to hold her, and she could only sit with her knees crooked up. But the warm water felt wonderful and there was a cake of lavender soap that smelled heavenly.

A few moments later, the door opened and James stepped inside. He was carrying a tray, which he placed on the nearest table. The heat in his eyes sparked a slow burn inside Blythe. Their gazes held as he walked toward her while stripping off his coat and then his shirt, letting them fall to the floor.

She slowly ran the cake of soap over her breasts. James watched, his eyes at half mast, as he sat on a stool to remove his boots. Then he sauntered closer while unbuttoning his breeches. He shucked off the garment, giving her a spectacular view of him in full arousal. Blythe lifted a hand out of the water to touch him, but he knelt beside the tub.

"Not yet," he said, taking the soap.

He plunged his hands into the water and began to wash her. She tilted her head back against the rim of the tub and reveled in the slick glide of his fingers over her body. He teased her for a time before commencing a more intimate exploration that soon had her crying out from the pulsating bliss of release.

As she lay relaxed and happy, James lifted her dripping from the tub. He wrapped her in a linen towel and carried her to the bed. There, he stood over her and dabbed the moisture from her body, bending down to kiss her all over. Then Blythe took charge by drawing him down beside her and commencing an investigation of her own. She reveled in their differences; where he was hard, she was soft. Discovering all the ways to pleasure him imbued her with joy. When at last he entered her, their first joining as man and wife held whispered words of love and the perfection of mutually shared ecstasy.

Afterward, James brought over the tray and they ate cold chicken and cheese in bed, talking and laughing about inconsequential matters. There was even a bottle of red wine and two glasses.

Blythe sat wrapped in a blanket, which by artful design kept slipping low on her breasts. Oh, she relished the way James looked at her. She enjoyed gazing at him, too, watching the gleam of candlelight on the muscles of his naked chest. Nothing tonight would interrupt them. . . .

"Minx!" she said suddenly. "Where is she?"

"The lone stable boy on staff is watching her. When I left the kitchen, he was already spoiling her with table scraps. And speaking of feeding"—James leaned forward to pop a morsel of chicken into Blythe's mouth—"I've had fantasies about serving you like this."

"Mm." She ate the bite while regarding him curiously. "Odd, how you've never really seemed like a footman to me."

He lowered his gaze to the slice of bread he was buttering. "Perhaps because the position has never appealed to me. I vastly prefer to be my own man, and to spend my time outdoors."

Blythe watched him, wondering how to broach the topic of his prospects without offending his pride. "James, I intend to write to my parents on the morrow. I must plead our case with them and ask them to accept our marriage. You mentioned once going to India to make your fortune. I would very much like to invite my father to help you."

His face darkening, James shook his head. "After I stole his daughter? He will want nothing to do with me."

"But you could manage one of his offices there and learn about the shipping business—"

He pressed his finger to her lips. "I need no one's help in providing for you. And never mind the future just yet. All that matters is now."

Pushing away the tray, he pulled her into his arms and touched his lips to hers. He tasted of wine, and by the time he had thoroughly kissed her, she felt too happy to spoil the mood by quarreling.

"Oh, James, I do wish we could stay right here forever."

"As do I."

He left the bed to remove the tray and blow out the candles. In the semidarkness of the dying fire, he settled her against the length of his body, snuggling with her beneath the covers. "I want only your happiness, Blythe. I pray you always know what you mean to me." His voice lowered to a husky murmur. "You are the love of my life."

She basked in the glow of his words, while noticing how tightly he held her. Did he fear she could ever scorn him? "I love you, too. So very much. And don't *you* ever forget that, either."

⁂

The chirping of birds awakened Blythe. Daylight poured through a crack in the curtains, slanting across the canopied bed. A marvelous sense of well-being permeated her. She lay alone, and the pillow beside her still bore the impression of James's head.

She stretched luxuriously, enjoying the slide of the linens against her bare skin. How decadent it was to lie naked in the tangled sheets, to remember all the ways James had pleased her. Twice more during the night, they had made love, and it had been wonderful to awaken in the darkness to the caress of his hands on her body. Each time they had fallen asleep together, her back to his chest.

You are the love of my life.

She looked forward to sharing a bed with him forever. Her husband. To think that a few months ago, she hadn't even known James existed. Now, she couldn't imagine life without him.

Where had he gone? Perhaps to take Minx out for a walk on the grounds? James had an energetic vitality that demanded action of him. He must have let her sleep late on purpose, to make up for the days of travel and their vigorous activity during the night.

But she would not waste a single moment of this day.

Blythe slid out of bed, her bare toes curling against the chilly floorboards. She drew open the draperies and glanced outside. There was no clock in the chamber, but the slant of the sun told her it was mid-morning. Did James intend for them to stay here for a time? She hoped so. It was the perfect place for their honeymoon.

She strolled into the dressing room to ready herself. Having no maidservant to assist her, she chose a pale blue gown because it had the fewest buttons. Unfortunately, it was sadly wrinkled from being stuffed in her portmanteau. There had been precious little space for her belongings. But she didn't mind giving up her vast wardrobe. In her new life, she would have no use for fancy ball gowns.

Humming under her breath, Blythe returned to the window. While arranging her hair in a loose knot, she looked out over the rolling front lawn. The pastoral scene enhanced her sense of contentment. Sheep cropped the grass, and a stream glinted in a distant copse of trees.

Gradually, the noise of hoof beats and rattling wheels caught her attention. Having finished her hair, she leaned on the stone casement and gazed out in curiosity as a fine black coach appeared around a bend in the drive.

It was heading toward the house.

Blythe drew back in faint alarm. Had one of the neighbors learned of their arrival? Would there be sticky questions about their presence here?

She mustn't worry. She and James had a perfect right to stay at Crompton Abbey. Any visitor would have to be received and placated and then sent on their way.

The coachman drew the vehicle to a stop in front of the porch. Her gaze went to the footman who jumped down to lower the step. His blue livery looked disturbingly familiar. . . .

At the same moment, the door opened. Two people emerged from the coach, a woman in a dark hooded cloak and a middle-aged man in a top hat and overcoat.

Her mother and father.

Chapter 29

Her hand stifling a gasp, Blythe backed away from the window. All the happiness leached out of her, leaving her cold and anxious. How in the world had her parents found them so swiftly? Had she and James been spotted on the road? Even so, it seemed impossible for anyone to have guessed where they had been going.

Perhaps her parents were merely stopping here on their way to Gretna Green. They might have no idea at all that she and James were staying here.

But not even that made sense. Why not head straight to Scotland?

One thing was certain. She would not cower like a child here in the bedchamber. Explanations must be made to her parents, their feelings soothed, their objections overcome. They must be coaxed into understanding that she had chosen James as her husband and they would accept him—or lose her forever.

With trembling hands, she checked her appearance in the pier glass. Oh, how she wished she'd asked Mrs. Grimshaw to iron her gown. Blythe wanted to be dressed in her very finest for this difficult interview. Mama might infer that a slovenly appearance reflected upon Blythe taking up with a man of the lower classes.

Nothing could be more wrong. They simply *must* be made to see the goodness in James.

Where was he, anyway? Perhaps it was best if he had gone for a walk. A long walk would keep him away from the house for a while. By making haste, she might be able to plead her case and calm her parents somewhat before they confronted him.

Oh, heavens! Papa would be furious that she'd run off with a footman. He might even attempt to punch James. Papa had nearly done that very thing when Colin had kidnapped Portia two years ago—and Colin was a peer of the realm.

How much worse James would fare!

Blythe hurried down the broad oak staircase. The great hall was empty, but the sound of voices drew her down the corridor to the library. Her heart pounding, she stepped through the doorway.

There, she halted in dismay. James already faced her parents in the center of the room. Papa stood rigidly at attention in front of a massive stone fireplace. He gave Blythe a troubled stare, but his lips were taut and she wasn't sure if he would welcome a hug from her.

She was startled to see her mother curtsying to James. "Your Highness," she said. "We came as soon as we could."

Blythe swallowed an hysterical laugh. Of course, her parents knew him as Prince Nicolai.

James must not have mentioned in his note to them that he was a footman. Perhaps he had feared to anger them even further.

She went to James and slipped her arm through his. "Mama, Papa, I'm sorry you had to travel halfway across the country. I never wanted to cause you any worry. But now that you're here, I would like you to meet my—"

"Blythe," James cut in. "Go back upstairs. I'll handle this matter."

"No. I won't leave you here to suffer their recriminations alone."

"We are not so terribly unhappy," Mrs. Crompton said with a wan smile, as she removed her gloves and cloak and set them on a chair. "After all, you are now Princess Blythe of Ambrosia."

"But Mama, I'm *not*. You don't understand—"

"Do you mean to say he hasn't married you?" Her father stepped toward them. He shook his fist at James. "You lied in your letter summoning us here. Have you ruined her, then? By God! Royal or not, you're a bounder of the worst sort!"

James half pushed her toward the door. "Go," he ordered. *"Now."*

She balked, digging in her heels. His tone held a harshness that she couldn't comprehend. "Do stop, James! It's very gallant of you, but you needn't protect me from my own parents."

"James?" her mother asked. "Why are you calling him James?"

"He isn't Prince Nicolai, Mama. He never was. It was merely a silly ruse. His name is James Ryding, and we were married yesterday."

The effect on her parents was stunning. Her father froze in his tracks, his face turning deathly pale, his fist falling to his side. Her mother staggered back a step and clapped her hand to her mouth. Both of them were gazing wide-eyed at James.

As if they'd seen a ghost.

"James Ryding," her mother whispered. "Oh, dear God . . ."

A clock bonged somewhere in the bowels of the house.

Blythe looked from her parents to James. They were staring at him as if they'd forgotten her presence here. She sensed an undercurrent that puzzled her.

"Then you *do* realize that James is a footman?" she asked.

Papa gave her the oddest look. "A footman?"

"Yes," James said coolly. "I've been employed in your London house since the start of the season."

He again took Blythe by the arm and steered her toward the open doorway. There, he caressed her cheek as if willing her to obey. "It's best you go upstairs, truly it is. I beg you, darling, trust me on this."

Blythe hardly knew what to think. What was going on that he was trying to protect her from knowing?

A noise came from the passageway behind her: the shuffle of feet.

James cursed under his breath.

Coming down the corridor was a thin old woman dressed in homespun garb and assisted by an elderly gentleman. There was something about the man that tugged at her memory.

James's fingers pressed into her back. "In the name of God, *go*."

Urgency glittered in his dark eyes. She had the strangest feeling that whatever was happening here would finally provide the key to understanding him. "No, James. I'm staying."

⁂

Bleak with despair, James watched her walk back into the library. Her presence dealt a mortal blow to any hope he'd had of shielding her from this confrontation. Short of using bodily force, he could not eject her from the room.

The note of instruction he'd left for her parents had specified this appointment here today. They were to arrive not a moment earlier or later than the designated time. Surmising that Edith would be too fearful to come to Lancashire, James had signed the letter as Prince Nicolai, on the theory that she would not be able to resist assuring herself of a marriage between her daughter and the prince.

There had only been the problem of how to safeguard Blythe.

God! She had been slumbering peacefully when he'd left her. While making love to her half the night, he had been desperate to imbue her with a fire that could never be extinguished. He'd wanted her to remain abed until this interview was over and her parents gone. Then he could find some means to gently break the story of his true identity.

Yet perhaps this way was for the best. It would be a fast, if devastating, blow. She would learn the whole sordid story. There would be no more secrets between them.

She also would find out who her parents really were. She would know who he was.

And that knowledge would destroy her trust in him.

He waved the approaching pair to a bench just outside the door. "Wait here," he murmured.

Fighting dread, James stepped back into the library.

Blythe was guiding her mother to a wing chair. "Do sit, Mama. You look as if you're about to swoon. I never meant to upset you so."

"Blythe," her father said heavily. "You should obey . . . your husband. Leave this room."

"I'm staying," she reaffirmed. "There is nothing any of you can say to stop me." Going to her father, she briefly rested her head on his shoulder. "Oh, Papa, I promise you will like James if only you give him a chance. He may be a footman, but you'll see he's more a gentleman than any of the lords I met in society."

Watching them, James faced the ugly moment of truth. The moment when Blythe would find out just how she had been duped.

"Blythe, I *am* a gentleman by birth," he said. "I was merely posing as a footman."

She gazed at him blankly. "What?"

"Your parents know precisely who I am." He turned his gaze on George Crompton. "I would venture to guess my name was a topic of great interest to them over the years."

George—or whoever he was—said nothing. Edith caught an audibly ragged breath.

"I don't understand," Blythe said. "Why would they know your name?"

Hardening his heart, he met her gaze without flinching. "I was born James Ryding Crompton. George Crompton is—or *was*—my cousin."

He watched the terrible light of comprehension enter her beautiful eyes. Little did she know, it would be worse in a few minutes.

Far worse.

"But . . ." Blythe shook her head in denial. "That would mean . . . we're related by blood."

"No, we are not. You'll understand in a moment." Hands on his hips, he walked back and forth in front of the doorway. "As you know, my father died when I was sixteen. Ever since, I've been living in the West Indies on a plantation that was my only inheritance. About a year ago, I received a letter from Percy Thornton, the retired estate agent here at Crompton Abbey. He told me that he had visited George Crompton in London to ask him for a pension. Thornton had reason to suspect that the man was not my cousin at all. He believed George was an imposter—as was his wife."

Blythe made a small sound of disbelief. She sank onto the edge of a chair as if her legs would no longer hold her upright. Her incredulous gaze flitted to her parents, then back to him. "Imposters? Papa—and Mama? Why would you believe such a ludicrous tale?"

"I didn't at first. I hadn't seen them since I was a boy of ten, so I sought a position in their house where I could observe them. Eventually, I was able to determine that Thornton was correct in his assumption."

"I remember you now," George said coldly. "You were snooping in Edith's bedchamber one night, while she was away at a ball."

"Yes." James held the man's gaze until he looked away in obvious guilt.

Staring down at the unlit hearth, Blythe's father ran his fingers through his thinning hair. "I knew it would eventually come to this," he muttered. "We should never have returned to England."

"Hush," Edith said fiercely. "I deny these allegations. They are *false*. He cannot prove any of it."

"I have the letter," James said. "The one from your prayer book."

Edith gave him a stark look of horror.

He stepped to the doorway and motioned to the old couple. Percy Thornton helped the woman into the library. Frail and white-haired, Mrs. Bleasdale had difficulty walking. Despite the infirmity, however, her hazel eyes held a spark of vitality in the wrinkled landscape of her face.

It was a look that James recognized well.

God help him. She was Blythe's grandmother. He had been so absorbed in his scheme that he'd overlooked that fact.

Blythe had no notion of it, either. When he glanced at her, she regarded him with wary reproach. Her expression was skeptical, as if she suspected him of making all this up for some evil, unknown purpose.

He wanted desperately to take her into his arms, to reassure her of his love. But he had destroyed her faith in him. When she realized the full ramifications of her situation, it would only make matters worse.

Yet he had no choice but to see this through.

He took the woman's arm and guided her to Edith. "This is the woman whose letter you saved for years. Your mother, Mrs. Hannah Bleasdale. You wrote to her and told her that her daughter, Mercy, was dead."

Edith sat rigidly in the chair. Her fingers gripped like claws to the arms. She had the frightened look of a cornered animal.

"Are ye my little Mercy? Can it really be true?" A quavering smile on her elfin face, Mrs. Bleasdale reached out a palsied hand. "Why, ye are, praise be to God! Here ye are alive and garbed like a fancy lady!"

Edith buried her face in her hands. Her slim body shook with silent sobs.

Mrs. Bleasdale shuffled forward and wrapped her arms around Edith. "There, there, my girl. 'Tis a day for celebration, not tears. My little Mercy, home again after all these years."

James had anticipated this moment for weeks. By allowing the woman to embrace her, Edith had as much as admitted Mrs. Bleasdale was her mother. Thornton stood by the door as his witness. James now had the proof of foul play.

But instead of satisfaction, he felt hollow inside. Edith continued to weep noiselessly, and he could not take pleasure in her downfall.

Blythe stared wide-eyed at the pair of them. "Papa, I don't understand. Is she really . . . my grandmother?"

George stood with his shoulders bowed, his hands gripping the back of a chair. "Yes, my dear, she is."

"Why did you not tell me? You and Mama always said we had no living relatives."

"He didn't dare admit the truth," James said. "Because to do so would be to acknowledge his own crime—that he and Mercy Bleasdale had taken over the lives of my cousin and his wife." Burning with renewed anger, James took a step toward him. "You will confess the rest of this sordid story. I want to know who you are and what you know about the disappearance of my cousin and his wife in India."

Blythe sprang up from the chair. "What are you saying?" she cried out. "Do you dare to suggest that my father is a murderer?"

Her outrage was a blow to his heart. But he could not back down now. "That question is for him to answer."

George lifted his head, his face desolate. "I assure you, sir, I am no killer. But you're right, it *is* time the truth be known. It has been a millstone around my neck all these years."

"*No,*" Edith whispered, pulling away from Mrs. Bleasdale. "Keep silent, George, you mustn't say a word."

He slashed his hand through the air to silence her. "Enough! The charade is over." He turned his somber gaze on James. "As you've already guessed, my wife is really Mercy Bleasdale. She was personal maid to your cousin's wife when they sailed to Calcutta. At the time of their arrival, I was a shipping agent in George's firm. I was known then as Timothy Arkwright."

Blythe made a strangled sound of distress. She was sitting on the edge of her chair again, her eyes fixed on her father, her fingers gripping the folds of her skirt. She did not even look at James. How devastated she must be to learn that her own father had been born with a different name, that he had been living a lie.

Just as James had lied to her, too.

"Mercy and I met and married," Arkwright went on. "Shortly thereafter, there was an outbreak of cholera. People were healthy in the morning and dead by nightfall. Since the Cromptons had two young daughters, they decided to take the children out of the city and to the hills, where they would be safe from contagion. I went along, as did Mercy. But we were not far down the road when George and Edith took ill. Neither of them lasted the night."

Was that the truth? James had to conclude so. George—Timothy Arkwright—looked too haunted to be lying. And this time, he had no trouble meeting James's eyes.

"Why did you not report their deaths?"

"People were dying by the hundreds. Everything was chaos, we were traveling . . . and so we decided to pretend to *be* George and Edith, just for a time. The ruse began for the purpose of protecting the girls, so that no other English authorities we encountered might attempt to take them from us. Eventually, we decided to continue the deception. Instead of returning to Calcutta, we traveled to the other side of India, to Bombay, where no one would know us." He opened his hands. "You must understand, Portia and Lindsey were so very young, hardly more than babies. We couldn't abandon them to strangers."

"You might have brought them back to England," James said.

Edith lifted her head from her hands. "There was only your father," she said scornfully. "He was a known profligate. Were we to send two innocent children to live with such a man?"

James conceded the point, although he suspected she'd

also been driven by her own ambition to live as a wealthy lady. "So Blythe is your only true daughter, then."

"Yes, she was born shortly thereafter," Arkwright said, directing a beseeching look at her. "But I assure you, all three girls were raised as sisters. I never showed any favoritism. I love them equally."

Blythe turned her head away, her eyes tightly closed. Her beautiful face was a mask of anguish. James had to leash the frantic need to console her. And not just about the crime of her parents. She must be horrified to learn that Portia and Lindsey were not her sisters by blood.

"I had a knack for trade and commerce," Arkwright went on. "As George Crompton, I had the means to build his shipping company into an extremely successful enterprise. So you see, it is not so terrible a tale. Edith—Mercy—and I acted with the best of intentions."

"The best?" James mocked. "You stole my cousin's identity. You took my inheritance, as well. All of the property should have come to me upon my cousin's death."

Arkwright regarded him steadily. "No. Your father was still alive then, and it would have gone to him. He would have squandered the lot at dicing and cards. Instead, I have increased the Crompton wealth tremendously. The girls were able to make excellent marriages—"

He broke off, no doubt reflecting on the bad marriage his youngest daughter had made in being duped by James.

"We've done no wrong," Edith said brokenly. "No one was harmed. George, he must not be allowed to take everything from us."

"I'm afraid he has the right to do so," Arkwright told her. "The wealth is not ours—it never was. It belongs to him—and to Portia and Lindsey. They are the blood relatives."

Tears in her eyes, Blythe glared at James. "I see now why you eloped with me. You needed me as a pawn in order to lure my parents here. So that Mama could come face to face with"—she glanced at Mrs. Bleasdale—"my grandmother. You did it for the money."

Damn it! Every word she spoke was true. James knew he deserved to be castigated by her. Yet it wrenched his chest to see her look at him so. "Blythe, let me explain. I *did* start out to deceive you. But then I fell in love—"

"No!" She stood up, her fists gripped at her sides. "There will be no more deceit. Not from you . . . not from any of you."

At that moment, Edith also surged to her feet. "He mustn't be allowed to ruin us," she cried out. "I won't let him!"

She lifted her arm and something glinted in her hand. A tiny pistol. It was pointed straight at James.

Chapter 30

Her mother's feral-eyed look shocked Blythe to the core. James stood across the library, near the door. Too far away to save himself.

Blythe acted on instinct. She charged at her mother and seized her arm, thrusting it upward.

A shot exploded. The bullet went wild, striking one of the bookcases. Dust and bits of paper fluttered down from the top shelf.

In the ringing silence, Blythe felt her heart beating so fast that spots swam before her eyes. The acrid scent of gunpowder hung in the air. Dropping the spent pistol, her mother sagged against Blythe.

Papa rushed to take hold of his wife. "Have you gone mad? You could have killed someone!"

"We're ruined, George. *Ruined*. I can't bear it. I simply can't."

Appalled, Blythe stepped back until she bumped into a table. Her legs felt as insubstantial as jelly. Sickness roiled in her belly. Her mother had nearly *killed* James. For the sake of money and status, no less!

Mrs. Bleasdale hovered in the background, her hands to her wrinkled cheeks. Looking at the stooped old woman, Blythe felt separated from reality. Because of her parents' deception, she had never even known her grandmother existed.

Strong arms clasped her from behind. The scent and warmth of James enveloped her. For the barest moment, she leaned into him, craving his comfort. Only hours ago, they had found such perfect happiness together.

But he, too, had been deceiving her.

Swallowing hard, she thrust him away. Tears blurred her vision. "Don't! Don't come near me."

Grim-faced, James regarded her. "I never meant to hurt you, Blythe. I've no excuses to offer except that . . . I had to find out the truth. I can only hope you'll find it in your heart to forgive me."

He extended his hand to her in supplication. As if he expected her to forget his betrayal just like that.

Holding her weeping mother, her father said, "This is my fault. I should never have embarked on such a deception. I blame myself."

"As well you should," Blythe said, needing an outlet for her pain. "Now I know why you and Mama pushed me to marry the duke. So that you'd be above suspicion and no one would ever dare to question your presence in society."

Her father made no reply. He bowed his head, which told her more than mere words could never express.

Heartsick, Blythe glared at all of them.

At her mother, who would kill for profit.

At her father, who was a common thief.

At her husband, who had orchestrated her seduction.

Half an hour ago, they had been the dearest people in the world to her, yet she had not known who they really were. She had been living an illusion, believing herself loved, never doubting her place in the world. But it had just been a charade.

"You are strangers to me, all of you," she lashed out. "I hope never to see any of you ever again."

Then she turned and ran from the library.

⁂

Blythe found herself outdoors. She could not remember opening the door or going down the front steps. But she was sprinting into the hills, following a drystone fence, clutching her skirts to keep from tripping on the uneven ground.

She could scarcely see for the tears in her eyes. The world had become a watery blur of blue sky, green grass, and wretched despair. The need to escape drove her onward. She wanted only to put as much distance as possible between her and the people she no longer knew.

If only she could outrun the anguish in her heart.

Nearing a copse of willows by a stream, she grew aware of a thrashing in the bushes behind her. Had James come after her? How dare he!

Stumbling in a rabbit hole, Blythe caught her balance and furiously dashed away her tears. Devil take him! She would give him a dressing-down unlike anything he'd ever known. She hated him for being a liar, despised him for tricking her into loving him . . .

She glanced back over her shoulder. A small furry shape bounded in her wake. Minx!

Slowing to a stop, Blythe sank to the ground. Her breath came in ragged gasps that hurt her lungs. The mutt trotted straight to her, tail wagging.

With a cry of despair, she gathered the dog close. As if sensing her unhappiness, Minx solemnly licked her chin and snuggled in her arms.

All the wild energy of running abruptly left Blythe.

Holding the dog, she lay on the bank of the stream and wept in great noisy sobs. Every thought stabbed into her; every memory caused fresh agony. Laughing with her sisters, who were not her sisters anymore. Playing with little Arthur, who was not her nephew. Holding baby Ella, who was no longer her niece. What if she never saw them again?

The possibility was too unbearable to contemplate.

What would happen to Mama and Papa? They were servants who had assumed the identities of a dead gentleman and his wife. They had stolen a fortune and two young children. The very notion of their deception made Blythe sick.

Would James bring charges against her parents? Would they be tried before a judge and go to prison? Or be transported to one of the colonies? Worse, would they be sentenced to death?

No.

No, she could not imagine even James being so cruel. Perhaps he would just take her father's money and let her parents walk away free.

Where would they go?

She shouldn't care what happened to them, but she did. Her affection for them was too deeply ingrained to ignore. But they were not the honorable people she'd believed them to be.

Nor was James.

How she hated him! He had tricked her into believing his words of affection. He had made love to her so passionately. All the while, he had been lying to her. He had lied about being a servant, he had lied about being poor, he had lied about saving every penny to go to India. He had just been trying to worm information out of her about her parents.

She recalled the night when he'd come into her father's office and they had kissed for the first time. James had made an excuse about needing to check the lamps. But his true purpose must have been to find proof to implicate her parents.

Dear God! James had ripped apart the fabric of her family. She had no one left. No one at all.

It was too much to absorb.

Hugging Minx, Blythe felt drained and empty. Weariness settled over her, and she didn't want to think anymore. She closed her eyes and concentrated on the trill of birdsong, the burbling of the stream. The hard ground was more welcome than the pain in her heart. So was the blessed oblivion of sleep.

⁂

Upon awakening, Blythe didn't know why she was lying outside beneath the trees. Pushing up onto her elbow, she felt stiff and chilled. The position of the sun told her it must be mid-afternoon.

Memory struck like a fist. The awful confrontation. The shocking discovery that her parents were criminals. The jolt of learning that James was a wealthy gentleman, and not an impoverished servant.

They had all lied to her.

Too heartsore to think about it, she rose to her feet. Where had Minx gone? If the dog had abandoned her, too . . .

As if summoned by her thoughts, a small furry shape appeared over a grassy slope. Tail wagging, the mutt yapped at her, then vanished again on the other side of the hill.

Blythe trudged after the dog. When she reached the top, she could see Crompton Abbey in the distance. Her throat closed with pain. There was no sign of life around the ivy-covered manor house. Her parents' coach was no longer in front. Had they left—or had the vehicle merely been moved to the stables? And where was James?

She didn't want to know. He could die for all she cared.

Catching a glimpse of Minx trotting away from the house, Blythe followed. She had no purpose in mind except to avoid those who had hurt her. She trudged across hillocks and through dips, uncaring that the undergrowth snagged at her skirts. Once, she crossed a brook by balancing on flat stones. The occasional grazing sheep paid her no heed.

Every now and then, she caught sight of Minx roaming far ahead. The dog would stop and look back as if to make certain Blythe was still in pursuit. Eventually, she came to a road and saw the dog trotting several hundred yards ahead. Cresting a hill, Blythe spied rooftops in the distance and the stone steeple of a church.

She had no wish to encounter people in her bedraggled, woebegone state. But she feared Minx might become lost, so she walked faster. At the last bend in the road before the village, the mutt sat down and waited. As Blythe approached, the dog ran briskly down a narrow lane that had been hidden by a field of daffodils.

"Minx! Come back!"

Worried, Blythe hastened down the dirt track. All of a sudden, she came upon a thatch-roofed cottage with roses climbing up the sides. A low stone fence surrounded the place, and a riotous garden grew in a pleasing tangle. Several chickens pecked at the earth.

Blythe stopped at the gate. It was opened a crack and Minx was heading up the flagstone path to the door. The dog barked. Blythe hurried into the garden to retrieve the animal just as the door opened.

A stooped old woman emerged from the cottage. Her

white hair and frail appearance hit Blythe with a shock of recognition.

Mrs. Bleasdale. Her grandmother.

"My, look who's here. Ye've come back fer another treat, have ye?"

The woman was speaking to Minx. Curious, Blythe ventured closer. "Have you met Minx, then?"

"Oh, aye. When yer young man came by."

Her chest tightened. James had been here. Had he been looking for her? And Minx had accompanied him. It must have happened while Blythe had been napping by the stream. At least that explained the mystery of how the dog knew this place.

Mrs. Bleasdale beckoned with a gnarled hand. "Come in, dearie. Ye look fair draggled. I'll fix ye a hot cuppa tea."

The old woman shuffled back into the cottage.

Blythe hesitated. A part of her balked at the notion of accepting any companionship. Her emotions felt too raw for her to exchange pleasantries with the grandmother who had so abruptly appeared in her life.

But the bond they shared went beyond blood. They had both been duped by Blythe's mother, Mercy Bleasdale.

Blythe went inside. She found herself in a snug room with a low, beamed ceiling and several windows that were open to the breeze. An earthenware vase of mixed flowers sat on a small table in the corner. Minx sat waiting on a rag rug that covered the wide-plank floor.

Mrs. Bleasdale stood at the large brick hearth on one wall. She ladled hot water from a bubbling iron pot into a mug, to which she added a pinch of tea leaves. She hobbled to the table, set down the cup, and pulled out a wooden chair.

"Come, dearie," she said with a smile. "Do sit down."

Blythe sat. Oddly, she found the invitation more welcome than any issued by a grand London hostess. Society would be agog to see her now, the premier heiress of the season drinking tea in her grandmother's tiny cottage.

But Blythe was no longer an heiress. She was penniless. It didn't matter that she had married James. He could keep his precious money. By heavens, she would not ask him for tuppence.

Mrs. Bleasdale bustled around the cottage, fetching a small pitcher of cream and a plate of golden scones. When Minx came begging, the old woman crumbled one of the pastries for her.

"'Tis still warm from the oven," she said, using a knife to slather a scone with butter and blackberry jam. "There, ye'll feel better when ye eat."

Blythe had no interest in food, at least not until the delicious aroma penetrated the haze of her unhappiness. For the first time, she realized she'd had nothing to eat all day.

She took a bite that melted in her mouth. Trying not to appear ravenous, she consumed the scone quickly. "Thank you, Mrs. Bleasdale. You're very kind."

The old woman settled onto the other chair. "Ye must call me Granny. Such a wondrous day this is, to have ye here to visit."

The waiflike woman had deep seams in her face and a sparkle in her hazel eyes. Blythe added cream to her tea and took the mug in her hands, hoping to warm the coldness inside her.

"Granny . . . how can you be so happy after what my mother did to you? She sent news long ago claiming that your daughter had died of cholera. How can you ever forgive her for doing such a terrible wrong?"

"Mercy has arisen from the dead. Is that not cause for rejoicing? 'Tis like the story of Lazarus in my Bible." Mrs. Bleasdale buttered another scone and placed it on

Blythe's plate. "And she has given ye into my life, my only grandchild."

Anger penetrated Blythe's pain. "But she kept me from you. We've been back in England for three years. I could have been visiting you all this time."

"Ye're here now, and naught else matters. 'Tis truly a blessing."

Blythe's eyes filled with tears. Perhaps her grandmother was right, and she should look on the bright side. She had gained a grandmother, after all. Yet there was so very much she had lost today.

Her parents. Her sisters. Her husband.

A tear slid down her cheek, and she wiped it away.

Clucking in sympathy, Mrs. Bleasdale patted Blythe's hand. "Ye've had a trying day, dearie. Just married, too, were ye?"

The floodgates opened and Blythe poured out the story of how James had taken the post of footman under false pretenses, charmed her into falling in love with him, and convinced her to run off to Scotland to be married. His elaborate scheme had involved luring her parents to Lancashire, all so that he could regain his inheritance by proving Mama was really Mercy Bleasdale.

"Even as a wee girl, my Mercy was never satisfied with her lot in life," Mrs. Bleasdale said with a mournful shake of her head. "She always wanted more. Many a time I told her, ye'll never be content that way."

Blythe could see that her mother's ambitions had sprung from a need to deny a lowly past. Yet she felt no sympathy. The shock of betrayal was still too painful. Bitterly, she said, "It's no wonder my parents wanted me to marry a duke. It was to protect their position in society."

" 'Tis better the truth has come out," Mrs. Bleasdale said. "A wound left to fester will only poison a body.

Now ye can heal. Come outside now and sit for a bit. The sunshine will cheer ye."

Blythe doubted that anything could make her happy ever again. She settled herself on a stool with Minx at her feet, while her grandmother tended the roses and hollyhocks. The sun hung low in the sky. At this time the previous day, she and James had arrived at Crompton Abbey and she had looked forward to their wedding night.

Pushing away the memory, she stood up abruptly. "May I help?"

Her grandmother showed her how to pull weeds and trim the dead foliage. Having never gardened, Blythe found it a welcome distraction from her troubled thoughts. Her world narrowed to leaves and twigs and cool, pungent earth. Kneeling in front of a flower bed, she was feeling marginally better when the sound of hoofbeats came from the lane.

A man on horseback wheeled to a stop in front of the gate.

The sight of James caused a terrible lurch in her heart. She sat back on her heels, her hands dirty and her senses raw. It was too late to dash into the cottage. Blast him, she wouldn't hide, anyway.

Their gazes met and held. His grave expression showed no hint of the deviltry that had lured her into loving him. He looked unbearably handsome in his coffee-brown coat and white cravat, a fine gentleman on a ride through his estate.

Fury broke free from the tangle of her emotions. She no longer knew who he was. The man who had claimed her heart didn't exist.

He made a move to dismount.

Blythe surged to her feet. "Do *not* set foot here," she snapped. "There is *nothing* you can say that I wish to hear."

He gave her a cool nod. "I wanted only to assure myself of your well-being," he said. "I am going to London for a week or so. You are welcome to accompany me if you like."

He must be anxious to claim her father's money, she thought in disgust. There would be legal papers to sign, perhaps even reports to be filed with the magistrate. What would happen to her parents? She could only hope that Portia or Lindsey had the connections to help them.

Blythe lifted her chin. "Accompany you? I can think of nothing I would like *less*. Pray God you never return here."

James gazed bleakly at her for another moment, then he turned the horse around and set off at a canter.

Minx whined at the latched gate, scratching with her paw. It was painfully obvious that she wanted to run after James.

Blythe caught up the dog in a hug. "No, Minx. I couldn't bear to lose you, too."

She would *not* weep. She *would not*. Such a scoundrel wasn't worth a single tear. But when her grandmother came down the path and put her frail arms around Blythe, she clung to her granny and wept wretchedly.

⁂

Five days later, the letters began arriving. Not from James, but from her sisters.

Portia wrote that Papa had come to them the previous afternoon and confessed the whole sordid story. It had been a terrible shock to learn the hidden truth about their past. They were all still grappling with disbelief over the matter. Their mother had taken to her bed with a megrim and had refused to see anyone.

We remain your loving sisters, Portia wrote at the

end. *It doesn't matter what our bloodlines are. Nothing has changed in our hearts.*

Lindsey wrote that she had suspected something fishy all along about James, for he had played the role of Prince Nicolai far too convincingly. She now regretted keeping silent, for she had not realized that Blythe's heart had become so engaged with him.

We love you, dear sister, and we miss you terribly. You will always have a home here with us.

Lindsey enclosed enough coins to cover Blythe's fare back home.

Sitting in the cottage, Blythe bowed her head and wept. In the last week, she had become a veritable watering pot. These tears were not from the pain of loss and betrayal, but from relief. How could she have ever thought, even for a moment, that her sisters might shun her?

The next day, more letters arrived. Portia related amusing little stories about the children. Arthur had picked up a pretty brown stone in the garden, only to howl in aggrieved surprise when it had uncurled into an earthworm. Ella had laughed for the first time, and her happy disposition had made her the delight of the household.

Lindsey wrote that Kasi had known about the ruse from the start, for she had been the girls' *ayah* on the journey when the real George and Edith Crompton had died of cholera. All these years, Kasi had kept silent in order to protect the three sisters from the taint of scandal.

The letters continued to be delivered, day after day. Portia kept Blythe updated with news about the children, and every now and then mentioned James. In one, she said that he had dined with the family.

Pray don't be angry with us for receiving him. He is,

after all, our brother-in-law and second cousin to Lindsey and me. Perhaps you won't wish to hear this, but James is not a happy man. I do believe he is suffering greatly for his ill treatment of you.

Suffering!

Thrusting the letter away, Blythe stomped into the garden and yanked out weeds. Her grandmother was clipping the ivy on the stone wall. "News of yer husband, I reckon?"

"I don't know *how* my sisters can like him," Blythe burst out. "He's a heartless villain with no honor at all."

"Ye fell in love with him," Granny said with a wise smile. "Perhaps ye might try to remember why."

Blythe recalled far too much. Every night as she lay in her little cot under the eaves where her mother had slept as a child, memories of him would haunt her. The glint of mischief in his eyes. His brash smile and teasing remarks. And oh, the feel of his hands on her body . . .

Instead of diminishing with the passage of time, the memories intensified, so that she would wake up in the dark, longing for the warmth of his arms around her.

Foolish, foolish, foolish!

In her next letter, Lindsey reported that Lady Davina had been in a snit ever since Prince Nicolai's proposal to Blythe. Then James had made an appearance at a ball, and just as the duke's daughter was curtsying to him in front of all of society, he'd revealed he was not a prince at all; he had played the role to win a private wager with Lord Mansfield. James had apologized most charmingly for the hoax.

Everyone but Lady Davina had been amused.

Amused!

Blythe tossed the letter down and went to the table to make scones, using her granny's recipe. She measured the flour into a wooden bowl and cracked an egg. Adding currants and a pinch of salt, she wondered why her sisters were helping James gain a place in society.

Did the ton know that James had married her? Did they wonder why she had vanished? Were all the ladies flirting with him?

Mixing the dough, she denied a stab of white-hot jealousy. It shouldn't matter anymore how he conducted his life. But if he dared to turn that heart-stopping smile on any other woman . . .

As the days passed, more letters arrived, including one from her father, who begged her forgiveness. He went on at length about how considerate James had been in not bringing them before a magistrate, and how generous he was in allowing them to keep Crompton House. *He will accept only your dowry and the estate in Lancashire, nothing more.*

The news was so earthshaking that Blythe hastened outside to find her grandmother, who sat knitting beneath the shade of a tree while Minx pursued a butterfly through the garden. "James didn't send my parents to prison, after all," Blythe said breathlessly. "Nor did he claim my father's fortune. I don't understand it."

"Why, dearie, 'tis simple. He must love ye very much."

Blythe hardly knew what to say to that. Was it possible he had done this for *her*? Oh, how she wished she could know for certain. Her insides felt like a roiling mass of anxiety.

"Granny, how can you always be so wise and so content?"

Those hazel eyes smiled. "The happiest people don't always have the best of everything. They make the best of everything they have."

Blythe pondered that. It was time to stop brooding

over the past and make the best of *her* life. As much as she liked staying here with her grandmother, she could not hide any longer from her family—or James.

It was time for her to return to London.

Chapter 31

"Lady Mansfield and Lady Ratcliffe are in the nursery," a footman informed Blythe. "I will inform them at once that you are here."

"It's quite all right. I know the way."

As Blythe started up the grand staircase at Pallister House, she marveled at the enormity of the entrance hall. Only weeks ago she had wanted to become mistress of such a fine house as her sister's. But after a month spent in the cozy quarters of her grandmother's cottage, she had learned what truly mattered in life.

The happiest people don't always have the best of everything. They make the best of everything they have.

Such a sensible woman, her granny. They'd shared a tearful goodbye two days ago, and Blythe had promised to return very soon. She had left Minx there as a companion to her grandmother. If all went well, they would be together again soon.

On the long journey here, Blythe had thought much about James. He must have had a reason for asking her father for the deed to the Lancashire house. Did James hope she would agree to live there with him? Or did he just want something to offer to her as restitution for the pain he'd caused in her life?

The desire to see him again burned like a fire in her heart.

But first, she needed to visit her sisters, to thank them for their loving support. From them, she would find out where James was staying.

She reached the upper floor and headed down the corridor. Curiously, no sounds of laughter or conversation emanated from the nursery. It was mid-afternoon. Perhaps her sisters were putting the children down for their naps.

In the doorway of the schoolroom, she halted. A man stood by the windows. *James.*

His presence here caught her by surprise. Her throat squeezed so tightly she could scarcely breathe. James didn't notice her. His full attention was focused downward on the bundle in his arms. He cradled Ella to his broad chest and murmured to her.

As he stroked his finger over her face, the baby happily waved her arms. He caught one tiny flailing fist and kissed it. Ella giggled and cooed.

Blythe's heart melted. In all of her life, she had never witnessed a more beautiful sight. It only served to reaffirm the fact that for better or for worse, she loved James.

But did he truly love her? Oh, she prayed so!

The sound of voices came from an adjoining room. Laughing and talking, her sisters and their husbands came out of the wing that housed the children's bedchambers.

Lindsey spied her first. "My stars, it's the prodigal sister!"

"Blythe!" Portia said with a cry of joy. "You're back!"

Both rushed toward her, and Blythe hastened to meet them halfway. The three of them embraced in a tearful, happy reunion.

"We didn't know you were coming," Lindsey said, "or we'd have been watching for you."

"Have a care while hugging me," Portia said, holding

up her hands to show smudges of black on her fingers. "Arthur was supposed to be napping, but he found a piece of charcoal and drew all over the wall."

"I set him to work helping the maid wash it off," Colin said. "Alas, the little imp seems to be enjoying his punishment too much."

James stood unmoving, cradling Ella and staring at Blythe.

"Speaking of washing," Portia said, with a glance at him, "I'm afraid I shall have to go do something about my hands."

Lindsey took her daughter from James. "It's nearly time for Ella's feeding. I'll take her downstairs."

She sent her husband a meaningful frown.

"Colin and I will be off to my club, then." Thane cast a sly look at James. "I don't suppose we could interest you in accompanying us, old chap?"

"What? No."

While speaking, James had not taken his eyes off Blythe. The fierce intensity of his dark eyes thrilled her to the core. The rest of the family vanished out the door. Alone, they stood gazing at each other from halfway across the room.

James took a step toward her. "Blythe, I realize you came to visit your sisters, not me. But . . . oh God, I feared I might never see you again."

"I gave you no cause to think otherwise." She remembered their last meeting, when he had come on horseback to her grandmother's cottage. "James, I know that I spoke harshly to you. I was hurt and angry—"

"I deserved every word of your reprimand." He closed the distance between them and stood before her. "I would very much like to speak to you in private. Will you trust me enough to come to my bedchamber?"

Surprise flitted through her. "You're staying *here*?"

"Your sisters can be quite formidable. They said it was wise to keep a close eye on one's enemy."

As they walked down one flight of stairs, Blythe knew her sisters had only been teasing him. They didn't regard James as an enemy. Not if Portia and Colin treated him with the warmth of family. Not if Lindsey and Thane had trusted him to hold their precious baby daughter.

Blythe felt a rush of gladness that her family approved of him. It gave her hope that she and James could right the wrongs between them.

He opened a door and ushered her into a bedchamber with sumptuous blue hangings and a large four-poster bed.

Stepping inside, she was assailed by a pang of memory. "This is the room where you changed into the garb of Prince Nicolai."

"Yes, which is why your sisters have taken to calling it the Ambrosia Bedchamber."

She watched him close the door. "You were reluctant to play the prince, even when I offered to pay you fifty pounds. My scheme must have complicated your plan to search my parents' house."

He grimaced. "It was clever of you to dangle a reward in front of me. Had I refused, you might have guessed I wasn't really a footman."

The thought of his deception still hurt. Blythe crossed her arms to hug herself. "All that time, I believed you were a servant, James. I fought against my feelings for you because I thought you were forbidden to me. But I never knew who you really were."

But she knew now—didn't she? She had experienced his warmth when he had made love to her. She had learned his character when her father had written to say James had refused the money. And she had known his heart when she had seen him holding baby Ella.

James led her to a chaise, the same one where he had

told her that enchanting story about Princess Amora of Ambrosia, who had been captured by an ogre and rescued by a stable lad. "Please sit," he said. "I do hope you'll hear me out."

She sat. Despite the remnants of pain, it was a pleasure just to look at him again. And she did so want to know what was in his heart.

"From the moment we met, I've done everything wrong," he said, walking back and forth in front of her, his hands clasped behind his back. "I should never have posed as a servant. I should have confronted your father directly, without the subterfuge. I've done a terrible wrong to your parents."

"A *wrong*?" she asked, unable to keep the bitterness from her voice. "James, their crime needed to be exposed. They lied to me all these years. They are not George and Edith Crompton. They are Timothy Arkwright and Mercy Bleasdale."

"Yet there are mitigating circumstances to take into account. Your *ayah* made that quite clear to me shortly after I returned to London."

Lindsey had written that Kasi had known about the ruse from the start. "What did she say?"

James flashed Blythe a troubled look. "She told the same tale that your parents related, though in more detail. It was quite grim to hear how my cousin and his wife contracted cholera on the road, while caught up in a mass exodus from Calcutta. Kasi said they begged your parents with their dying breath to watch over their two young daughters. How can I despise your mother and father for doing just that?"

Blythe bowed her head. She could imagine the utter chaos of panicked people fleeing the city, her mother as a frightened maidservant charged with the care of two babies. How awful it must have been. . . .

James came to stand before her. "Blythe, I've come to see that your parents are not the villains I thought them to be. They acted as they did to protect your sisters."

She lifted her chin to look up at him. "How can you ever forgive them, though? They stole your fortune."

"Had they not done so, there would be nothing left of it, anyway. My father was still alive at the time. Had the inheritance gone to him, it would have been squandered at the dice table."

"But Mama would have *shot* you, James. I don't know that I can ever absolve her of that."

He shrugged. "We all make mistakes. It was a tremendous shock to her to see her whole life being snatched away. She has since apologized to me, and there can be nothing gained from harboring ill will toward her."

He was right, of course. Besides, Blythe, too, had made her share of mistakes, when she had pursued the duke instead of following her heart.

She felt the lightening of a burden. To know that James was as wise as her granny only made her fall more deeply in love with him. She longed to feel his arms around her, but when she would have risen, he waved her back onto the chaise.

"That is not all I've done wrong," he went on. "These past weeks I've had ample time to reflect on my dishonorable behavior toward you, Blythe. I should have courted you honestly as a gentleman. Instead, I seduced you and took your innocence. I lured you from your home under false pretenses. I tricked you into marrying me."

"You did deceive me," she allowed. "However, the seduction was mutual."

He fell to his knees. Taking her hands in his, he gently kissed her fingers. "Blythe, I love you with all my heart. I don't know if you're willing to live with me as my wife, but if by the grace of God you are, we can have a proper wedding here in London with all the ton."

She touched his cheek. "James, I love you, too. I'm perfectly happy with the wedding we had. Besides, all the bother would only stop us from returning to Lancashire."

His dark eyes searched hers as if he could not quite believe she was his. "There will be no more lies from me, I swear it. I only wish there was some way to make up for all my duplicity."

"There *is* something."

"By God," he said passionately, "tell me, and I'll do it."

She rose from the chaise, strolled to the bed, and smiled at him. "You can give me a kiss so perfect and passionate that it will be immortalized by the bards for a thousand years to come."

And so he did.

AVAILABLE FROM ROUGE:

WHEN BLOOD CALLS

J. K. Beck

Attorney Sara Constantine is thrilled with her promotion – until she finds out that the criminals she will be prosecuting are in fact vampires and werewolves. She is even more surprised when she learns that her first defendant is Lucius Dragos, the sexy stranger with whom she recently shared an explosive night of ecstasy.

But what starts as a simple kiss ignites into an all-consuming passion. Charged with murder, Lucius knows that Sara is determined to see him locked away – unless he can convince her that he's not a monster. And that might mean making the ultimate sacrifice...

Red-hot romance...

www.rougeromance.co.uk